D0790398

MANY PEOPLES, MANY FATES—

"Apartness" by Vernor Vinge—Sometimes vengeance is just a matter of letting your enemy's hatred do him in. . . .

"Of Space-Time and the River" by Gregory Benford—When the aliens came to Egypt, their idea of souvenirs might turn the Earth itself topsy-turvy. . . .

"The Quiet" by George Guthridge—Will the Moon prove a haven to endangered tribes . . . or a deadly danger to their protectors?

"The Pale Thin God" by Mike Resnick—When Africa's most ancient powers confront the West's most worshiped Lord, who will prove mightier?

These are just a few of the voyages of discovery that await you as you journey down the twisting streams of time in—

FUTURE EARTHS: UNDER AFRICAN SKIES

**Other Imagination-Gripping Anthologies
Brought to You by DAW:**

WHATDUNITS *edited by Mike Resnick.* All-original stories by such inventive science fiction sleuths as Pat Cadigan, Judith Tarr, Katharine Kerr, Jack Haldeman, and Esther Friesner. Match wits with the masters to make human, alien, robot, clone, and android perpetrators fit the crime.

ALADDIN: Master of the Lamp *edited by Mike Resnick and Martin H. Greenberg.* An all-original collection of tales, some serious, some scary, some humorous, but all recounting either the adventures of Aladdin himself or of other people who gain control of his magical lamp—and must then try to outwit the djinn imprisoned within it to gain their wishes without paying the price.

MICROCOSMIC TALES *Selected by Isaac Asimov, Martin H. Greenberg, and Joseph P. Olander.* One hundred short science fiction stories by such masters of the genre as Arthur C. Clarke, Larry Niven, Robert Silverberg, James Tiptree, Jr., Harry Harrison, Lester del Rey, and, of course, Isaac Asimov himself.

FUTURE EARTHS:
UNDER AFRICAN SKIES

EDITED BY

Mike Resnick
and
Gardner Dozois

DAW BOOKS, INC.
DONALD A. WOLLHEIM, FOUNDER
375 Hudson Street, New York, NY 10014

**ELIZABETH R. WOLLHEIM
SHEILA E. GILBERT
PUBLISHERS**

Copyright © 1993 by Mike Resnick and Gardner Dozois.

All Rights Reserved.

Cover art by Peter Gudynas.

DAW Book Collectors No. 905.

If you purchase this book without a cover you should be aware that
this book may have been stolen property and reported as ''unsold and
destroyed'' to the publisher. In such case neither the author nor the
publisher has received any payment for this ''stripped book.''

First Printing, February 1993

1 2 3 4 5 6 7 8 9

DAW TRADEMARK REGISTERED
U.S. PAT OFF AND FOREIGN COUNTRIES
—MARCA REGISTRADA,
HECHO EN U.S.A.

PRINTED IN THE U.S.A.

ACKNOWLEDGMENTS

Acknowledgment is made for permission to print the following material:

"Introduction" © 1993 by Mike Resnick.

"For I Have Touched the Sky," by Mike Resnick. Copyright © 1989 by Mercury Press, Inc. First published in *The Magazine of Fantasy and Science Fiction*, December 1989. Reprinted by permission of the author.

"Apartness," by Vernor Vinge. Copyright © 1965 by *New Worlds SF*. First published in *New Worlds*, 1965. Reprinted by permission of the author.

"Termites," by Dave Smeds. Copyright © 1987 by David Smeds. First published in *Isaac Asimov's Science Fiction Magazine*, May 1987. Reprinted by permission of the author.

"The Finger," by Naomi Mitchison. Copyright © 1980 by Naomi Mitchison. First published in *Edges* (Pocket Books). Reprinted by permission of the author.

"The Lions Are Asleep This Night," by Howard Waldrop. Copyright © 1986 by Omni Publications International, Ltd. First published in *Omni*, August 1986. Reprinted by permission of the author.

"Etoundi's Monkey," by Janet Dubois. Copyright © 1989 by Judith Logsdon Dubois. First published in *The Magazine of Fantasy and Science Fiction*, February 1989. Reprinted by permission of the author.

"Dry Niger," by M. Shayne Bell. Copyright © 1990 by M. Shayne Bell. First published in *Isaac Asimov's Science Fiction Magazine*, August 1990. Reprinted by permission of the author.

"A Transect," by Kim Stanley Robinson. Copyright © 1986 by Mercury Press, Inc. First published in *The Magazine of Fantasy and Science Fiction*, May 1986. Reprinted by permission of the author.

"Of Space-Time and the River," by Gregory Benford. Copyright © 1986 by Abbenford Associates. First published in *Isaac Asimov's Science Fiction Magazine*, February 1986. Reprinted by permission of the author.

"Still Life With Scorpion," by Scott Baker. Copyright © 1984 by Davis Publications, Inc. First published in *Isaac Asimov's Science Fiction Magazine*, May 1984. Reprinted by permission of the author.

"The Quiet," by George Guthridge. Copyright © 1981 by Mercury Press, Inc. First published in *The Magazine of Fantasy and Science Fiction*, July 1981. Reprinted by permission of the author.

"Dinner in Audoghast," by Bruce Sterling. Copyright © 1985 by Davis Publications, Inc. First published in *Isaac Asimov's Science Fiction Magazine*, May 1985. Reprinted by permission of the author.

"A Passive Victim of a Random Genetic Accident," by Janet Gluckman. Copyright © 1983 by Janet Gluckman. First published in *Owlflight 4*. Reprinted by permission of the author.

"The Pale Thin God," by Mike Resnick. Copyright © 1992 by Mike Resnick. First published in *Xanadu* (Tor). Reprinted by permission of the author.

"Toward Kilimanjaro," by Ian McDonald. Copyright © 1990 by Davis Publications, Inc. First published in *Isaac Asimov's Science Fiction Magazine*, August 1990. Reprinted by permission of the author.

for
PAT CADIGAN
—because She Is There

The Editors would like to thank the following people for their help and support:

Susan Casper, Carol Resnick, Lawrence Person, Janet Kagan, Pat Cadigan, Edward Ferman, Audrey Ferman, Sheila Williams, Ian Randall Strock, Scott Towner, Ellen Datlow, Jan Burke, Rachel Holman, Richard Curtis, Scott Baker, Janet Gluckman, Dave Smeds, and special thanks to our own editor, Sheila Gilbert.

CONTENTS

Introduction
by Mike Resnick   11

For I Have Touched the Sky
by Mike Resnick   15

Apartness
by Vernor Vinge   45

Termites
by Dave Smeds   67

The Finger
by Naomi Mitchison   87

The Lions Are Asleep This Night
by Howard Waldrop   97

Etoundi's Monkey
by Judith Dubois   122

Dry Niger
by M. Shayne Bell   149

A Transect
by Kim Stanley Robinson   160

Of Space-Time and the River
by Gregory Benford   174

Still Life with Scorpion
by Scott Baker   209

The Quiet
by George Guthridge   227

Dinner in Audoghast
  by *Bruce Sterling*   243

A Passive Victim of a Random Genetic Accident
  by *Janet Gluckman*   259

The Pale Thin God
  by *Mike Resnick*   271

Toward Kilimanjaro
  by *Ian McDonald*   275

Further Reading About Africa   315

INTRODUCTION
by Mike Resnick

Okay, science fiction fans, let's play a little guessing game:

1. What science fiction story features an active business in slave-trading a full century after it has been outlawed everywhere in human society?

2. What science fiction story postulates crucifixion and boiling in oil as legal punishments in an otherwise-enlightened day and age?

3. What science fiction story tells of a ruler who erects a statue of Adolph Hitler in front of his palace, tortures and kills hundreds of thousands of his own supporters, and divorces and dismembers his wives?

4. What science fiction story describes a rite-of-passage ritual in which more than half the young women of an alien world voluntarily undergo clitoridectomy operations?

5. What science fiction story tells of an emperor who personally mows down his country's schoolchildren with a machine gun?

6. What science fiction story portrays a modern society in which females of the species have so few rights that their language has no word for ''woman'' or its equivalent?

All right. Think about your answers, and while you're doing so, let's discuss Africa, since this is an anthology of science fiction stories about that exotic and mysterious continent.

Let's begin with the postulate that almost all science

fiction writers, no matter what their politics, share one basic belief: that if we can reach the stars, sooner or later we will colonize them.

This in turn leads to the not-unlikely supposition that, somewhere along the way, we're going to come into contact—and into cultural conflict—with alien races.

Now, since science fiction is supposed to be extrapolated from known facts, its writers have more and more frequently turned their eyes toward Africa, a remarkable continent that offers not one, not two, but fully half a hundred examples of cultures in conflict and of the effects of colonization on both the colonizers and the colonized.

Originally Africa was the setting only for romantic daydreams spun by such dream weavers as H. Rider Haggard and Edgar Rice Burroughs, as well it should have been. To put matters in perspective, an enormous part of Africa was unmapped and unexplored at the dawn of this century. In 1890, not a single East African language had a word for "wheel," because nobody had ever seen one. In fact, the first professional hunting safari did not leave Nairobi until the year before Ronald Reagan's birth. John F. Kennedy had already started shaving by the time a specially-provisioned car became the first vehicle ever to cross the Sahara Desert. When Elvis Presley recorded "Heartbreak Hotel," only one sub-Saharan country (there are more than forty of them) had achieved independence.

But as we know, science tends to make the world smaller, and today there is almost no section of Africa that hasn't been thoroughly explored, there is no African nation that is not the master (however inefficiently) of its own fate, there are no lost tribes or cities, no hidden civilizations. There are no undiscovered animals, nor are there any secret rituals that haven't been videotaped, translated, and codified in someone's doctoral thesis.

But while Africa has lost some of the mystery and romance of Haggard's and Burroughs' day, it now provides thoroughly documented examples of some of the most fascinating people and societies any writer, searching for the new and the different and the alien, could hope to find.

You think not? Let's examine those six science fiction stories I asked you about.

By now, of course, you've probably figured out that I cheated. They are not science fiction stories at all, but merely some representative people and facts that can be (and have been) turned into science fiction.

1. In 1991, more than 15,000 members of the Dinka tribe of Somalia were sold into slavery, most of them winding up in Ethiopia.

2. In the Sudan, the legal custom of "Sharia" still exists, whereby a murder victim's family can choose the murderer's punishment. Since 1990 both crucifixion and boiling in oil have been chosen and lawfully administered.

3. It was Idi Amin, of course, who erected the statue of Hitler, killed 300,000 of his countrymen, and dismembered some of his wives. (But how many of you know that his two successors, Dr. Obote and Gen. Okello, each killed more of their fellow Ugandans than Amin did?)

4. Female circumcision, as it is called, is a ritual that to this day is willingly undergone by almost 80% of all adolescent black African women living in the forty-plus nations south of the Sahara.

5. It was the self-proclaimed Emperor Bokassa of the Central African Republic who killed more than one hundred impoverished schoolchildren when they protested that they did not have enough money to buy the school uniforms that he insisted they wear (and which were made in his own factory).

6. There is no word for "woman" in Swahili, the *lingua franca* of Kenya, Tanzania, Uganda, and parts of Zambia. The closest one can come to it is "manamouki," a word that means "female property," and equally describes women, mares, sows, and ewes.

Interesting story material, isn't it? (And we haven't even begun to touch on *apartheid.*)

Is there anyone out there who still thinks Africa isn't alien enough?

Surely not the writers of science fiction. During the period 1988–1991, eighty-two novels, novellas, novelettes, and short stories were nominated for the Hugo Award, which is voted upon by the World Science Fiction Convention; of them, eight were set in Africa or were African in theme. With all of the universe to play with, almost 10% of the best science fiction was about things African.

Lest you think we have somehow skewed the figures, let's look at the Nebula Awards, presented by the Science Fiction and Fantasy Writers of America, for the period of 1989–1992 (our publication schedule allows us to know the 1992 Nebula nominees, though not the Hugo nominees.) Of the ninety-nine novels, novellas, novelettes, and short stories nominated during that four-year period, ten of them, slightly more than 10%, were set in Africa or were concerned with African themes.

There are a trillion galaxies out there.

There are a billion stars in our own galaxy.

There are a million possible planets on which to set science fiction stories.

Even on Earth, there are six continents (or seven, depending on your schoolteacher), and close to two hundred countries.

And yet 10% of the very best stories keep getting set in Africa.

Why should that be, you ask?

Well, if this introduction hasn't shown you, read the stories we've assembled here, and long before you're through you'll know the answer.

FOR I HAVE TOUCHED
THE SKY

by Mike Resnick

Mike Resnick is one of the best-selling authors in science fiction, and one of the most prolific. His many novels include The Dark Lady, Stalking The Unicorn, Paradise, Santiago, *and* Ivory, *and, as editor,* Whatdunits, *as well as* Aladdin: Master of the Lamp *and* Alternate Presidents, *co-edited with Martin H. Greenberg (several more Resnick/Greenberg anthologies are on the way, including* Alternate Warriors *and* Alternate Outlaws). *He won the Hugo Award in 1989 for "Kirinyaga," one of the most controversial and talked-about stories in recent years (in fact, I'd be willing to bet that the amount of space since devoted to analyzing it and arguing about it in various critical journals exceeds by a good margin the wordage of the original story itself!). He won another Hugo Award last year for another story in the Kirinyaga series, "The Manumouki," and another Kirinyaga story, "One Perfect Morning, With Jackals," is on the final Hugo ballot for 1992. His most recent novel was the well-received* Soothsayer. *He lives with his family, a whole bunch of dogs—he and his wife, Carol, run a kennel—and at least one computer, in Cincinnati, Ohio.*

An experienced Africa hand, Resnick has probably done more hard thinking about the future of that troubled continent than any other science fiction writer, and his work often reflects the knowledge that there are no easy answers to Africa's problems—that, in fact, every "solution" raises a host of new questions, and new chal-

lenges, that must then be dealt with in their turn. So it is with Kirinyaga, an attempt to create a Utopian society in an orbiting space colony that has been remade in the likeness of ancient Kenya, an attempt to find the future of Africa by going back to its past, to the way things were before the invasion of the Europeans. But, as you will see in "For I Have Touched the Sky," one of the best and certainly one of the most moving of the Kirinyaga stories, unexpected areas of cultural conflict crop up in even the most well-managed of Utopias, and sometimes the price that must be paid by those who quest after knowledge is a terrible price indeed. . . .

There was a time when men had wings.

Ngai, who sits alone on His throne atop Kirinyaga, which is now called Mount Kenya, gave men the gift of flight, so that they might reach the succulent fruits on the highest branches of the trees. But one man, a son of Gikuyu, who was himself the first man, saw the eagle and the vulture riding high upon the winds, and, spreading his wings, he joined them. He circled higher and higher, and soon he soared far above all other flying things.

Then, suddenly, the hand of Ngai reached out and grabbed the son of Gikuyu.

"What have I done that you should grab me thus?" asked the son of Gikuyu.

"I live atop Kirinyaga because it is the top of the world," answered Ngai, "and no one's head may be higher than my own."

And so saying, Ngai plucked the wings from the son of Gikuyu, and then took wings away from *all* men, so that no man could ever again rise higher than His head.

And that is why all of Gikuyu's descendents look at the birds with a sense of loss and envy, and why they no longer eat the succulent fruits from the highest branches of the trees.

* * *

We have many birds on the world of Kirinyaga, which was named for the holy mountain where Ngai dwells. We brought them along with our other animals when we received our charter from the Eutopian Council and departed from a Kenya that no longer had any meaning for true members of the Kikuyu tribe. Our new world is home to the marabou and the vulture, the ostrich and the fish eagle, the weaver and the heron, and many other species. Even I, Koriba, who am the *mundumugu*—the witch doctor—delight in their many colors, and find solace in their music. I have spent many afternoons seated in front of my *boma*, my back propped up against an ancient acacia tree, watching the profusion of colors and listening to the melodic songs as the birds come to slake their thirst in the river that winds through our village.

It was on one such afternoon that Kamari, a young girl who was not yet of circumcision age, walked up the long, winding path that separates my *boma* from the village, holding something small and gray in her hands.

"*Jambo,* Koriba," she greeted me.

"*Jambo,* Kamari," I answered her. "What have you brought to me, child?"

"This," she said, holding out a young pygmy falcon that struggled weakly to escape her grasp. "I found him in my family's *shamba*. He cannot fly."

"He looks fully fledged," I noted, getting to my feet. Then I saw that one of his wings was held at an awkward angle. "Ah!" I said. "He has broken his wing."

"Can you make him well, *mundumugu*?" asked Kamari.

I examined the wing briefly, while she held the young falcon's head away from me. Then I stepped back.

"I can make him well, Kamari," I said. "But I cannot make him fly. The wing will heal, but it will never be strong enough to bear his weight again. I think we will destroy him."

"No!" she exclaimed, pulling the falcon back. "You will make him live, and I will care for him!"

I stared at the bird for a moment, then shook my head. "He will not wish to live," I said at last.

"Why not?"

"Because he has ridden high upon the warm winds."

"I do not understand," said Kamari, frowning.

"Once a bird has touched the sky," I explained, "he can never be content to spend his days on the ground."

"I will *make* him content," she said with determination. "You will heal him, and I will care for him, and he will live."

"I will heal him, and you will care for him," I said. "But," I added, "he will not live."

"What is your fee, Koriba?" she asked, suddenly businesslike.

"I do not charge children," I answered. "I will visit your father tomorrow, and he will pay me."

She shook her head adamantly. "This is *my* bird. *I* will pay the fee."

"Very well," I said, admiring her spirit, for most children—and *all* adults—are terrified of their *mundumugu,* and would never openly contradict or disagree with him. "For one month you will clean my *boma* every morning and every afternoon. You will lay out my sleeping blankets, and keep my water gourd filled, and you will see that I have kindling for my fire."

"That is fair," she said after a moment's consideration. Then she added: "What if the bird dies before the month is over?"

"Then you will learn that a *mundumugu* knows more than a little Kikuyu girl," I said.

She set her jaw. "He will not die." She paused. "Will you fix his wing now?"

"Yes."

"I will help."

I shook my head. "You will build a cage in which to confine him, for if he tries to move his wing too soon, he will break it again, and then I will surely have to destroy him."

She handed the bird to me. "I will be back soon," she promised, racing off toward her *shamba.*

I took the falcon into my hut. He was too weak to

struggle very much, and he allowed me to tie his beak shut. Then I began the slow task of splinting his broken wing and binding it against his body to keep it motionless. He shrieked in pain as I manipulated the bones together, but otherwise he simply stared unblinking at me, and within ten minutes the job was finished.

Kamari returned an hour later, holding a small wooden cage in her hands.

"Is this large enough, Koriba?" she asked.

I held it up and examined it.

"It is almost too large," I replied. "He must not be able to move his wing until it has healed."

"He won't," she promised. "I will watch him all day long, every day."

"You will watch him all day long, every day?" I repeated, amused.

"Yes."

"Then who will clean my hut and my *boma*, and who will fill my gourd with water?"

"I will carry his cage with me when I come," she replied.

"The cage will be much heavier when the bird is in it," I pointed out.

"When I am a woman, I will carry far heavier loads on my back, for I shall have to till the fields and gather the firewood for my husband's *boma*," she said. "This will be good practice." She paused. "Why do you smile at me, Koriba?"

"I am not used to being lectured to by uncircumcised children," I replied with a smile.

"I was not lecturing," she answered with dignity. "I was *explaining*."

I held up a hand to shade my eyes from the afternoon sun.

"Are you not afraid of me, little Kamari?" I asked.

"Why should I be?"

"Because I am the *mundumugu*."

"That just means you are smarter than the others," she said with a shrug. She threw a stone at a chicken that was approaching her cage, and it raced away, squawking its annoyance. "Someday I shall be as smart as you are."

"Oh?"

She nodded confidently. "Already I can count higher than my father, and I can remember many things."

"What kind of things?" I asked, turning slightly as a hot breeze blew a swirl of dust about us.

"Do you remember the story of the honey bird that you told to the children of the village before the long rains?"

I nodded.

"I can repeat it," she said.

"You mean you can remember it."

She shook her head vigorously. "I can repeat every word that you said."

I sat down and crossed my legs. "Let me hear it," I said, staring off into the distance and idly watching a pair of young men tending their cattle.

She hunched her shoulders, so that she would appear as bent with age as I myself am, and then, in a voice that sounded like a youthful replica of my own, she began to speak, mimicking my gestures.

"There is a little brown honey bird," she began. "He is much like a sparrow, and as friendly. He will come to your *boma* and call to you; and as you approach him, he will fly up and lead you to a hive, and then wait while you gather grass and set fire to it and smoke out the bees. But you must *always*"—she emphasized the word, just as I had done—"leave some honey for him, for if you take it all, the next time he will lead you into the jaws of *fisi*, the hyena, or perhaps into the desert, where there is no water and you will die of thirst." Her story finished, she stood upright and smiled at me. "You see?" she said proudly.

"I see," I said, brushing away a large fly that had lit on my cheek.

"Did I do it right?" she asked.

"You did it right."

She stared at me thoughtfully. "Perhaps when you die, I will become the *mundumugu*."

"Do I seem that close to death?" I asked her.

"Well," she answered, "you are very old and bent and wrinkled, and you sleep too much. But I will be just as happy if you do not die right away."

"I shall try to make you just as happy," I said ironically. "Now take your falcon home."

I was about to instruct her concerning his needs, but she spoke first.

"He will not want to eat today. But starting tomorrow, I will give him large insects, and at least one lizard every day. And he must always have water."

"You are very observant, Kamari."

She smiled at me again, and then ran off toward her *boma*.

She was back at dawn the next morning, carrying the cage with her. She placed it in the shade, then filled a small container with water from one of my gourds and set it inside the cage.

"How is your bird this morning?" I asked, sitting close to my fire, for even though the planetary engineers of the Eutopian Council had given Kirinyaga a climate identical to Kenya's, the sun had not yet warmed the morning air.

Kamari frowned. "He has not eaten yet."

"He will, when he gets hungry enough," I said, pulling my blanket more tightly around my shoulders. "He is used to swooping down on his prey from the sky."

"He drinks his water, though," she noted.

"That is a good sign."

"Can you not cast a spell that will heal him at once?"

"The price would be too high," I said, for I had foreseen her question. "This way is better."

"How high?"

"*Too* high," I repeated, closing the subject. "Now, do you not have work to do?"

"Yes, Koriba."

She spent the next few minutes gathering kindling for my fire and filling my gourd from the river. Then she went into my hut to clean it and straighten my sleeping blankets. She emerged a moment later with a book in her hand.

"What is this, Koriba?" she asked.

"Who told you that you could touch your *mundumugu*'s possessions?" I asked sternly.

"How can I clean them without touching them?" she replied with no show of fear. "What is it?"

"It is a book."

"What is a book, Koriba?"

"It is not for you to know," I said. "Put it back."

"Shall I tell you what I think it is?" she asked.

"Tell me," I said, curious to hear her answer.

"Do you know how you draw signs on the ground when you cast the bones to bring the rains? I think that a book is a collection of signs."

"You are a very bright little girl, Kamari."

"I *told* you that I was," she said, annoyed that I had not accepted her statement as a self-evident truth. She looked at the book for a moment, then held it up. "What do the signs mean?"

"Different things," I said.

"*What* things?"

"It is not necessary for the Kikuyu to know."

"But you know."

"I am the *mundumugu*."

"Can anyone else on Kirinyaga read the signs?"

"Your own chief, Koinnage, and two other chiefs can read the signs," I answered, sorry now that she had charmed me into this conversation, for I could foresee its direction.

"But you are all old men," she said. "You should teach me, so when you all die, someone can still read the signs."

"These signs are not important," I said. "They were created by the Europeans. The Kikuyu had no need for books before the Europeans came to Kenya; we have no need for them on Kirinyaga, which is our own world. When Koinnage and the other chiefs die, everything will be as it was long ago.''

''Are they evil signs, then?'' she asked.

''No,'' I said. ''They are not evil. They just have no meaning for the Kikuyu. They are white man's signs.''

She handed the book to me. ''Would you read me one of the signs?''

''Why?''

''I am curious to know what kind of signs the white men made.''

I stared at her for a long minute, trying to make up my mind. Finally I nodded my assent.

''Just this once,'' I said. ''Never again.''

''Just this once,'' she agreed.

I thumbed through the book, which was a Swahili translation of English poetry, selected one at random, and read it to her:

> *Live with me, and be my love,*
> *And we will all the pleasures prove*
> *That hills and valleys, dales and fields,*
> *And all the craggy mountains yields.*
> *There will we sit upon the rocks,*
> *And see the shepherds feed their flocks,*
> *By shallow rivers, by whose falls*
> *Melodious birds sing madrigals.*
> *There will I make thee a bed of roses,*
> *With a thousand fragrant posies,*
> *A cap of flowers, and a kirtle*
> *Embroider'd all with leaves of myrtle.*
> *A belt of straw and ivy buds,*
> *With coral clasps and amber studs;*
> *And if these pleasures may thee move,*
> *Then live with me and be my love.*

Kamari frowned. ''I do not understand.''

''I told you that you would not,'' I said. ''Now put the book away and finish cleaning my hut. You must still work in your father's *shamba*, along with your duties here.'

She nodded and disappeared into my hut, only to burst forth excitedly a few minutes later.

"It is a *story*!" she exclaimed.

"What is?"

"The sign you read! I do not understand many of the words, but it is a story about a warrior who asks a maiden to marry him!" She paused. "You would tell it better, Koriba. The sign doesn't even mention *fisi*, the hyena, and *mamba*, the crocodile, who dwells by the river and would eat the warrior and his wife. Still, it is a story! I had thought it would be spell for *mundumugus*."

"You are very wise to know that it is a story," I said.

"Read another to me!" she said enthusiastically.

I shook my head. "Do you not remember our agreement? Just that once and never again."

She lowered her head in thought, then looked up brightly. "Then teach *me* to read the signs."

"That is against the law of the Kikuyu," I said. "No woman is permitted to read."

"Why?"

"It is a woman's duty to till the fields and pound the grain and make the fires and weave the fabrics and bear her husband's children," I answered.

"But I am not a woman," she pointed out. "I am just a little girl."

"But you will become a woman," I said, "and a woman may not read."

"Teach me now, and I will forget how when I become a woman."

"Does the eagle forget how to fly, or the hyena to kill?"

"It is not fair."

"No," I said. "But it is just."

"I do not understand."

"Then I will explain it to you," I said. "Sit down, Kamari."

She sat down on the dirt opposite me and leaned forward intently.

"Many years ago," I began, "the Kikuyu lived in the shadow of Kirinyaga, the mountain upon which Ngai dwells."

"I know," she said. "Then the Europeans came and built their cities."

"You are interrupting," I said.

"I am sorry, Koriba," she answered. "But I already know this story."

"You do not know all of it," I replied. "Before the Europeans came, we lived in harmony with the land. We tended our cattle and plowed our fields, and we produced just enough children to replace those who died of old age and disease, and those who died in our wars against the Maasai and the Wakamba and the Nandi. Our lives were simple but fulfilling."

"And *then* the Europeans came!" she said.

"Then the Europeans came," I agreed, "and they brought new ways with them."

"Evil ways."

I shook my head. "They were not evil ways for the Europeans," I replied. "I know, for I have studied in European schools. But they were not good ways for the Kikuyu and the Maasai and the Wakamba and the Embu and the Kisi and all the other tribes. We saw the clothes they wore and the buildings they erected and the machines they used, and we tried to become like Europeans. But we are not Europeans, and their ways are not our ways, and they do not work for us. Our cities became overcrowded and polluted, and our land grew barren, and our animals died, and our water became poisoned, and finally, when the Eutopian Council allowed us to move to the world of Kirinyaga, we left Kenya behind and came here to live according to the old ways, the ways that are good for the Kikuyu." I paused. "Long ago the Kikuyu had no written language, and did not know how to read, and since we are trying to create a Kikuyu world here on Kirinyaga, it is only fitting that our people do not learn to read or write.''

"But what is good about not knowing how to read?'' she asked. "Just because we didn't do it before the Europeans came doesn't make it bad.''

"Reading will make you aware of other ways of thinking and living, and then you will be discontented with your life on Kirinyaga.''

"But you read, and you are not discontented.''

"I am the *mundumugu*,'' I said. "I am wise enough to know that what I read are lies.''

"But lies are not always bad,'' she persisted. "You tell them all the time.''

"The *mundumugu* does not lie to his people,'' I replied sternly.

"You call them stories, like the story of the lion and the hare, or the tale of how the rainbow came to be, but they are lies.''

"They are parables,'' I said.

"What is a parable?''

"A type of story.''

"Is it a true story?''

"In a way.''

"If it is true in a way, then it is also a lie in a way, is it not?'' she replied, and then continued before I could answer her. "And if I can listen to a lie, why can I not read one?''

"I have already explained it to you.''

"It is not fair,'' she repeated.

"No,'' I agreed. "But it is true, and, in the long run, it is for the good of the Kikuyu.''

"I still don't understand why it is good,'' she complained.

"Because we are all that remain. Once before, the Kikuyu tried to become something that they were not, and we became not city-dwelling Kikuyu, or bad Kikuyu, or unhappy Kikuyu, but an entirely new tribe called Kenyans. Those of us who came to Kirinyaga came here to preserve the old ways—and if women start reading, some of them will become discontented, and they will leave, and then one day there will be no Kikuyu left.''

"But I don't want to leave Kirinyaga!" she protested. "I want to become circumcised, and bear many children for my husband, and till the fields of his *shamba,* and someday be cared for by my grandchildren."

"That is the way you are supposed to feel."

"But I also want to read about other worlds and other times."

I shook my head. "No."

"But—"

"I will hear no more of this today," I said. "The sun grows high in the sky, and you have not yet finished your tasks here, and you must still work in your father's *shamba* and come back again this afternoon."

She rose without another word and went about her duties. When she finished, she picked up the cage and began walking back to her *boma.*

I watched her walk away, then returned to my hut and activated my computer to discuss a minor orbital adjustment with Maintenance, for it had been hot and dry for almost a month. They gave their consent, and, a few moments later, I walked down the long, winding path into the center of the village. Lowering myself gently to the ground, I spread my pouchful of bones and charms out before me and invoked Ngai to cool Kirinyaga with a mild rain, which Maintenance had agreed to supply later in the afternoon.

Then the children gathered about me, as they always did when I came down from my *boma* on the hill and entered the village.

"*Jambo,* Koriba!" they cried.

"*Jambo,* my brave young warriors," I replied, still seated on the ground.

"Why have you come to the village this morning, Koriba?" asked Ndemi, the boldest of the young boys.

"I have come here to ask Ngai to water our fields with His tears of compassion," I said, "for we have had no rain this month, and the crops are thirsty."

"Now that you have finished speaking to Ngai, will you tell us a story?" asked Ndemi.

I looked up the sun, estimating the time of day.

"I have time for just one," I replied. "Then I must walk through the fields and place new charms on the scarecrows, that they may continue to protect your crops."

"What story will you tell us, Koriba?" asked another of the boys.

I looked around, and saw that Kamari was standing among the girls.

"I think I shall tell you the story of the Leopard and the Shrike," I said.

"I have not heard that one before," said Ndemi.

"Am I such an old man that I have no new stories to tell?" I demanded, and he dropped his gaze to the ground. I waited until I had everyone's attention, and then I began:

"Once there was a very bright young shrike, and because he was very bright, he was always asking questions of his father.

" 'Why do we eat insects?' he asked one day.

" 'Because we are shrikes, and that is what shrikes do,' answered his father.

" 'But we are also birds,' said the shrike. ''And do not birds such as the eagle eat fish?'

" 'Ngai did not mean for shrikes to eat fish,' said his father, 'and even if you were strong enough to catch and kill a fish, eating it would make you sick.'

" 'Have you ever eaten a fish?' asked the young shrike.

" 'No,' said his father.

" 'Then how do you know?' said the young shrike, and that afternoon he flew over the river and found a tiny fish. He caught it and ate it, and he was sick for a whole week.

" 'Have you learned your lesson now?' asked the shrike's father, when the young shrike was well again.

" 'I have learned not to eat fish,' said the shrike. 'But I have another question.'

" 'Why are shrikes the most cowardly of birds?' asked

the shrike. 'Whenever the lion or the leopard appears, we flee to the highest branches of the trees and wait for them to go away.'

" 'Lions and leopards would eat us if they could,' said the shrike's father. 'Therefore, we must flee from them.'

" 'But they do not eat the ostrich, and the ostrich is a bird,' said the bright young shrike. 'If they attack the ostrich, he kills them with his kick.'

" 'You are not an ostrich,' said his father, tired of listening to him.

" 'But I am a bird, and the ostrich is a bird, and I will learn to kick as the ostrich kicks,' said the young shrike, and he spent the next week practicing kicking any insects and twigs that were in his way.

"Then one day he came across *chui*, the leopard, and as the leopard approached him, the bright young shrike did not fly to the highest branches of the tree, but bravely stood his ground.

" 'You have great courage to face me thus,' said the leopard.

" 'I am a very bright bird, and I am not afraid of you,' said the shrike. 'I have practiced kicking as the ostrich does, and if you come any closer, I will kick you and you will die.'

" 'I am an old leopard, and cannot hunt any longer,' said the leopard. 'I am ready to die. Come kick me, and put me out of my misery.'

"The young shrike walked up to the leopard and kicked him full in the face. The leopard simply laughed, opened his mouth, and swallowed the bright young shrike.

" 'What a silly bird,' laughed the leopard, 'to pretend to be something that he was not! If he had flown away like a shrike, I would have gone hungry today—but by trying to be what he was never meant to be, all he did was fill my stomach. I guess he was not a very bright bird, after all.' "

I stopped and stared straight at Kamari.

"Is that the end?" asked one of the other girls.

"That is the end," I said.

"Why did the shrike think he could be an ostrich?" asked one of the smaller boys.

"Perhaps Kamari can tell you," I said.

All the children turned to Kamari, who paused for a moment and then answered.

"There is a difference between wanting to be an ostrich, and wanting to know what an ostrich knows," she said, looking directly into my eyes. "It was not wrong for the shrike to want to know things. It was wrong for him to think he could become an ostrich."

There was a momentary silence while the children considered her answer.

"Is that true, Koriba?" asked Ndemi at last.

"No," I said, "for once the shrike knew what the ostrich knew, it forgot that it was a shrike. You must always remember who you are, and knowing too many things can make you forget."

"Will you tell us another story?" asked a young girl.

"Not this morning," I said, getting to my feet. "But when I come to the village tonight to drink *pombe* and watch the dancing, perhaps I will tell you the story about the bull elephant and the wise little Kikuyu boy. Now," I added, "do none of you have chores to do?"

The children dispersed, returning to their *shambas* and their cattle pastures, and I stopped by Juma's hut to give an ointment for his joints, which always bothered him just before it rained. I visited Koinnage and drank *pombe* with him, and then discussed the affairs of the village with the Council of Elders. Finally I returned to my own *boma,* for I always take a nap during the heat of the day, and the rain was not due for another few hours.

Kamari was there when I arrived. She had gathered more wood and water, and was filling the grain buckets for my goats as I entered my *boma.*

"How is your bird this afternoon?" I asked, looking at the pygmy falcon, whose cage had been carefully placed in the shade of my hut.

"He drinks, but he will not eat," she said in worried tones. "He spends all his time looking at the sky."

"There are things that are more important to him than eating," I said.

"I am finished now," she said. "May I go home, Koriba?"

I nodded, and she left as I was arranging my sleeping blanket inside my hut.

She came every morning and every afternoon for the next week. Then, on the eighth day, she announced with tears in her eyes that the pygmy falcon had died.

"I told you this would happen," I said gently. "Once a bird has ridden upon the winds, he cannot live on the ground."

"Do all birds die when they can no longer fly?" she asked.

"Most do," I said. "A few like the security of the cage, but most die of broken hearts, for, having touched the sky, they cannot bear to lose the gift of flight."

"Why do we make cages, then, if they do not make the birds feel better?"

"Because they make *us* feel better," I answered.

She paused, and then said: "I will keep my word and clean your hut and your *boma*, and fetch your water and kindling, even though the bird is dead."

I nodded. "That was our agreement," I said.

True to her word, she came back twice a day for the next three weeks. Then, at noon on the twenty-ninth day, after she had completed her morning chores and returned to her family's *shamba*, her father, Njoro, walked up the path to my *boma*.

"*Jambo*, Koriba," he greeted me, a worried expression on his face.

"*Jambo*, Njoro," I said without getting to my feet. "Why have you come to my *boma*?"

"I am a poor man, Koriba," he said, squatting down next to me. "I have only one wife, and she has produced no sons and only two daughters. I do not own as large a *shamba* as most men in the village, and the hyenas killed three of my cows this past year."

I could not understand his point, so I merely stared at him, waiting for him to continue.

"As poor as I am," he went on, "I took comfort in the thought that at least I would have the bride-prices from my two daughters in my old age." He paused. "I have been a good man, Koriba. Surely I deserve that much."

"I have not said otherwise," I replied.

"Then why are you training Kamari to be a *mundumugu*?" he demanded. "It is well known that the *mundumugu* never marries."

"Has Kamari told you that she is to become a *mundumugu*?" I asked.

He shook his head. "No. She does not speak to her mother or myself at all since she has been coming here to clean your *boma*."

"Then you are mistaken," I said. "No woman may be a *mundumugu*. What made you think that I am training her?"

He dug into the folds of his *kikoi* and withdrew a piece of cured wildebeest hide. Scrawled on it in charcoal was the following inscription:

> *I AM KAMARI*
> *I AM TWELVE YEARS OLD*
> *I AM A GIRL*

"This is writing," he said accusingly. "Women cannot write. Only the *mundumugu* and great chiefs like Koinnage can write."

"Leave this with me, Njoro," I said, taking the hide, "and send Kamari to my *boma*."

"I need her to work my *shamba* until afternoon."

"Now," I said.

He sighed and nodded. "I will send her, Koriba." He paused. "You are certain that she is not to be a *mundumugu*?"

"You have my word," I said, spitting on my hands to show my sincerity.

He seemed relieved, and went off to his *boma*. Kamari came up the path a few minutes later.

"*Jambo*, Koriba," she said.

"*Jambo*, Kamari," I replied. "I am very displeased with you."

"Did I not gather enough kindling this morning?" she asked.

"You gathered enough kindling."

"Were the gourds not filled with water?"

"The gourds were filled."

"Then what did I do wrong?" she asked, absently pushing one of my goats aside as it approached her.

"You broke your promise to me."

"That is not true," she said. "I have come every morning and every afternoon, even though the bird is dead."

"You promised not to look at another book," I said.

"I have not looked at another book since the day you told me that I was forbidden to."

"Then explain *this*," I said, holding up the hide with her writing on it.

"There is nothing to explain," she said with a shrug. "I wrote it."

"And if you have not looked at books, how did you learn to write?" I demanded.

"From your magic box," she said. "You never told me not to look at it."

"My magic box?" I said, frowning.

"The box that hums with life and has many colors."

"You mean my computer?" I said, surprised.

"Your magic box," she repeated.

"And it taught you how to read and write?"

"*I* taught me—but only a little," she said unhappily. "I am the shrike in your story—I am not as bright as I thought. Reading and writing is very difficult."

"I told you that you must not learn to read," I said,

resisting the urge to comment on her remarkable accomplishment, for she had clearly broken the law.

Kamari shook her head.

"You told me I must not look at your books," she replied stubbornly.

"I told you that women must not read," I said. "You have disobeyed me. For this, you must be punished." I paused. "You will continue your chores here for three more months, and you must bring me two hares and two rodents, which you must catch yourself. Do you understand?"

"I understand."

"Now come into my hut with me, that you may understand one thing more."

She followed me into the hut.

"Computer," I said. "Activate."

"Activated," said the computer's mechanical voice.

"Computer, scan the hut and tell me who is here with me."

The lens of the computer's sensors glowed briefly.

"The girl, Kamari wa Njoro, is here with you," replied the computer.

"Will you recognize her if you see her again?"

"Yes."

"This is a Priority Order," I said. "Never again may you converse with Kamari wa Njoro verbally or in any known language."

"Understood and logged," said the computer.

"Deactivate." I turned to Kamari. "Do you understand what I have done, Kamari?"

"Yes," she said, "and it is not fair. I did not disobey you."

"It is the law that women may not read," I said, "and you have broken it. You will not break it again. Now go back to your *shamba*."

She left, head held high, youthful back stiff with defiance, and I went about my duties, instructing the young boys on the decoration of their bodies for their forthcoming circumcision ceremony, casting a counter-spell for old Siboki (for he had found hyena dung within his *boma,* which is one of the surest signs of a *thahu,* or curse), instructing Maintenance to make another minor orbital adjustment that would bring cooler weather to the western plains.

By the time I returned to my hut for my afternoon nap, Kamari had come and gone again, and everything was in order.

For the next two months, life in the village went its placid way. The crops were harvested, old Koinnage took another wife and we had a two-day festival with much dancing and *pombe*-drinking to celebrate the event, the short rains arrived on schedule, and three children were born to the village. Even the Eutopian Council, which had complained about our custom of leaving the old and the infirm out for the hyenas, left us completely alone. We found the lair of a family of hyenas and killed three whelps, then slew the mother when she returned. At each full moon, I slaughtered a cow—not merely a goat, but a large, fat cow—to thank Ngai for His generosity, for truly He had graced Kirinyaga with abundance.

During this period I rarely saw Kamari. She came in the mornings when I was in the village, casting bones to bring forth the weather, and she came in the afternoons when I was giving charms to the sick and conversing with the Elders—but I always knew she had been there, for my hut and my *boma* were immaculate, and I never lacked for water or kindling.

Then, on the afternoon after the second full moon, I returned to my *boma* after advising Koinnage about how he might best settle an argument over a disputed plot of land, and as I entered my hut, I noticed that the computer screen was alive and glowing, covered with strange symbols. When I had taken my degrees in England and America, I had learned English and French and Spanish, and of course I knew Kikuyu and Swahili, but these symbols represented no known language, nor, although they used numerals as well as letters and punctuation marks, were they mathematical formulas.

"Computer, I distinctly remember deactivating you this morning," I said, frowning. "Why does your screen glow with life?"

"Kamari activated me."

"And she forgot to deactivate you when she left?"

"That is correct."

"I thought as much," I said grimly. "Does she activate you every day?"

"Yes."

"Did I not give you a Priority Order never to communicate with her in any known language?" I said, puzzled.

"You did, Koriba."

"Can you then explain why you have disobeyed my directive?"

"I have not disobeyed your directive, Koriba," said the computer. "My programming makes me incapable of disobeying a Priority Order."

"Then what is this that I see upon your screen?"

"This is the Language of Kamari," replied the computer. "It is not among the 1,732 languages and dialects in my memory banks, and hence does not fall under the aegis of your directive."

"Did you create this language?"

"No, Koriba. Kamari created it."

"Did you assist her in any way?"

"No, Koriba, I did not."

"Is it a true language?" I asked. "Can you understand it?"

"It is a true language. I can understand it."

"If she were to ask you a question in the Language of Kamari, could you reply to it?"

"Yes, if the question were simple enough. It is a very limited language."

"And if that reply required you to translate the answer from a known language to the Language of Kamari, would doing so be contrary to my directives?"

"No, Koriba, it would not."

"Have you in fact answered questions put to you by Kamari?"

"Yes, Koriba, I have," replied the computer.

"I see," I said. "Stand by for a new directive."

"Waiting. . . ."

I lowered my head in thought, contemplating the problem. That Kamari was brilliant and gifted was obvious: she had not only taught herself to read and write, but had actually created a coherent and logical language that the computer could understand and in which it could respond. I had given orders, and without directly disobeying them, she had managed to circumvent them. She had no malice within her, and wanted only to learn, which in itself was an admirable goal. All that was on the one hand.

On the other was the threat to the social order we had labored so diligently to establish on Kirinyaga. Men and women knew their responsibilities and accepted them happily. Ngai had given the Maasai the spear, and He had given the Wakamba the arrow, and He had given the Europeans the machine and printing press; but to the Kikuyu, He had given the digging-stick and the fertile land surrounding the sacred fig tree on the slopes of Kirinyaga.

Once before we had lived in harmony with the land, many long years ago. Then had come the printed word. It turned us first into slaves, and then into Christians, and then into soldiers and factory workers and mechanics and politicians, into everything that the Kikuyu were never meant to be. It had happened before; it could happen again.

We had come to the world of Kirinyaga to create a perfect Kikuyu society, a Kikuyu Utopia: could one gifted little girl carry within her the seeds of our destruction? I could not be sure, but it was a fact that gifted children grew up. They became Jesus, and Mohammed, and Jomo Kenyatta—but they also became Tippoo Tib, the greatest slaver of all, and Idi Amin, butcher of his own people.

Or, more often, they became Friedrich Nietzsche and Karl Marx, brilliant men in their own right, but who influenced less brilliant, less capable men. Did I have the right to stand aside and hope that her influence upon our society would be benign, when all history suggested that the opposite was more likely to be true?

My decision was painful, but it was not a difficult one.

"Computer," I said at last, "I have a new Priority Order that supersedes my previous directive. You are no longer allowed to communicate with Kamari under any circumstances whatsoever. Should she activate you, you are to tell her that Koriba has forbidden you to have any contact with her, and you are then to deactivate immediately. Do you understand?"

"Understood and logged."

"Good," I said. "Now deactivate."

When I returned from the village the next morning, I found my water gourds empty, my blankets unfolded, my *boma* filled with the dung of goats.

The *mundumugu* is all-powerful among the Kikuyu, but he is not without compassion. I decided to forgive this childish display of temper, and so I did not visit Kamari's father, nor did I tell the other children to avoid her.

She did not come again in the afternoon. I know, because I waited beside my hut to explain my decision to her. Finally, when twilight came, I sent for the boy, Ndemi, to fill my gourds and clean my *boma*, and although such chores are woman's work, he did not dare disobey his *mundumugu*, although his every gesture displayed contempt for the tasks I had set for him.

When two more days had passed with no sign of Kamari, I summoned Njoro, her father.

"Kamari has broken her word to me," I said when he arrived. "If she does not come to clean my *boma* this afternoon, I will be forced to place a *thahu* upon her."

He looked puzzled. "She says that you have already

placed a curse on her, Koriba. I was going to ask you if we should turn her out of our *boma.*"

I shook my head. "No," I said. "Do not turn her out of your *boma.* I have placed no *thahu* on her yet—but she must come to work this afternoon."

"I do not know if she is strong enough," said Njoro. "She has had neither food nor water for three days, and she sits motionless in my wife's hut." He paused. "*Someone* has placed a *thahu* on her. If it's not you, perhaps you can cast a spell to remove it."

"She has gone three days without eating or drinking?" I repeated.

He nodded.

"I will see her," I said, getting to my feet and following him down the winding path to the village. When we reached Njoro's *boma,* he led me to his wife's hut, then called Kamari's worried mother out and stood aside as I entered. Kamari sat at the farthest point from the door, her back propped against a wall, her knees drawn up to her chin, her arms encircling her thin legs.

"*Jambo,* Kamari," I said.

She stared at me but said nothing.

"Your mother worries for you, and your father tells me that you no longer eat or drink."

She made no answer.

"Listen to my words, Kamari," I said slowly. "I made my decision for the good of Kirinyaga, and I will not recant it. As a Kikuyu woman, you must live the life that has been ordained for you." I paused. "However, neither the Kikuyu nor the Eutopian Council are without compassion for the individual. Any member of our society may leave if he wishes. According to the charter we signed when we claimed this world, you need only walk to that area known as Haven, and a Maintenance ship will pick up you and transport you to the location of your choice."

"All I know is Kirinyaga," she said. "How am I to choose a new home if I am forbidden to learn about other places?"

"I do not know," I admitted.

"I don't *want* to leave Kirinyaga!" she continued. "This is my home. These are my people. I am a Kikuyu girl, not a Maasai girl or a European girl. I will bear my husband's children and till his *shamba;* I will gather his wood and cook his meals and weave his garments; I will leave my parents' *shamba* and live with my husband's family. I will do all this without complaint, Koriba, if you will just let me learn to read and write!"

"I cannot," I said sadly.

"But *why*?"

"Who is the wisest man you know, Kamari?" I asked.

"The *mundumugu* is always the wisest man in the village."

"Then you must trust to my wisdom."

"But I feel like the pygmy falcon," she said, her misery reflected in her voice. "He spent his life dreaming of soaring high upon the winds. I dream of seeing words upon the computer screen."

"You are not like the falcon at all," I said. "He was prevented from being what he was meant to be. You are prevented from being what you are not meant to be."

"You are not an evil man, Koriba," she said solemnly. "But you are wrong."

"If that is so, then I shall have to live with it," I said.

"But you are asking *me* to live with it," she said, "and that is your crime."

"If you call me a criminal again," I said sternly, for no one may speak thus to the *mundumugu,* "I shall surely place a *thahu* on you."

"What more can you do?" she said bitterly.

"I can turn you into a hyena, an unclean eater of human flesh who prowls only in the darkness. I can fill your belly with thorns, so that your every movement will be agony. I can—"

"You are just a man," she said wearily, "and you have already done your worst."

"I will hear no more of this," I said. "I order you to

eat and drink what your mother brings to you, and I expect to see you at my *boma* this afternoon.''

I walked out of the hut and told Kamari's mother to bring her banana mash and water, then stopped by old Benima's *shamba*. Buffalo had stampeded through his fields, destroying his crops, and I sacrificed a goat to remove the *thahu* that had fallen upon his land.

When I finished, I stopped at Koinnage's *boma*, where he offered me some freshly brewed *pombe* and began complaining about Kibo, his newest wife, who kept taking sides with Shumi, his second wife, against Wambu, his senior wife.

"You can always divorce her and return her to her family's *shamba*," I suggested.

"She cost twenty cows and five goats!" he complained. "Will her family return them?"

"No, they will not."

"Then I will not send her back."

"As you wish," I said with a shrug.

"Besides, she is very strong and very lovely," he continued. "I just wish she would stop fighting with Wambu."

"What do they fight about?" I asked.

"They fight about who will fetch the water, and who will mend my garments, and who will repair the thatch on my hut." He paused. "They even argue about whose hut I should visit at night, as if I had no choice in the matter."

"Do they ever fight about ideas?" I asked.

"Ideas?" he repeated blankly.

"Such as you might find in books."

He laughed. "They are *women*, Koriba. What need have they for ideas?" He paused. "In fact, what need have any of us for them?"

"I do not know," I said. "I was merely curious."

"You look disturbed," he noted.

"It must be the *pombe*," I said. "I am an old man, and perhaps it is too strong."

"That is because Kibo will not listen when Wambu

tells her how to brew it. I really should send her away"—
he looked at Kibo as she carried a load of wood on her
strong, young back—"but she is so young and so lovely."
Suddenly his gaze went beyond his newest wife to the
village. "Ah!" he said. "I see that old Siboki has finally
died."

"How do you know?" I asked.

He pointed to a thin column of smoke. "They are
burning his hut."

I stared off in the direction he indicated. "That is not
Siboki's hut," I said. "His *boma* is more to the west."

"Who else is old and infirm and due to die?" asked
Koinnage.

And suddenly I knew, as surely as I knew that Ngai
sits on His throne atop the holy mountain, that Kamari
was dead.

I walked to Njoro's *shamba* as quickly as I could. When
I arrived, Kamari's mother and sister and grandmother
were already wailing the death chant, tears streaming
down their faces.

"What happened?" I demanded, walking up to Njoro.

"Why do you ask, when it was you who destroyed
her?" he replied bitterly.

"I did not destroy her," I said.

"Did you not threaten to place a *thahu* on her just this
morning?" he persisted. "You did so, and now she is
dead, and I have but one daughter to bring the bride-
price, and I have had to burn Kamari's hut."

"Stop worrying about bride-prices and huts and tell
me what happened, or you shall learn what it means to
be cursed by a *mundumugu*!"

"She hanged herself in her hut with a length of buffalo
hide."

Five women from the neighboring *shamba* arrived and
took up the death chant.

"She hanged herself in her hut?" I repeated.

He nodded. "She could at least have hanged herself
from a tree, so that her hut would not be unclean and I
would not have to burn it."

"Be quiet!" I said, trying to collect my thoughts.

"She was not a bad daughter," he continued. "Why did you curse her, Koriba?"

"I did not place a *thahu* upon her," I said, wondering if I spoke the truth. "I wished only to save her."

"Who has stronger medicine than you?" he asked fearfully.

"She broke the law of Ngai," I answered.

"And now Ngai has taken His vengeance!" moaned Njoro fearfully. "Which member of my family will He strike down next?"

"None of you," I said. "Only Kamari broke the law."

"I am a poor man," said Njoro cautiously, "even poorer now than before. How much must I pay you to ask Ngai to receive Kamari's spirit with compassion and forgiveness?"

"I will do that whether you pay me or not," I answered.

"You will not charge me?" he asked.

"I will not charge you."

"Thank you, Koriba!" he said fervently.

I stood and stared at the blazing hut, trying not to think of the smoldering body of the little girl inside it.

"Koriba?" said Njoro after a lengthy silence.

"What now?" I asked irritably.

"We do not know what to do with the buffalo hide, for it bore the mark of your *thahu,* and we were afraid to burn it. Now I know that the marks were made by Ngai and not you, and I am afraid even to touch it. Will you take it away?"

"What marks?" I said. "What are you talking about?"

He took me by the arm and led me around to the front of the burning hut. There, on the ground, some ten paces from the entrance, lay the strip of tanned hide with which Kamari had hanged herself, and scrawled upon it were more of the strange symbols I had seen on my computer screen three days earlier.

I reached down and picked up the hide, then turned to Njoro. "If indeed there is a curse on your shamba," I said, "I will remove it and take it upon myself, by taking Ngai's marks with me."

"Thank you, Koriba!" he said, obviously much relieved.

"I must leave to prepare my magic," I said abruptly, and began the long walk back to my *boma*. When I arrived, I took the strip of buffalo hide into my hut.

"Computer," I said. "Activate."

"Activated."

I held the strip up to its scanning lens.

"Do you recognize this language?" I asked.

The lens glowed briefly.

"Yes, Koriba. It is the Language of Kamari."

"What does it say?"

"It is a couplet:

> *I know why the caged birds die—*
> *For, like them, I have touched the sky.*"

The entire village came to Njoro's *shamba* in the afternoon, and the women wailed the death chant all night and all of the next day, but before long Kamari was forgotten, for life goes on, and she was, after all, just a little Kikuyu girl.

Since that day, whenever I have found a bird with a broken wing, I have attempted to nurse it back to health. It always dies, and I always bury it next to the mound of earth that marks where Kamari's hut had been.

It is on those days, when I place the birds in the ground, that I find myself thinking of her again, and wishing that I were just a simple man, tending my cattle and worrying about my crops and thinking the thoughts of simple men, rather than a *mundumugu* who must live with the consequences of his wisdom.

APARTNESS
by Vernor Vinge

*This masterful short story, amazingly enough Vinge's first
sale, is as powerful a look at one possible future Africa
as you are likely to find. In it, Vinge shows us that, sadly,
the more things change, the more they remain the
same. . . .*

Born in Waukesha, Wisconsin, Vernor Vinge now lives
in San Diego, California, where he is an associate professor of math sciences at San Diego State University. He
sold his first story, "Apartness," to New Worlds in 1965,
and since then has become a frequent contributor to Analog; he has also sold to Orbit, Far Frontiers, If, Stellar,
and other markets. His novella "True Names" was a
finalist for both the Nebula and Hugo awards in 1981,
and these days Vinge is regarded as one of the best of
the new breed of "hard science" writers, along with people such as Charles Sheffield and Greg Bear. His novels
include Tatia Grimm's World, The Witling, and the well-
received The Peace War and Marooned in Realtime, Hugo
finalists, which have been released in an omnibus volume
as Across Realtime. His most recent books include the
novel A Fire Upon the Deep, and two short story collections, True Names and Other Dangers, and Threats and
Other Promises.

". . . But he saw a light! *On the coast.* Can't you understand what that means?" Diego Ribera y Rodrigues
leaned across the tiny wooden desk to emphasize his
point. His adversary sat in the shadows and avoided the
weak glow of the whale oil lamp hung from the cabin's

ceiling. During the momentary pause in the argument, Diego could hear the wind keening through the masts and rigging above them. He was suddenly, painfully conscious of the regular rolling of the deck and slow oscillations of the swinging lamp. But he continued to glare at the man opposite him, and waited for an answer. Finally Capitán Manuel Delgado tilted his head out of the shadows. He smiled unpleasantly. His narrow face and sharp black mustache made him look like what he was: a master of power—political, military, and personal.

"It means," Delgado answered, "people. So what?"

"That's right. People. On the Palmer Peninsula. The Antarctic Continent is inhabited. Why, finding humans in Europe couldn't be any more fantastic—"

"*Mire,* Señor Professor. I'm vaguely aware of the importance of what you say." There was that smile again. "But the *Vigilancia*—"

Diego tried again. "We simply have to land and investigate the light. Just consider the scientific importance of it all—" The anthropologist had said the wrong thing.

Delgado's cynical indifference dropped away and his young, experienced face became fierce. "Scientific import! If those slimy Australian friends of yours wanted to, they could give us all the scientific knowledge ever known. Instead they have their sympathizers"—he jabbed a finger at Ribera—"run all about the South World doing 'research' that's been done ten times as well more than two centuries ago. The pigs don't even use the knowledge for their own gain." This last was the greatest condemnation Delgado could offer.

Ribera had difficulty restraining a bitter reply, but one mistake this evening was more than enough. He could understand though not approve Delgado's bitterness against a nation which had been wise (or lucky) enough not to burn its libraries during the riots following the North World War. *The Australians have the knowledge, all right,* thought Ribera, *but they also have the wisdom to know that some fundamental changes must be made in human society before this knowledge can be reintro-*

*duced, or else we'll wind up with a South World War and
no more human race.* This was a point Delgado and many
others refused to accept. "But, really. Señor Capitán, we
are doing original research. Ocean currents and populations change over the years. Our data are often quite different from those we know were gathered before. This
light Juarez saw tonight is the strongest evidence of all
that things are different." And for Diego Ribera, it was
especially important. As an anthropologist he had had
nothing to do during the voyage except be seasick. A
thousand times during the trip he had asked himself why
he had been the one to organize the ecologists and ocean-
ographers and get them on the ship; now he knew. If he
could just convince this bigoted sailor . . .

Delgado appeared relaxed again. "And too, Señor
Professor, you must remember that you 'scientists' are
really superfluous on this expedition. You were lucky to
get aboard at all."

That was true. El Presidente Imperial was even more
hostile to scientists of the Melbourne School than Delgado was. Ribera didn't like to think of all the boot-
licking and chicanery that had been necessary to get his
people on the expedition. The anthropologist's reply to
the other's last comment started out respectfully, almost
humbly. "Yes, I know you are doing something truly
important here." He paused. *To hell with it,* he thought,
suddenly sick of his own ingratiating manner. *This fool
won't listen to logic or flattery.* Ribera's tone changed.
"Yeah, I know you are doing something *truly* important
here. Somewhere up in Buenos Aires the Chief Astrologer to el President Imperial looked at his crystal ball or
whatever and said to Alfredo IV in sepulchral tones: 'Señor Presidente, the stars have spoken. All the secrets of
joy and wealth lie on the floating Isle of Coney. Send
your men southward to find it.' And so you, the *Vigilancia NdP,* and half the mental cripples in Sudamérica are
wandering around the coast of Antarctica looking for Coney Island." Ribera ran out of breath and satire at the

same time. He knew his long-caged temper had just ruined all his plans and perhaps put his life in danger.

Delgado's face seemed frozen. His eyes flickered over Ribera's shoulder and looked at a mirror strategically placed in the space between the door frame and the top of the cabin's door. Then he looked back at the anthropologist. "If I weren't such a reasonable man you would be orca meat before morning." Then he smiled, a sincere friendly grin. "Besides, you're right. Those fools in Buenos Aires aren't fit to rule a pigsty, much less the Sudamérican Empire. Alfredo I was a man, a superman. Before the war-diseases had died out, he had united an entire continent under one fist, a continent that no one had been able to unite with jet planes and automatic weapons. But his heirs, especially the one that's in now, are superstitious tramps. . . . Frankly, that's why I can't land on the coast. The Imperial Astrologer, that fellow Jones y Urrutia, would claim when we returned to Buenos Aires that I had catered to your Australian sympathizers and el Presidente would believe him and I would probably end up with a one-way ticket to the Northern Hemisphere."

Ribera was silent for a second, trying to accept Delgado's sudden friendliness. Finally he ventured, "I would've thought you'd *like* the astrologers; you seem to dislike us scientists enough."

"You're using labels, Ribera. I feel nothing toward labels. It is success that wins my affection, and failure my hate. There may have been some time in the past when a group calling themselves astrologers could produce results. I don't know, and the matter doesn't interest me, *for I live in the present.* In our time the men working in the name of astrology are incapable of producing results, are conscious frauds. But don't be smug: your own people have produced damn few results. And if it should ever come that the astrologers are successful, I will take up their arts without hesitation and denounce you and your Scientific Method as superstition—for that is what it would be in the face of a more successful method."

The ultimate pragmatist, thought Ribera. *At least there is one form of persuasion that will work.* "I see what you mean, Señor Capitán. And as to success: there is one way that you could land with impunity. A lot can happen over the centuries." He continued half-slyly, "What was once a floating island might become grounded on the shore of the continent. If the astrologers could be convinced of the idea . . ." He let the sentence hang.

Delgado considered, but not for long. "Say! that is an idea. And I personally would like to find out what kind of creature would prefer this icebox over the rest of the South World.

"Very well, I'll try it. Now get out. I'm going to have to make this look like it's all the astrologers' idea, and you are likely to puncture the illusion if you're around when I talk to them."

Ribera lurched from his chair, caught off balance by the swaying of the deck and the abruptness of his dismissal. Without a doubt, Delgado was the most unusual Sudamérican officer Ribera had ever met.

"*Muchisimas gracias,* Señor Capitán." He turned and walked unsteadily out the door, past the storm light by the entrance, and into the wind-filled darkness of the short Antarctic night.

The astrologers did indeed like the idea. At two-thirty in the morning (just after sunrise) the *Vigilancia, Nave del Presidente,* changed course and tacked toward the area of coast where the light had been. Before the sun had been up six hours, the landing boats were over the side and heading for the coast.

In his eagerness, Diego Ribera y Rodrigues had scrambled aboard the first boat to be launched, not noticing that the Imperial Astrologers had used their favored status on the expedition to commandeer the lead craft. It was a clear day, but the wind made the water choppy and frigid salt water was splattered over the men in the boat. The tiny vessel rose and fell, rose and fell with a monotony that promised to make Ribera sick.

"Ah, so you are finally taking an interest in our Quest," a reedy voice interrupted his thoughts. Ribera turned to face the speaker, and recognized one Juan Jones y Urrutia, Subassistant to the Chief Astrologer to El Presidente Imperial. No doubt the vapid young mystic actually believed the tales of Coney Island, or else he would have managed to stay up in Buenos Aires with the rest of the hedonists in Alfredo's court. Beside the astrologer sat Capitán Delgado. The good captain must have done some tremendous persuading, for Jones seemed to regard the whole idea of visiting the coast as his own conception.

Ribera endeavored to smile. "Why yes, uh—"

Jones pressed on. "Tell me; would you have ever suspected life here, you who don't bother to consult the True Fundamentals?"

Ribera groaned. He noticed Delgado smiling at his discomfort. If the boat went through one more rise-fall, Ribera thought he'd scream; it did and he didn't.

"I guess we couldn't have guessed it, no." Ribera edged to the side of the boat, cursing himself for having been so eager to get on the first boat.

His eyes roamed the horizon—anything to get away from the vacuous, smug expression on Jones' face. The coast was gray, bleak, covered with large boulders. The breakers smashing into it seemed faintly yellow or red where they weren't white foam—probably coloring from the algae and diatoms in the water; the ecology boys would know.

"Smoke ahead!" The shout came thinly through the air from the second boat. Ribera squinted and examined the coast minutely. There! Barely recognizable as smoke, the wind-distorted haze rose from some point hidden by the low coastal hills. What if it turned out to be some sluggishly active volcano? That depressing thought had not occurred to him before. The geologists would have fun, but it would be a bust as far as he was concerned. . . . In any case, they would know which it was in a few minutes.

Capitán Delgado appraised the situation, then spoke several curt commands to the oarsmen. The crew's cadence shifted, and the boat turned ninety degrees to move parallel to the shore and breakers five hundred meters off. The trailing boats imitated the lead craft's maneuver.

Soon the coast bent sharply inward, revealing a long, narrow inlet. The night before, the *Vigilancia* must have been directly in line with the channel in order for Juarez to see the light. The three boats moved up the narrow channel. Soon the wind died. All that could be heard of it was a chill whistle as it tore at the hills which bordered the channel. The waves were much gentler now and the icy water no longer splashed into the boats, though the men's parkas were already caked with salt. Earlier the water had seemed faintly yellow; now it appeared orange and even red, especially farther up the inlet. The brilliant bacterial contamination contrasted sharply with the dull hills, hills that bore no trace of vegetation. In the place of plant life, uniformly gray boulders of all sizes covered the landscape. Nowhere was there snow; that would come with the winter, still five months in the future. But to Ribera, this "summer" landscape was many times harsher than the bleakest winter scene in Sudamérica. Red water, gray hills. The only things that seemed even faintly normal were the brilliant blue sky, and the sun which cast long shadows into the drowned valley; a sun that seemed always at the point of setting even though it had barely risen.

Ribera's attention wandered up the channel. He forgot the sea sickness, the bloody water, the dead land. He could see *them;* not an ambiguous glow in the night, but people! He could see their huts, apparently made of stone and hides, and partly dug into the ground. He could see what appeared to be leather-hulled boats or kayaks along with a larger, white boat (now what could that be?), lying on the ground before the little village. He could see people! Not the expressions on their faces nor the exact manner of their clothing, but he could see them and that was enough for the instant. Here was something truly new;

something the long dead scholars of Oxford, Cambridge, and UCLA had never learned, could never have learned. Here was something that mankind was seeing for the first and not the second or third or fourth time around!

What brought these people here? Ribera asked himself. From the few books on polar cultures that he had read at the University of Melbourne, he knew that generally populations are forced into the polar regions by competing peoples. What were the forces behind this migration? Who were these people?

The boats swept swiftly forward on the quiet water. Soon Ribera felt the hull of his craft scrape bottom. He and Delgado jumped into the red water and helped the oarsmen drag the boat onto the beach. Ribera waited impatiently for the two other boats, which carried the scientists, to arrive. In the meantime, he concentrated his attention on the natives, trying to understand every detail of their lives at once.

None of the aborigines moved; none ran; none attacked. They stood where they had been when he had first seen them. They did not scowl or wave weapons, but Ribera was distinctly aware that they were not friendly. No smiles, no welcome grimness. They seemed a proud people. The adults were tall, their faces so grimy, tanned, and withered that the anthropologist could only guess at their race. From the set of their lips, he knew that most of them lacked teeth. The natives' children peeped around the legs of their mothers, women who seemed old enough to be great grandmothers. If they had been Sudaméricans, he would have estimated their average age as sixty or seventy, but he knew that it couldn't be more than twenty or twenty-five.

From the pattern of fatty tissues in their faces, Ribera thought he could detect evidence of cold adaption; maybe they were Eskimos, though it would have been physically impossible for that race to migrate from one pole to the other while the North World War raged. Both their parkas and the kayaks appeared to be made of seal hide. But the parkas were ill-designed and much bulkier than the Eskimo outfits he had seen in pictures. And the harpoons they held were much less ingenious than the designs he remembered. If these people were of the supposedly extinct Eskimo race, they were an extraordinarily primitive branch of it. Besides, they were much too hairy to be full-blooded Indians or Eskimos.

With half his mind, he noticed the astrologers glance at the village and dismiss it. They were after the Isle of Coney, not some smelly aborigines. Ribera smiled bitterly; he wondered what Jones' reaction would be if the astrologer ever learned that Coney had been an amusement park. Many legends had grown up after the North World War and the one about Coney Island was one of the weirdest. Jones led his men up one of the nearer hills, evidently to get a better view of the area. Capitán Delgado hastily dispatched twelve crewmen to accompany the mystics. The good sailor obviously recognized what a position he would be in if any of the astrologers were lost.

Ribera's mind returned to the puzzle: Where were these people from? How had they gotten here? Perhaps that was the best angle on the problem: people don't just sprout from the ground. The pitiful kayaks—they weren't true kayaks; they didn't enclose the lower body of the user—could hardly transport a person ten kilometers over open water. What about that large white craft, further up the beach? It seemed a much sturdier vessel than the hide and bone "kayaks." He looked at it more closely—the white craft might even be made of fiberglass, a pre-War construction material. Maybe he should get a closer look at it.

A shout attracted Ribera's attention; he turned. The second landing craft, bearing the majority of the scientists, had grounded on the rocky beach. He ran down the beach to the men piling out of the boat, and gave them the gist of his conclusions. Having explained the situation, Ribera selected Enrique Cardona and Ari Juarez, both ecologists, to accompany him in a parley with the natives. The three men approached the largest group of natives, who watched them stonily. The Sudaméricans stopped several paces before the silent tribesmen. Ribera raised his hands in a gesture of peace. "My friends, may we look at your beautiful boat yonder? We will not harm it." There was no response, though Ribera thought he sensed a greater tenseness among the natives. He tried again, making the request in Portuguese, then in English. Cardona attempted the question in Zulunder, as did Juarez in broken French. Still no acknowledgement, but the harpoons seemed to quiver, and there was an all but imperceptible motion of hands toward bone knives.

"Well, to hell with them," Cardona snapped finally. "C'mon Diego, let's have a look at it." The short-tempered ecologist turned and began walking toward the mysterious white boat. This time there was no mistaking hostility. The harpoons were raised and the knives drawn.

"Wait, Enrique," Ribera said urgently. Cardona stopped. Ribera was sure that if the ecologist had taken one more step he would have been spitted. "Wait," Diego Ribera y Rodrigues continued. "We have plenty of time. Besides, it would be madness to push the issue." He indicated the natives' weapons.

Cardona noticed the weapons. "All right. We'll humor them for now." He seemed to regard the harpoons as an embarrassment rather than a threat. The three men retreated from the confrontation. Ribera noticed that Delgado's men had their pistols half drawn. The expedition had narrowly avoided a blood-bath.

The scientists would have to content themselves with a peripheral inspection of the village. In one way this was more pleasant than direct examination, for the ground about the huts was littered with filth. In a century or so this area would have the beginnings of a soil. After ten minutes or so the adult males of the tribe resumed their work mending the kayaks. Apparently they were preparing for a seal hunting expedition; the area around the village had been hunted free of the seals and sea birds that populated most other parts of the coast.

If only we could communicate with them, thought Ribera. The aborigines themselves probably knew (at least by legend) what their origins were. As it was, Ribera had to investigate by the most indirect means. In his mind he summed up the facts he knew: the natives were of an indeterminate race; they were hairy, and yet they seemed to have some of the physiological cold weather adaptions of the extinct Eskimos. The natives were primitive in every physical sense. Their equipment and techniques were far inferior to the ingenious invention of the Eskimos. And the natives spoke no currently popular language. One other thing: the fire they kept alive at the center of the village was an impractical affair, and probably served a religious purpose only. Those were the facts; now, who the hell were these people? The problem was so puzzling that for the moment he forgot the dreamlike madness of the gray landscape and the ''setting'' noonday sun.

A half hour and more passed. The geologists were mildly ecstatic about the area, but for Ribera the situation was becoming increasingly exasperating. He didn't dare approach the villagers or the white boat, yet these were the things he most wanted to do. Perhaps this impatience made him especially sensitive, for he was the first of the scientists to hear the clatter of rolling stones and the sound of voices over the shrill wind.

He turned and saw Jones and company descending a néarby hill at all but breakneck speed. One misstep and the entire group would have descended the hill on their backs rather than their feet. The rolling stones cast loose by their rush preceded them into the valley. The astrologers reached the bottom of the hill far outdistancing the sailors delegated to protect them, and continued running.

''Wonder what's trying to eat them,'' Ribera asked Juarez half-seriously.

As he plunged past Delgado, Jones shouted, ''—think we may have found it, Capitán—something man-made rising from the sea.'' He pointed wildly toward the hill they had just descended.

The astrologers piled into a boat. Seeing that the mystics really intended to leave, Delgado dispatched fifteen men to help them with the craft, and an equal number to go along in another boat. In a couple of minutes, the two boats were well into the channel and rowing fast toward open water.

"What the hell was that about?" Ribera shouted to Capitán Delgado.

"You know as much as I. Señor Professor. Let's take a look. If we go for a little walk—"he nodded to the hill—"we can probably get within sight of the 'discovery' before Jones and the rest reach it by boat. You men stay here." Delgado turned his attention to the remaining crewmen. "If these primitives try to confiscate our boat, demonstrate your firearms to them—on them.

"The same goes for you scientists. As many men as possible are going to have to stay here to see that we don't lose that boat; it's a long, wet walk back to the *Vigilancia*. Let's go, Ribera. You can take a couple of your people if you want."

Ribera and Juarez set out with Delgado and three ship's officers. The men moved slowly up the slope, which was made treacherous by its loose covering of boulders. As they reached the crest of the hill the wind beat into them, tearing at their parkas. The terrain was less hilly but in the far distance they could see the mountains that formed the backbone of the peninsula.

Delgado pointed. "If they saw something in the ocean, it must be in that direction. We saw the rest of the coast on our way in."

The six men started off in the indicated direction. The wind was against them and their progress was slow. Fifteen minutes later they crossed the top of a gentle hill, and reached the coast. Here the water was a clean bluish-green and the breakers smashing over the rocky beach could almost have been mistaken for Pacific waters sweeping into some bleak shore in the Province of Chile. Ribera looked over the waves. Two stark, black objects broke the smooth, silver line of the horizon. Their uncompromising angularity showed them to be artificial.

Delgado drew a pair of binoculars from his parka. Ribera noted with surprise that the binoculars bore the mark of the finest optical instruments extant: U.S. Naval war surplus. On some markets, the object would have brought a price comparable to that of the entire ship *Vigilancia*. Capitán Delgado raised the binoculars to his eyes and inspected the black forms in the ocean. Thirty seconds passed. *"Madre del Presidente!"* he swore softly but with feeling. He handed the binocs to Ribera. "Take a look, Señor Professor."

The anthropologist scanned the horizon, spotted the black shapes. Though winter sea ice had smashed their hulls and scuttled them in the shallow water, they were obviously ships—atomic or petroleum powered, pre-War ships. At the edge of his field of vision, he noticed two white objects bobbing in the water; they were the two landing boats from the *Vigilancia*. The boats disappeared every few seconds in the trough of a wave. They moved a little closer to the two half-sunken ships, then began to pull away. Ribera could imagine what had happened: Jones had seen that the hulks were no different from the relics of the Argentine navy sunk off Buenos Aires. The astrologer was probably fit to be tied.

Ribera inspected the wrecks minutely. One was half capsized and hidden behind the other. His gaze roamed along the bow of the nearer vessel. There were letters on that bow, letters almost worn away by the action of ice and water upon the plastic hull of the ship.

"My God!" whispered Ribera. The letters spelled: S—*Hen*—k—*V*—*woe*—d. He didn't need to look at the other vessel to know that it had once been called *Nation*. Ribera dumbly handed the binoculars to Juarez.

The mystery was solved. He knew the pressures that had driven the natives here. "If the Zulunders ever hear about this . . ." Ribera's voice trailed off into silence.

"Yeah." Delgado replied. He understood what he had seen, and for the first time seemed somewhat subdued. "Well, let's get back. This land isn't fit for . . . it isn't fit."

The six men turned and started back. Though the ship's officers had had an opportunity to use the binoculars, they didn't seem to understand exactly what they had seen. And probably the astrologers didn't realize the significance of the discovery, either. That left three, Juarez, Ribera, and Delgado, who knew the secret of the natives' origin. If the news spread much further, disaster would result, Ribera was sure.

The wind was at their backs but it did not speed their progress. It took them almost a quarter-hour to reach the crest of the hill overlooking the village and the red water.

Below them, Ribera could see the adult male natives clustered in a tight group. Not ten feet away stood all the scientists, and the crewmen. Between the two groups was one of the Sudaméricans. Ribera squinted and saw that the man was Enrique Cardona. The ecologist was gesturing wildly, angrily.

"Oh, no!" Ribera sprinted down the hill, closely followed by Delgado and the rest. The anthropologist moved even faster than the astrologers had an hour before, and almost twice as fast as he would have thought humanly possible. The tiny avalanches started by his footfalls were slow compared to his speed. Even as he flew down the slope, Ribera felt himself detached, analytically examining the scene before him.

Cardona was shouting, as if to make the natives understand by sheer volume. Behind him the ecologists and biologists stood, impatient to inspect the village and the natives' boat. Before him stood a tall, withered native, who must have been all of forty years old. Even from a distance the natives' bearing revealed intense, suppressed anger. The native's parka was the most impractical of all those Ribera had seen; he could have sworn that it was a crude, seal-skin imitation of a double-breasted suit.

Almost screaming, Cardona cried, "God damn it, why can't we look at your boat?" Ribera put forth one last burst of speed, and shouted at Cardona to stop his provocation. It was too late. Just as the anthropologist arrived at the scene of the confrontation, the native in the strange parka drew himself to his full height, pointed to all the Sudaméricans, and screeched (as nearly as Ribera's Spanish-thinking mind could record), *"—in di nam niutrantsfals mos yulisterf—"*

The half-raised harpoons were thrown. Cardona went down instantly, transfixed by three of the weapons. Several other men were hit and felled. The natives drew their knives and ran forward, taking advantage of the confusion which the harpoons had created. A painfully loud *BAM* erupted beside Ribera's ear as Delgado fired his pistol, picking off the leader of the natives. The crewmen recovered from their shock, began firing at the aborigines. Ribera whipped his pistol from a pouch at his side and blasted into the swarm of primitives. Their single shot pistols emptied, the scientists and crew were reduced to knives. The next few seconds were total chaos. The knives rose and fell, gleaming more redly than the water in the cove. The anthropologist half stumbled over squirming bodies. The air was filled with hoarse shouts and sounds of straining men.

The groups were evenly matched and they were cutting each other to pieces. In some still calm part of his mind Ribera noticed the returning boats of the astrologers. He glimpsed the crewmen aiming their muskets, waiting for a clear shot at the primitives.

The turbulence of the fray whirled him about, out of the densest part of the fight. They had to disengage; another few minutes and there wouldn't be one man in ten left standing on the beach. Ribera screamed this to Delgado. Miraculously the man heard him and agreed; retreat was the only sane thing to do. The Sudaméricans ran raggedly toward their boat, with the natives close behind. Sharp cracking sounds came from over the water. The crewmen in the other boats were taking advantage of the dispersion between pursuers and pursued. The Sudaméricans reached their boat and began pushing it into the water. Ribera and several others turned to face the natives. Musket fire had forced most of the primitives back, but a few still ran toward the shore, knives drawn. Ribera reached down and snatched a small stone from the ground. Using an almost forgotten skill of his "gentle" childhood, he cocked his arm and snapped the rock forward in a flat trajectory. It caught one of the natives dead between the eyes with a sharp *smack*. The man plunged forward, fell on his face, and lay still.

Ribera turned and ran into the shallow water after the boat. He was followed by the rest of the rearguard. Eager hands reached out from the boat to pull him aboard. A couple more feet and he would be safe.

The blow sent him spinning forward. As he fell, he saw with dumb horror the crimson harpoon which had emerged from his parka just below the right side pocket.

Why? Must we forever commit the same blunders over and over, and over again? Ribera didn't have time to wonder at this fleeting incongruous thought, before the redness closed about him.

A gentle breeze, carrying the happy sounds of distant parties, entered the large windows of the bungalow and caressed its interior. It was a cool night, late in summer. The first mild airs of fall made the darkness pleasant, inviting. The house was situated on the slight ridge which marked the old shore line of La Plata; the lawns and hedges outside fell gently away toward the general plain of the city. The faint though delicate light from the oil lamps of that city defined its rectangular array of streets, and showed its buildings uniformly one or two stories high. Further out, the city lights came to an abrupt end at the waterfront. But even beyond that there were the moving, yellow lights of boats and ships navigating La Plata. Off to the extreme left burned the bright fires surrounding the Naval Enclosure, where the government labored on some secret weapon, possibly a steam-powered warship.

It was a peaceful scene, and a happy evening; preparations were almost complete. His desk was littered with the encouraging replies to his proposals. It had been hard work but a lot of fun at the same time. And Buenos Aires had been the ideal base of operations. Alfredo IV was touring the western provinces. To be more precise, el Presidente Imperial and his court were visiting the pleasure spots in Santiago (as if Alfredo had not built up enough talent in Buenos Aires itself). The Imperial Guard and the Secret Police clustered close by the monarch (Alfredo was more afraid of a court coup than anything else), so Buenos Aires was more relaxed than it had been in many years.

Yes, two months of hard work. Many important people had to be informed, and confidentially. But the replies had been almost uniformly enthusiastic, and it appeared that the project wasn't known to those who would destroy its goal; though of course the simple fact that so many people had to know increased the chances of disclosure. But that was a risk that had to be taken.

And, thought Diego Ribera, *it's been two months since the Battle of Bloody Cove.* (The name of the inlet had arisen almost spontaneously). He hoped that the tribe hadn't been scared away from that spot, or, infinitely worse, driven to the starvation point by the massacre. If that fool Enrique Cardona had only kept his mouth shut, both sides could have parted peacefully (if not amicably) and some good men would still be alive.

Ribera scratched his side thoughtfully. Another inch and he wouldn't have made it himself. If that harpoon had hit just a little further up. . . . Someone's quick thinking had added to his initial good luck. That someone had slashed the thick cord tied to the harpoon which had hit Ribera. If the separation had not been made, the cord would most likely have been pulled back and the harpoon's barb engaged. Even as miraculous was the fact that he had survived the impalement and the poor medical conditions on board the *Vigilancia*. Physically, all the damage that remained was a pair of neat, circular scars. The whole affair was enough to give you religion, or, conversely, scare the hell out of you. . . .

And come next January he would be headed back,

along with the secret expedition which he had been so energetically organizing. Nine months was a long time to wait, but they definitely couldn't make the trip this fall or winter, and they really did need time to gather just the right equipment.

Diego was taken from these thoughts by several dull thuds from the door. He got up and went to the entrance of the bungalow. (This small house in the plushiest section of the city was evidence of the encouragement he had already received from some very important people). Ribera had no idea who the visitor could be, but he had every expectation that the news brought would be good. He reached the door, and pulled it open.

"Mkambwe Lunama!"

The Zulunder stood framed in the doorway, his black face all but invisible against the night sky. The visitor was over two meters tall and weighed nearly one hundred kilos; he was the picture of a superman. But then, the Zulunder government made a special point of using the super-race type in its dealings with other nations. The procedure undoubtedly lost them some fine talent, but in Sudamérica the myth held strong that one Zulunder was worth three warriors of any other nationality.

After his first outburst, Ribera stood for a moment in horrified confusion. He knew Lunama vaguely as the Highman of Trueness—propaganda—at the Zulunder embassy in Buenos Aires. The Highman had made numerous attempts to ingratiate himself with the academic community of la Universidad de Buenos Aires. The efforts were probably aimed at recruiting sympathizers against that time when the disagreements between the Sudamérican Empire and the Reaches of Zulund erupted into open conflict.

Wildly hoping that the visit was merely an unlucky coincidence, Ribera recovered himself. He attempted a disarming smile, and said, "Come on in, Mkambwe. Haven't seen you in a long time."

The Zulunder smiled, his white teeth making a dazzling contrast with the rest of his face. He stepped lightly into the room. His robes were woven of brilliant red, blue and green fibers, in defiance of the more somber hues of Sudamérican business suits. On his hip rested a Mavimbelamake 20 mm. *revolver.* The Zulunders had their own peculiar ideas about diplomatic protocol.

Mkambwe moved lithely across the room and settled in a chair. Ribera hurried over and sat down by his desk, trying unobtrusively to hide the letters that lay on it from the Zulunder's view. If the visitor saw and understood even one of those letters, the game would be over.

Ribera tried to appear relaxed. "Sorry I can't offer you a drink, Mkambwe, but the house is as dry as a desert." If the anthropologist got up, the Zulunder would almost certainly see the correspondence. Diego continued jovially, desperately trying to dredge up reminiscences. ("Remember that time your boys whited their faces and went down to la Casa Rosada Nueva and raised hell with the—").

Lunama grinned. "Frankly, old man, this visit is business." The Zulunder spoke with a dandyish, pseudo-Castilian accent, which he no doubt thought aristocratic.

"Oh," Ribera answered.

"I hear that you were on a little expedition to Palmer Peninsula this January."

"Yes," Ribera replied stonily. Perhaps there was still a chance; perhaps Lunama didn't know the whole truth. "And it was supposed to be a secret. If el Presidente Imperial found out that your government knew about it—"

"Come, come, Diego. That isn't the secret you are thinking of. I know that you found what happened to the *Hendrik Verwoerd* and the *Nation.*"

"Oh," Ribera replied again. "How did you find out?" he asked dully.

"You talked to many people, Diego," he waved vaguely. "Surely you didn't think that every one of them would keep your secret. And surely you didn't think you could keep something this important from us." He looked beyond the anthropologist and his tone changed.

"For three hundred years we lived under the hells of those white devils. Then came the Retribution in the North and—"

What a quaint term the Zulunders use for the North World War, thought Ribera. It had been a war in which every trick of destruction—nuclear, biological, and chemical—had been used. The mere residues from the immolation of China had obliterated Indonesia and India. Mexico and América Central had disappeared with the United States and Canada. And North Africa had gone with Europe. The gentlest wisps from that biological and nuclear hell had caressed the Southern Hemisphere and nearly poisoned it. A few more megatons and a few more disease strains and the war would have gone unnamed, for there would have been no one to chronicle it. This was the Retribution in the North which Lunama so easily referred to.

"—and the devils no longer had the protection of their friends there. Then came the Sixty-Day struggle for Freedom."

There were both black devils and white devils in those sixty days—and saints of all colors, brave men struggling desperately to avert genocide. But the years of slavery were too many and the saints lost, not for the first time.

"At the beginning of the Rising we fought machine guns and jet fighters with rifles and knives," Lunama continued, almost self-hypnotized. "We died by the tens of thousands. But as the days passed *their* numbers were reduced, too. By the fiftieth day *we* had the machine guns, and *they* had the knives and rifles. We boxed the last of them up at Kapa and Durb," (he used the Zulunder terms for Capetown and Durban) "and drove them into the sea."

Literally, added Ribera to himself. *The last remnants of White Africa were physically pushed from the wharves and sunny beaches into the ocean.* The Zulunders had succeeded in exterminating the Whites, and thought they succeeded in obliterating the Afrikaner culture from the continent. Of course they had been wrong. The Afrikaners had left a lasting mark, obvious to any unbiased observer; the very name Zulunder, which the present Africans cherished fanatically, was in part a corruption of English.

"By the sixtieth day, we could say that not a single White lived on the continent. As far as we know, only one small group evaded vengeance. Some of the highest ranking Afrikaner officials, maybe even the Prime Minister, commandeered two luxury vessels, the *SR Hendrik Verwoerd* and the *Nation*. They left many hours before the final freedom drive on Kapa."

Five thousand desperate men, women and children crammed into two luxury ships. The vessels had raced across the South Atlantic, seeking refuge in Argentina. But the government of Argentina was having troubles of its own. Two light Argentine patrol boats badly damaged the *Nation* before the Afrikaners were convinced that Sudamérica didn't offer shelter.

The two ships had turned south, possibly in an attempt to round Tierra del Fuego and reach Australia. That was the last anyone had heard of them for more than two hundred years—till the *Vigilancia*'s exploration of the Palmer Peninsula.

Ribera knew that an appeal to sympathy wouldn't dissuade the Zulunder from ordering the destruction of the pitiful colony. He tried a different tack. "What you say is so true, Mkambwe. But please, please don't destroy these descendants of your enemies. The tribe on the Palmer Peninsula is the only polar culture left on Earth." Even as Ribera said the words, he realized how weak the argument was; it could only appeal to an anthropologist like himself.

The Zulunder seemed surprised, and with a visible effort shelved the terrible history of his continent. "Destroy them? My dear fellow, whyever would we do that? I just came here to ask if we might send several observers from the Ministry of Trueness along on your expedition. To report the matter more fully, you know. I think that

Alfredo can probably be convinced, if the question is put persuasively enough to him.

"Destroy them?" He repeated the question. "Don't be silly! They are *proof* of destruction. So they call their piece of ice and rock Nieutransvaal, do they?" He laughed. "And they even have a Prime Minister, a toothless old man who waves his harpoon at Sudaméricans." Apparently Lunama's informant had actually been on the spot. "And they are even more primitive than Eskimos. In short, they are savages living on seal blubber."

He no longer spoke with foppish joviality. His eyes flashed with an old, old hate, a hate that was pushing Zulund to greatness, and which might eventually push the world into another hemispheric war (unless the Australian social scientists came through with some desperately needed answers). The breeze in the room no longer seemed cool, gentle. It was cold and the wind was coming from the emptiness of death piled upon megadeath through the centuries of human misery.

"It will be a pleasure for us to see them enjoy their superiority." Lunama leaned forward even more intensely. "They finally have the apartness their kind always wanted. *Let them rot in it—*"

TERMITES
by Dave Smeds

*Before turning to writing, Dave Smeds made his living
as a commercial artist. He made his first fiction sale in
1980, and has subsequently sold stories to Isaac Asimov's Science Fiction Magazine, Far Frontiers, Full
Spectrum, Dragons of Light, In the Field of Fire, Pulphouse, and Sword and Sorceress, as well as to many
men's magazines. He has published two novels, The Sorcery Within and The Schemes of Dragons, and is at work
on several more. He lives with his family in Santa Rosa,
California.*

*In the brilliant and disturbing story that follows, he
postulates an ingenious cure for humankind's oldest enemy, an enemy that haunts today's Africa and is all too
likely to haunt the Africa of the future as well: hunger.
But, as you will see, the cost of the cure may turn out to
be one that is too high to pay. . . .*

August, 2011

When I first arrived in the Cherangani Hills of northwestern Kenya as a young woman, the mountains had
been green and tawny, cloaked in lush bush, dotted with
the cultivated plots of the Pokot tribe that I had come to
study. Now I could hardly recognize the place where I
had lived my life between the ages of twenty-two and
twenty-eight. The drought had turned the Great Rift Valley into blistered, lunarlike terrain; the hills reminded
me of Ethiopia back in the eighties—steep mounds un-

intended for human habitation, withered, eroded, and above all, dry. Greg stopped the Land Rover and let me examine the scenery more carefully. But it was no use.

"I'm lost," I said.

He brushed a cloud of flies away from his face, callused fingers rasping against a four-day growth of tough, white beard. "I believe it's around the next promontory," he said, his clipped British inflections making the statement unequivocal, though in truth he knew the region far less than I.

His confidence made me try one more time. "Yes. Yes, I think you're right," I said.

When we rounded the flank of the hills, we saw the remnants of a village. All that remained of the huts were the firepits, the packed-earth floors, and ruptured holes where the branches that formed the walls had been anchored. And, of course, the sitting stones—it was improper for a man of the Pokot to sit on naked ground. In their stead were three hovels constructed of piled dung and animal hides, not true dwellings at all, merely places to get out of the sun. I saw a dozen or more people, all lying or sitting listlessly in the shade.

We felt the impact of their eyes, but aside from the stares, most of them did not react to our arrival. A single boy stood and began to approach the Land Rover. He was suffering from the early stages of marasmus, his limbs painfully thin, stomach bloated, skin hanging slack from his bones so that his face resembled that of an old man and not, so I estimated, a boy well short of puberty. His only garment was a pair of threadbare, stained khaki shorts.

Greg pulled out the .45 as we stopped rolling, keeping it in obvious view. But the boy emitted not even a flicker of belligerence; he was past those emotions. He gazed at us blankly, like a retardate. Only the fact that he had risen of his own accord gave me hope of obtaining a response from him.

"Do you know KoCherop?" I asked. I used the Pokot dialect, though the words came haltingly, with a bittersweet tang. The boy, if he had been schooled, could speak English or Swahili, but use of his home tongue might ingratiate me. "Do you know where she is?"

He turned his prematurely old eyes toward me, and I saw, to my surprise, a mind still capable of activity and calculation. "You are Chemachugwo," he said, using my Pokot name, his voice raspy but energetic.

"Yes." I did not know him, but I was not surprised that he had guessed my identity. There were no other middle-aged white women alive who could speak his language.

"I will tell you where to find KoCherop if you give me a piece of paper," he stated.

I hesitated a moment, then reached into a compartment under the seat and withdrew the bribe. I gave him a whole sheet. The boy ran his hands over it, apparently pleased with the rough, pulpy texture and sawdust-yellow color. He rolled it into a funnel, and with his empty hand pointed to a terrace plot far up the nearest mountain. "She is there."

I could make out a tendril of smoke. I signaled Greg to drive on.

I could see the boy and his piece of paper in the side mirror for a full thirty seconds. Just before the dust and the turns in the track obscured him I saw him bite off the end of the funnel and begin to chew it. I wanted to weep, but the past few days had left me incapable of tears. It was the village, I told myself. It had been so much like the one in which I had built my hut, almost forty years back.

The road narrowed and grew more steep, until the Land Rover would go no further. We faced a dilemma, for we couldn't leave the vehicle unattended.

"I'll stay," Greg said, handing me the .45. He pulled out one of the rifles for himself.

I hadn't reckoned on this development. I needed his plucky humor and stiff upper lip. But I had gone alone into the wilderness of East Africa before. I buckled on my holster and started up the path.

Climbing these hills had been easier in younger days. I stopped often, until I could no longer bear to gaze out over the valley, where I had once watched the herdsmen and their cattle. The air became cooler, though not enough to compensate for my exertion. I estimated it would take me two hours to reach the terrace. I thought of KoCherop.

January, 1978

"Now we are like sisters," she said, touching my belly. I jumped. The tattoo was still tender from the artist's needle. She jerked back her hand. "I'm sorry."

"It's all right. I was just surprised."

"It will only hurt for a little while," she said encouragingly. "Then you will be happy because you have become more beautiful." She pointed at the spectacular, star-shaped design carved around her navel. The blood still congealed around it. "All the other girls will be jealous of me," she said firmly. "Now that I am a woman, I will add more all along here." She brushed her fingers up and down her midriff.

I concealed my shiver. KoCherop—she still used her childhood name, Chesinen, at that point—had a sleek body and perfect, rich brown complexion. It needed no accentuation. Along with clitoridectomy, scarification was one of the practices that tempted me to drop my anthropologist's reserve.

"Many of the girls nowadays are leaving their bellies smooth," I said.

"Those girls must be looking for Kikuyu husbands," she said with disdain. She smeared her face with red ocher and ghee, and offered to do the same for me. I accepted.

She lavished it over my nose and cheeks. "Trust me. One day a handsome man with much land will look at your belly and admire what you have had done."

I chuckled, staring down at the tattoo. I had to admit it was pretty. It was a tiny butterfly, etched in six colors of ink, excellent artistry considering that it had been performed by a traveling craftsman. In my own way, I *would* enjoy owning it; otherwise I would never have done something so permanent to my body. But it most certainly had not been done to attract a husband. I had done it for my Pokot sister, because her father had become like my own, and because she, though ten years my junior, had made me feel instantly welcome in a sea of strange black faces.

"Oh, no one will marry me," I said. "I always burn the porridge."

August, 2011 continued

I passed terrace after terrace of abandoned land. The farms extended far up the slope ahead of me, each family tilling parcels at not one but several elevations, the better to guard against crop failure. Some could be found as high as seven or eight thousand feet, among the peaks where, in former times, the mist would gather, moistening the land, dispelling the aridity of the Great Rift Valley. Now all I could see growing were gnarled hardwoods whose resins made them impossible to eat, or thorn thickets and brambles not worth the pain to molest. Dust crawled up my shoes and into the cuffs of my trousers.

Breathless, aching in my calves, I reached the terrace that the boy had indicated. Nothing was left of the fields but irrigation channels waiting for water that had not come. KoCherop was seated on a flat stone beside a firepit. An empty porridge kettle sat over dying coals. Beside her was a gourd of water and a small sack of maize or millet.

She stared at me with wide eyes, perhaps thinking that she had died and met a ghost. I spoke her name.

She bowed her head. "I am called only Ko, now."

"Ko" means grandmother. Her full name meant Grandmother of Daughter of Rain, which she had adopted upon the birth of her first granddaughter. It was a declaration that Cherop was dead.

KoCherop, in her typically Pokot way, did not display overt grief. It was enough to have made the statement. In a culture in which the lives of the women of the tribe revolve so deeply around those of their children that they rename themselves each time a new generation is established, no loss could have been sharper.

"I'm sorry," I said, trying to keep my voice steady. "Lokomol told me."

"He sent you, didn't he? I told him not to do that." Her voice softened. "He is well? And the little ones?"

"There is food in the refugee camp, for the moment. He wouldn't accept help. But he did beg me to come to you."

"And you have come. What will you do now?"

"Greg and I plan to take you to back to Kampala," I said. "We want you to live with us."

"I live here," she said, standing up. She had always been thin and spare; now the effect was more extreme, but the vigor—and determination—in her body was still obvious.

"What happens when that sack is empty?" I asked, pointing at her food supply. It was nearly depleted already.

She ground a toe into the dust, and dislodged a hidden stick. She tossed it in the firepit. "I am waiting for the government workers, coming to tell me that now I can eat dirt."

I started to speak, lost my momentum, paused.

"What is there for me in Kampala, Chemachugwo?" she continued. "Do they have grindstones? Can you farm there?"

"Can you farm *here*?" I found my tongue. "Do you remember the time you had the fever? I started to leave the hut one night, but you begged me not to go. Do you remember what you said?"

She faced me for the first time. "You are not fair, Janet."

"You said you didn't want to die alone. Have you changed your mind after all these years?"

The flies were devils. KoCherop, with her African composure, paid them no mind, even when they sipped fluid from the rim of her eyelids. "Lokomol should not have sent you."

"But he did." I reached out and clasped her shoulder. She leaned into my hand. "We won't have to stay in the city all the time. You can come with us when I do my field work in the Ituri forest. The pygmies will call you a giant."

KoCherop, who was rather short, smiled faintly, then lost it. I could feel her tremble through my palm. "Yes. Yes, Janet, I will come. But give me one more night. I must say good-bye to Cherop."

I am ashamed to say that, for an instant, I did not believe her. I envisioned her hiding from us when the time came to leave. But if she did, I would have to respect that choice, so I told her where the truck was and climbed down the mountain.

February, 1988

KoCherop was giving her two-year-old son Lokomol a bath Pokot style: squirting water out of her mouth in a pencil-thin stream and scrubbing him with her fingers. The baby wailed, watching forlornly as the mud he'd so diligently splattered over his skin was rinsed away. Not far away his slightly older sister laughed at his discomfiture, while KoCherop's three other children clambered up and down the acacia tree under which we sat.

"You have been married for half a year, Chemachugwo," she said. "Why aren't you pregnant?" I knew she was scolding me; she reserved use of my Pokot name for times when she wanted to lecture or argue.

I paused, keeping my glance on Lokomol, marveling at how much he had grown in the year and a half since I had last visited my tribal friends. "Greg and I don't plan to have any children just yet."

"You are over thirty years—well over. You could be a grandmother by now."

I thought of the crow's feet in the corners of my eyes and the strands of gray hair that I'd found a couple of months back. I didn't need KoCherop's reminder.

"What about you?" I asked. "Are you going to stop at five?"

"Oh, no!" she said emphatically, sending Lokomol off to his siblings with an affectionate pat on the butt. "Seven, eight, nine—whatever luck brings me. I am already behind. KamaChepkech already has six," she said of her younger sister.

KoCherop was twenty-four years old.

August, 2011 continued

Morning arrived with the suddenness of the tropics. I, lying awake on the bed of the Land Rover, watched the sun illuminate the tracks of the snakes that had crawled past the vehicle in the night. I head footsteps scuffing the path and my heart began to pound.

KoCherop had come.

She had brought her sack and her gourd. She stood like a statue, her wide, Nilo-Hamitic features impassive. She was dressed in the traditional style: a skirt of thick brown muslin covering her from the base of her rib cage to her knees, huge hoop earrings, and a cornucopia of bright, multi-colored beads in the form of belts, anklets, bracelets, armbands, a headband, and row after row of necklaces draping her collar, shoulders, and upper chest, leaving her breasts bare. This was her best outfit, and a rare sight in days when most Pokot women had long since begun to mimic Western fashions.

"When we get to Kampala, they will know I am a Pokot," she explained.

I pursed my lips. They would know, all right.

I saw her glance wistfully at the hills. "It will be temporary," I said rapidly. "The rain will come. It has to come. Lokomol and his brothers will plant new crops. You can return then."

"And maybe my granddaughter will be born again," she replied.

I sighed. It was hard not to agree with her pessimism. The rain *would* come again—no doubt far more of it than the vegetationless soil could withstand—and some of the million Pokot refugees would reestablish their homes, but for vast numbers, the old way of life had ended forever.

Greg grumbled up out of his sleep, saw KoCherop, and gave me a questioning glance.

"Start her up," I said. "There's no reason to stay here."

July, 1990

As I watched the first news broadcast concerning the Termite bacteria, I remembered Grape Nuts. In a flashback to my childhood Euell Gibbons appeared, white-haired, fatherly, pouring a bowlful of cereal. "Ever eat a pine tree?" he asked in his backwoods accent.

The geneticists explained how they had developed a strain of *E. coli* capable of converting cellulose into sugar. Doctors calculated that the effects, though disconcerting, would not be dangerous in the long term. Politicians justified its release into test populations in East Africa and Bangladesh on the grounds that it hailed the end of world hunger, a new chance for the stricken nations of the Third World.

I kept thinking of Marie Antoinette. *Let them eat wood.*

August, 2011 continued

We made our way to the main road, a dirt track that would take us down the valley, past Mt. Elgon to Lake Victoria, and eventually across the border into Uganda. The grimy windshield showed us a view of bleak mountains and dust, broken by an occasional cactus or bit of scrub brush.

KoCherop sat between Greg and me, taking no note of the surroundings, a contagious gloom that kept my husband and me from saying more than ten words to each other all morning. It was as if each mile enervated her, until it was all she could do to simply sit.

We approached Sigor, the district's marketing center, the only "big town" KoCherop had ever visited. It was little more than a collection of dung huts with tin sheet roofs. Nowhere on the wind-whipped ground was there a tree or a blade of grass, only dust, rusting old drums, black requiem birds, a scent of human poverty. In temperate climates, poverty smells sour, but in hot regions it is sickeningly sweet. Small knots of people gathered at the periphery of the street as we rolled through: sad black faces, pleading eyes.

We kept our weapons visible, but here, as with the boy the day before, no one had the energy to threaten us. They simply stood with the passivity of the starving, hoping that perhaps we were famine relief workers. I did not look at their faces. Though we had an ample supply of food in the Land Rover, we didn't dare stop and try to share it, or the spell holding them back would have been broken. Our food stayed hidden inside plastic, metal, and canvas, as inconspicuous as we could make it.

It couldn't save them. There were too many. What mattered now was KoCherop. I could, God willing, rescue one person, if she would let me.

She paid no attention to the audience, though they stared at her beads and naked breasts, which in their minds marked her as more primitive, and therefore poorer, than they. Perhaps they were wondering why she, and not they, deserved to ride. We didn't stop until long after the village had merged with the dust of the horizon.

February, 1992

"You don't have to do that anymore," I said.

KoCherop continued picking bits of stems and stalks out of the sorghum she was grinding. She looked at me with skepticism.

"You don't have to separate the chaff," I clarified. "Just grind it in. The bacteria will allow you to digest it, just like the grain."

"It is meant for cattle, not people," she said firmly. "You talk like the government workers."

"The crop's been very poor this year. You don't have much to waste."

"Do they eat chaff in California?" she asked. She knew that I had just returned from a visit to my home-town in the San Joaquin Valley.

"No. North America hasn't been infected yet. But it will be. There's no way to stop *E. coli*. Eventually it'll get everyone. We'll all be Termites. I'm one already. So are you."

"No, I am not."

"Yes, you are. It's even gotten into your cattle. That's why the dung burns so poorly," I said, pointing at the smoldering fire underneath the kettle of porridge. There wasn't enough fiber left in the cow pies to serve as fuel. "Don't tell me you haven't noticed a big difference in how food passes through your system."

Not being Caucasian, her blush didn't show, but the expression was the same. I, too, had been embarrassed by the sudden, violent cycles of diarrhea and constipation, and most of all by the methane, though more recently my body had begun to adjust.

"I will keep doing it this way," she insisted. "This is the way my mother taught me."

August, 2011 continued

We began to catch up with the refugee caravans by mid-afternoon. The first contained about fifty people, shuffling along at a pace of perhaps a kilometer an hour. It was much worse than in Sigor, for they made no effort to get out of the way of the Land Rover—many, I suspected, would not have cared if they had been run over—and it took a considerable length of time to weave our way through them, all the while aware of their eyes an arm's length outside the windows. Their lighter coloring and thinner features told me that they were Samburu. They had come even further than we, from the vicinity of Lake Turkana, where the normally bountiful supplies of fish had become exhausted from the excessive demand.

At least they were away from the water and its mosquitoes. Fewer would die from malaria.

In due course we came upon another, somewhat larger group, readily distinguishable because some of them still carried significant possessions, either in carts, on packs, or slung on poles. They even drove a pair of oxen and a few bony cows ahead of them. I noticed four men huddled around a bowl of milk and blood, a traditional meal of the pastoralists of the Rift Valley, while a knot of women and children watched, quiet with envy. My hands, lubed with perspiration, slid along the stock of my rifle. Greg gave me a glance, and I knew he saw what I did: these tribesmen had enough strength left to cause trouble should they wish.

Three young men, painfully lean but still muscular, were very slow to get out of our path. They glowered at us as we passed. I pretended to be distracted by the constant bouncing from the ruts and chuck holes, but I could feel their eyes riveted to us. It was like the sensation a woman gets when a man blatantly undresses her in his mind.

The last obstacle was a boy who strode behind one of the oxen with a thin whip. For a full two minutes, though it was obvious he knew we were behind him, he refused to move himself or his animal out of the way. Finally the track widened and Greg began to pull around. Suddenly the boy began lashing at us. The sound of leather on metal made me jump. The boy shouted—a guttural, wordless roar. The tip of his lash struck the steering wheel.

Greg stepped firmly on the throttle, shooting us into the clear, and didn't let up until the irregularity of the road shook us more than our aging bones could tolerate.

He eased off, put the .45 back into its holster on the dash, got out his handkerchief, and wiped his forehead. The boy, his image shrinking out of sight in the mirror, was laughing that his whip had spurred us so well. His poor ox could not have been so vigorous.

"Bloody little blighter," Greg cursed.

My hands were shaking. I turned to share a sigh of relief with KoCherop, only to find her gazing ahead, lips pursed, as if nothing of importance had occurred. Greg noticed and, like me, his eyebrows drew together.

Ahead in the distance, well away from the Samburu, an escarpment loomed. "We'll pull over when we reach that," Greg announced, pointing. "Time for a rest."

September, 2001

We were walking down a trail between two plots of farmland, one belonging to KoCherop's uncle, the other to her brother. For once, the rain had come in full vigor, and neither locusts nor the flocks of marauding queleas had come to steal the grain. Dozens of tribesmen worked the fields, the glistening brown backs of both men and women happily bending down to harvest a bumper crop.

"Why do you do what you do?" KoCherop asked suddenly.

The question had come from out of the blue. "You mean, why am I an anthropologist?"

She nodded. "See my people with their scythes? See this mountain? I am in my place. Why do you live so far from your parents? Why do you go to the forest to study the pygmies, instead of having children? You are too old now to start a family. How can you be happy?"

There were occasional times, as menopause approached and I wondered what would have happened if I had married my college sweetheart and stayed in the United States, that I wasn't totally content with the alternative I'd chosen. But I was able to answer KoCherop honestly, "I do what I do because I want to. My work fulfills me."

She shook her head, mystified. "I could never be like that. Take me from my clan and this dirt and I would die."

August, 2011 continued

We stopped in the shade of the escarpment, where we were relatively inconspicuous but nevertheless had an unobstructed view of the road. Greg got out quickly, looked toward the rear of the truck, and groaned.

"I thought that last mile was a mite rough," he said. I walked around to his side, and saw that we had a flat tire.

"A gift from the Samburu?" I suggested.

"Could be. Most likely the frigging road." He opened up the rear of the Land Rover. "Last spare," he said, which we both knew already. I checked the map to measure the distance to Lake Victoria, and gnawed at my inner lip.

I began to help him, but he convinced me to relax, and in exchange I would drive the remaining short leg until sundown. KoCherop and I found a relatively comfortable spot in the talus a few yards away, where I spread out the last of our fresh fruit, as well as bread and, most important of all, a jug of water. The flies were overjoyed at the repast.

KoCherop ate a piece of fruit, a treat even in good seasons and a part of her diet of which she had surely been totally deprived lately, drank her fill, and turned to look at the plain.

"Have more," I said.

She didn't answer. Occasionally her glance would dart toward the north, where we had now left the last of the Pokot lands behind. She began taking apart her headband, running the beads off the ends of their threads one by one and flicking them away.

I am ashamed to confess that my own appetite was ravenous, and when I was certain my friend was not going to touch another bite, I saw to it that the ants had nothing more than stems and gleaned rinds to attack. The sand at the edge of the talus was now vivid with specks of color, an inadvertent piece of artwork created by KoCherop's cast-off beads, each one a particle of the life she knew, gone. I made sure not to disturb it as I walked back to check on Greg.

He was cinching the last nut. I handed him his canteen. He drained it. "Next time we bring a chauffeur," he joked, slightly breathless.

"We're losing her," I told him. "She's just waiting until the wind calls her name and takes her away."

He stowed the tire iron. "Well," he murmured, "the choice is hers now, isn't it? You can't make it for her."

The words seemed callous, but I had no answer for them at the time. KoCherop was waiting for the world to conform to her desires, not unlike the scientists who had created the Termite bacteria. But the world has ways of turning the tables back around. Now it was man's, and KoCherop's, turn to adapt, and she was refusing.

Brooding, I assisted Greg in lifting the flat tire into the Land Rover. The winds of upper Kenya had arrived with their usual vigor, hurrying us toward the next leg of our journey.

March, 2007

We were walking along the bank of a river. The drought had been severe for three years, and now the watercourse contained only sand, pocked with pits where the tribespeople had dug to reach the watertable. Now even those holes were desiccated. Thirty years before, when I had still lived here, the river had been lined with grass and overhung by broad, leafy acacias. Now even the stumps were gone.

Ironically, it was the industrialized nations that had benefitted from the modified *E. coli*. The sugar industry no longer had to boil away ninety percent of the raw cane during refining. Grains no longer had to be as thoroughly processed. But in the Third World bureaucrats became dangerously lax in educating the people about the need for population control, and the added demand for wood exacerbated the already severe deforestation problem. The climate had rebelled.

Cherop, the granddaughter for whom my friend had been renamed, skipped along ahead of us, always alert for a sunning lizard or a pretty stone. We were solemn in spite of the child's exuberance. KoCherop's husband had died two months before. This was my first visit since that event, and our conversation had awakened some of KoCherop's sense of loss. Now we just walked, thinking about the changes brought by time. It was young Cherop who broke the silence.

"Look!" she cried, pointing. Not far off the path, partially hidden in a thorn bramble, stood a termite mound.

Assured that we were watching, she ran over to it and began climbing. The mound was nearly three times as tall as she, rising into a dozen eroded towers. A hyena or aardwolf had dug a burrow at its base; birds had done the same, on a smaller scale, in his heights. The termites themselves had abandoned the site. Cherop explored the structure as much as the thorns would allow, no doubt hoping that one of the nests would still contain something interesting.

I smiled. The girl gave me a big, toothless grin, breaking off a small projection to demonstrate her strength, offering the dust to the wind.

I turned to KoCherop, and stage by stage my smile faded. I had never seen such a bitter look on her face.

"What's wrong?"

"I wish that all the termites had died ten thousand years ago. Then maybe your people would never have thought of a way to make us like insects."

It felt like I had been stung. The worst part of it was that she seemed unaware that she was hurting me. I could not avoid blurting out a response.

"Maybe if your people had stopped having so many babies, my people wouldn't have tried to solve your problems."

August, 2011 continued

We reached an armed checkpoint shortly before dusk. An overweight minor officer, skin so oily it gleamed, examined our papers with a frown, peering repeatedly at our vehicle's contents. He spared KoCherop a disinterested glance, mostly toward her breasts. Greg bribed him with two packs of American cigarettes and we were on our way. "Wish it could be that easy at the border," said my husband. We camped not far down the road, reasoning that bandits might be discouraged by the proximity of the checkpoint.

It was crowded in the back of the Land Rover. I slept between Greg and KoCherop, listening to the wind moan and the crickets trill, unable to sleep. KoCherop's scent evoked memories. It is strange that an entire tribe can have an identifiable essence. When I had lived with them year round I had become oblivious to it.

I thought about the city, trying to picture KoCherop walking to the supermarket, wearing a cotton smock, smelling the civilized odors of cement and auto exhaust. What kind of fool was I to think that, simply because I loved her, I could succeed in transferring a human being from her culture into mine?

Greg woke and crawled out of the vehicle. Soon I heard the muffled, rain-on-the-roof sound of urine splattering dust. I glanced at KoCherop. Even in the dim illumination I could see the determined, stubborn tension in her shoulders, and I became angry.

"Damn it," I murmured. "What more do you want me to do? *It's not my fault.*"

She didn't stir, but something in the stillness of her breathing hinted that she was awake. But after Greg returned and began snoring, I convinced myself that I had imagined it.

In the distance, I was certain I heard a hyena laughing, like a ghost of Africa of old.

July, 2011

The refugee camp was a sea of humanity. Our guide was a young doctor who, judging from his haggard cheeks and the red in his eyes, had not slept in four days. Somehow he kept his humor as we threaded through the crowd from checkpoint to checkpoint, trying to find Lokomol and the rest of KoCherop's family.

A little girl, bloated with kwashiorkor, stared at me as I passed. I turned away—from her and from all the faces, keeping my glance on the doctor. Here and there sat a lucky family with a tent or blanket to shade themselves; for the most part the refugees simply lay on the packed ground beneath an open sky, waiting until the next shipment of food arrived at the distribution point, or until the doctors received a fresh supply of basic medicines.

Some attempt had been made to funnel members of various tribal groups into specific areas of the camp. Otherwise we might never have found Lokomol.

He was sitting with his youngest daughter propped in his lap. I spotted him immediately; his lean features and long fingers closely resembled his mother. He was, much to my relief, apparently in good health.

"We came as soon as we got your message," I said. "We've arranged for transportation to take you to the camp near Kampala. It's much better supplied than this one."

"You have always been good to us, Chemachugwo," he answered pensively. "But it is for my mother that I sent for you."

"Why isn't she with you?"

He shrugged.

Knowing KoCherop, I understood completely. "You want me to try to bring her?"

He nodded. "I am ashamed to ask this of you, but you are the only person I have ever known who can make my mother listen."

August, 2011 continued

"Wake up, Janet."

It was Greg's voice, coming from the other end of a long tunnel. I peeled my eyes open. The morning light was unforgivably bright.

"Time for breakfast," Greg said for the second time. "I want to get to the border well before dusk."

I moaned, rubbed the grit from my lashes, and went about the meal like a zombie, hoping that my headache would soon go away. KoCherop sat nearby. I noticed that she ate a full share this time, but otherwise I avoided paying much attention to her. The border crossing was enough to think about, I told myself.

"You are sad, Janet," KoCherop said during a moment when Greg was out of hearing range.

"That's true," I replied, and turned to clean my bowl.

"Janet?"

"Yes?"

"I am sorry."

I looked at her, frowned, and climbed into the Land Rover. I was sorry, too, but what good was that? I didn't answer her. She had nothing to add, and we didn't speak for the rest of the morning.

By noon we began to see grass and brush. The air closed in, a sign of humidity. Greg spotted a flamingo in flight. Suddenly we crested a hill and saw Lake Victoria sprawling into the distance.

KoCherop's eyes went wide. It was easy to understand why.

"Where is the other side?" she whispered.

The shore to which she referred was over two hundred miles away, lost over the horizon. The lake was so vast that it could generate its own climate, moistening the adjacent countryside that would otherwise have been as arid as the region from which we had emerged.

It was one more new thing to overwhelm her, I thought bitterly.

KoCherop stared at the lake for almost an hour, while

I stayed locked in my own preoccupations. She startled me when she called for us to stop.

"I want to look at that," she said.

We had reached a particularly good vantage point from which to view the lake. KoCherop got out of the vehicle and walked to the edge of the road. Just in front of her the land dropped off abruptly. I could see jagged rocks down below. My friend stood where one more step would send her tumbling over the edge. Suddenly my insides clenched.

"Greg!" I cried.

"Give her a moment," he said in a voice that struck me as far too calm.

I held my breath, prepared at any time to shut my eyes and cover my ears. Again Greg, though observing carefully, seemed much too unruffled. Then, bit by bit, I began to see it as he did.

Her posture was no longer stiff. She stared at the lake not as if overwhelmed or contemplating suicide, but as I had the first time I had seen this, the second largest body of fresh water in the world—with awe and delight. I realized then that her demeanor had been different all day, but I, in my melancholy, had failed to notice.

She turned and walked toward me, her back straight, her eyes bright.

"Will I have my own room in Kampala?" she asked.

I felt a smile tugging at my lips. This was the Ko-Cherop I had once known, someone with hope for the years to come. "Yes," I replied. "A big one."

"Good," she said crisply, and climbed into the Land Rover. I thought back to the beads she had cast away the previous day. Not particles of life, thrown away in order to embrace Death, but bits of the past, dropped by the wayside to make room for the future. KoCherop was willing to adapt. The tightness in my throat melted away.

"Let's go home," I told Greg.

THE FINGER

by Naomi Mitchison

*In this chilling little story of authentic tribal magic and
medicine murder, the Good Man is actually the bad man,
one who is busily insinuating his corruption into the modern world of post-colonial Africa, the practitioner of kgogela . . . sorcery.*

*Here a boy must confront implacable evil with nothing
more than the vulnerability—and strength—of inno-
cence. . . .*

*British novelist Naomi Mitchison, sister of physicist
J.B. Haldane, was once a tribal adviser to the Bakgatla
tribe of southeast Botswana. She is the author of more
than ten books, including the well-known* Memories of a
Spacewoman, The Corn King or the Spring Queen, *and*
To the Chapel Perilous, *an idiosyncratic retelling of the
Arthurian legend, which some critics consider to be an
underground classic. Her most recent book is the novel*
Not by Bread Alone.

Kobedi had a mother but no father. When he was old
enough to understand such things someone said that his
father was the Good Man. By that they meant the Bad
Man, because, so often, words, once they are fully
known, have meanings other or opposite to their first ap-
pearance. Kobedi, however, hoped that his father was the
fat man at the store. Sometimes his mother went there
and brought back many things, not only the needful meal
and oil, but tea and sugar and beautiful tins with pictures, and almost always sweets for himself. Once, when
he was a quite little boy, he had asked his mother where

she kept the money for this and she answered "Between my legs." So, when she had drunk too much beer and was asleep on her back and snoring, he lifted her dress to see if he could find this money and take a little. But there was nothing there except a smell which he did not like. He had two small sisters, both fat and flat-nosed like the man at the store. But his own nose was thin, and the Good Man also had a thin nose as though he could cut with it.

Kobedi went to school and he thought he now understood what his mother had meant though he did not wish to think of it; at least she paid the school fees, though she grumbled about them. He was in Standard Three and there were pictures on the wall which he liked; now he wrote sentences in his jotter and they were ticked in red because they were correct. That was good. But in a while he became aware that things were happening around him which were not good. First it was the way his mother looked at him, and sometimes felt his arms and legs, and some of her friends who came and whispered. Then came the time he woke in the blackest of the night, for there was a smell which made him feel sick and the Good Man was there, sitting on the stuffed and partly torn sofa under the framed picture of white Baby Jesus. He was wearing skins of animals over his trousers, and his toes, which had large nails, clutched and burrowed in the rag rug Kobedi's mother had made. The Good Man saw that Kobedi was awake because his eyes were open and staring; he pointed one finger at him. That was the more frightening because his other hand was under the skirt of a young girl who was sitting next to him, snuggling. The pointing finger twitched and beckoned and slowly Kobedi unrolled himself from his blanket and came over naked and shaking.

The Good Man now withdrew his other hand and his dampish fingers crawled over Kobedi. He took out two sinews from a bundle, rubbing them in the sweat of his own skin until they became thin and hard and twisted and dipped them into a reddish medicine powder he had and spat on them and he pointed the finger again and Kobedi slunk back and pulled the blanket over his head.

The next day the tied-on sinews began to make his skin itch. He tried to pull them off but his mother slapped him, saying they were strong medicine and he must keep them on. He could not do any arithmetic that day. The numbers had lost their meaning and his teacher beat him.

The next time he became aware of that smell in the night he carefully did not move nor open his eyes, but pulled the blanket slowly from his ears so that he could hear the whispering. Again it was the Good Man and his mother and perhaps another woman or even two women. They were speaking of a place and a time, and at that place and time, a happening. The words were so dressed as to mean something else, as when speaking of a knife they called it a little twig, when they spoke of the heart it was the cooking pot, when they spoke of the liver it was the red blanket, and when they spoke of the fat it was the beer froth. And it became clear to Kobedi that when they spoke of the meal sack it was of himself they were speaking. Death, death, the whispers said, and the itching under the sinews grew worse.

The next morning all was as always. The little sisters toddled and played and their mother pounded meal for the porridge and called morning greetings to her neighbors across the walls of the lapa. Then she said to him: "After the school is finished you are to go to the store and get me one packet tea. Perhaps he will give you sweets. Here is money for tea."

It was not much money, but it was a little and he knew he had to go and fast. He passed by the school and did not heed the school bell calling to him and he walked to the next village and on to the big road. He waited among people for a truck and fear began to catch up on him; by now he was hungry and he bought fatty cakes for five cents. Then he climbed in at the back of the truck with the rest of the people. Off went the truck, north, south, he did not know. Only there was a piece of metal in the bottom of the truck, some kind of rasp, and he worked with this until he had got the sinew off his ankle and he dropped it over the side so that it would be run over by many other trucks. It was harder to get at the arm one and he only managed to scrape his own skin before the truck stopped in a big town.

Now it must be said that Kobedi was lucky; after a short time of hunger and fear he got a job sweeping out a small shop and going with heavy parcels. He was also allowed to sleep on a pile of sacks under the counter, though he must be careful to let nobody know, especially not the police. But under the sacks was a loose board and below it he had a tin, and into this he put money out of his wages, a few cents at a time. He heard about a school that was held in the evenings after work; he did not speak to anyone about it, and indeed he had no friends in the big town because it seemed to him that friends meant losing one's little money at playing dice games or taking one's turn to buy a coke; and still his arm itched.

When he had enough money he went one evening to the school and said he had been in Standard Three and he wanted to go on with education and had money to buy it. The white man who was the head teacher asked him where he came from. He said from Talane, which was by no means the name of his village, and also that his father was dead and there was no money to pay for school. The truth is too precious and dangerous to be thrown anywhere. So the man was sorry for him and said well, he could sit with the others and try how he did.

At this time Kobedi worked all day and went to classes in the evening and still he was careful not to become too friendly, in case the friend was an enemy. There was a knife in the shop, but it was blunt, and though he sawed at the sinew on his arm he could not get it off. Sometimes he dreamed about whispering in the night and woke frozen. Sometime he thought his mother would come suddenly through the door of the shop and claim him. If she did, could the night school help him?

One of the Botswana teachers took notice of him and

let him come to his room to do homework, since this was
not possible in the shop. There were some books in the
teacher's room and a photograph of himself with others
at the T.T.C.; after a while Kobedi began to like this
teacher, Mr. Tshele, and half thought that one day he
would tell him what his fears were. But not yet. There
came an evening when he was writing out sentences in
English, at one side of the table where the lamp stood.
Mr. Tshele had a friend with him; they were drinking
beer. He heard the cans being opened and smelled the
fizzing beer. At a certain moment he began to listen because Mr. Tshele was teasing his friend, who was hoping
for a post in the civil service and had been to a doctor
to get a charm to help him. "You believe in that!" said
Mr. Tshele. "You are not modern. You should go to a
cattle post and not to the civil service!"

"Everyone does the same," said his friend, "perhaps
it helps, perhaps not. I do not want to take risks. It is
my life."

"Well, it is certainly your money. What did he charge
you?" The friend giggled and did not answer; the beer
cans chinked again. "I am asking you another thing,"
said Mr. Tshele, "This you have done at least brings no
harm. But what about sorcery? Do you believe?"

The friend hesitated. "I have heard dreadful things,"
he said. "What they do. Perhaps they are mad. Perhaps
it no longer happens. Not in Botswana. Only perhaps—
well, perhaps in Lesotho. Who knows? In the mountains."

Mr. Tshele leaned back in his chair. Kobedi ducked
his head over his paper and pencil and pretended to be
busy writing. "There is a case coming up in the High
Court," said Mr. Tshele. "My cousin who is a lawyer
told me. A man is accused of medicine murder. The trial
will be next week. They are looking for witnesses, but
people are afraid to come forward."

"But they must have found—something?"

"Yes, a dead child. Cut in a certain way. Pieces taken

out. Perhaps even while the child was alive and screaming for help.''

"This is most dreadful,'' said the friend, ''and most
certainly the man I went to about my civil service inter-
view would never do such a thing!''

"Maybe not,'' said Mr. Tshele, ''not if he can get
your money a safer way! Mind you, I myself went to a
doctor who was a registered herbalist when I had those
headaches, and he threw the *ditaola* and all that, but most
certainly he did not murder.''

"Did he cure your headaches?''

"Yes, yes, and it was cheaper than going to the chem-
ist's shop. He rubbed the back of my neck and also gave
me a powder to drink. Two things. It was a treatment, a
medical treatment, not just a charm. I suppose you also
go for love charms?''

Again the friend giggled, and Kobedi was afraid they
would now only speak about girls. He wanted to know
more, more, about the man who had cut out the heart—
and the liver—and stripped off the fat for rubbing, as he
remembered the whispering in the night. But they came
back to it. "This man, the one you spoke of who is to
be tried, he is from where?'' the friend asked. And Mr.
Tshele carelessly gave the name of the village. His village. The name, the shock, the knowledge, for it must
indeed and in truth be the Good Man. Kobedi could not
speak, could not move. He stared at the lamp and the
light blurred and pulsed with the strong terrible feeling
he had in him like the vomiting of the soul.

He did not speak that evening. Nor the next. He wondered if the Good Man was in a strong jail, but if so
surely he could escape, taking some form, a vulture, a
great crow? And his mother? And the other women, the
whisperers? But the evening after that, in the middle of
a dusty open space near the school where nobody could
be hiding to listen, he touched Mr. Tshele's coat and
looked up at him, for he did not yet come to a man's
shoulder height. Mr. Tshele bent down, thinking this was
some school trouble. It was then that Kobedi whispered

the name of his village and when Mr. Tshele did not immediately understand: "Where *that one* who is to be tried comes from. I know him."

"You? How?" said Mr. Tshele and then Kobedi began to tell him everything and the dust blew round them and he began to cry and Mr. Tshele wiped his dusty tears away and took him to a shop at the far side of the open space and gave him an ice lolly on a stick. He had seen boys sucking them, but for him it was the first time and great pleasure.

Then Mr. Tshele said, "Come with me," and took him by the hand and they went together to the house of his cousin the lawyer, which was set in a garden with fruit trees and tomato plants and flowers and a thing which whirled water. Inside it was as light as a shop and Kobedi's bare feet felt a soft and delicious carpet under them. "Here is your witness in the big case!" said Mr. Tshele, and then to Kobedi: "Tell him!" But Kobedi could not speak of it again.

But they gave him a drink that stung a little on the tongue and was warm in the stomach, and in a while Kobedi was able to say again what he had said to his teacher and it came more easily. "Good," said the cousin who was a lawyer. "Now, little one, will you be able to say this in the Court? If you can do it you will destroy a great evil. Modimo will be glad of you." Kobedi nodded and then he whispered to Mr. Tshele, "It will come better if you take this off me," and he showed them the sinew with the medicine. The two men looked at one another and the lawyer fetched a strong pair of scissors and cut through the sinew; then he took it into the kitchen, and before Kobedi's eyes he put it with his own hand into the stove and poked the wood into a blaze so that it was consumed altogether. After that Kobedi told the lawyer the shop where he worked. "So now," said the lawyer, "no word to any other person. This is between us three. *Khudu Thamaga.*"

That night Kobedi slept quickly without dreaming. Two days later a big car stopped at the shop where he was

sweeping out the papers and dirt and spittle of the customers. The lawyer came to the door and called him:
"You have not spoken? Good. But in Court you will
speak." Then the lawyer gave some money to the man
at the shop to make up for taking his servant, and when
they were in the car he explained to Kobedi how it would
be. The accused here, the witness there. "I will ask you
questions," he said, "and you will answer and it will be
only the truth. Look at the Judge in the high seat behind
the table where men write. Do not look at the accused
man. Never look at him. Do you understand?" Kobedi
nodded. The lawyer went on, "Speak in Setswana when
I question you, even if you know some English words
which my cousin says you have learnt. These things of
which you will tell cannot be spoken in English. But
show also that you know a little. You can say to the Judge,
'I greet you, Your Honor'. Repeat that. Yes, that is right.
Your Honor is the English name for a Judge and this is a
most important Judge."

So in a while the car stopped and Kobedi was put into
a room and given milk and sandwiches with meat in them
and he waited. The time came when he was called into
the Court and a man helped him and told him not to be
afraid. He kept his eyes down and saw nothing, but the
man touched his shoulder and said, "This is His Honor
the Judge." So Kobedi looked up bravely and greeted
the Judge, who smiled at him and asked if he knew the
meaning of an oath. At all times there was an interpreter
in the Court and there seemed to be very many people,
who sometimes made a rustling sound like dry leaves of
mealies, but Kobedi carefully looked only at the Judge.
So he took his oath; there was a Bible, such as he had
seen at his first school. And then the lawyer began to ask
him questions and he answered, so that the story grew
like a tree in front of the Judge.

Now it came to the whisperers in the midnight room
and what they had shown him of their purpose; the lawyer asked him who there were besides the accused. Kobedi answered that one was his mother. And as he did

so there was a scream and it came from his mother herself. "Wicked one, liar, runaway, oh how I will beat you!" she yelled at him until a policewoman took her away. But he had turned towards her, and suddenly he had become dreadfully unhappy. And in his unhappiness he looked too far and in a kind of wooden box half a grown person's height, he saw the Good Man.

Before he could take his eyes away the Good Man suddenly shot out his finger over the top of the box and it was as though a rod of fire passed between him and Kobedi. "It is all lies," shouted the Good Man. "Tell them you have lied, lied, lied!" And a dreadful need came onto Kobedi to say just this thing and he took a shuffling step towards the Good Man, for what had passed between them was *kgogela*, sorcery, and it had trapped him. But there was a great noise from all round and he heard the lawyer's voice and the Judge's voice and other voices and he felt a sharp pain in the side of his stomach.

Now after this Kobedi was not clear what was happening, only he shut his eyes tight, and then it seemed to him that he still wore those sinews which the Good Man had fastened onto him. And the pain in his stomach seemed to grow. But the *kgogela* had been broken and he did not need to undo his words and he was able to open his eyes and look at the Judge and to answer three more questions from his friend the lawyer. Then he was guided back to the room where one waited and he did not speak of the pain, for he hoped it might go.

But it was still there. After a time his friend the lawyer came in and said he had done well. But somehow Kobedi no longer cared. When he was in the car beside the lawyer he had to ask for it to stop so that he could get out and vomit into a bush, for he could not dirty such a shining car. On the way to the Court he had watched the little clocks and jumping numbers in the front of the car, but now they did not speak to him. He had become tired all over and yet if he shut his eyes he saw the finger pointing. "I will take you to Mr. Tshele," said the lawyer and stopped to buy milk and bread and sausage; but

Kobedi was only a little pleased and he began less and less to be able not to speak of his pain.

After a time of voices and whirling and doctors, he began to wake up and he was in a white bed and there was a hospital smell. A nurse came and he felt pain, but not of the same deep kind, not so bad. Then a doctor came and said all was well and Mr. Tshele came and told Kobedi that now he was going to live with him and go properly to school in the daytime and have new clothes and shoes. He and the lawyer would become, as it were, Kobedi's uncles. ''But,'' said Kobedi, ''tell me—the one—the one who did these things?''

''The Judge has spoken,'' said Mr. Tshele. ''That man will die and all will be wiped out.''

''And—the woman?'' For he could not now say mother.

''She will be put away until the evil is out of her.'' Kobedi wondered a little about the small sisters, but they were no longer in his life so he could forget them and forget the house and forget his village forever. He lay back in the white bed.

After a while a young nurse came in and gave him a pill to swallow. Kobedi began to question her about what happened, for he knew by now that the doctors had cut the pain out of his stomach. The young nurse looked round and whispered: ''They took out a thing like a small crocodile, but dead,'' she said.

''That was the sorcery,'' said Kobedi. Now he knew and was happy that it was entirely gone.

The young nurse said, ''We are not allowed to believe in sorcery.''

''I do not believe in it any longer,'' said Kobedi, ''because it is finished. But that was what it was.''

THE LIONS ARE ASLEEP THIS NIGHT

by Howard Waldrop

Howard Waldrop is widely considered to be one of the best short-story writers in the business, and his famous story "The Ugly Chickens" won both the Nebula and the World Fantasy Awards in 1981. His work has been gathered in three collections: Howard Who?, All About Strange Monsters Of The Recent Past: Neat Stories By Howard Waldrop, *and* Night of the Cooters: More Neat Stories By Howard Waldrop, *with more collections in the works. Waldrop is also the author of the novel* The Texas-Israeli War: 1999, *in collaboration with Jake Saunders, and of two solo novels,* Them Bones *and* A Dozen Tough Jobs. *He is at work on a new novel, tentatively entitled* The Moon World. *Waldrop lives in Austin, Texas.*

Waldrop is widely known for his ingenious Alternate Histories, such as "Ike At the Mike," in which Eisenhower becomes a jazz musician instead of a military man, or "Custer's Last Jump," (written with Steve Utley), in which the Sioux use fighter biplanes to defeat Custer's zeppelin-borne parachute troops at Little Big Horn. In the story that follows, one of Waldrop's most elegant, eloquent, and richly inventive Alternate Histories, he shows us what a future Africa might have been like if the Europeans had never arrived at all. . . .

The white man was drunk again. Robert Oinenke crossed the narrow, graveled street and stepped up on the boardwalk at the other side. Out of the corner of his eyes

he saw the white man raving. The man sat, feet out, back
against a wall, shaking his head, punctuating his monologue with cursing words.

Some said he had been a mercenary in one of the
boarder wars up the coast, one of those conflicts in which
two countries had become one; or one country, three.
Robert could not remember which. Mr. Lemuel, his history teacher, had mentioned it only in passing.

Since showing up in Onitsha town the white man had
worn the same khaki pants. They were of a military cut,
now torn and stained. The shirt he wore today was a
dashiki, perhaps variegated bright blue and red when
made, now faded purple. He wore a cap with a foreign
insignia. Some said he had been a general; others, a ser-
geant. His loud harangues terrified schoolchildren. Robert's classmates looked on the man as a forest demon.
Sometimes the constables came and took him away;
sometimes they only asked him to be quiet, and he would
subside.

Mostly he could be seen propped against a building,
talking to himself. Occasionally somebody would give
him money. Then he would make his way to the nearest
store or market stall that sold palm wine.

He had been in Robert's neighborhood for a few
months. Before that he had stayed near the marketplace.

Robert did not look at him. Thinking of the marketplace, he hurried his steps. The first school bell rang.

"You will not be dawdling at the market," his mother
had said as he readied himself for school. "Miss Mbene
spoke to me of your tardiness yesterday."

She took the first of many piles of laundry from her
wash baskets and placed them near the ironing board.
There was a roaring fire in the hearth, and her irons were
lined up in the racks over it. The house was already hot
as an oven and would soon be as damp as the monsoon
season.

His mother was still young and pretty but worn. She
had supported them since Robert's father had been killed

in an accident while damming a tributary of the Niger. He and forty other men had been swept away when a cofferdam burst. Only two of the bodies had ever been found. There was a small monthly check from the company her husband had worked for, and the government check for single mothers.

Her neighbor Mrs. Yortebe washed, and she ironed. They took washing from the well-to-do government workers and business people in the better section.

"I shan't be late," said Robert, torn with emotions. He knew he wouldn't spend a long time there this morning and be late for school, but he did know that he would take the long route that led through the marketplace.

He put his schoolbooks and supplies in his satchel. His mother turned to pick up somebody's shirt from the pile. She stopped, looking at Robert.

"What are you going to do with *two* copybooks?" she asked.

Robert froze. His mind tried out ten lies. His mother started toward him.

"I'm nearly out of pages," he said. She stopped. "If we do much work today, I shall have to borrow."

"I buy you ten copybooks at the start of each school year and then again at the start of the second semester. Money does not grow on the breadfruit trees, you know?"

"Yes, Mother," he said. He hoped she would not look in the copybooks, see that one was not yet half-filled with schoolwork and that the other was still clean and empty. His mother referred to all extravagance as "a heart-tearing waste of time and money."

"You have told me not to borrow from others. I thought I was using foresight."

"Well," said his mother, "see you don't go to the marketplace. It will only make you envious of all the things you can't have. And do not be late to school one more time this term, or I shall have you ever ironing."

"Yes, Mother," he said. Running to her, he rubbed his nose against her cheek. "Good-bye."

"Good day. And don't go near that marketplace!"
"Yes, Mother."

The market! Bright, pavilioned stalls covered a square Congo mile of ground filled with gaudy objects, goods, animals, and people. The Onitsha market was a crossroads of the trade routes, near the river and the railway station. Here a thousand vendors sold their wares on weekdays, many times that on weekends and holidays.

Robert passed the great piles of melons, guinea fowl in cages, tables of toys and geegaws, all bright and shiny in the morning light.

People talked in five languages, haggling with each other, calling back and forth, joking. Here men from Senegal stood in their bright red hats and robes. Robert saw a tall Waziri, silent and regal, indicating the prices he would pay with quick movements of his long fingers, while the merchant he stood before added two more each time. A few people with raised tattoos on their faces, backcountry people, wandered wide-eyed from table to table, talking quietly among themselves.

Scales clattered, food got weighed, chickens and ducks rattled, a donkey brayed near the big corral where larger livestock was sold. A goat wagon delivered yams to a merchant, who began yelling because they were still too hard. The teamster shrugged his shoulders and pointed to his bill of lading. The merchant threw down his apron and headed toward Onitsha's downtown, cursing the harvest, the wagoners, and the food cooperatives.

Robert passed by the food stalls, though the smell of ripe mangoes made his mouth water. He had been skipping lunch for three weeks, saving his Friday pennies. At the schoolhouse far away the ten-minute bell rang. He would have to hurry.

He came to the larger stalls at the far edge of the market where the booksellers were. He could see the bright paper jackets and dark type titles and some of the cover pictures on them from fifty yards away. He went toward the stall of Mr. Fred's Printers and High-Class Bookstore, which was his favorite. The clerk, who knew him by now, nodded to Robert as he came into the stall area. He was a nice young man in his twenties, dressed in a three-piece suit. He looked at the clock.

"Aren't you going to be late for school this fine morning?"

Robert didn't want to take the time to talk but said, "I know the books I want. It will only be a moment."

The clerk nodded.

Robert ran past the long shelves with their familiar titles: *Drunkards Believe the Bar Is Heaven; Ruth, the Sweet Honey That Poured Away; Johnny, the Most-Worried Husband; The Lady That Forced Me to Be Romantic; The Return of Mabel, in a Drama on How I Was About Marrying My Sister,* the last with a picture of Miss Julie Engebe, the famous drama actress, on the cover, which Robert knew was just a way to get people to buy the book.

Most of them were paper covered, slim, about fifty pages thick. Some had bright stenciled lettering on them, others drawings; a few had *photographios.* Robert turned at the end of the shelf and read the titles of others quickly: *The Adventures of Constable Joe; Eddy, the Coal-City Boy; Pocket Encyclopedia of Etiquette and Good Sense; Why Boys Never Trust Money-Monger Girls; How to Live Bachelor's Life and a Girl's Life Without Too Many Mistakes; Ibo Folktales You Should Know.*

He found what he was looking for: *Clio's Whips* by Oskar Oshwenke. It was as thin as the others, and the typefaces on the red, green, and black cover were in three different type styles. There was even a different *i* in the word *whips.*

Robert took it from the rack (it had been well thumbed, but Robert knew it was the only copy in the store.) He went down two more shelves, to where they kept the dramas, and picked out *The Play of the Swearing Stick* by Otuba Malewe and *The Raging Turk, or Bajazet II* by Thomas Goffe, an English European who had lived three hundred years ago.

Robert returned to the counter, out of breath from his dash through the stall. "These three," he said, spreading them out before him.

The clerk wrote figures on two receipt papers. "That will be twenty-four new cents, young sir," he said.

Robert looked at him without comprehension. "But yesterday they would have been twenty-two cents!" he said.

The clerk looked back down at the books. Then Robert noticed the price on the Goffe play, six cents, had been crossed out and eight cents written over that in big, red pencil.

"Mr Fred himself came through yesterday and looked over the stock," said the clerk. "Some prices he raised, others he liberally reduced. There are now many more two-cent books in the bin out front," he said apologetically.

"But . . . I only have twenty-two new cents." Robert's eyes began to burn.

The clerk looked at the three books. "I'll tell you what, young sir. I shall let you have these three books for twenty-two cents. When you get two cents more, you are to bring them *directly* to me. If the other clerk or Mr. Fred is here, you are to make no mention of this matter. Do you see?"

"Yes, yes. Thank you!" he handed all his money across. He knew it was borrowing, which his mother did not want him to do, but he wanted these books so badly.

He stuffed the pamphlets and receipts into his satchel. As he ran from the bookstall he saw the nice young clerk reach into his vest pocket, fetch out two pennies, and put them into the cashbox. Robert ran as fast as he could toward school. He would have to hurry or he would be late.

Mr Yotofeka, the principal, looked at the tardy slip.

"Robert," he said, looking directly into the boy's eyes, "I am very disappointed in you. You are a bright pupil.

Can you give me one good reason why you have been late to school three times in two weeks?''

"No, sir," said Robert. He adjusted his glasses, which were taped at one of the earpieces.

"No reason at all?"

"It took longer than I thought to get to school."

"You are thirteen years old, Robert Oinenke!" His voice rose. "You live less than a Congo mile from this schoolhouse, which you have been attending for seven years. You should know by now how long it takes to get from your home to the school.!"

Robert winced. "Yessir."

"Hand me your book satchel, Robert."

"But I . . ."

"Let me see."

"Yessir." He handed the bag to the principal, who was standing over him. The man opened it, took out the schoolbooks and copybooks, then the pamphlets. He looked down at the receipt, then at Robert's record file, which was open like the big book of the Christian Saint Peter in heaven.

"Have you been not eating to buy this trash?"

"No, sir."

"No, yes? Or yes, no?"

"Yes. I haven't."

"Robert, two of these are pure trash. I am glad to see you have brought at least one good play. But your other choices are just, just . . . You might as well have poured your coppers down a civet hole as buy these." He held up *Clio's Whips*. "Does your mother know you read these things? And this play! *The Swearing Stick* is about the primitive superstitions we left behind before independence. You want people to believe in this kind of thing again? You wish blood rituals, tribal differences to come back? The man who wrote this was barely literate, little more than just come in from the brush country."

"But . . ."

"But me no buts. Use the library of this schoolhouse, Robert, or the fine public one. Find books that will uplift you, appeal to your higher nature. Books written by learned people, who have gone to university.'' Robert knew that Mr. Yotofeka was proud of his education and that he and others like him looked down on the bookstalls and their books. He probably only read books published by the universities or real books published in Lagos or Cairo.

Mr. Yotofeka became stern and businesslike. ''For being tardy you will do three days detention after school. You will help Mr. Labuba with his cleaning.''

Mr Labuba was the custodian. He was large and slow and smelled of old clothes and yohimbe snuff. Robert did not like him.

The principal wrote a note on a form and handed it to Robert. ''You will take this note home to your hardworking mother and have her sign it. You will return it to me before *second* bell tomorrow. If you are late again, Robert Oinenke, it will not be a *swearing* stick I will be dealing with you about.''

''Yes, sir,'' said Robert.

When he got home that afternoon Robert went straight to his small alcove at the back of the house where his bed and worktable were. His table had his pencils, ink pen, eraser, ruler, compass, protractor, and glue. He took his copybooks from his satchel, then placed the three books he'd bought in the middle of his schoolbook shelf above the scarred table. He sat down to read the plays. His mother was still out doing the shopping as she always was when he got out of school.

Mr. Yotofeka was partly right about *The Play of the Swearing Stick*. It was not a great play. It was about a man in the old days accused of a crime. Unbeknownst to him, the real perpetrator of the crime had replaced the man's swearing stick with one that looked and felt just like it. (Robert knew this was implausible.) But the false swearing stick carried out justice anyway. It rose up from its place on the witness cushion beside the innocent man when he was questioned at the chief's court. It went out the window and chased the criminal and beat him to death. (In the stage directions the stick is lifted from the pillow by a technician with wires above the stage and disappears out of the window, and the criminal is seen running back and forth yelling and holding his head, bloodier each time he goes by.)

Robert really liked plays. He watched the crowds every afternoon going toward the playhouse in answer to the drums and horns sounded when a drama was to be staged. He had seen the children's plays, of course—*Big Magic, The Trusting Chief, Daughter of the Yoruba.* He had also seen the plays written for European children—*Cinderella, Rumpelstiltskin, Nose of Fire.* Everyone his age had—the Niger Culture Center performed the plays for the lower grades each year.

But when he could get tickets, through the schools or his teachers, he had gone to see real plays, both African and European. He had gone to folk plays for adults, especially *Why the Snake Is Slick,* and he had seen Ourelay the Congo playwright's *King of All He Surveyed* and *Scream of Africa.* He had seen tragedies and comedies from most of the African nations, even a play from Nippon, which he had liked to look at but in which not much happened. (Robert had liked the women actresses best, until he found out they weren't women; then he didn't know what to think.) But it was the older plays he liked best, those from England of the early 1600's.

The first one he'd seen was *Westward for Smelts!* by Christopher Kingstone, then *The Pleasant Historie of Darastus and Fawnia* by Rob Greene. There had been a whole week of Old English European plays at the Culture Hall, at night, lit by incandescent lights. His school had gotten free tickets for anyone who wanted them. Robert was the only student his age who went to all the performances, though he saw several older students there each night.

There had been *Caesar and Pompey* by George Chapman, *Mother Bombay* by John Lyly, *The Bugbears* by John Jeffere, *The Tragicall History of Romeus and Juliet*

by Arthur Broke, *Love's Labour Won* by W. Shaksper,
The Tragedy of Dido, Queen of Carthage by Marlow and
Nash, and on the final night, and best of all, *The Spar-
agus Garden* by Richard Brome.

That such a small country could produce so many good
playwrights in such a short span of time intrigued Robert, especially when you consider that they were fighting
both the Turks and the Italians during the period. Robert
began to read about the country and its history in books
from the school library. Then he learned that the Onitsha
market sold many plays from that era (as there were no
royalty payments to people dead two hundred fifty years.)
He had gone there, buying at first from the penny bin,
then the two-cent tables.

Robert opened his small worktable drawer. Beneath
his sixth-form certificate were the pamphlets from Mr.
Fred's. There were twenty-six of them; twenty of them
plays, twelve of those from the England of three hundred
years before.

He closed the drawer. He looked at the cover of
Thomas Goffe's play he had bought that morning—*The
Raging Turk, or Bajazet II*. Then he opened the second
copybook his mother had seen that morning. On the first
page he penciled, in his finest hand:

MOTOFUKO'S REVENGE:
A Play in Three Acts
By Robert Oinenke

After an hour his hand was tired from writing. He had
gotten to the place where King Motofuko was to consult
with his astrologer about the attacks by Chief Renebe on
neighboring tribes. He put the copybook down and began
to read the Goffe play. It was good, but he found that
after writing dialogue he was growing tired of reading it.
He put the play away.

He didn't really want to read *Clio's Whips* yet; he
wanted to save it for the weekend. But he could wait no
longer. Making sure the front door was closed, though it

was still hot outside, he opened the red, green, and black covers and read the title page:

CLIO'S WHIPS: The Abuses of Historie
by the White Races
By Oskar Oshwenke

"So the Spanish cry was Land Ho! and they sailed in the three famous ships, the *Nina,* the *Pinta,* and the *Elisabetta* to the cove on the island. Colon took the lead boat, and he and his men stepped out onto the sandy beach. All the air was full of parrots, and it was very wonderful there! But they searched and sailed around for five days and saw nothing but big bunches of animals, birds, fish, and turtles.

"Thinking they were in India, they sailed on looking for habitations, but on no island where they stopped were there any people at all! From one of the islands they saw far off the long lines of a much bigger island or a mainland, but tired from their search, and provendered from hunting and fishing, they returned to Europe and told of the wonders they had found, of the New Lands. Soon everyone wanted to go there."

This was exciting stuff to Robert. He reread the passage again and flipped the pages as he had for a week in Mr. Fred's. He came to his favorite illustration (which was what made him buy this book rather than another play.) It was the picture of a hairy elephant, with its trunk raised and with that magical stuff, snow, all around it. Below was a passage Robert had almost memorized:

"The first man then set foot at the Big River (now the New Thames) of the Northern New Land. Though he sailed from the Portingals, he came from England (which had just given the world its third pope), and his name was Cromwell. He said the air above the Big River was a darkened profusion of pigeons, a million and a million times a hundred hundred, and they covered the skies for hours as they flew.

''He said there were strange humped cattle there (much like the European wisents) that fed on grass, on both sides of the river. They stood so thickly that you could have walked a hundred Congo miles on their backs without touching the ground.

''And here and there among them stood great hairy mammuts, which we now know once lived in much of Europe, so much like our elephant, which you see in the game parks today, but covered with red-brown hair, with much bigger tusks, and much more fierce-looking.

''He said none of the animals were afraid of him, and he walked among them, petting some, handing them tender tufts of grass. They had never seen a man or heard a human voice, and had not been hunted since the very beginning of time. He saw that a whole continent of skins and hides lay before European man for the taking, and a million feathers for hats and decorations. He knew he was the first man ever to see this place, and that it was close to Paradise. He returned to Lisboa after many travails, but being a good Catholic, and an Englishman, he wasn't believed. So he went back to England and told his stories there.''

Now Robert went back to work on his play after carefully sharpening his pencil with a knife and setting his eraser close at hand. He began with where King Motofuko calls in his astrologer about Chief Renebe:

MOTOFUKO: Like to those stars which blaze forth overhead, brighter even than the seven ordered planets? And having waxed so lustily, do burn out in a week?
ASTROLOGER: Just so! Them that awe to see their burning forget the shortness of their fire. The moon, though ne'er so hot, stays and outlasts all else.
MOTOFUKO: Think you then this Chief Renebe be but a five months' wonder?
ASTROLOGER: The gods themselves do weep to see his progress! Starts he toward your lands a blazing beacon, yet will his followers bury his ashes and cinders in some

poor hole 'fore he reaches the Mighty Niger. Such light makes gods jealous.

Robert heard his mother talking with a neighbor outside. He closed his copybook, put *Clio's Whips* away, and ran to help her carry in the shopping.

During recess the next morning he stayed inside, not joining the others in the playground. He opened his copybook and took up the scene where Chief Renebe, who has conquered all King Motofuko's lands and had all his wives and (he thinks) all the king's children put to death, questions his general about it on the way to King Motofuko's capital.

RENEBE: And certaine, you, all his children dead, all his warriors sold to the Moorish dogs?
GENERAL: As sure as the sun doth rise and set, Your Highness. I myself his children's feet did hold, swing them like buckets round my conk, their limbs crack, their necks and heads destroy. As for his chiefs, they are now sent to grub ore and yams in the New Lands, no trouble to you forevermore. Of his cattle we made great feast, his sheep drove we all to the four winds.

This would be important to the playgoer. King Motofuko had escaped, but he had also taken his four-year-old-son, Motofene, and tied him under the bellwether just before the soldiers attacked in the big battle of Yotele. When the soldiers drove off the sheep, they sent his son to safety, where the shepherds would send him far away, where he would grow up and plot revenge.

The story of King Motofuko was an old one any Onitsha theatergoer would know. Robert was taking liberties with it—the story of the sheep was from one of his favorite parts of the *Odyssey*, where the Greeks were in the cave of Polyphemus. (The real Motofene had been sent away to live as hostage-son to the chief of the neighboring state long before the attack by Chief Renebe.) And

Robert was going to change some other things, too. The trouble with real life, Robert thought, was that it was usually dull and full of people like Mr. Yotofeka and Mr. Labuba. Not like the story of King Motofuko should be at all.

Robert had his copy of *Clio's Whips* inside his Egyptian grammar book. He read:

"Soon all the countries of Europe that could sent expeditions to the New Lands. There were riches in its islands and vast spaces, but the White Man had to bring others to dig them out and down the mighty trees for ships. That is when the Europeans really began to buy slaves from Arab nations, and to send them across to the Warm Sea to skin animals, build houses, and to serve them in all ways.

"Africa was raided over. Whole tribes were sold to slavery and degradation; worse, wars were fought between black and black to make slaves to sell to the Europeans. Mother Africa was raped again and again, but she was also traveled over and mapped: Big areas marked 'unexplored' on the White Man's charts shrank and shrank so that by 1700 there were very few such places left."

Miss Mbene came in from the play yard, cocked an eye at Robert, then went to the slateboard and wrote mathematical problems on it. With a groan, Robert closed the Egyptian grammar book and took out his sums and ciphers.

Mr. Labuba spat a stream of yohimbe-bark snuff into the weeds at the edge of the playground. His eyes were red and the pupils more open than they should have been in the bright afternoon sun.

"We be pulling at grasses," he said to Robert. He handed him a big pair of gloves, which came up to Robert's elbows. "Pull steady. These plants be cutting all the way through the gloves if you jerk."

In a few moments Robert was sweating. A smell of desk polish and eraser rubbings came off Mr. Labuba's shirt as he knelt beside him. They soon had cleared all along the back fence.

Robert got into the rhythm of the work, taking pleasure when the cutter weeds came out of the ground with a tearing pop and a burst of dirt from the tenacious, octopuslike roots. Then they would cut away the runners with trowels. Soon they had made quite a pile near the teetertotters.

Robert was still writing his play in his head; he had stopped in the second act when Motofuko, in disguise, had come to the forgiveness-audience with the new King Renebe. Unbeknownst to him, Renebe, fearing revenge all out of keeping with custom, had persuaded his stupid brother Guba to sit on the throne for the one day when anyone could come to the new king and be absolved of crimes.

"Is he giving you any trouble?" asked the intrusive voice of Mr. Yotofeka. He had come up and was standing behind Robert.

Mr. Labuba swallowed hard, the yohimbe lump going down chokingly.

"No complaints, Mr. Yotofeka," he said, looking up.

"Very good, Robert, you can go home when the tower bell rings at three o'clock."

"Yes, sir."

Mr. Yotofeka went back inside.

Mr Labuba looked at Robert and winked.

MOTOFUKO: Many, many wrongs in my time. I pray you, king, forgive me. I let my wives, faithful all, be torn from me, watched my children die, while I stood by, believing them proof from death. My village dead, all friends slaves. Reason twisted like hemp.

GUBA: From what mad place came you where such happens?

MOTOFUKO: *(Aside)* Name a country where this is not the standard of normalcy. *(To Guba)* Aye, all these I have done. Blinded, I went to worse. Pray you, forgive my sin.

GUBA: What could that be?

MOTOFUKO: *(Uncovering himself)* Murdering a king. *(Stabs him)*

GUBA: Mother of gods! Avenge my death. You kill the wrong man. Yonder—*(Dies)*

(Guards advance, weapons out.)

MOTOFUKO: Wrong man, when all men are wrong? Come, dogs, crows, buzzards, tigers. I welcome barks, beaks, claws, and teeth. Make the earth one howl. Damned, damned world where men fight like jackals over the carrion of states! Bare my bones then; they call for rest.

(Exeunt, fighting. Terrible screams off. Blood flows in from the wings in a river.)

SOLDIER: *(Aghast)* Horror to report. They flay the ragged skin from him whole!

"But the hide and fishing stations were hard to run with just slave labor. Not enough criminals could be brought from the White Man's countries to fill all the needs.

"Gold was more and more precious, in the hands of fewer and fewer people in Europe. There was some, true, in the Southern New Lands, but it was high in the great mountain ranges and very hard to dig out. The slaves worked underground till they went blind. There were revolts under those cruel conditions.

"One of the first new nations was set up by slaves who threw off their chains. They called their land Freedom, which was the thing they had most longed for since being dragged from Mother Africa. All the armies of the White Man's trading stations could not overthrow them. The people of Freedom slowly dug gold out of the mountains and became rich and set out to free others, in the Southern New Land and in Africa itself. . . .

"Rebellion followed rebellion. Mother Africa rose up. There were too few white men, and the slave armies they sent soon joined their brothers and sisters against the White Man.

"First to go were the impoverished French and Spanish dominions, then the richer Italian ones, and those of the British. Last of all were the colonies of the great German banking families. Then the wrath of Mother Africa turned on those Arabs and Egyptians who had helped the White Man in his enslavement of the black.

"Now they are all gone as powers from our continent and only carry on the kinds of commerce with us which put all the advantages to Africa."

ASHINGO: The ghost! The ghost of the dead king!

RENEBE: What! What madness this? Guards, your places! What means you, man?

ASHINGO: He came, I swear, his skin all strings, his brain a red cawleyflower, his eyes empty holes!

RENEBE: What portent this? The old astrologer, quick. To find what means to turn out this being like a goat from our crops.

(Alarums without. Enter Astrologer.)

ASTROLOGER: Your men just now waked me from a mighty dream. Your majesty was in some high place, looking over the courtyard at all his friends and family. You were dressed in regal armor all of brass and iron. Bonfires of victory burned all around, and not a word of dissent was heard anywhere in the land. All was peace and calm.

RENEBE: Is this then a portent of continued long reign?

ASTROLOGER: I do not know, sire. It was *my* dream.

His mother was standing behind him, looking over his shoulder.

Robert jerked, trying to close his copybook. His glasses flew off.

"What is that?" She reached forward and pulled the workbook from his hands.

"It is extra work for school," he said. He picked up his glasses.

"No, it is not." She looked over his last page. "It is wasting your paper. Do you think we have money to burn away?"

"No, Mother. Please . . ." He reached for the copybook.

"First you are tardy. Then you stay detention after school. You waste your school notebooks. Now you have *lied* to me."

"I'm sorry. I . . ."

"What is this?"

"It is a play, a historical play."

"What are you going to do with a play?"

Robert lowered his eyes. "I want to take it to Mr. Fred's Printers and have it published. I want it acted in the Niger Culture Hall. I want it to be sold all over Niger."

His mother walked over to the fireplace, where her irons were cooling on the racks away from the hearth.

"What are you going to *do*!!?" he yelled.

His mother flinched in surprise. She looked down at the notebook, then back at Robert. Her eyes narrowed.

"I was going to get my spectacles."

Robert began to cry.

She came back to him and put her arms around him. She smelled of the marketplace, of steam and cinnamon. He buried his head against her side.

"I will make you proud of me, Mother. I am sorry I used the copybook, but I *had* to write this play."

She pulled away from him. "I ought to beat you within the inch of your life, for ruining a copybook. You are going to have to help me for the rest of the week. You are not to work on this until you have finished every bit of your schoolwork. You should know Mr. Fred nor nobody is going to publish anything written by a schoolboy."

She handed him the notebook. "Put that away. Then go out on the porch and bring in those piles of mending. I am going to sweat a copybook out of your brow before I am through."

Robert clutched the book to him as if it were his soul.

RENEBE: O rack, ruin, and pain! Falling stars and the winds do shake the foundation of night itself! Where my soldiers, my strength? What use taxes, tribute if they buy not strong men to die for me?

(*Off*): Gone. All Fled.

RENEBE: Hold! Who is there? (*Draws*)

MOTOFENE: (*Entering*) He whose name will freeze your blood's roots.

RENEBE: The son of that dead king!

MOTOFENE: Aye, dead to you and all the world else, but alive to me and as constant as that star about which the groaning axletree of the earth does spin.

(*Alarums and excursions off.*)

Now hear you the screams of your flesh and blood and friendship, such screams as those I have heard awake and fitfully asleep these fourteen years. Now hear them for all time.

RENEBE: Guards! To me!

MOTOFENE: To you? See those stars which shower to earth out your fine window: At each a wife, child, friend does die. You watched my father cut away to bone and blood and gore and called not for the death stroke! For you I have had my Vulcans make you a fine suit. All iron and brass, as befits a king! It you will wear, to look out over the palace yard of your dead, citizens and friends. You will have a good high view, for it is situate on cords of finest woods. (*Enter Motofene's soldiers.*) Seize him gently. (*Disarm*) And now, my former king, outside. Though full of hot stars, the night is cold. Fear not the touch of the brass. Anon you are garmented, my men will warm the suit for you.

(*Exeunt and curtain.*)

Robert passed the moaning white man and made his way down the street, beyond the market. He was going to Mr. Fred's Printers in downtown Onitsha. He followed broad New Market Street, bring careful to stay out of the way of the noisy streetcars that steamed on their rails toward the center of town.

He wore his best clothes, though it was Saturday morning. In his hands he carried his play, recopied in ink in yet another notebook. He had learned from the clerk at the market bookstall that the one sure way to find Mr. Fred was at his office on Saturday forenoon, when the Onitsha *Weekly Volcano* was being put to bed.

Robert saw two *wayway* birds sitting on the single telegraph wire leading to the relay station downtown. In the old superstitions one *wayway* was a bad omen, two were good, three a surprise.

"Mr. Fred is busy," said the woman in the *Weekly Volcano* office. Her desk was surrounded by copies of all the pamphlets printed by Mr. Fred's bookstore, past headlines from the *Volcano*, and a big picture of Mr. Fred, looking severe in his morning coat, under the giant clock, on whose face was engraved the motto in Egyptian: TIME IS BUSINESS.

The calendar on her desk, with the picture of a Niger author for each month, was open to October 1894. A listing of that author's books published by Mr. Fred was appended at the bottom of each page.

"I should like to see Mr. Fred about my play," said Robert.

"Your play?"

"Yes. A rousing historical play. It is called *Motofuko's Revenge*."

"Is your play in proper form?"

"Following the best rules of dramaturgy," said Robert.

"Let me see it a moment."

Robert hesitated.

"Is it a papertypered?" she asked.

A cold chill ran down Robert's spine.

"All manuscripts must be papertypered, two spaces between lines, with wide margins," she said.

There was a lump in Robert's throat. "But it is in my very finest book-hand," he said.

"I'm sure it is. Mr. Fred reads everything himself, is a very busy man, and insists on papertypered manuscripts."

The last three words came crashing down on Robert like a mud-wattle wall.

"Perhaps if I spoke to Mr. Fred . . ."

"It will do you no good if your manuscript isn't papertypered."

"Please. I . . ."

"Very well. You shall have to wait until after one. Mr. Fred has to put the *Volcano* in final form and cannot be disturbed."

It was ten-thirty.

"I'll wait," said Robert.

At noon the lady left, and a young man in a vest sat down in her chair.

Other people came, were waited on by the man or sent into another office to the left. From the other side of the shop door, behind the desk, came the sound of clanking, carts rolling, thumps, and bells. Robert imagined great machines, huge sweating men wrestling with cogs and gears, books stacked to the ceiling.

It got quieter as the morning turned to afternoon. Robert stood, stretched, and walked around the reception area again, reading the newspapers on the walls with their stories five, ten, fifteen years old, some printed before he was born.

Usually they were stories of rebellions, wars, floods, and fears. Robert did not see one about the burst dam that had killed his father, a yellowed clipping of which was in the Coptic Bible at home.

There was a poster on one wall advertising the fishing resort on Lake Sahara South, with pictures of trout and catfish caught by anglers.

At two o'clock the man behind the desk got up and pulled down the windowshade at the office. "You shall have to wait outside for your father," he said. "We're closing for the day."

"Wait for my father?"

"Aren't you Meletule's boy?"

"No. I have come to see Mr. Fred about my play. The lady . . ."

"She told me nothing. I thought you were the printer's devil's boy. You say you want to see Mr. Fred about a play?"

"Yes. I . . ."

"Is it papertypered?" asked the man.

Robert began to cry.

"Mr. Fred will see you now," said the young man, coming back in the office and taking his handkerchief back.

"I'm sorry," said Robert.

"Mr. Fred only knows you are here about a play," he said. He opened the door to the shop. There were no mighty machines there, only a few small ones in a dark, two-story area, several worktables, boxes of type and lead. Everything was dusty and smelled of metal and thick ink.

A short man in his shirtsleeves leaned against a workbench reading a long, thin strip of paper while a boy Robert's age waited. Mr. Fred scribbled something on the paper, and the boy took it back into the other room, where several men bent quietly over boxes and tables filled with type.

"Yes," said Mr. Fred, looking up.

"I have come here about my play."

"Your play?"

"I have written a play, about King Motofuko. I wish you to publish it."

Mr. Fred laughed. "Well, we shall have to see about that. Is it papertypered?"

Robert wanted to cry again.

"No, I am sorry to say, it is not. I didn't know . . ."

"We do not take manuscripts for publication unless . . ."

"It is in my very best book-hand, sir. Had I known, I would have tried to get it papertypered."

"Is your name and address on the manuscript?"

"Only my name. I . . ."

Mr. Fred took a pencil out from behind his ear. "What is your house number?"

Robert told him his address, and he wrote it down on the copybook.

"Well, Mr.—Robert Oinenke. I shall read this, but not before Thursday after next. You are to come back to the shop at ten a.m. on Saturday the nineteenth for the manuscript and our decision on it."

"But . . ."

"What?"

"I really like the books you publish, Mr. Fred, sir. I especially liked *Clio's Whips* by Mr. Oskar Oshwenke."

"Always happy to meet a satisfied customer. We published that book five years ago. Tastes have changed. The public seems tired of history books now."

"That is why I am hoping you will like my play," said Robert.

"I will see you in two weeks," said Mr. Fred. He tossed the copybook into a pile of manuscripts on the workbench.

"Because of the legacy of the White Man, we have many problems in Africa today. He destroyed much of what he could not take with him. Many areas are without telegraphy; many smaller towns have only primitive direct current power. More needs to be done with health and sanitation, but we are not as badly off as the most primitive of the White Europeans in their war-ravaged countries or in the few scattered enclaves in the plantations and timber forests of the New Lands.

"It is up to you, the youth of Africa of today, to take our message of prosperity and goodwill to these people, who have now been as abused by history as we Africans once were by them. I wish you good luck."

Oskar Oshwenke,
Onitsha, Niger, 1889

Robert put off going to the market stall of Mr. Fred's bookstore as long as he could. It was publication day.

He saw that the nice young clerk was there. (He had paid him back out of the ten Niger dollar advance Mr. Fred had had his mother sign for two weeks before. His mother still could not believe it.)

"Ho, there, Mr. Author!" said the clerk. "I have your three free copies for you. Mr. Fred wishes you every success."

The clerk was arranging his book and John-John Motulla's *Game Warden Bob and the Mad Ivory Hunter* on the counter with the big starburst saying: JUST PUBLISHED!

His book would be on sale throughout the city. He looked at the covers of the copies in his hands:

The TRAGICALL DEATH OF KING
MOTOFUKO
and HOW THEY WERE SORRY
a drama by Robert Oinenke
abetted by
MR. FRED OLUNGENE
"The Mighty Man of the Press"
for sale at Mr. Fred's High-Class Bookstore
300 Market, and the *Weekly Volcano*
Office, 12 New Market Road
ONITSHA, NIGER
price 10¢ N.

On his way home he came around the corner where a group of boys was taunting the white man. The man was drunk and had just vomited on the foundation post of a store. They were laughing at him.

"Kill you all. Kill you all. No shame," he mumbled, trying to stand.

The words of *Clio's Whips* came to Robert's ears. He walked between the older boys and handed the white man three Niger cents. The white man looked up at him with sick, grey eyes.

"Thank you, young sir," he said, closing his hand tightly.

Robert hurried home to show his mother and the neighbors his books.

ETOUNDI'S MONKEY
by Judith Dubois

Here's a bittersweet and moving story about a young scientist who makes a far greater discovery than she'd bargained for in a remote corner of Africa, and an old native woman who takes on far more responsibility than she ever thought she'd need to bear. . . .

New writer Janet Dubois went to Cameroon in West Africa as a Peace Corps volunteer in 1967, and met and married her husband there. They now have four children and are living in the country in southern France, where she teaches English. She has a Master's Degree from the University of Bordeaux in France, and has made sales so far to The Magazine of Fantasy and Science Fiction *and* Stories. *She has finished her first novel, and is at work on another.*

Aunt Nyah was visiting Hiroko. She enjoyed looking at the Japanese girl's photo albums, intrigued by pictures of Hiroko's mother in a kimono. She shuffled through a collection of postcards representing the carved demons and heroes of a famous temple, mimicking the statues' grimaces. Hiroko laughed behind her fingers.

A Pygmy hunter sauntered up to the door and called out in a loud voice, *"Koh-koh-koh."* That is how Pygmies knock, perhaps because their huts have no doors. It was not unusual for small men dressed in symbolic rags and a wide grin to show up at the Japanese student's cabin with monkey heads. She already had a large crate of skulls ready to be shipped to the Primate Research Institute of the University of Kyoto. She gave the hunters a few coins, and they went away chuckling at the foolish foreign woman who paid for scraps they usually threw to the dogs.

Hiroko recognized Johnny, one of her regular guides, and told him to enter. But when he held up his strange head, she started and rushed to grab the gory trophy. She examined it in the sunlight, then brought it into the cabin and began measuring it with jerky, feverish movements. The head was almost as big as a gorilla's, but had little else in common with the big apes. The murky yellow eyes were huge, like those of a nocturnal lemur, yet there were no visible pupils. Long gray fur of a peculiar texture grew thickly over the head and lower face except for an narrow mask of short hairs around the eyes. There was neither muzzle nor chin. It was a weird-looking creature, but what excited Hiroko most was the absence of anything resembling a mouth or nose.

She questioned the Pygmy hunter, but her excitement and limited pidgin vocabulary hampered her. She turned to Aunt Nyah.

"Please, ask Johnny what he knows about this animal, where he found it."

Puzzled, Aunt Nyah walked over to the table, but was careful not to touch the head. She stared at it, then crossed herself.

"What kind of animal is it?" asked Hiroko.

"Witchcraft. Must be. I've never seen anything like that come out of the forest."

"Please ask Johnny about it."

Aunt Nyah stiffened. "Better send him away and have nothing to do with it. It's bad luck."

"It's tremendous good luck for my thesis. Please. This is very serious."

"Mais oui, mais oui." The elderly African woman shook her head. "Everything *Mademoiselle* Hiroko does is serious. *Mademoiselle* is a serious girl. Much too *serieuse.*"

Hiroko grinned. "I have to behave myself. Naughty girls don't get study grants."

The African woman waggled her turban. "Naughty girls have fun. At your age you should be having fun, not following monkeys in the forest to collect their turds."

The Japanese girl laughed at the description of her research. "Please, ask Johnny where he found the creature. Do his people have a name for it?"

"Na fo ou sye you don find dis beef?"

Johnny replied in rapid pidgin, and Aunt Nyah interpreted. His band of hunters had discovered the *beef* in the forest, a long trot from the village. It was a large *beef* and had made a delicious stew. Pidgin, like the other local languages, made no distinction between "meat" and "animal," using the word *beef* to indicate anything that might go into the soup pot. Johnny promised to show Hiroko where they had found the creature. He shrugged at her next question. He didn't know whether or not they could find others. Perhaps. He grinned. But it would be difficult work. Much more difficult than tracking the mandrills Hiroko occasionally hired him to find. She would have to pay more. The *beef* was fierce when attacked. It had fought viciously. Even the little one. . . .

Hiroko interrupted with a startled question.

Yes, the creature was carrying its young when they found it.

Shaking her head sadly, the student turned to her interpreter. "Please. You must make him understand. His family has made stew out of two priceless specimens. This animal has never been observed or reported before. I don't even know what family it belongs to. He must not let his hunters harm any others they come across. The government will want to protect the species."

"If you think Johnny and his hunters care about government regulations. . . ."

"They'll be paid for their forbearance. Such an animal is more valuable than a dozen chimpanzees."

Seeing how urgent Hiroko was, Aunt Nyah convinced Johnny that if he caught any more of the strange beasts, they would be worth more to him alive than in the stew-pot. The little hunter gave her a worried frown.

"Fo one small beef like so, how much she fit give me! She fit give me twenty thousand?"

Hiroko's Oriental eyes widened. She understood pidgin better than she spoke it. "Does he still have the infant, Aunt Nyah? Is that what he is saying? Of course I'll give him twenty thousand francs. My university will be willing to pay much more than that."

When the old woman relayed this information to Johnny, he woefully shook his head. *"I don be one fool-ish man. I don sell dis thing fo Massa Etoundi. Massa Etoundi, he don thief me plenty. He never pay me so good price."*

"*Monsieur* Etoundi?" asked Hiroko. "*Monsieur* Etoundi bought it? I'll go see him right away. I'll explain to him how important. . . ."

"That wouldn't be a wise thing to do," interrupted Aunt Nyah. She held the girl by the shoulders to keep her in her chair. "If you want that animal, that's not the way to go about it. As soon as my brother-in-law sees how eager you are, he'll start raising his price; and the more you offer him, the more he'll ask; and when you agree to his highest price, he'll grow suspicious and de-cide he's not asking enough, that he can get more from someone else. Etoundi is so clever he outsmarts himself. Let me handle this. I'll find out how much he wants, and let him think a Hausa trader has asked me to buy for him."

Hiroko hesitated, then agreed. "While you bargain with *Monsieur* Etoundi, I shall go into the forest with Johnny. Perhaps he can find other creatures like this one."

"*Très bien,*" replied Aunt Nyah. "While you're in the Pygmy camp, try to buy me a small piece of smoked meat. But don't let them rob you."

The old woman went to the hut in which she lived alone to prepare for a formal visit to her sisters-in-law.

In one corner of the room, a cast-iron kettle simmered over a small fire amidst three stones. Nyah squatted beside it, took off the lid, and sniffed. Whisky, the old bitch she kept for company, approached and wagged an interested tail. Thick red palm oil floated on the surface of a rich stew made with gumbo, tender white mushrooms, a small piece of zebu tail, and plenty of hot pepper. "It's not for you, Whisky, and not for me, either." Nyah sighed and spooned the stew into a gaudily painted tin dish. The small, short-haired dog returned to its corner with a disappointed slouch.

Nyah washed in a basin and opened the battered metal chest that contained her wardrobe. Most of her dresses dated from her brief marriage to Etoundi's brother. She saved her bride's finery for special occasions and wore hand-me-downs given her by Etoundi's wives for everyday wear.

She chose a black lace gown, to remind her hosts that she was a widow and not a cast-off wife. After his brother's death, Etoundi had inherited Nyah as a second wife. It was an old custom meant to provide for women who had neither husbands nor grown sons. But the young widow had bitterly resented his claims. Her hostility soon discouraged him; his accusations that she was barren, insolent, and bad-tempered frightened other suitors. When a new kitchen was built, Nyah carried her cot into the old hut, gathered palm branches to rethatch the roof, and repaired the crumbling walls with a fresh coat of adobe. She cleared her own garden and lived on what she was able to earn selling vegetables and fried pastries in the market. Etoundi took other, younger, wives and forgot his prerogatives over his brother's widow. The village children, constantly in and out of the little shack, called her Aunt Nyah.

She finished knotting a scarf over her gray braids and picked up the dish of stew. As she crossed the yard, she admired the blossomlike bracts of a flaming red bougainvillea that arched over the roof of her brother-in-law's house. Etoundi was sitting alone on his veranda, listen-

ing to a soccer game on the radio. The healer wore sandals and a large pagne knotted under his bulging paunch.
It left bare his womanish breasts and their sparse growth
of hair. His plump, cheerful face was belied by the
shrewd eyes behind gold-rimmed spectacles. On market
days, dressed in a Tergal suit, he looked more like a
prosperous merchant or a retired bureaucrat than a witch
doctor. But the fawning court of young apprentices that
followed him about showed more respect than an ordinary mortal could command.

Nyah walked by him without stopping. *"I hangwe,
mbolopehe."*

Etoundi nodded and returned her greeting with a
mumbled, *"Sitah, mbolo."* His attention was riveted to
the game going on inside his over-sized transistor. The
radio announcer began to scream incoherently as Nyah
rounded the corner of the house.

She found the healer's present three wives in the
kitchen hut. Over the years, some had come and some
had gone. Madjoli, Etoundi's first wife, was a heavy,
middle-aged woman in a faded pagne tied over her
breasts. The hair on one side of her head stood out in
spikes while a younger co-wife worked on the other side,
twisting small tufts into intricate braids that lay flat
against her skull. A girl still in her teens sat on a leather
cushion and nursed a chubby baby. Madjoli had once
hated the pretty Nyah as a rival. Now, accustomed to co-
wives who shared the work and honored her as head wife,
she greeted Nyah kindly and had her sit on the bench at
her side. She was pleased by the gift of stew. It was not
difficult to get her to talk about her husband's recent purchase from the Pygmies.

"This is even more important than I thought, Aunt
Nyah." Hiroko was trembling with emotion, making tight
knots of her fingers in an effort to stay calm. "Johnny
showed me where they captured the creature, and not far
away, we discovered a burned-out crater. There seems to
be something metal at the bottom of it, but it's so melted

I could tell little about it.'' She paused and gulped air before going on. ''It is possible that the creature Johnny and his hunters killed was an extraterrestrial, that it came from outer space, another world.''

The African woman nodded wisely. The radio said men had gone to the moon and returned, and people from the city said this was true. It was no more difficult to believe that strange creatures from other worlds could visit the earth.

''We must convince Etoundi to turn the infant over to the authorities. As quickly as possible. I am going to send a telegram to my director in the capital city. He will. . . .''

Aunt Nyah held up a hand to stop the girl. She was sorry to disappoint her. Hiroko was still young enough to care deeply about many things. ''Etoundi will never give it up. He believes it is a powerful fetish, that it will make him a great healer, a very rich healer. He will not let the postmaster send your telegram. If you bring in the authorities, he will only hide the creature and show them a chimpanzee in a cage until they go away. This is his village. He will do as he pleases.''

''He can ask his price. . . .''

''Such a fetish has no price. It is useless to worry yourself about it. The creature will not live long enough to make such a fuss over it.'' She shrugged at Hiroko's look of dismay. ''Madjoli says it refuses to eat and is very weak. Etoundi does not care if it dies. He will dry the meat and skin, grind up the bones, and sell it to his customers, sliver by sliver, pinch by pinch.''

Hiroko grabbed Aunt Nyah's knee. ''Please. You are my only true friend in the village. I can count on no one else. Please arrange to let me see the animal. If I can show the authorities a photograph, they will act, perhaps in time to save its life. Our best scientists should be studying it, trying to help it survive.''

Nyah looked down at the hand on her knee. The Japanese girl had tiny hands, like a child's. She seemed too young to have come so far from her parents and family.

Nyah would never have let a daughter of hers go away to live among strangers. Most of the village viewed the foreign student with suspicion, but Aunt Nyah had been a helpful ally from the beginning. The old woman patted Hiroko's little fingers. "I shall take you to see it. But we must. . . ." She hunched her shoulders and mimicked a sneak. ". . . go in the night like thieves. No one must see us."

Hiroko nodded soberly. "If it were not so important to the entire world to learn what the animal is and save it if it can be saved, I would not ask this of you."

The African woman smiled, suddenly unveiling the handsome young bride that had been brought to the village many years ago. "If I did not detest Etoundi so thoroughly, perhaps I would not do it."

That night the village emptied to attend a wake four kilometers away. The deceased was a man of importance, a former postmaster in town, who had been buried a week earlier. Now the family was holding a wake to keep his ghost from returning to haunt them. Etoundi's village set out in high spirits. A proper wake included plenty to eat and drink, music, dancing, and storytelling until dawn.

Aunt Nyah left with a group of younger cousins. She was gay and talkative for the first two kilometers so that they would remember her walking to the wake with them. Afterward she fell silent and let them outpace her. Once they were out of sight, she left the road and followed a network of footpaths through the cacao plantations and gardens back to the village.

As soon as she reached Hiroko's cabin, the Japanese girl wanted to go to Etoundi's house. The older woman refused. "We must wait. The second wife, Mouadakou-kou, did not go to the wake. They say she is ill. We must be certain she is asleep before we attempt to enter the house."

Hiroko showed her the drawings she had been making of the head. To preserve it, she had put it in a large jar filled with alcohol. Aunt Nyah preferred looking at the photo albums. It was past midnight when she heard an owl hoot nearby, and glanced up with a worried frown. She shuddered.

"That's an evil bird. It sings when it smells death."

Hiroko smiled. "I think it smells only a fat rat."

Displeased, Aunt Nyah shrugged. "Well, let us be going. If she's an honest wife, Mouadakoukou is asleep by now. Bring a flashlight." She blew out the kerosene lamp, and they left the little hut to enter a world painted with a palette of muted grays. The full moon illuminated the village; its magical light banished the timid night shadows to their holes under the eaves and within corners and crooked angles. Pale gray fringes of silk waved in the banana groves; the village roofs gleamed silver, the barren yards were smooth courts of slate and iron. The two women circled the houses on a narrow, moonlit path that meandered through sprawling gardens to approach Etoundi's house from the rear.

The back door was unlatched. Aunt Nyah gave a small tisk of disapproval and led the way into the house. Moonlight coming through the open door dimly illuminated a long hall that ran the full length of the building. Nyah counted the doors until she reached the storeroom. Etoundi often bought baby monkeys and chimpanzees from the Pygmies to resell to Europeans in town. He kept his sad little prisoners in the storeroom next to his bedroom.

Of course the door was locked. She pointed to Madjoli's room across the hall. The first wife kept the storeroom keys.

Nyah and the Japanese girl entered the room and shut the door. Wooden shutters kept the moonlight out and the room dark. Nyah turned on the flashlight. Its beam slid over the bed shrouded in mosquito netting, metal chests stacked one on top of the other, and a small table with a kerosene lamp next to the bed. Madjoli was a well-organized person who rarely changed her habits. Most of the village knew where she kept her keys. A blue vase stood flowerless on the little table. Nyah turned it upside down, and a bundle of keys fell out.

The two women furtively crossed the hall. For long, exasperating minutes they tried the keys on the lock one after another without any success, until at last they heard a tumbler click. They entered the storeroom and quickly closed the door behind them.

The creature was lying at the bottom of a wooden crate. Its huge eyes reflected the flashlight beam. As they approached, they were almost overpowered by its stench. Its fur was matted and damp with liquid, greenish fecal matter that also covered the cage floor. It was aware of them and made one brief, feeble effort to stir, then lapsed into apathy.

"*Eeyah,*" said Aunt Nyah, moved by pity.

"It must be properly cared for," whispered Hiroko. "We cannot just let it die."

Nyah shrugged. The creature belonged to Etoundi, and he did not really care whether it lived or died.

"We could take it," said Hiroko. "I could take it to my director in the city. He would see that it received treatment. It would still be Etoundi's property, of course, but it might live, with proper care."

Nyah was shocked by the intensity of the girl's voice. She turned the flashlight on Hiroko's smooth, round face, but it told her very little. She shrugged doubtfully. Getting to take pictures of the creature was one thing, but she could not let the foreign student steal it. "Take your pictures," she whispered. "I can hear voices coming along the road."

Hiroko hesitated. "Surely. . . ."

"Hush!" Aunt Nyah turned off the flashlight.

There was loud laughter outside the window. Then a door in the house slammed open, and someone ran past the storeroom. They heard a man shout in surprise, then a loud commotion. The high, frightened voice of a woman was crying. "Thief! Thief!" An angry voice they recognized as Etoundi's drowned out the woman's until she began screaming.

"What is happening?" asked Hiroko.

Aunt Nyah chuckled. "Etoundi returned, and Mouadakoukou must have had a lover in her room. Etoundi saw him run out of the house. Mouadakoukou is trying to convince him that it was a thief he saw. He's beating her. If she sticks to her story, Etoundi will at least pretend to believe her, to save face."

The Japanese girl winced at a particularly loud scream.

"He's enjoying himself," muttered Nyah. "That is why I moved out of his house."

After a while the blows stopped, and the woman's screams faded to muffled sobs. Etoundi was making an angry, indignant speech. Doors began to open and slam closed in the hallway. Nyah pulled Hiroko to the back of the storeroom and made her crouch beside her.

"He's searching the house," she explained. "To see if the thief took anything. I forgot the key on the outside."

"He's going to find us."

"Perhaps not. In the dark he may take us for a couple of sacks of cacao."

The door to Madjoli's room across the way slammed open, then slammed shut again.

The storeroom door opened. Etoundi's short, stocky figure stood in the doorway holding a kerosene lamp. The two women cringed in the dark shadows and stopped breathing.

They waited. The healer held up his lamp and entered the storeroom. He was not looking at the women and did not seem to suspect their presence. His gaze was on the strange creature in the cage. But as he raised his lamp higher, its yellow glow struck the bright print of Aunt Nyah's dress. Etoundi started, then gave a surprised grunt.

Nyah stood and stepped forward, hoping she could mask the Japanese girl crouching behind her. But Hiroko did not have the sense to go on hiding. She stood up and came to stand beside the African woman. Etoundi stared at them.

"We did not come to steal," said Hiroko. "I had to see the animal you bought from the Pygmies. I believe it may be a sentient, sapient being. It may come from another world. It appears to be unrelated to any life-form known on earth. It needs care. It is very valuable, perhaps priceless. You must let experts care for it, try to keep it alive. You will be paid. . . ."

"Shut up!" Etoundi cried. His growing fury had gotten the better of his amazement and whatever awe he might have had for the foreign scholar. "I know how the government pays: With promises. The fetish is mine! I bought it. Get out of my house!" He grabbed Hiroko's arm and yanked her across the storeroom and out the door. Seeing the camera she held, he tore it out of her grasp and smashed it on the floor. Then he stomped on it. When nothing was left but debris, he looked up at the Japanese girl. His eyes were cold and hostile, his voice lethal.

"If I find you in my house again, I will report you to the authorities. I'll tell them . . . enough to have you expelled within twenty-four hours!"

Hiroko tried to protest, but Etoundi pushed her brutally down the hall. Over his shoulder she saw Aunt Nyah signaling her to go quietly. She let herself be shoved out of the healer's house.

Etoundi returned to attack the woman he had once claimed as a wife. "You brought her here. Insolent whore. You opened the storeroom for her, showed her my fetish! How could you dare? Who was the man that was with you?"

Nyah said nothing, sensing his anger, originally provoked by Mouadakoukou, had carried him too far, that he was beyond listening, beyond reason. He approached. His eyes were bloodshot. His breath and body stank of alcohol, as if the evening's many drinks had soured and turned to a poisonous liquor that seeped from his pores. She could not keep the repulsion, the hatred, she felt for him out of her eyes.

He slapped her. She staggered but continued to glare

at him. Then Etoundi hit her with his fist and struck her again as she fell. Using both fists, he buffeted her from side to side like a limp sandbag.

For fear Hiroko would hear, return, and be punished in the same manner, Nyah held back her cries. Quickly, she realized that her silence was depriving Etoundi of a pleasure he had counted on; he wanted to hear her scream. She bit her lips tightly. It was not courage that kept her mute but spite.

Village children are not trained to stoicism; it is not expected of adults. When in pain, they cry, scream, and howl without shame. Nyah's silence under his blows infuriated Etoundi. He hit her harder, letting the hatred and anger her pride inspired take over, yielding to a mindless, sensual pleasure in giving pain. He continued beating the old woman until someone grabbed him and pushed him away from his victim.

Madjoli, his first wife, was holding his arms and screaming at him.

"Fool! You've killed her!"

He stared at Nyah's inert body sprawled indecently among the canned goods and tins of kerosene. For an instant, panic gripped him. He had not meant to kill her, only to punish her for betraying him to the foreign woman. If she had cried out, if she had wept and pleaded, he would have stopped.

"Hush!" said Madjoli suddenly. She turned a flashlight on Nyah's body. The bloodied lips quivered with a faint moan.

The man turned away, more relieved than he wished to show. "Get her out of here. I don't want to ever see her again. She must leave the village. When my brother died, I did my duty by her and took her into my home. When she refused to respect me as her husband and bear my children, I tolerated her insolence for my brother's sake. But tonight she came into my house as a thief, to steal the fetish. The foreign woman must have bribed her. She does not deserve my trust. She must leave the village."

"She has no other family," objected Madjoli.

"Let her go where she will!" shouted Etoundi. "Let her go to the city. If she's too old to play the whore, let her beg in the streets. I promise you, woman, that if I see her around here again, she won't survive the next beating I give her. She's a demon, Satan's wife, not mine. She tried to use the evil eye on me, but my magic was too strong for her." He left the storeroom, still shouting. Soon Madjoli could hear him out in the yard, relating to his apprentices and the rest of the village Nyah's shocking betrayal. She could not see him, but she could imagine the expressive, dramatic gestures he was using. Etoundi was a good orator. Passion made his voice loud and convincing. The village would believe him and accept Nyah's exile.

Madjoli knelt and put her arm under Nyah's head. She slipped the other arm under Nyah's knees and managed to stand, the tall, slim body she had once envied cradled against her large breasts like an ungainly child. She had to carry the unconscious woman back to her hut alone. No one else dared touch the bearer of the evil eye.

Aunt Nyah heard Whisky whining, and struggled to sit up. Her body ached with a sullen, throbbing pain, an alien thing that burrowed deep within her and would not be dislodged. She undid her corsage and saw bruises on her arms and breasts, dark splotches on the light mahogany of her skin. She tasted blood. Her lips were cut and swollen. Two teeth wobbled. Her left eye would not open. She gingerly touched the sore and puffy skin around it and moaned.

Whisky laid her head on her mistress's knees. Aunt Nyah bent over the bitch and embraced her with sore, aching arms. She began to weep, keening shrilly her grief and misery. Salty tears stung the cut and torn flesh of her lips. The dog whined again and tried to comfort her with wet licks.

"Nyah."

Madjoli stood in the doorway with unhappy eyes.

"*Eeeyah.* Why do you anger him so? Why do you seek out sorrows?" She came in, carrying a basket that she set on the floor beside Nyah's low bamboo cot. It contained cotton and a disinfectant, ointment and bandages. Gently, she forced Nyah to lay down again, and began cleaning the cuts left by Etoundi's rings. "If you have the evil eye, you use it against none but yourself."

"Who says I have the evil eye?" Aunt Nyah's swollen lips blurred her words.

"Etoundi. He says you must leave the village. If he sees you again, he will beat you again. He claims you tried to use the evil eye on him. People believe him. No one will buy your pastries or plaintain in the market."

"*Eeeyah!*" Aunt Nyah wailed, heedless of who might hear her now.

"Patience, patience," murmured Madjoli. Her words were Africa's eternal reply to sorrow. They did not advise to be patient and hope for better, but rather to be patient and accept fate. Etoundi's wife began to rub ointment into the inky bruises. "*Eeeyah,* Nyah. How I hated you when first you came to the village. So lovely and proud, you walked like a princess. My husband wanted you; if you had wished, he would have repudiated me, sent me back to my father, and kept you as his only wife."

"Until he took another."

Madjoli shrugged. "Perhaps. Men are like that."

The woman lying on the cot grunted.

"You could have been happy with him. He would have given you children. If you had a son to care for you now. . . ."

"*Eeeyah.*" Nyah gripped her friend's hand tightly. "Say no more. You are touching a deep, old wound. Etoundi's blows did not hurt as much."

Madjoli sighed and continued the massage. After a short silence she asked, "When will you leave?"

"Tomorrow. I'll take the Mammy wagon that goes to the city."

"Have you any money?"

"Just enough for a ticket."

"I have brought you some." She frowned at Nyah's surprised protest. "It is not mine. Mouadakoukou sends it to you. She . . . she is grateful that you did not tell Etoundi that the man who ran out of the house was not with you."

Nyah sat up and stared at the heavy, worn woman. "Why? Why did you tell me this? If your husband's wife is misbehaving, why do you not tell him?"

"Did you see the man who ran away?"

"No."

Madjoli shook her head. "It was my young brother, Bikanda. He is wild and foolish. Mouadakoukou is unhappy since her husband has a new favorite. I was the one that told Etoundi that she was too sick to go to the wake last night. They would have met whatever I did; I hoped to make it discreet."

Nyah touched Madjoli's hand. Etoundi's first wife had borne him eight children. She remembered the stout, cheerful girl suffering through her pregnancies, grieving over the three babies she had lost, working hard in her fields to feed her children, being forced to accept the pretty young co-wives that Etoundi installed under his roof. Nyah had envied her the children and grandchildren that would comfort her old age, but knew they had been paid for with tribulations she had not shared. She hesitated, then said, "I would ask one thing of you. I am ashamed. You have done much for me, and I would ask more."

"Ask what you will. I cannot refuse you. Etoundi truly believes that the man he saw was helping you. For my brother's sake, I can refuse you nothing."

"I have no right to ask. You may say no, and I will still kiss you good-bye and bless you for your kindness. But I would punish Etoundi for the beating he gave me. I did not go into his house to steal; I only wanted to show the fetish to the foreign woman."

Madjoli waited. When Nyah failed to continue, she said, "Yes?"

''Bring me the fetish.'' Nyah's words were abrupt and brutal.

Madjoli frowned. ''You are asking me to steal from my husband.''

Nyah did not protest. She looked aside. ''Yes, I am.''

The heavy woman stood and walked to the door. ''What would you do with it?''

''I will sell it to the foreign woman. She said it is worth much money. I will give the money to your son, Ntonga. Perhaps he will let me live with him. Students are always in need of money.''

Madjoli turned to gaze at the little fire in the corner of the hut. ''Etoundi promised to send Ntonga money from the coffee harvest, but used it all to pay the dowry he owed for Nyake. I will bring you the fetish. But I do not believe you will get much money for it.''

''Why?''

''It is dying. It cannot eat. It has no mouth to eat with.''

A flame flickered over the smoldering stub of a branch amidst three stones, dimly lighting the small hut. Aunt Nyah sat on her coat and looked around her. The shelves were bare, the many hooks set in the beams empty. She had lived there for over thirty years, and it had taken only a couple of hours to pack all her belongings. The tin chest sat by the door. She held a small bundle knotted in a piece of pagne on her lap. She waited.

The night that crouched beyond her open door was quiet. Nyah stared at the dying fire. No one from the village had come to say good-bye. At dusk, everyone had gone to bed early, locking their doors and closing their shutters. Fear of the evil eye had made them forget the years of friendship and the many sweet pastries she had shared with their children. She remembered the greedy little faces crowded around the pot of red palm oil bubbling on her fire while she ladled off the golden globs of fried dough as they rose to the surface. She had been

Aunt Nyah then. Now she was a barren old woman alone, a stranger to be shunned.

"Koh-koh-koh."

Madjoli stood in the doorway and waited for Nyah's nod before she entered. The heavy woman crossed to the fire, squatted, and unwrapped the bundle she carried. Nyah came to her side, and the two women stared at Etoundi's strange fetish.

Its damp, matted fur stank with an acrid, nauseating odor. Its large eyes were veiled with a thin gray membrane. The ribs of the creature's emaciated chest stood out in ridges under the soiled fur, ridges that ran the wrong way. It had four limbs, hollow, boneless tubes of muscle like an elephant's trunk, and no tail. Madjoli poked at her offering in disgust. It stirred weakly and at once subsided.

"It's dying," said Nyah.

Etoundi's first wife nodded. "It's starving to death. It has no mouth. How could we feed it?"

"I'll have to clean it. They won't let me on the Mammy wagon with something that smells so badly."

Madjoli stood. "I must go back now." She hesitated. "Etoundi sent some of his apprentices to the foreign woman's cabin. They smashed things, frightened her. They took the head she bought from the Pygmies. She has gone to the mission."

"They did not hurt her."

"No. Etoundi only wanted to scare her and get the head she had."

Nyah embraced her friend. "Madjoli, you have been kind to me. Will you care for Whisky? She's a good watchdog, and she doesn't eat much."

Madjoli nodded. Suddenly tears stood in her eyes. She hugged Nyah tightly. *"Walka fine, sitah."*

"Walka fine, sitah, my sister. May God be kind to you." Nyah watched her friend leave the hut and disappear in the darkness.

The creature at her feet mewed. She stooped over it, dismayed at its feebleness. Then she remembered discarding a small brush used to wash clothes. She found it, built up her fire, and moved the cot closer to its light. She took off the good dress she had put on for traveling and hung it on a hook. She spread a rag over her bare knees and took the dying infant onto her lap.

At first she was fearful of touching it, still half believing it a creature of witchcraft, sent by an enemy to bring about her doom. But it was so feeble and miserable that pity vanquished her hesitation. It lay against her skin, trembling like a frightened kitten. Its bones were as light as a bird's. She wished it could live, but she did not know how to feed something that had no mouth.

She brushed it thoroughly, methodically, starting at the head and working her way down. The creature did not struggle or resist her. For a reason she could not have explained, she felt that it took some comfort in her handling. Its fur became soft and silky when clean. She was so absorbed in her work that only when she had finished did she notice the end of one of its tubular arms fastened to her waist. Gently, she pried it loose, breaking the suction. The gray membranes over the strange, pupilless eyes flickered, then the creature wrapped its limbs around itself in a ball and lay still.

"It feels better now that it's clean," she thought. She examined the spot on her waist. The firelight revealed no mark, but the skin was tender and a bit sore. She shrugged. Etoundi had given her more painful bruises.

She did not want to be noticed carrying the creature or even a suspicious bundle. She decided to conceal it under the loose folds of her Mother Hubbard dress. Using an old pagne, she tied the sleeping creature to her waist just below her breasts. Then she put on the dress. Its five yards of material hung in full gathers from her shoulders. The bulge on her stomach was not noticeable. She felt and shared the faint rhythm of the creature's breathing.

Long before dawn, Aunt Nyah stood by the edge of the road waiting for the Mammy wagon. An owl hooted, and she shivered, wondering whose death the bird of evil omen was prophesying, her own or that of the small beast cradled under her breasts.

The wind freshened and began to blow harder. She could hear rain falling on the forest across the valley, a dull roar like the marching of an army approaching in the night. She clutched her shawl tighter against the chill wind.

Suddenly distant headlights appeared, drilling a round well of light through the night under the giant trees. A roar, a sputtering explosion, and a creaking rumble were followed by the screech of gears shifting. The Mammy wagon, a battered old bus, lumbered to a stop beside her. It was a lugubrious, top-heavy silhouette in the dark. An agile motorboy hopped out the back door and scrambled up to the roof. The driver picked up Aunt Nyah's tin chest and passed it to the motorboy. He found a place for it among the suitcases, clusters of bananas, demijohns of palm wine, baskets of chickens, and a pair of bleating goats. After the ritual protestations over the price, Aunt Nyah paid the driver and climbed into his bus. In the back a fat Bamileke merchant grudgingly squeezed against his neighbor, a Hausa trader, to free a small place for her on the narrow metal bench they occupied. The driver started his motor; the bus roared and lurched forward. She looked out the window, but the village was already hidden behind the forest and the night. She clasped the little beast she carried, and imagined that it stirred and snuggled closer to her.

The rain caught up with them, enclosing the crowded bus with heavy curtains of water. Nyah stared past the dozing passengers around her into the dark forest. The headlights, their beams compressed and stifled by the rain, barely lit the dirt road. The bus bumped and rolled through a faint tunnel of light while the night's dark gullet pursued it.

She hunched her shoulders and settled back on her spine, trying to find a comfortable position on the narrow ledge of a seat she had been allowed. They would reach the mission shortly after dawn. Her thoughts whirled in

her head like leaves caught in a wind dervish. The cuts
and bruises Etoundi had given her ached. She could see
his face, contorted with hate and rage. Then she saw
herself in the city, a skinny old woman dressed in rags
stiff with dirt, begging from foreigners.

The strange little creature cradled against her stomach
stirred and kissed her with warm lips. Grateful for its
affection, Nyah cuddled it closer before she wondered
how something that had no mouth could kiss. The soft
lips touched her again and clung gently to her. She remembered how one of the peculiar hollow limbs had held
to her while she cleaned the creature. And felt another
mouth grip her flesh. She laughed. They had been looking for a mouth in the usual place, and had refused to
see that the strange animal had four very obvious mouths.
Its touch was not disagreeable. The lips were soft, warm,
and gentle. She sat quietly and waited. After a while the
beast released its hold.

Unexplainable despair gripped Nyah. "It is too weak
to feed," she thought. "Or I'm not giving it the nourishment it needs." Suddenly the tears she had not shed on
leaving the village stung her eyes. She was a useless old
woman, good for nothing, loved by no one, incapable of
even keeping alive this fragile being that trusted her.

One of its arms brushed against her in a light caress
and gripped her skin. Its hold seemed stronger than before. Now she could feel it sucking, pulling its nourishment through her skin. Another took hold, and another.
With one hand she cautiously felt its body through the
folds of her dress. All four of its limbs were fastened to
her. She tugged on one gently without breaking its hold.

Contentment settled over the old woman. She had never
had a child to feed at her breast and had often been intrigued by an absent look on the faces of friends nursing
their babies. They seemed to withdraw into a private
world of peace. Now she was entering that world, tasting
the bliss of being needed.

"My *mouna,* my little one," she murmured. After a
while the furry infant stopped sucking and slept. Later it

awoke and began to feed again. Nyah felt it recovering, gaining strength; life was returning with the nourishment she was giving. A smile of pride lit her battered face. As the lopsided bus dodged potholes and stumbled along the forest track, she willingly shared her strength with the orphaned stranger.

The Mammy wagon reached the top of a high hill, and Nyah saw the first faint light of dawn. Then the road dipped into the forest again, and the world of night briefly returned. The morning mists were rising when they reached the mission, a group of red-brick buildings set among lawns and flowers. Smoke spiraled from a cluster of native huts behind the mission where women were starting their cooking fires.

The Dutch priest was having breakfast and grumbling at his cook, a sly-looking Ngoumba who grumbled back at him. Nyah asked for *Mademoiselle* Hiroko, saying she had brought something for her. The cook led her down a long veranda and knocked on a door.

The Japanese girl opened the door and cried out at the sight of Aunt Nyah. She bowed first, then remembered to shake hands, staring in dismay at the African woman's face. "What have they done to you? You must see a doctor. Forgive me for getting you involved in this. I did not know. . . ."

"Hush, child. I got myself involved with this. If I had let you go to Etoundi at once as you wished, he would have thrown you out, but I wouldn't have earned myself a beating. He enjoyed it so much I wonder why he waited so long. Don't worry. By next week I'll be almost pretty again." She sat down on the narrow bed. "Close the door."

Hiroko obeyed. "Would you care for some tea?"

Nyah remembered the bitter green tea that Hiroko drank without sugar. "No. I would rather have coffee. And some whiskey."

Hiroko looked surprised, but she nodded and smiled. "I'll ask the priest for some. Please wait here."

As soon as she left, Aunt Nyah lifted her dress to look

at the tiny beast she carried. It seemed to be sleeping peacefully. Its fur gleamed like soft gray silk. She touched it gently, and the large yellow eyes opened to hold her gaze. They no longer beamed an aura of misery and suffering. She heard a step in the hall outside and quickly lowered her dress.

Hiroko entered carrying a loaf of bread, a small jar of instant coffee, and a bottle of Johnnie Walker. While she heated water and laid out dishes for breakfast, Nyah remained silent. She was grateful for the Japanese girl's innate courtesy that permitted her to withdraw into her own thoughts and lay her plans for the future with as much privacy as if she had occupied a separate room.

The African woman drank a cup of hot coffee, ate some bread, and then poured herself a glass of brown and gold liquor. She smiled at Hiroko, poured part of the whiskey out on the floor, and laughed. "It's for the old spirits." She swallowed what was left in the glass. It burned, but the taste it left in her mouth was good. She savored it. Then began to speak somewhat formally. "*Mademoiselle* Hiroko, if I had been able to bring you Etoundi's monkey, what would you have done with it?"

"I would have taken it to my director in the city. He would have notified other scientists. We would have studied it, tried to learn everything possible about it, about where it came from, about what it is."

Aunt Nyah nodded. "Do you think they would have put it in a cage?"

Hiroko looked perplexed. "Perhaps. Probably. To make sure it wasn't stolen or didn't run away. It would have been a comfortable cage, nothing like the crate Etoundi has it in."

The old woman nodded again. "What are you going to do now?"

The Japanese girl grimaced. "Set up a new study site near here. I can't stay in the village if Etoundi doesn't want me there. You know they threatened me, took the head I had. I have nothing to show my director but some drawings and a wild tale."

Aunt Nyah gave the girl a sly, teasing smile. "I've learned the Pygmies may have another one of the animals. If you can give me some money, I'll go to their camp and see if I can buy it."

"I shall go! Which camp?"

"No. They do not trust you; Etoundi has told them lies about you. I must go alone. They know me."

Hiroko nodded sadly. "Yes. How much money do you need? Are you certain they have another one?"

"No, I am not certain. They may be lying. But they will not fool me as easily as they would you. I think I will need at least twenty thousand. That is what Johnny wanted from Etoundi and didn't get. Maybe more. Since you told him it was worth more."

Hiroko nodded and went to take the money from her handbag. She gave Aunt Nyah thirty thousand. "This is all I can spare now. But if you really do find another of the animals, I can get more money from my director. Even a dead corpse would be valuable to us."

Aunt Nyah stood up and smiled, looking smug and mischievous. "I shall stay in the Pygmy camp. I shall be living with them."

Hiroko gave her a puzzled frown. "I thought you would go to the city. Life with the Pygmies would be hard on you. What if they won't have you?"

Aunt Nyah wrinkled her nose in distaste. "What would an old woman like me do in the city? Besides, the Mammy wagons stink. The little men have gentle hearts; they will not chase me away. They like my fried pastries, and I know how to bandage their children's cuts and sores. They won't let me starve." She grinned. "I'll eat meat more often than I did in the village."

Hiroko remained sober. "When the hunting is good. They are not like your people. They are different; they do not stay long in one place. I cannot believe you will stay with them."

"Why not? They will not beat me and send me away. I have been to the city and seen the filthy, crazy old women who sleep on porches and scare little children. I

saw them begging in front of the stores and quarreling
with dogs over garbage. No. The Pygmies will be kinder
to me than that.''

"I hope so. I feel responsible. If there is anything I
can do to help you. . . .''

Aunt Nyah said nothing, but she smiled. She could feel
the fragile creature under her breasts beginning to feed
again.

During the morning a Pygmy hunter came to the mission to sell smoked meat. He agreed to lead Aunt Nyah
to his camp.

She walked behind him on a narrow path that had been
traced by forest buffalo going to a stream to drink. What
few belongings she could carry were tied up in a bundle
that balanced on top of her head. The tin chest remained
behind in the mission. Pygmies did not encumber themselves with useless goods. She would have to learn to
share their indifference.

As she walked, she devised how to send the money
she had with her to Madjoli's son. The head wife had
taken a great risk; it would not be unrewarded. Nyah did
not worry about lying to Hiroko. Foreigners had more
money than they knew what to do with, anyway. The
Japanese girl shouldn't expect her to return with either
the creature or the money. If Nyah had asked for money
for herself, Hiroko would probably have given it to her,
feeling guilty and embarrassed while the African woman
felt humiliated. Nyah smiled. The story about bargaining
with the Pygmies for another one of the strange beasts
permitted both friends to save face. Hiroko was more of
an accomplice than a dupe.

The hunter stopped and signed to her for silence. She
traced his rapt gaze to a dense black shadow in the lower
branches of an azobe tree. It coughed once, a loud, cav-
ernous noise; Nyah realized that she was staring at a
gorilla. The Pygmy was raising his rifle, preparing to
shoot. Nyah made the sign of the cross. If the hunter
missed or merely wounded the ape, it would charge them.

One of her cousins had been slapped by a gorilla, and half his face was missing. But Pygmies were fearless and did not hesitate to attack any "beef" they crossed in the forest. Johnny's brother had been killed by an elephant he had attacked alone, armed only with a lance. The family insisted the elephant must have used witchcraft to vanquish such a great hunter.

Something in the higher branches of the azobe grunted and was answered with a guttural snarl from nearby. The Pygmy lowered his rifle without firing and squatted behind a bush. A whole troop of gorillas nested in the trees ahead of them. Nyah imitated the hunter and shrank to the ground, making herself as small as possible, grateful that her guide was not foolish enough to provoke half a dozen adults with their young. The gorillas continued their siesta while she sat and the hunter crouched among the ferns and vines on the forest floor and waited.

A cub cried out. The gorilla nearest to them grunted quietly to soothe it. Nyah studied the dark mass among the leaves more closely. The cub whimpered again, and they heard greedy slurping noises. She could make out the mother's head bent over its infant. The beast's powerful shoulders and arms formed a protective circle around its nursing cub. Nyah recognized the fierce devotion of its attitude.

Her hidden passenger stirred. She felt one of its mouths open and cling to her skin, then release its hold in a sleepy, affectionate embrace. She cradled it tenderly. She would protect the small creature both from Etoundi and from the foreign scientists who would keep it in a cage. Life with the Pygmies would be harsh, but it would afford her some dignity and the seclusion she needed to care for the creature.

The mother gorilla swung to the ground with her little one clinging to her waist. The rest of the band imitated her, grunting quietly among themselves. Soon the huge beasts were moving away, going deeper into the forest.

The Pygmy waited until they had been out of sight for

several minutes before he stood. He shook his head and grinned with regret. *"Na fine beef, dat!"*

She nodded, laughing at his greed, and they resumed their journey.

DRY NIGER
by M. Shayne Bell

Here's a picture of another all-too-likely future Africa, one locked even more tightly and disastrously into the grip of drought and ever-increasing desertification than today's Africa. But there's one thing still green here in this dusty, arid landscape, the thing that makes us human—hope.

M. Shayne Bell first came to public attention in 1986, when he won first place in that year's Writers of the Future contest. Since then he has published widely in Isaac Asimov's Science Fiction Magazine, Amazing, The Magazine of Fantasy and Science Fiction, Pulphouse, *and elsewhere, and published a well-received first novel,* Nicoji. *"Dry Niger" is one of a loosely connected series of stories about life in a future Africa that he has sold to various markets, and which he plans to meld into a new novel, tentatively entitled* The Sound of the River. *He is also working on a fantasy novel called* To a Changeling Sea, *and a young-adult SF novel set among the Eskimo of the future. Bell has an M.A. degree in English from Brigham Young University, and lives in Salt Lake City, Utah.*

That spring, the Niger had gone dry. Ahmid, my castrato driver, careened our jeep down the riverbank and sped northwest up the dusty riverbed. "All the roads out of Niamey are blown in with sand," he said. "We will make better time here."

I had read the night before in *Le Sahel* of a military caravan that found a jeep, just like the one I was in, stuck

in a sand dune that had blown over the main road to
Tahoua. No one was in the jeep, or near the jeep, and
the soldiers found no sign of driver or occupants. The
wind had blown sand over all their tracks and eventually,
no doubt, them. "Maybe they saw the mirage of an oasis
within walking distance," one of the soldiers theorized.
It was a terrible story. I was glad to be driving up the
riverbed.

We passed under the Kennedy Bridge, and in the brief
moment we were in its shadow I felt cold. "You will not
shiver again today," Ahmid said, very serious.

I looked back at the bridge and saw a thin man start
across it from the south, driving three goats before him.
Behind him came a woman carrying on her head a bundle
of the black cloth favored by the Tuareg. We were getting
a late start. But the jeep wouldn't start in the night, and
though the minister of mines herself, Aissa Seibou, had
come with the mechanic and waited with me and Ahmid
in the shed while we watched the mechanic work, it took
time to change a fuel pump, and then the water pump
just in case, and then to put on the new belt I insisted
on. "I will follow you in two days," the minister had
said. "By then you will have seen and studied these uranium fields as I have, and you will agree with me."

Such confidence. But I was prepared to believe her
because I had read URANIGER's reports on the potential
of these mines, and the World Bank was prepared to believe me and back my recommendation when I gave it.
The Bank had money to fund only one project that year
in West Africa. The directors had narrowed their choices
to two projects: one, a loan to help develop uranium
mines in Niger's Zermaganda province, eighty kilometers northeast of Sinder, the other, a reforestation project
in the highlands of Guinea around the source of the Niger
so that rainfall might increase and in forty years the river
might flow again to the sea, not dry up at Lake Debo in
Mali. The reforestation project offered enormous long-
term benefits decades after its start. But exploitable uranium lay waiting in the desert now. West Africa needed

help now. Aissa Seibou was probably justified in feeling confident.

I turned back around and watched the riverbed ahead of us. "How often do you get flash floods?" I asked.

"That Allah should send us rain," Ahmid said, with almost a laugh. But after maybe ten minutes he looked hard at me. "If you see any cloud, however small, tell me," he said.

Ah, I thought. So we *would* have to get out of the riverbed. Fast.

We careened around a bend, and there were four women ahead of us, digging in the dirt. Ahmid sped past them, blowing them with dust, but I looked in the hole they were digging and could see a fifth woman in it scooping dirt into a bucket and lifting it up to those above her.

"Have you found any water?" I yelled in French.

But the women just waved.

"They will not find water," Ahmid said.

We drove through all the heat of that day and toward evening were approaching Sansanne-Hausa, where they were building a camp for the Tuareg. The Tuareg were finally coming into camp, driven this time by a famine that would not end. Ahead of us I could see great mounds of dirt piled up in the riverbed and maybe twenty Zerma women. "Stop the jeep," I told Ahmid.

He stopped it. I climbed out and pushed through the women that rushed up around us, left Ahmid to keep them away from our water, and climbed up a mound of dirt twice as tall as me. At the top I could look down into a great hole maybe forty feet deep. Three women were digging down there, tying their buckets to ropes. I pulled one up for them. "Have you found any water?" I yelled down, first in French, then in Hausa which they could understand.

"No," one of them yelled back.

That night I dreamt I was walking in the Gaoueyé district of Niamey, though I had never gone with African

whores, not after geneticists in Lagos won the War of the
Sahel for the coastal dictatorships by spraying the Sahelian troops with mutated viruses that had since spread
among whores all over the continent, some of whom
could live for fifteen years with the viruses in their
bodies. Those viruses could kill a European like me before a doctor could diagnose which virus had attacked
me and get the antidote.

But I let a woman lead me up rickety stairs to her tiny
room that looked out over the banks of the dry Niger.
Her room was filled with plants and flowers that must
have cost her a fortune to water. The room smelled clean,
and she smelled clean, and I wanted to keep touching her
but she pulled back and told me that if I held this certain
cloth over my eyes I would see the Niger with water in
it. It was the blue cloth she wadded on the floor to keep
sand from blowing in under the door. She played these
games with me. I knew that. I suddenly knew it was not
the first time I had been with her, that I knew her well.

I put the cloth over my eyes. Nothing happened, of
course. I thought she would kiss me after a minute, but
she didn't so I took the cloth away.

"No. Put it back," she said.

She looked so serious. No smile. This was an odd
game. I put the cloth back, then felt her small hands
press down over my eyes to hold the cloth there, tight.

So I relaxed and lay back on her bed that smelled of
her and thought I would play this game out, whatever
happened, whatever she wanted.

And gradually heard water flowing by outside in the
Niger, lapping the riverbank. I pulled her hands away,
and the cloth, and looked out the window at water.

"I didn't know if you could see it," she said, and she
smiled, happy that I could see the water.

She had sprinkled some drug onto the cloth and I was
hallucinating, I thought, but the hallucination was lovely.
She led me back down the stairs that were somehow sturdier now, and we walked to the river. The water was
cold, and clean. I drank it.

"You will not get sick," she said, and she drank some water herself, then gave me water to drink out of her hands, then more water, then more. I drank it all.

And woke sweating in my hot room in Sansanne-Hausa. I got up and drank real water from the flask I'd carried in from the jeep, then walked to the window and looked out. The Tuareg camp lay black outside the city, a sea of tents, no fires among them. That sedentary camp marked the death of nomadic Tuareg civilization.

We got another late start that morning because Mai Maïgana, mayor of Sansanne-Hausa, insisted on feeding me breakfast. It really was very good: a mango imported from Brasil, dates, goats-milk cheese, water. "You can tell the monsieurs of the World Bank that Sansanne-Hausa will meet its population quota," he said.

I murmured something polite.

"All of Niger will," he said. "When we began this, when the Bank gave us our quotas, some said 'how can a country drop from sixteen million people to four hundred thousand in two generations,' but we are doing it and without massacres like those in Mali."

The Mali had massacred their Tuareg who would not submit to population control.

"But the Tuareg do worry me," he went on.

I looked up at him.

"They do not believe in a never-ending famine until they walk to the Niger and see that it is dry. They believe the camps are set up to castrate their men."

"Aren't they?"

"Only if they father unlicensed children. But it is dangerous to go out there to abort babies and castrate men, or to castrate the illegal male babies that somehow get born. A doctor was murdered in that camp just last month. I have to send the doctors in with troops."

Castrati troops, no doubt, who, like my driver, had been illegal babies themselves. Such men were supposedly the most efficient at that sort of work.

"We will meet our population quota," Mai Maïgana said.

We drove all day, but the riverbed Sansanne-Hausa seemed to wind more, and it was rocky and difficult to drive over. Once we drove up what had been a long ox-bow that dead-ended, so we had to backtrack. By night, when even with the weak headlights we could not see well enough to drive, we were still maybe forty kilometers from Sinder. So we stopped and slept in the jeep. "We can be in Sinder tomorrow by noon," Ahmid said. If we were delayed much beyond that, I knew, someone would come driving down the Niger looking for us. We built no fire. The day had been hot, and now the night was hot. Ahmid took the first watch.

Sometime later he shook me awake. "You had better wake up," he said. I thought it was my turn to watch, but I looked at my wristwatch and saw that it was just after midnight.

"Get up," he said again.

I sat up and saw that veiled Tuareg men were standing around our jeep. Some had guns pointed at us, others had drawn knives. One started talking to me, fast, commanding, repeating one word over and over: *attini, attini.*

"What does he want?" I asked Ahmid, hoping he could understand Tamasheq.

"Our water," he said. "And your boots, and your shirt, and our food, the blankets, my belt, our extra clothes."

Then I remembered what *attini* meant in Tamasheq: *give me.*

"Do you speak French?" I asked the Tuareg, thinking I could reason with them, tell them I was here to help them, but not one of them would talk to me in French. I tried Hausa, and the little Yoruba I knew, but they would speak only Tamasheq, and I knew only a few words in that language. I could not speak it. Ahmid had to translate for me.

One of the Tuareg reached in the back of the jeep and took out our water. I let him.

"They want your boots and shirt," Ahmid said.

I took off my boots and handed them to the man who had spoken Tamasheq at me. I handed him my shirt. They took the other things they wanted and walked away behind us, tall, regal. It was as if we were a caravan and had paid them tribute to pass through their lands.

"Why didn't they take the jeep?" I asked.

"The army would find that," Ahmid said.

I looked back at the Tuareg, but in their black robes they were already indistinguishable from the shadows of the riverbanks. I suddenly felt sorry for them. They had taken tribute from us, but they had no future outside of the government camps.

Ahmid slept fitfully while I watched. We both wondered if the Tuareg would come back or if others would come along and rob us a second time. Ahmid finally gave up trying to sleep, and we started off for Sinder long before dawn, driving very slowly, creeping around the rocks and holes in the riverbed till it grew light enough to see to drive faster. We had nothing for breakfast, and no water to drink. Once the sun was up, I could not stay awake. I dreamed again of my whore in Niamey. She pressed the blue cloth to my eyes, and when I could see the river we went walking along its banks.

She had brought a picnic of melons, clean, juicy, and bright green. We ate on the grassy riverbank, in cool shade under a great tree, and I marveled at the beautiful greenery all around me. I no longer believed I was drugged.

"Is this what was, or what might have been?" I asked.

She just smiled at me, and when she smiled I wanted to love her, there, on the banks of a watery Niger. I took her in my arms and held her, tight.

"Love me," she said.

"I do," I said.

"Love me for a long time, not just today," she said.

"I will."

She broke away from me, picked a leaf from the tree above us, and pressed it into my palm.

"Love me," she said again.

And I did.

I woke sweating, and sunburned. The Tuareg had taken everything I could have put over me to keep off the sun.

"We are soon at Sinder," Ahmid said. "They will have creams for your skin there, and a shirt."

I sat up straight and rubbed the sweat off my face—but regretted that. My face was so sunburned it hurt to touch it.

"Were you dreaming?" Ahmid asked.

I nodded. "Of a beautiful woman."

He looked concerned. "A woman, you say?"

"Yes, Ahmid." I regretted mentioning women to him, a castrato. He could never know the things I knew. I did not want to hurt him.

"You do not understand what such a dream could mean," he said. "The Djenoun blow about on winds across these empty lands till they find a man's mind to inhabit. If one troubles you, tell me and I will pray to Allah for your protection. Allah can protect you, even in your dreams."

I could not believe that he believed what he was telling me about the Djenoun. Yet for one moment I wondered if Tuareg superstitions could be true, and if a Djenoun were haunting my mind. If she were, I would not ask Ahmid to pray to have her taken from me.

I looked at the palm of my hand, but there was no leaf in it. I looked at the dry riverbanks above us on either side and wondered what they would look like wooded. Then I realized I had come on this trip with my mind made up. I was going to recommend the uranium mines to the World Bank. I had never seriously considered the trees.

* * *

We passed four Tuareg women in the streets of Sinder. One looked like the woman in my dreams, then I thought all four did, then I thought every woman I saw—Songhai, Hausa, Fulani, Tuareg—all looked like that woman. The old French nurse who doctored my sunburn at the clinic looked like that whore. They were all beautiful. I thought that I had never looked at women like this before, that I had never realized that all women were beautiful. I loved them all. We got water, food, gas, clothes, and struck out across the erg to the Zermaganda uranium fields.

And they were everything I had been promised. UR-ANIGER had set off one thousand seismic charges which proved the deposits greater than those at Arlit, the mines that made Niger the world's fifth largest uranium producer. The Zermaganda mines would make them the largest. I spent two days studying the ore and the results of the seismic charges, talking with the geologists and walking with them over flat-topped gara and down dry wadis to the best sites. But I spent my nights studying the reports on reforestation. I realized that plan was too modest. The source of the Niger needed to be reforested, yes, but so did the sources of five of the major tributaries. If that happened, and if the rainfall increased as might be expected, the river might flow.

Aissa Seibou arrived late that second day, and though tired from the journey from Niamey, I could see the enthusiasm in her eyes. She looked beautiful to me, like my whore.

"What do you think?" she asked.

I smiled. "I think this deposit will be everything you dream of," I said.

"You will help us, then. You will recommend us?"

That was the question.

"Money from these mines would give us money to import water from the sea," she said. "The coastal dictatorships are killing us for water."

It was what the War of the Sahel had been fought over. By international law, every nation had rights to water from the sea, including landlocked nations like Niger,

Mali, Burkina Fasso. But the costal nations were reluctant to give them land for desalination plants—they wanted to sell them water. Taxes for road repairs on the roads used to truck water inland, charges from the trucking firms, tariffs were not enough. International law was not enough. And the Sahelian nations had lost their war and now had no choice but to pay for water trucked in from the coast.

"You have seen what this country has become," she said. "If even four hundred thousand people can live here we need money. We need these mines."

"Have you studied the reforestation proposals?" I asked.

"You can't be serious," she said. "There is nothing to reforest in Niger."

"But there is in Guinea, Burkina Fasso, Mali. If it works you would have the Niger again, and be freed of the stranglehold of the coast."

"In forty years," she said, incredulous.

I dreamed that night of my whore in Niamey, and she was big with child. "You fathered her," she said. "She will be your daughter."

This was an unlicensed child, and I was horrified to think that it would be aborted.

"Only if you tell the authorities will it be aborted," she said. "Otherwise all people will love her when they see her."

"You can look in the blue cloth and go to the Niger with water," I said, "and stay there."

"And wait for you to come," she said.

Then I understood that the blue cloth did not show what was or what might have been. It showed what could be, and, I hoped, what would be.

"Name your daughter *Fecund*," she said.

I thought that name more beautiful than any I had ever heard. "I will come to you," I said. "Down this river when it flows again, to these trees."

She smiled, and behind her I saw the desert greening.

* * *

I made my recommendation to the World Bank, and they accepted it. But Aissa Seibou did not leave me in anger. I agreed to stay on with her in Niamey through the summer to help her find outside funding to develop the Zermaganda mines. Ahmid and I followed her jeep back to Niamey, down the dry Niger. We stayed maybe half a kilometer behind her, out of her dust.

Once we rounded a bend and ahead of us, against the bank, I could see the whitened bones of some great animal.

"Hippopotamus," Ahmid said. "Extinct here now, forever."

"Maybe not," I said.

"Ah, that Allah should send us hippopotamus again," Ahmid said.

I had him stop by the bones, and we walked over to them. The skull was gone. "It is worth money in the markets of Niamey," Ahmid explained.

All that was left were the ribs and leg bones, a few neck vertebrae. Dry leaves had blown in under the hips. I pulled out a handful of leaves and crumpled them.

"We should go," Ahmid said. "Aissa Seibou will be far ahead of us."

I picked up one dry leaf to take with me. We walked to the jeep and started driving again for Niamey. I held the leaf in my fingers, but it crumbled away piece by piece and blew off into the dust billowing behind us.

A TRANSECT
by Kim Stanley Robinson

Here's a subtle, mysterious, and deceptively quiet little story that suggests that the view is quite different, depending on where you're viewing it from—and who you happen to be. . . .

Kim Stanley Robinson sold his first story in 1976, and quickly established himself as one of the most respected and critically-acclaimed writers of his generation. His story "Black Air" won the World Fantasy Award in 1984, and his novella "The Blind Geometer," won the Nebula Award in 1987. His excellent novel The Wild Shore *was published in 1984 as the first title in the resurrected Ace Special line. Other Robinson books include the novels* Icehenge, The Memory of Whiteness, A Short, Sharp Shock, The Gold Coast, *and* The Pacific Shore, *and the landmark collections* The Planet on the Table *and* Escape From Kathmandu, *His most recent book is a new collection,* Remaking History. *Upcoming is a trilogy of novels set on a future Mars. Robinson and his family are back in their native California again, after several years of exile in Switzerland and Washington, D.C.*

After he had secured a windowseat in the Amtrack coach, he set his dark brown leather briefcase in his lap and unlocked it. *Clunk. Clunk.* He liked the way the gold-plated hasps snapped open. About fifty times more power in the springs than was necessary. Sign of a well-tooled briefcase: big, heavy, powerful. Expensive. Something for clients to note with approval. Part of their confidence in him.

Riffling through his account files was depressing. Nothing in there but bad news. No one was buying fine paper in quantity these days; he had to bust a gut just to stay even. Northeast Section Marketing and Sales Vice President, forever and ever amen. He sighed; at times like this he felt utterly stuck. No chance of advancement whatsoever. Stuck at forty-five thousand a year for good, and with wife and kids throwing it away faster than he could make it. Lucky his credit was good, he could spend his future right up to his death and beyond, no doubt. Ah, the end of a long, hard trip: he needed a drink.

The train came out of its hole and he looked into the industrial yards of Montreal. Beyond them was the city center where he had spent the day selling. Sun setting behind it. Funny how much Canada looked like the States (he always thought that). He let his files accordion back into the briefcase and pulled out his copy of the day's *Wall Street Journal*. Up and down the train car, other copies of the same paper were blooming over the plush maroon seats, covering the businessmen behind them. A young punk wearing earphones sat in the aisle seat beside him, cramping his reading. Faint whispers of percussive music joined the rustling of newspapers in the strangely hushed car.

Nothing in the day's *Journal* was of interest. He folded it and put it in his lap. They were out of the industrial district, in the trees between suburbs. Too late in the fall: the half-bare trees looked bedraggled, the leaf-matted ground wet and boggy. He folded his suit jacket over twice and used it as a pillow against the inner window. It would have to be dry-cleaned anyway; he had spilled a few drops of Burgundy on it at lunch, right on the top of the right cuff, where clients would see it when he signed things.

"*Hei broer!* Watch out where you going when you walking backwards like that! Here, you need a hand with those?"

"Thanks, I got them." He heaved up on the straps tied around his two boxes and pulled them past the old man

down the center of the train. The benches on both sides
were crowded with migrant workers going home, jammed
together hip to hip. Their boxes and bags were stacked
on the wooded floor, leaving him just enough room to
maneuver to the end of the car. There, because it was
the last car on the train, he could set his two boxes in the
middle of the aisle and sit on them, as several other men
had already done. He greeted them with a lift of his chin.

"Where you from, *broer*?"

"Mzimhlophe Hostels. I did my eleven months there—
now I going home. Home to Kwa-Xhosa."

"Home," said a thin colored man bitterly. "Just how
is Kwa-Xhosa Bantustan your home?"

"My folks is there," he said with a shrug.

"Your folks is there because the government moved
them there," the man said. "Me, my home is Robben
Island. It been my home nine years, and all because of
one night's A.N.C. meeting at my house. They gave me
two and a half years for taking subscriptions, one and a
half years for meeting, and five years for distributing
pamphlets. All the same night!" He laughed harshly.
"Now I'm out, and they ban me! Clearly I must be meeting a whole bunch of Communists in those nine years,
for they ban me the moment I out! Ban me to Kwa-Xhosa,
where I never been in my whole life, where I can never
see my family, for five long years."

The others laughed their sympathy. "That too bad,
Pieter!" "You got to watch all those bad phone calls you
make from the island, man!"

The conversation focused on the newcomer. "What
your name?"

"Norman."

"What did you do in Soweto?"

"Bricklayer," Norman said.

The train jerked twice and they rolled out of Park Station.

"That against the law, you know," Pieter said. "If
they pay attention to their own law, you could not have
job, *Nie kaffir* bricklayers, *nie*!"—this with the heavy

Afrikaaner tone. The men laughed. Several in the car turned on transistor radios, and the hard rhythms clashed. The train cleared the outskirts of Johannesburg and clattered through the outlying townships.

Norman looked out the window and saw three women sitting on a step, leaning in on each other in a stupor. Empty bottles. Blank faces under the streetlight. He recognized in the slump of their shoulders that moment of exhaustion and peace, and felt his own shoulders relax with it. He was on his way home.

The train swayed as it took a sharp turn. One last view of Montreal. He put his suit jacket on the chair arm and pulled a Sherman cigarette from the box in his briefcase. The punk next to him appeared to be asleep, although faint music still whispered from his earphones. He lit the Sherman with the gold lighter his boss had given him, and felt a certain uneasiness leave him, breath by breath. Hard to sleep on a train. Another station stop. The people in his car were mostly commuters. Briefcases, cuff links, polished shoes. The *swish-swish* of nyloned legs rubbing together; his head shifted so he could see the tight dress between the two seat backs in front of him. She sat two seats ahead. A man with a cough sat behind him. Muted voices came from the car behind theirs, until a door hissed shut.

When the Sherman was finished, he took a last look at the night lights of Montreal. The company's awards dinner had been in Montreal, just a month earlier, in the fashionable district downtown. He had expected to win the regional sales award for the year, because things were tough everywhere and he did have some big regular clientele. He took his wife along. All that backslapping and joking about the awards at the cocktail party before, as if no one cared about them, as if they were bowling trophies or something—when everyone knew they were a strong indicator of what the upper echelon thought of your prospects. So that in that sense they represented thousands of dollars—careers, even. So that looking around the room there was a part of him that hated all his colleagues, his competitors. Even more so afterwards, when he had to do like all the rest and go up to congratulate the winner, George Dulak, head of the Midwestern Section (which in itself was an advantage): beaming winner surrounded by envious admirers, shiny gold pen set cradled in one hand. . . . Finally he had gone away to get a drink. It was just like management to make the work a contest like this, to get them all at each other's throats. Competition more productive than teamwork: the American way!

"On Robben Island," Pieter said, "the *agter-nyer* is the one the warden uses to control the rest—he the guard inside, and gets the little extras you know, tobacco and such. But our *agter-nyer* was not a bad man, he help to get us food sometimes. And one night we was entertaining one another, Solly, he acting out the various guards and the wardens—all without one word, you see, but just watching him we knew exactly who he mean. And we giggling and brushing—we never clapped, you see, for fear of the guards' attentions, so to applaud we rubbed our hands together like so." They heard nothing of Pieter's prison applause over the talk and the radios. "And we in such a state we never in the world hear the guard coming, but for the *agter-nyer* sitting on the cement at the door watching for them. He been standing watch for us all those nights, and never let us know till he had to." He laughed. "A good man!"

"I been living in a prison, too, these last eleven months," Norman said suddenly, surprising them all, including himself. "A prison called the Mzimhlophe Hostels."

Most of them had been living around Soweto in the men's dormitories that house the migrant laborers from the bantustans, and some said, "We hear that, *broer*!" But Pieter quickly disagreed—"nothing's prison but prison, man"—and continued telling stories of Robben Island. Norman was not listening to Pieter anymore, however; he was back in the hostels, looking over row after row of low gray brick dorms, their chimneys jutting out of asbestos roofs into the sky. One morning after a Friday night's drinking, he had gotten up and stumbled out of the dorm to the toilets in the next building—in the door, past the cement troughs for washing dishes and clothes, to the open toilet basins, there to retch miserably. As he returned to his dorm, he felt so sick he was sure he would die before his eleven months' stint of work in Soweto was up. That certainly gave him new eyes as he entered the dorm and crossed the dusty concrete floor, past the low concrete slabs on metal struts that were their tables, past the benches also made of concrete slabs to the sleeping cubicles, where men slept on the doorlike lids of the brick trunks that held all their possessions. In the gloom it seemed they slept on coffins. Beyond in the kitchen cubicle, men were still playing guitars connected to little amplifiers, and the low electric twangs were the only signs that the men sitting around the small stove were still awake, still alive—a single candle on the slab beside them, shadows everywhere in the dim air, drying shirts hung overhead—and bitterly he thought, what a place to die in.

Perhaps he would get a drink. The restaurant car was only two ahead, and he was thirsty and needed to wash down some aspirin. He needed a drink. He stood and managed to step over the sleeping punk; debated taking the briefcase with him, but after all it was locked and no one was going anywhere anyway. Hopefully by his presence the punk would guard it.

Down the car. His balance was shaky; something wrong with him this night. He should have gotten a sleeper. Too much pride in his endurance as a traveler. Out of the soundproofed compartment and into the cold, jouncing passageway between cars. Here you could believe the train was really moving. Back into the hush of the next car. Only half the overhead lights were still on here, and most of the occupants were asleep. Some read or listened to earphones. Half their heads were shaved or tinted green or purple, it seemed. Craziness. His daughter, only fourteen years old, had brought one of those home once. He hadn't known how to express his disgust; he left it to Vicki, tried to forget about it.

There was a line at the little bar in the restaurant car. The two black bartenders went at the work casually, chatting to each other about vacationing in Jamaica, just as if there weren't a line. When one of them asked him what he wanted, he curtly ordered a gin and tonic and a foil bag of nuts, but his disapproval didn't seem to register. He sipped the gin and tonic—a weak one—to give himself some room for jiggling while he walked, then saw that the woman in the tight dress was sitting at one of the little tables. He sat at another and watched her as he drank. Not actually very good-looking. When he finished the drink, it felt like a million miles separated him from everyone else there. He stood and returned to his seat. Should have gotten a sleeper. Something wrong with him, some kind of tension somehow . . . had to avoid that kind of thing, or it was back to the Tagamet for him.

Back in his seat he stared through his reflection in the window at the world outside. Clanking red lights at railroad crossings, time after time. A sleeping town, even the neon off. Loading docks, laundromat, Village Video Rental. You saw a lot of those video places these days, even in the little backwoods towns. "Movies in the privacy of your own home!" and then it was gone. The drink began to go to his head, and the repeated hoot of the train's horn—so distant, so muted—was like the cry of some mournful beast, lulling him toward sleep and then calling him back, time after time.

The beauty of the Witwatersrand took his breath away. He had forgotten that such open, clean land existed in South Africa, and at the sight of it something in his chest hurt. White clouds sprawled across a cobalt sky, and there in the yellowwoods and Camdeboo stinkwoods dotting the sere grass of the veldt flew loeris, doves, hoepoe, and drongos, with small white hawks circling far above. Wild gardenia growing by the tracks. It affected all the men similarly, and they threw open the windows and laughed and shouted at the sky, aware suddenly that they really were going home. They danced in the aisle to the fast mbaqanga beat and sang American spirituals. "Swing Low, Sweet Chariot," accompanied by a fifteen-year-old boy playing harmonica for all he was worth—it was grand.

Then the train pulled into Vereeninging Station. Still in a celebratory mood, the men stuck their heads out the train window and shouted for the platform hawkers. "Dresses and aprons for your loved ones at only five rand, *broers!*" "Not a chance, *suster,* you bore me with your dresses, let that *bierman* through to us." They bought dumpies of beer at an extortionate price, and downed most of them before the train rattled off again. Then through the outskirts of town: corrugated iron, donkeys, pigs, children, Indian corner groceries, paw-paw trees, women with washtubs, prickly pears, and scraps of paper everywhere, all over the hard-packed earth of the streets. "Oh, how I hate this town, the most hateful town in the world to me," one man cried. "My wife got off the train at this station and I never saw her again up to this very day." The men whooped their sympathy. "Wasn't that Georgina the hippo left you, man?" "She found you were undermining her interest with that girl in Joburg, didn't she? You lucky you didn't see snake's butt that day instead!" And the man laughed "hee, hee, hee," as he shook his head to deny them.

The man in the seat behind him could not stop coughing. A couple minutes' labored breathing, the strained efforts to control it—then *kar! karugh! urrkhktaugh!* He couldn't believe it. Next time, he thought, I'll drive. To hell with this. His throat was beginning to tickle a little, right there below his Adam's apple, and briefly he glanced over his shoulder in irritation. Old pasty-faced man with dark rings under his eyes, in a shabby gray suit. Italian-looking. Incredibly inconsiderate of him to travel sick and infect everyone else on the train. He really was coming down with it! He swallowed over and over. There was only a single light on in the car—some insomniac businessman reading *In Search of Excellence,* still looking fresh and unruffled at 2 AM. Yeah, you'll win the award, he thought angrily, and me, I'll just catch a cold. And all because of the luck of seating availability. He hated being sick. You couldn't possibly make a good impression with a cold. Sales out of the question. Might as well stay at home and watch Vicki take care of things. More coughs; it was enough to make him envy the sleeping punk his earphones. Although that would still be no protection for his throat.

Abruptly he stood and took a walk toward the restaurant car. It was closed for the night. Back between cars, in the cold passageway, he noticed that the train was moving very slowly. He looked through the thick little window in the passageway door. They were over water; Lake Champlain, he guessed. The railroad bridge was so old and rickety that the train had to cross at about ten miles an hour. Looking down he couldn't even see the bridge, it was so narrow. White mist lay over the water, swirling eerily under the half-moon. He shivered convulsively: something *odd* about this night, the hush too quiet, the distances too great . . . he must be getting ill. Or . . . something. For the last few years he had gotten his life into such a groove, such a routine of day to day activities, each day resembling its predecessor from the week before, Mondays all alike, Fridays all alike, Saturdays . . . that he had found himself with time on his hands. It seemed he could live his life on a sort of automatic pilot, leaving him all sorts of time to just . . . think. Like he really never had before. And once or twice in this new thinking he had wondered what it (*it* being his life, the world, everything) was all about. No great answer had jumped immediately to mind; often he was left with just this sort of uneasy feeling. Out there, was that another train? No, just mist. A lake of white cotton. . . .

Nothing for it but to return to his seat. As the night progressed he fell in and out of a half-sleep that resembled a trance. Several times they stopped at stations briefly, and once he woke completely when the police boarded to check everyone's passbooks. Two big white security police, making an old black ticket taker do most of the work. The migrants dug through their possessions for their reference books. Tins, boxes, old water drums bound with straps, all heavily loaded with basic groceries to help out the families on the bantustans. Norman's boxes were full of sugar, salt, and tea, all placed under his extra shirt and pants. His passbook was in the spare shirt's pocket; he pulled it out and bent the corners back down. All his stamps were in order, and he gave the ticket taker the book without looking up. Out the window Cape fig trees shaded the tiny veldt station, flanking the tracks like a hedge. Signs marked the entrances to the station house: BLANKES. NIE-BLANKES.

One of the security police took Pieter's passbook from the ticket-taker's hand and inspected it closely. Suddenly no one in the car was talking. The radios babbled in Zulu and Xhosa. Then the policeman showed it to his companion and laughed. *"Robben vir Kwa-Xhosa! Die lewe is swaar né, Pieter!"*

"Ja, my baas," Pieter said, looking at the floor of the corridor. "Life is hard, all right."

"Listen to me, *seuntjie,"* the policeman said, and gave Pieter a little lecture: more God, *volk* and trek, as someone said when they were gone. Pieter resolutely stared at the floor. When the policeman finished, Pieter looked up at him, the hatred clear in his eyes. "My stamps are good, *ja baas*?"

"Ja, seuntjie," the big man said easily, and tossed Pieter his passbook. The two police led the ticket taker out of the car, laughing over something, the pass check already forgotten. "Capetown whores are best." "Moering haffirs will kill you in bed, though!"

Then they were gone, and everyone started breathing properly again. Only now could they be sure that all the passbooks were really in order; often they were not, and so one didn't discuss the matter. There had been a good chance someone on the car would be dragged off to jail. But they were all legal this time, and the talk began again.

"They stick him on the tenth floor by the open window, you know, but he refuse the jump and so he in jail and his kids is starving with hungry—"

"—you ever try sharing a bed with such a hippo? You got to sleep like a flea, ready to jump quick. And the fatter she got the worse her temper! Man I kissed Mother Earth daily living with her. Ha! Ha! She ransack me good sometime—"

"—*ja*, and if you get out, it's to the labor bureau like me, to sell yourself off to the coal mines of Witbank a thousand miles from home. We had a bad one at our labor bureau—he says, which of you boys wants a job, and of course we all jumping up and down like dogs, pick me *baas*, pick me, and he pick one after another to tell them no, they not good enough. Then he pick and look through my workbook, won't your wife sleep around while you gone, boy, I bet she sleep with me for giving you this job, until he tire of the game and give me the joy of eleven months work away from my folks."

"And that better still than prison," Pieter took it up; but Norman turned from Pieter's bitter comedies and looked out the window. Train noising out of the station with hard jerks, as if the engine were yanking on it. An old man sitting in the dirt by a wheelbarrow stacked with baskets; too late in the day to sell anymore, but still he sat, in that twilight moment. . . . SLEGS BLANKES.

He got up to go to the bathroom, feeling distant, disoriented. Stepping over the punk was getting easy—the kid was slumped lower every time. Once again, trouble with balance. Something wrong. Everything too hushed, almost silent. Like cotton in his ears. Everything a great distance away.

The bathroom at the front of the car was occupied. He turned and went to the car behind, the last one of the train. Maneuvered through all the tight turns and heavy narrow doors between cars, found an empty bathroom. For the disabled, but he used it anyway. Not *exclusively* for the disabled, right? Down the iron toilet he could see the track ties flashing beneath the train. When he was done he looked at himself in the cracked coppery mirror: hair mussed, face stubbly, some odd disquiet in his eyes. . . .

The beer wanted out of him, and he stood up to use the lavatory at the end of the next car up. By now the travelers were drowsy with beer and fatigue, and he had to step over men sleeping in the aisles. Somehow they sprawled in a way that always left footing just where it was needed. Outside in the dusk the hillocks bordering the Orange River were etched against a moonless blue sky. Igqili River, he said to himself, mother of my country Azania. He stepped through the doorway into the connecting corridor, over the shifting joints of the iron floor. The joints squealed loudly and looking down at them he almost ran into the man coming his way. A white, from one of the first-class cars: confused, he said, "Sorry, *baas*."

The black kid muttered something under his breath, so sullenly that he was suddenly afraid he might be mugged right there between the two cars. The wheels rolling over the track were loud, no one would hear him: "Sorry about that," he said hastily, feeling dizzy, and yielded to the right. The train jerked and they bumped together hard; the black man reached out a hand to hold him steady, then withdrew as if shocked, his frightened eyes round and white in the gloom. Their gazes met and held.

The look.

Dark brown iris, the whites a bit yellowed; pale blue iris, the whites a bit bloodshot. And the pupils identical round black holes, the windows of the soul, through which one can fall, spinning dizzily, to land cut, confused, stunned, in a new place; and all with a look—

. . . He wasn't sure how long the kid's feral stare had held him still, when he jerked free and pulled himself, staggering slightly, away. The doors were heavy and had to be pulled into the walls to right and left. Back in his car the hush seemed more pronounced than ever. Unsteadily he stepped back over the sleeping punk, feeling utterly shaken. The plush maroon velvet of his seat arm.

Silvery ashtray, sliding in and out of the arm. Long brown cigarette butts wasted inside. Looking around: such incredible, excessive luxury—and this was just a train! He stared. . . .

The migrants swayed with the train like luggage as he made his way in some confusion back to his boxes. Smell of sweat, beer, the hot veldt night. He ended his *dwaal* on his boxes and looked at his companions. Their clothes were frayed and dirty. Their shoes were broken and full of holes. They slept, or slumped in stupors of non-thought; and suddenly it seemed he could read what pain had chiseled in each worn face. The boy still hummed thoughtfully into his harmonica—bleak falling chords—

Finally they slid into the labyrinth of Penn Station. Darkness, trains passing by, their lit windows making them look like submarines. Then track lights everywhere. The punk woke and stood up. Everyone standing, stretching. He put his coat on in the aisle, feeling its smooth texture. The sick man was struggling to get his suitcase off the overhead racks, and awkwardly he helped him get it down. A haggard smile for thanks; he nodded quickly, embarrassed. A press of people (he held his briefcase close by his side), and he was out of the train, onto the long, crowded platform. Up a set of stairs, turn and follow everyone else to the next set. Up again. Into the light and glare of Penn Station's big central waiting area, with the businessmen and the students and the cops and the cleaning men and the bums. And then suddenly his wife was upon him, with a quick hug and kiss. Strong scent of perfume. She laughed at his exhaustion and held his arms as they made their way up to the street, chattering over something or other and pleased that she had found a legal spot to park their car. She drove, and he sat back in the deep seat and looked at the bright dashboard, at her: glossy cap of blonde hair, blush on her cheeks like two bruises, upper eyelids blue, purple, lashes spiky black. He thought: she's mine. This is mine. I'm safe. At a red light she glanced over at him and laughed again, lips dark red, teeth perfectly white, and quick leaned over to steady themselves as the old train clattered up the grade and out of the hills. Night passed, dawn arrived, they were in Kwa-Xhosa now and it was as if S.A. Railways had been a time machine, taking a century into the past overnight. Women they passed wore white turbans and led donkeys on dirt paths. On the plains before the blue mountains on the horizon were villages of circular thatched rondewels, whitewashed under the thatch and around the doors. Finally the train clanked into e'Negobo, past some men on donkeys and around the last curve to the small wooden building and platform that served as the train station. As the train rolled in, all the men stuck their heads out the windows on the right to look; but under the harsh morning light they saw that the station platform stood deserted, white splintered dusty planks utterly empty in the sun. Not a single soul was there to greet them. *And Thabo said to me, "So many had gone and come back, and so many had gone and never come back again, that no one waited anymore."*

OF SPACE-TIME AND
THE RIVER

by Gregory Benford

*Gregory Benford is one of the modern giants of the
field. His 1980 novel* Timescape *won the Nebula Award,
the John W. Campbell Memorial Award, the British Science Fiction Association Award, and the Australian
Ditmar Award, and is widely considered to be one of
the classic novels of the last two decades. His other
novels include* The Stars In Shroud, In The Ocean Of
Night, Against Infinity, Artifact, *and* Across The Sea
Of Suns. *His most recent novels are the bestselling*
Great Sky River, *and* Tides Of Light. *He has recently
become one of the regular science columnists for* The
Magazine of Fantasy and Science Fiction. *Benford is a
professor of physics at the University of California, Irvine.*

*Here, in one of the most strange and daring visions of
the future in this book, he takes us to the shadow of the
Pyramids for an encounter with a race of enigmatic aliens
who are strangely fascinated with Egypt's ancient
past. . . .*

Dec. 5, Monday, 2048

We took a limo to Los Angeles for the 9 A.M. flight, LAX
to Cairo.

On the boost up we went over 1.4 G, contra-reg, and
a lot of passengers complained, especially the poor thins

in their clank-shank rigs, the ones that keep you walking even after the hip replacements fail.

Joanna slept through it all, seasoned traveler, and I occupied myself with musing about finally seeing the ancient Egypt I'd dreamed about as a kid, back at the turn of the century.

> If thou be'st born to strange sights,
> Things invisible to see,
> Ride ten thousand days and nights,
> Till age snow white hairs on thee.

I've got the snow powdering at the temples and steadily expanding waistline, so I guess John Donne applies. Good to see I can still summon up lines I first read as a teenager. There are some rewards to being a Prof. of Comp. Lit. at UC Irvine, even if you do have to scrimp to afford a trip like this.

The tour agency said the Quarthex hadn't interfered with tourism at all—in fact, you hardly noticed them, they deliberately blended in so well. How a seven-foot insectoid thing with gleaming russet skin can look like an Egyptian I don't know, but what the hell, Joanna said, let's go anyway.

I hope she's right. I mean, it's been fourteen years since the Quarthex landed, opened the first diplomatic interstellar relations, and then chose Egypt as the only place on Earth where they cared to carry out what they called their "cultural studies." I guess we'll get a look at that, too. The Quarthex keep to themselves, veiling their multi-layered deals behind diplomatic dodges.

As if six hours of travel wasn't numbing enough, including the orbital delay because of an unannounced Chinese launch, we both watched a holoD about one of those new biotech guys, called *Straight from the Hearts*. An unending string of single-entendre jokes. In our stupefied state it was just about right.

As we descended over Cairo it was clear and about

15°C. We stumbled off the plane, sandy-eyed from riding ten thousand days and nights in a whistling aluminum box.

The airport was scruffy, instant third world hubbub, confusion, and filth. One departure lounge was filled exclusively with turbaned men. Heavy security everywhere. No Quarthex around. Maybe they do blend in.

Our bus across Cairo passed a decayed aqueduct, about which milled men in caftans, women in black, animals eating garbage. People, packed into the most unlikely living spots, carrying out peddler's business in dusty spots between buildings, traffic alternately frenetic or frozen.

We crawled across Cairo to Giza, the pyramids abruptly looming out of the twilight. The hotel, Mena House, was the hunting lodge-cum-palace of 19th-century kings. Elegant.

Buffet supper was good. Sleep came like a weight.

Dec. 6

Keeping this journal is fun. Joanna says it's good therapy for me, might even get me back into the habit of writing again. She says every Comp. Lit. type is a frustrated author and I should just spew my bile into this diary. So be it:

> Thou, when thou return'st, wilt tell me
> All strange wonders that befell thee.

World, you have been warned.

Set off south today—to Memphis, the ancient capital lost when its walls were breached in a war and subsequent floods claimed it.

The famous fallen Rameses status. It looks powerful still, even lying down. Makes you feel like a pigmy tiptoeing around a giant, *a la* Gulliver.

Saqqara, principal necropolis of Memphis, survives three km. away in the desert. First Dynasty tombs, including the first pyramid, made of steps, five levels high. New Kingdom graffiti inside are now history themselves, from our perspective.

On to the Great Pyramid!—by camel! The drivers proved even more harassing than legend warned. We entered the Khefren pyramid, slightly shorter than that of his father, Cheops. All the 80 known pyramids were found stripped. These passages have a constricted vacancy to them, empty now for longer than they were filled. Their silent mass is unnerving.

Professor Alvarez from UC Berkeley tried to find hidden rooms here by placing cosmic ray detectors in the lower known rooms, and looking for slight increases in flux at certain angles, but there seem to be none. There are seismic and even radio measurements of the dry sands in the Giza region, looking for echoes of buried tombs, but no big finds so far. Plenty of echoes from ruins of ordinary houses, etc., though.

No serious jet lag today, but we nod off when we can. Handy, having the hotel a few hundred yards from the pyramids.

I tried to get Joanna to leave her wrist comm at home. Since her breakdown she can't take news of daily disasters very well. (Who can, really?) She's pretty steady now, but this trip should be as calm as possible, her doctor told me.

So of course she turns on the comm and it's full of hysterical stuff about another border clash between the Empire of Israel and the Arab Muhammad Soviet. Smart rockets vs. smart defenses. A draw. Some things never change.

I turned it off immediately. Her hands shook for hours afterward. I brushed it off.

Still, it's different when you're a few hundred miles from the lines. Hope we're safe here.

Dec. 7

Into Cairo itself, the Egyptian museum. The Tut Ankh
Amen exhibit—huge treasuries, opulent jewels, a sheer
wondrous plentitude. There are endless cases of beautiful
alabaster bowls, gold-laminate boxes, testifying to thousands of years of productivity.

I wandered down a musty marble corridor and then,
coming out of a gloomy side passage, there was the first
Quarthex I'd ever seen. Big, clacking and clicking as it
thrust forward in that six-legged gait. It ignored me, of
course—they nearly always lurch by humans as though
they can't see us. Or else that distant, distracted gaze
means they're ruminating over strange, alien ideas. Who
knows why they're intensely studying ancient Egyptian
ways, and ignoring the rest of us? This one was cradling
a stone urn, a meter high at least. It carried the black
granite in three akimbo arms, hardly seeming to notice
the weight. I caught a whiff of acrid pungency, the fluid
that lubricates their joints. Then it was gone.

We left and visited the oldest Coptic church in Egypt,
supposedly where Moses hid out when he was on the lam
out of town. Looks it. The old section of Cairo is
crowded, decayed, people laboring in every nook with
minimal tools, much standing around watching as others
work. The only sign of really efficient labor was a gang
of men and women hauling long, cigar-shaped yellow
things on wagons. Something the Quarthex wanted placed
outside the city, our guide said.

In the evening we went to the Sound & Light show at
the Sphinx—excellent. There is even a version in the
Quarthex language, those funny sputtering, barking
sounds.

Arabs say, "Man fears time; time fears the pyramids." You get that feeling here.

Afterward, we ate in the hotel's Indian restaurant; quite
fine.

Dec. 8

Cairo is a city being trampled to death.

It's grown by a factor of fourteen in population since the revolution in 1952, and shows it. The old Victorian homes which once lined stately streets of willowy trees are now crowded by modern slab concrete apartment houses. The aged buildings are kept going, not from a sense of history, but because no matter how rundown they get, somebody needs them.

The desert's grit invades everywhere. Plants in the courtyards have a weary, resigned look. Civilization hasn't been very good for the old ways.

Maybe that's why the Quarthex seem to dislike anything built since the time of the Romans. I saw one running some kind of machine, a black contraption that floated two meters off the ground. It was laying some kind of cable in the ground, right along the bank of the Nile. Every time it met a building it just slammed through, smashing everything to frags. Guess the Quarthex have squared all this with the Egyptian gov't, because there were police all around, making sure nobody got in the way. Odd.

But not unpredictable, when you think about it. The Quarthex have those levitation devices which everybody would love to get the secret of. (Ending sentence with preposition! Horrors! But this is vacation, dammit.) They've been playing coy for years, letting out a trickle of technology, with the Egyptians holding the patents. That must be what's holding the Egyptian economy together, in the face of their unrelenting population crunch. The Quarthex started out as guests here, studying the ruins and so on, but now it's obvious that they have free run of the place. They *own* it.

Still, the Quarthex haven't given away the crucial devices which would enable us to find out how they do it— or so my colleagues in the physics department tell me. It vexes them that this alien race can master space-time so completely, manipulating gravity itself, and we can't get the knack of it.

We visited the famous alabaster mosque. It perches on a hill called The Citadel. Elegant, cool, aloofly dominating the city. The Old Bazaar nearby is a warren, so much like the movie sets one's seen that it has an unreal, Arabian Nights quality. We bought spices. The calls to worship from the mosques reach you everywhere, even in the most secluded back rooms where Joanna was haggling over jewelry.

It's impossible to get anything really ancient, the swarthy little merchants said. The Quarthex have bought them up, trading gold for anything that might be from the time of the Pharaohs. There have been a lot of fakes over the last few centuries, some really good ones, so the Quarthex have just bought anything that might be real. No wonder the Egyptians like them, let them chew up their houses if they want. Gold speaks louder than the past.

We boarded our cruise ship, the venerable *Nile Concorde*. Lunch was excellent, Italian. We explored Cairo in mid-afternoon, through markets of incredible dirt and disarray. Calf brains displayed without a hint of refrigeration or protection, flies swarming, etc. Fun, especially if you can keep from breathing for five minutes or more.

We stopped in the Shepheard Hotel, the site of many Brit spy novels (Maugham especially). It has an excellent bar—Nubians, Saudis, etc., putting away decidedly non-Islamic gins and beers. A Quarthex was sitting in a special chair at the back, talking through a voicebox to a Saudi. I couldn't tell what they were saying, but the Saudi had a gleam in his eye. Driving a bargain, I'd say.

Great atmosphere in the bar, though. A cloth banner over the bar proclaims.

Unborn tomorrow and dead yesterday,
why fret about them if today be sweet.

Indeed, yes, ummm—bartender!

Dec. 9, Friday, Moslem holy day

We left Cairo at 11 P.M. last night, the city gliding past our stateroom windows, lovelier in misty radiance than in dusty day. We cruised all day. Buffet breakfast & lunch, solid Eastern and Mediterranean stuff, passable red wine.

A hundred meters away, the past presses at us, going about its business as if the pharaohs were still calling the tune. Primitive pumping irrigation, donkeys doing the work, women cleaning gray clothes in the Nile. Desert ramparts to the east, at spots sending sand fingers—no longer swept away by the annual flood—across the fields to the shore itself. Moslem tombs of stone and mud brick coast by as we lounge on the top deck, peering at the madly waving children through our binoculars, across a chasm of time.

There are about fifty aboard a ship with capacity of a hundred, so there is plenty of room and service as we sweep serenely on, music flooding the deck, cutting between slabs of antiquity; not quite decadent, just intelligently sybaritic. (Why so few tourists? Guide says people are maybe afraid of the Quarthex. Joanna gets jittery around them, but I don't know whether that's her old fears surfacing again.)

The spindly, ethereal minarets are often the only grace note in the mud-brick villages, like a lovely idea trying to rise out of brown, mottled chaos. Animal power is used everywhere possible. Still, the villages are quiet at night.

The flip side of this peacefulness must be boredom. That explains a lot of history and its rabid faiths, unfortunately.

Dec. 10

Civilization thins steadily as we steam upriver. The mud-brick villages typically have no electricity; there is ample power from Aswan, but the power lines and stations are too expensive. One would think that, with the Quarthex gold, they could do better now.

Our guide says the Quarthex have been very hard-nosed—no pun intended—about such improvements. They will not let the earnings from their patents be used to modernize Egypt. Feeding the poor, cleaning the Nile, rebuilding monuments—all fine (in fact, they pay handsomely for restoring projects). But better electricity—no. A flat no.

We landed at a scruffy town and took a bus into the western desert. Only a kilometer from the flat floodplain, the Sahara is utterly barren and forbidding. We visited a Ptolemaic city of the dead. One tomb has a mummy of a girl who drowned trying to cross the Nile and see her lover, the hieroglyphs say. Nearby are catacombs of mummified baboons and ibises, symbols of wisdom.

A tunnel begins here, pointing SE toward Akhenaton's capital city. The German discoverers in the last century followed it for 40 kilometers—all cut through limestone, a gigantic task—before turning back because of bad air.

What was it for? Nobody knows. Dry, spooky atmosphere. Urns of dessicated mummies, undisturbed. To duck down a side corridor is to step into mystery.

I left the tour group and ambled over a low hill—to take a leak, actually. To the west was sand, sand, sand. I was standing there, doing my bit to hold off the dryness, when I saw one of those big black contraptions come slipping over the far horizon. Chuffing, chugging, and laying what looked like pipe—a funny kind of pipe, all silvery, with blue facets running through it. The glittering shifted, changing to yellows and reds while I watched.

A Quarthex riding atop it, of course. It ran due south, roughly parallel to the Nile. When I got back and told

Joanna about it she looked at the map and we couldn't figure what would be out there of interest to anybody, even a Quarthex. No ruins around, nothing. Funny.

Dec. 11

Beni Hassan, a nearly deserted site near the Nile. A steep walk up the escarpment of the eastern desert, after crossing the rich flood plain by donkey. The rock tombs have fine drawings and some statues—still left because they were cut directly from the mountain, and have thick wedges securing them to it. Guess the ancients would steal anything not nailed down. One thing about the Quarthex, the guide says—they take nothing. They seem genuinely interested in restoring, not in carting artifacts back home to their neck of the galactic spiral arm.

Upriver, we landfall beside a vast dust plain, which we crossed in a cart pulled by a tractor. The mud brick palaces of Akhenaton have vanished, except for a bit of Nefertiti's palace, where the famous bust of her was found. The royal tombs in the mountain above are defaced—big chunks pulled out of the walls by the priests who undercut his monotheist revolution, after his death.

The wall carvings are very realistic and warm; the women even have nipples. The tunnel from yesterday probably runs under here, perhaps connecting with the passageways we see deep in the king's grave shafts. Again, nobody's explored them thoroughly. There are narrow sections, possibly warrens for snakes or scorpions, maybe even traps.

While Joanna and I are ambling around, taking a few snaps of the carvings, I hear a rustle. Joanna has the flashlight and we peer over a ledge, down a straight shaft. At the bottom something is moving, something damned big.

It takes a minute to see that the reddish shell isn't a sarcophagus at all, but the back of a Quarthex. It's planting sucker-like things to the walls, threading cables through them. I can see more of the stuff further back in the shadows.

The Quarthex looks up, into our flashlight beam, and scuttles away. Exploring the tunnels? But why did it move away so fast? What's to hide?

Dec. 12

Cruise all day and watch the shore slide by.

Joanna is right; I needed this vacation a great deal. I can see that, rereading this journal—it gets looser as I go along.

As do I. When I consider how my life is spent, ere half my days, in this dark world and wide . . .

The pell-mell of university life dulls my sense of wonder, of simple pleasures simply taken. The Nile has a flowing, infinite quality, free of time. I can *feel* what it was like to live here, part of a great celestial clock that brought the perpetually turning sun and moon, the perennial rhythm of the flood. Aswan has interrupted the ebb and flow of the waters, but the steady force of the Nile rolls on.

> Heaven smiles, and faiths and empires gleam,
> Like wrecks of a dissolving dream.

The peacefulness permeates everything. Last night, making love to Joanna, was the best ever. Magnifique!

(And I know you're reading this, Joanna—I saw you sneak it out of the suitcase yesterday! Well, it *was* the best—quite a tribute, after all these years. And there's tomorrow and tomorrow . . .)

> He who bends to himself a joy
> Does the winged life destroy;
> But he who kisses the joy as it flies
> Lives in eternity's sunrise.

Perhaps next term I shall request the Romantic Poets course. Or even write some of my own . . .

Three Quarthex flew overhead today, carrying what look like ancient rams-head statues. The guide says statues were moved around a lot by the Arabs, and of course the archeologists. The Quarthex have negotiated permission to take many of them back to their rightful places, if known.

Dec. 13

Landfall at Abydos—a limestone temple miraculously preserved, with its thick roof intact. Clusters of scruffy mud huts surround it, but do not diminish its obdurate rectangular severity.

The famous list of pharaohs, chiseled in a side corridor, is impressive in its sweep of time. Each little entry was a lordly pharaoh, and there are a whole wall jammed full. Egypt lasted longer than any comparable society, and the mass of names on that wall is even more impressive since the temple builders did not even give it the importance of a central location.

The list omits Hatchepsut, a mere woman, and Akhenaton the scandalous monotheist. Rameses II had all carvings here cut deeply, particularly on the immense columns, to forestall defacement—a possibility he was much aware of, since he was busily doing it to his ancestors' temples. He chiseled away earlier work, adding his own cartouches, apparently thinking he could fool the gods themselves into believing he had built them all himself. Ah, immortality.

Had an earthquake today. Shades of California!

We were on the ship, Joanna was dutifully padding back and forth on the main deck to work off the opulent lunch. We saw the palms waving ashore, and damned if there wasn't a small shock wave in the water, going east to west, and then a kind of low grumbling from the east. Guide says he's never seen anything like it.

And tonight, sheets of ruby light rising up from both east and west. Looked like an aurora, only the wrong directions. The rippling aura changed colors as it rose, then met overhead, burst into gold, and died. I'd swear I heard a high, keening note sound as the burnt-gold line flared and faded, flared and faded, spanning the sky.

Not many people on deck, though, so it didn't cause much comment. Joanna's theory is, it was a rocket exhaust.

An engineer says it looks like something to do with magnetic fields. I'm no scientist, but it seems to me whatever the Quarthex want to do, they can. Lords of space/time, they called themselves in the diplomatic ceremonies. The United Nations representatives wrote that off as hyperbole, but the Quarthex may mean it.

Dec. 14

Dendera. A vast temple, much less well known than Karnak, but quite as impressive. Quarthex there, digging at the foundations. Guide says they're looking for some secret passageways, maybe. The Egyptian gov't is letting them do what they damn well please.

On the way back to the ship, we pass a whole mass of people, hundreds, all dressed in costumes. I thought it was some sort of pageant or tourist foolery, but the guide frowned, saying he didn't know what to make of it. The mob was chanting something even the guide couldn't make out. He said the rough-cut cloth was typical of the old ways, made on crude spinning wheels. The procession was ragged, but seemed headed for the temple. They looked drunk to me.

The guide tells me that the ancients had a theology based on the Nile. This country is essentially ten kilometers wide and seven hundred kilometers long, a narrow band of livable earth pressed between two deadly deserts. So they believed the gods must have intended that, and the Nile was the center of the whole damned world.

The sun came from the east, meaning that's where things began. Ending—dying—happened in the west, where the sun went. Thus they buried their dead on the west side of the Nile, even 7000 years ago. At night, the sun swung below and lit the underworld, where everybody went finally. Kind of comforting, thinking of the sun doing duty like that for the dead. Only the virtuous dead, though. If you didn't follow the rules. . . .

> Some are born to sweet delight,
> Some are born to endless night.

Their world was neatly bisected by the great river, and they loved clean divisions. They invented the 24 hour day but, loving symmetry, split it in half. Each of the 12 daylight hours was longer in summer than in winter—and, for night, vice versa. They built an entire nation-state, an immortal hand or eye, framing such fearful symmetry.

On to Karnak itself, mooring at Luxor. The middle and late pharaohs couldn't afford the labor investment for pyramids, so they contented themselves with additions to the huge sprawl at Karnak.

I wonder how long it will be before someone rich notices that for a few million or so he could build a tomb bigger than the Great Pyramid. It would only take a million or so limestone blocks—or much better, granite—and could be better isolated and protected. If you can't conquer a continent or scribble a symphony, then pile up a great stack of stones.

> *L'eternité,*
> *ne fut jamais perdue.*

The light show this night at Karnak was spooky at times, and beautiful, with booming voices coming right out of the stones. Saw a Quarthex in the crowd. It stared straight ahead, not noticing anybody but not bumping into any humans, either.

It looked enthralled. The beady eyes, all four, scanned the shifting blues and burnt-oranges that played along the rising columns, the tumbled great statues. Its lubricating fluids made shiny reflections as it articulated forward, clacking in the dry night air. Somehow it was almost reverential. Rearing above the crowd, unmoving for long moments, it seemed more like the giant frozen figures in stone than like the mere mortals who swarmed around it, keeping a respectful distance, muttering to themselves.

Unnerving, somehow, to see

   . . . a subtler Sphinx renew
  Riddles of death Thebes never knew.

Dec. 15

A big day. The Valley of the Queens, the Nobles, and finally the Kings. Whew!

All are dry washes (wadis), obviously easy to guard and isolate. Nonetheless, all of the 62 known tombs except Tut's were rifled, probably within a few centuries of burial.

It must've been an inside job.

There is speculation that the robbing became a needed part of the economy, recycling the wealth, and providing gaudy displays for the next pharaoh to show off at *his* funeral, all the better to keep impressing the peasants. Just another part of the socio-economic machine, folks.

Later priests collected the pharaoh mummies and hid them in a cave nearby, realizing they couldn't protect the tombs. Preservation of Tuthmosis III is excellent. His hook-nosed mummy has been returned to its tomb—a big, deep thing, larger than our apartment, several floors in all, connected by ramps, with side treasuries, galleries, etc. The inscription above reads *You shall live again forever.*

All picked clean, of course, except for the sarcophagus, too heavy to carry away. The pyramids had portcullises, deadfalls, pitfalls, and rolling stones to crush the unwary robber, but there are few here. Still, it's a little creepy to think of all those ancient engineers, planning to commit murder in the future, long after they themselves are gone, all to protect the past.

Death, be not proud.

An afternoon of shopping in the bazaar. The old Victorian hotel on the river is atmospheric, but has few guests. Food continues good. No dysentery, either. We both took the EZ-Di bacteria before we left, so it's living down in our tracts, festering away, lying in wait for any ugly foreign bug. Comforting.

Dec. 16

Cruise on. We stop at Kom Ombo, a temple to the crocodile god, Sebek, built to placate the crocs who swarmed in the river nearby. (The Nile is cleared of them now, unfortunately; they would've added some zest to the cruise . . .) A small room contains 98 mummified crocs, stacked like cordwood.

Cruised some more. A few km. south, there were gangs of Egyptians working beside the river. Hauling blocks of granite down to the water, rolling them on logs. I stood on the deck, trying to figure out why they were using ropes and simple pulleys, and no powered machinery.

Then I saw a Quarthex near the top of the rise, where the blocks were being sawed out of the rock face. It reared up over the men, gesturing with those jerky arms, eyes glittering. It called out something in a halfway human voice, only in a language I didn't know. The guide came over, frowning, but he couldn't understand it, either.

The laborers were pulling ropes across ruts in the stone, feeding sand and water into the gap, cutting out blocks by sheer brute abrasion. It must take weeks to extract one at that rate! Further along, others drove wooden planks down into the deep grooves, hammering them with crude wooden mallets. Then they poured water over the planks, and we could hear the stone pop open as the wood expanded, far down in the cut.

That's the way the ancients did it, the guide said kind of quietly. The Quarthex towered above the human teams, that jangling, harsh voice booming out over the water, each syllable lingering until the next joined it, blending in the dry air, hollow and ringing and remorseless.

note added later

Stopped at Edfu, a well-preserved temple, buried 100 feet deep by Moslem garbage until the late 19th century. The best aspect of river cruising is pulling along a site, viewing it from the angles the river affords, and then stepping from your stateroom directly into antiquity, with nothing to intervene and break the mood.

Trouble is, this time a man in front of us goes off a way to photograph the ships, and suddenly something is rushing at him out of the weeds and the crew is yelling— it's a crocodile! The guy drops his camera and bolts.

The croc looks at all of us, snorts, and waddles back into the Nile. The guide is upset, maybe even more than the fellow who almost got turned into a free lunch. Who would reintroduce crocs into the Nile?

Dec. 17

Aswan. A clean, delightful town. The big dam just south of town is impressive, with its monuments to Soviet excellence, etc. A hollow joke, considering how poor the USSR is today. They could use a loan from Egypt!

The unforeseen side effects, though—rising water table bringing more insects, rotting away the carvings in the temples, rapid silting up inside the dam itself, etc.—are getting important. They plan to dig a canal and drain a lot of the incoming new silt into the desert, make a huge farming valley with it, but I don't see how they can drain enough water to carry the dirt, and still leave much behind in the original dam.

The guide says they're having trouble with it.

We then fly south, to Abu Simbel. Lake Nasser, which claimed the original site of the huge monuments, is hundreds of miles long. They enlarged it again in 2008.

In the times of the pharaohs, the land below these waters had villages, great quarries for the construction of monuments, trade routes south to the Nubian kingdoms. Now it's all underwater.

They did save the enormous temples to Rameses II—built to impress aggressive Nubians with his might and majesty—and to his queen, Nefertari. The colossal statues of Rameses II seem personifications of his egomania. Inside, carvings show him performing *all* the valiant tasks in the great battle with the Hittites—slaying, taking prisoners, then presenting them to himself, who is in turn advised by the gods—which include himself! All this, for a battle which was in fact an iffy draw. Both temples have been lifted about a hundred feet and set back inside a wholly artificial hill, supported inside by the largest concrete dome in the world. Amazing.

''Look upon my works, ye Mighty, and despair!''

Except that when Shelley wrote *Ozymandias*, he'd never seen Rameses II's image so well preserved.

Leaving the site, eating the sand blown into our faces by a sudden gust of wind, I caught sight of a Quarthex. It was burrowing into the sand, using a silvery tool that spat ruby-colored light. Beside it, floating on a platform, were some of those funny pipe-like things I'd seen days before. Only this time men and women were helping it, lugging stuff around to put into the holes the Quarthex dug.

The people looked dazed, like they were sleep-walking or something. I waved a greeting, but nobody even looked up. Except the Quarthex. They're expressionless, of course. Still, those glittering popeyes peered at me for a long moment, with the little feelers near its mouth twitching with a kind of anxious energy.

I looked away. I couldn't help but feel a little spooked

by it. I mean, it wasn't looking at us in a friendly way. Maybe it didn't want me yelling at its work gang.

Then we flew back to Aswan, above the impossibly narrow ribbon of green that snakes through absolute bitter desolation.

Dec. 18

I'm writing this at twilight, before the light gives out. We got up this morning and were walking into town when the whole damn ground started to rock. Mud huts slamming down, waves on the Nile, everything.

Got back to the ship but nobody knew what was going on. Not much on that radio. Cairo came in clear, saying there'd been a quake all right, all along the Nile.

Funny thing was, the captain couldn't raise any other radio station. Just Cairo. Nothing else in the whole Middle East.

Some other passengers think there's a war on. Maybe so, but the Egyptian army doesn't know about it. They're standing around, all along the quay, fondling their AK 47s, looking just as puzzled as we are.

More rumblings and shakings in the afternoon. And now that the light's about gone, I can see big sheets of light in the sky. Only it seems to me the constellations aren't right.

Joanna took some of her pills. She's trying to fend off the jitters and I do what I can. I hate the empty, hollow look that comes into her eyes.

We've got to get the hell out of here.

Dec. 19

I might as well write this down, there's nothing else to do.

When we got up this morning the sun was there all right, but the moon hadn't gone down. And it didn't, all day.

Sure, they can both be in the sky at the same time. But

all day? Joanna is worried, not because of the moon, but because all the airline flights have been cancelled. We were supposed to go back to Cairo today.

More earthquakes. Really bad this time.

At noon, all of a sudden, there were Quarthex everywhere. In the air, swarming in from the east and west. Some splashed down in the Nile—and didn't come up. Others zoomed overhead, heading south toward the dam.

Nobody's been brave enough to leave the ship—including me. Hell, I just want to go home. Joanna's staying in the cabin.

About an hour later, a swarthy man in a ragged gray suit comes running along the quay and says the dam's gone. Just *gone*. The Quarthex formed little knots above it, and there was a lot of purple flashing light and big crackling noises, and then the dam just disappeared.

But the water hasn't come pouring down on us here. The man says it ran *back the other way*. South.

I looked over the rail. The Nile was flowing north.

Late this afternoon, five of the crew went into town. By this time there were fingers of orange and gold zapping across the sky all the time, making weird designs. The clouds would come rolling in from the north, and these radiant beams would hit them, and they'd *split* the clouds, just like that. With a spray of ivory light.

And Quarthex, buzzing everywhere. There's a kind of high sheen, up above the clouds, like a metal boundary or something, but you can see through it.

Quarthex keep zipping up to it, sometimes coming right up out of the Nile itself, just splashing out, then zooming up until they're little dwindling dots. They spin around up there, as if they're inspecting it, and then they drop like bricks, and splash down in the Nile again. Like frantic bees, Joanna said, and her voice trembled.

A technical type on board, an engineer from Rockwell, says *he* thinks the Quarthex are putting on one hell of a light show. Just a weird alien stunt, he thinks.

While I was writing this, the five crewmen returned

from Aswan. They'd gone to the big hotels there, and then to police headquarters. They heard the TV from Cairo went out two days ago. All air flights have been grounded because of the Quarthex buzzing around and the odd lights and so on.

Or at least, that's the official line. The Captain says his cousin told him that several flights *did* take off two days back, and they hit something up there. Maybe that blue metallic sheen?

Anyway, one crashed. The others landed, even though damaged.

The authorities are keeping it quiet. They're not just keeping us tourists in the dark—they're playing mum with everybody.

I hope the engineer is right. Joanna is fretting and we hardly ate anything for dinner, just picked at the cold lamb. Maybe tomorrow will settle things.

Dec. 20

It did. When we woke, we went up on deck and watched the Earth rise.

It was coming up from the western mountains, blue-white clouds and patches of green and brown, but mostly tawny desert. We're looking west, across the Sahara. I'm writing this while everybody else is running around like a chicken with his head cut off. I'm sitting on deck, listening to shouts and wild traffic and even some gunshots coming from ashore.

I can see further east now—either we're turning, or we're rising fast and can see with a better perspective.

Where central Egypt was, there's a big, raw, dark hole.

The black must be the limestone underlying the desert. They've scraped off a rim of sandy margin enclosing the Nile valley, including us—and left the rest. And somehow, they're lifting it free of Earth.

No Quarthex flying around now. Nothing visible except that metallic blue smear of light high up in the air.

And beyond it—Earth, rising.

Dec. 22

I skipped a day.

There was no time to even think yesterday. After I wrote the last entry, a crowd of Egyptians came down the quay, shuffling silently along, like the ones we saw back at Abu Simbel. Only there were thousands.

And leading them was a Quarthex. It carried a big disc thing that made a humming sound. When the Quarthex lifted it, the pitch changed.

It made my eyes water, my skull ache. Like a hand squeezing my head, blurring the air.

Around me, everybody was writhing on the deck, moaning. Joanna, too.

By the time the Quarthex reached our ship I was the only one standing. Those yellow-shot, jittery eyes peered at me, giving nothing away. Then the angular head turned and went on. Pied piper, leading long trains of Egyptians.

Some of our friends from the ship joined at the end of the lines. Rigid, glassy-eyed faces. I shouted but nobody, not a single person in that procession, even looked up.

Joanna struggled to go with them. I threw her down and held her until the damned eerie parade was long past.

Now the ship's deserted. We've stayed aboard, out of pure fear.

Whatever the Quarthex did affects all but a few percent of those within range. A few crew stayed aboard, dazed but okay. Scared, hard to talk to.

Fewer at dinner.

The next morning, nobody.

We had to scavenge for food. The crew must've taken what was left aboard. I ventured into the market street nearby, but everything was closed up. Deserted. Only a few days ago we were buying caftans and alabaster sphinxes and beaten-bronze trinkets in the gaudy shops, and now it was stone cold dead. Not a sound, not a stray cat.

I went around to the back of what I remembered was

a filthy corner cafe. I'd turned up my nose at it while we were shopping, certain there was a sure case of dysentery waiting inside . . . but now I was glad to find some days-old fruits and vegetables in a cabinet.

Coming back, I nearly ran into a bunch of Egyptian men who were marching through the streets. Spooks.

They had the look of police, but were dressed up like Mardi Gras—loincloths, big leather belts, bangles and beads, hair stiffened with wax. They carried sharp spears.

Good thing I was jumpy, or they'd have run right into me. I heard them coming and ducked into a grubby alley. They were systematically combing the area, searching the miserable apartments above the market. The honcho barked orders in a language I didn't understand—harsh, guttural, not like Egyptian.

I slipped away. Barely.

We kept out of sight after that. Stayed below deck and waited for nightfall.

Not that the darkness made us feel any better. There were fires ashore. Not in Aswan itself—the town was utterly black. Instead, orange dots sprinkled the distant hillsides. They were all over the scrub desert, just before the ramparts of the real desert that stretches—or did stretch—to east and west.

Now, I guess, there's only a few dozen miles of desert, before you reach—what?

I can't discuss this with Joanna. She has that haunted expression, from the time before her breakdown. She is drawn and silent. Stays in the room.

We ate our goddamn vegetables. Now we go to bed.

Dec. 23

There were more of those patrols of Mardi Gras spooks today. They came along the quay, looking at the tour ships moored there, but for some reason they didn't come aboard.

We're alone on the ship. All the crew, the other tourists—all gone.

But that's not the big news. Around noon, when we were getting really hungry and I was mustering my courage to go back to the market street, I heard a roaring.

Understand, I hadn't heard an airplane in days. And those were jets. This buzzing, I suddenly realized, is a rocket or something, and it's in trouble.

I go out on the deck, checking first to see if the patrols are lurking around, and the roaring is louder. It's a plane with stubby little wings, coming along low over the water, burping and hacking and finally going dead quiet.

It nosed over and came in for a big splash. I thought the pilot was a goner, but the thing rode steady in the water for a while and the cockpit folded back and out jumps a man.

I yelled at him and he waved and swam for the ship. The plane sank.

He caught a line below and climbed up. An American, no less. But what he had to say was even more surprising.

He wasn't just some sky jockey from Cairo. He was an astronaut.

He was part of a rescue mission, sent up to try to stop the Quarthex. The others he'd lost contact with, although it looked like they'd all been drawn down toward the floating island that Egypt has become.

We're suspended about two Earth radii out, in a slowly widening orbit. There's a shield over us, keeping the air in and everything—cosmic rays, communications, space ships—out.

The Quarthex somehow ripped off a layer of Egypt and are lifting it free of Earth, escaping with it. Nobody had ever guessed they had such power. Nobody Earthside knows what to do about it. The Quarthex who were outside Egypt at the time just lifted off in their ships and rendezvoused with this floating platform.

Ralph Blanchard is his name, and his mission was to fly under the slab of Egypt, in a fast orbital craft. He was supposed to see how they'd ripped the land free. A lot of it had fallen away.

There was an array of silvery pods under the soil, he

says, and they must be enormous anti-gravity units. The same kind that make the Quarthex ships fly, and that we've been trying to get the secret of.

The pods are about a mile apart, making a grid. But between them, there are lots of Quarthex. They're building stuff, tilling soil and so on—upside down! The gravity works opposite on the underside. That must be the way the whole thing is kept together—compressing it with artificial gravity from both sides. God knows what makes the shield above.

But the really strange thing is the Nile. There's one on the underside, too.

It starts at the underside of Alexandria, where *our* Nile meets—met—the Mediterranean. It then flows back, all the way along the underside, running through a Nile valley of its own. Then it turns up and around the edge of the slab, and comes over the lip of it a few hundred miles upstream of here.

The Quarthex have drained the region beyond the Aswan dam. Now the Nile flows in its old course. The big temples of Rameses II are perched on a hill high above the river, and Ralph was sure he saw Quarthex working on the site, taking it apart.

He thinks they're going to put it back where it was, before the dam was built in the 1960s.

Ralph was supposed to return to Orbital City with his data. He came in close for a final pass and hit the shield they have, the one that keeps the air in. His ship was damaged.

He'd been issued a suborbital craft, able to do reentries, in case he could penetrate the airspace. That saved him. There were other guys who hit the shield and cracked through, guys with conventional deep-space shuttle tugs and the like, and they fell like bricks.

We've talked all this over but no one has a good theory of what is going on. The best we can do is stay away from the patrols.

Meanwhile, Joanna scavenged through obscure bins of the ship, and turned up an entire case of Skivaa, a cheap

Egyptian beer. So after I finish this ritual entry—who knows, this might be in a history book someday, and as a good academic I should keep it up—I'll go share it out in one grand bust with Ralph and Joanna. It'll do her good. She's been rocky. As well,

> Malt does more than Milton can
> To justify God's ways to man.

Dec. 24

This little diary was all I managed to take with us when the spooks came. I had it in my pocket.

I keep going over what happened. There was nothing I could do, I'm sure of that, and yet . . .

We stayed below decks, getting damned hungry again but afraid to go out. There was chanting from the distance. Getting louder. Then footsteps aboard. We retreated to the small cabins aft, third class.

The sounds got nearer. Ralph thought we should stand and fight but I'd seen those spears and hell, I'm a middle-aged man, no match for those maniacs.

Joanna got scared. It was like her breakdown. No, worse. The jitters built until her whole body seemed to vibrate, fingers digging into her hair like claws, eyes squeezed tight, face compressed as if to shut out the world.

There was nothing I could do with her, she wouldn't keep quiet. She ran out of the cabin we were hiding in, just rushed down the corridor screaming at them.

Ralph said we should use her diversion to get away and I said I'd stay, help her, but then I saw them grab her and hold her, not rough. It didn't seem as if they were going to do anything, just take her away.

My fear got the better of me then. It's hard to write this. Part of me says I should've stayed, defended her—but it was hopeless. You can't live up to your ideal self. The world of literature shows people summoning up courage, but there's a thin line between that and stupidity. Or so I tell myself.

The spooks hadn't seen us yet, so we slipped overboard, keeping quiet.

We went off the loading ramp on the river side, away from shore. Ralph paddled around to see the quay and came back looking worried. There were spooks swarming all over.

We had to move. The only way to go was across the river.

This shaky handwriting is from sheer, flat-out fatigue. I swam what seemed like forever. The water wasn't bad, pretty warm, but the current kept pushing us off course. Lucky thing the Nile is pretty narrow there, and there are rocky little stubs sticking out. I grabbed onto those and rested.

Nobody saw us, or at least they didn't do anything about it.

We got ashore looking like drowned rats. There's a big hill there, covered with ancient rock-cut tombs. I thought of taking shelter in one of them and started up the hill, my legs wobbly under me, and then we saw a mob up there.

And a Quarthex, a big one with a shiny shell. It wore something over its head, too. Supposedly Quarthex don't wear clothes, but this one had a funny rig on. A big bird head, with a long narrow beak and flinty black eyes.

There was madness all around us. Long lines of people carrying burdens, chanting. Quarthex riding on those lifter units of theirs. All beneath the piercing, biting sun.

We hid for a while. I found that this diary, in its zippered leather case, made it through the river without a leak. I started writing this entry. Joanna said once that I'd retreated into books as a defense, in adolescence. She was full of psychoanalytical explanations—it was a hobby. She kept thinking that if she could figure herself out, then things would be all right. Well, maybe I did use words and books and a quiet, orderly life as a place to hide. So what? It was better than this "real" world around me right now.

I thought of Joanna and what might be happening to her. The Quarthex can—

New Entry

I was writing when the Quarthex came closer. I thought we were finished, but they didn't see us. Those huge heads turned all the time, the glittering black eyes scanning. Then they moved away. The chanting was a relentless, singsong drone that gradually faded.

We got away from there, fast.

I'm writing this during a short break. Then we'll move on.

No place to go but the goddamn desert.

Dec. 25

Christmas.

I keep thinking about fat turkey stuffed with spicy dressing, crisp cranberries, a dry white wine, thick gravy—

No point in that. We found some food today in an abandoned construction site, bread at least a week old and some dried-up fruit. That was all.

Ralph kept pushing me on west. He wants to see over the edge, how they hold this thing together.

I'm not that damn interested, but I don't know where else to go. Just running on blind fear. My professorial instincts—like keeping this journal. It helps keep me sane. Assuming I still am.

Ralph says putting this down might have scientific value. If I can ever get it to anybody outside. So I keep on. Words, words, words. Much cleaner than this gritty, surreal world.

We saw people marching in the distance, dressed in loincloths again. It suddenly struck me that I'd seen that clothing before—in those marvelous wall paintings, in the tombs of the Valley of Kings. It's ancient dress.

Ralph thinks he understands what's happening. There

was an all-frequencies broadcast from the Quarthex when
they tore off this wedge we're on. Nobody understood
much—it was in that odd semi-speech of theirs, all the
words blurred and placed wrong, scrambled up. Something about their mission or destiny or whatever being to
enhance the best in each world. About how they'd made
a deal with the Egyptians to bring forth the unrealized
promise of their majestic past and so on. And that meant
isolation, so the fruit of ages could flower.

Ha. The world's great age begins anew, maybe—but
Percy Bysshe Shelley never meant it like this.

Not that I care a lot about motivations right now. I
spent the day thinking of Joanna, still feeling guilty. And
hiking west in the heat and dust, hiding from gangs of
glassy-eyed workers when we had to.

We reached the edge at sunset. It hadn't occurred to
me, but it's obvious—for there to be days and nights at
all means they're spinning the slab we're on.

Compressing it, holding in the air, adding just the right
rotation. Masters—of space/time and the river, yes.

The ground started to slope away. Not like going
downhill, because there was nothing pulling you down
the face of it. I mean, we *felt* like we were walking on
level ground. But overhead the sky moved as we walked.

We caught up with the sunset. The sun dropped for a
while in late afternoon, then it started rising again. Pretty
soon it was right overhead, high noon.

And we could see Earth, too, farther away than yesterday. Looking cool and blue.

We came to a wall of glistening metal tubes, silvery
and rippling with a frosty blue glow. I started to get
woozy as we approached. Something happened to gravity—it pulled your stomach as if you were spinning
around. Finally we couldn't get any closer. I stopped,
nauseated. Ralph kept on. I watched him try to walk
toward the metal barrier, which by then looked like luminous icebergs suspended above barren desert.

He tried to walk a straight line, he said later. I could
see him veer, his legs rubbery, and it looked as though

he rippled and distended, stretching horizontally while some force compressed him vertically, an egg man, a plastic body swaying in tides of gravity.

Then he started stumbling, falling. He cried out—a horrible, warped sound, like paper tearing for a long, long time. He fled. The sand clawed at him as he ran, strands grasping at his feet, trailing long streamers of glittering, luminous sand—but it couldn't hold him. Ralph staggered away, gasping, his eyes huge and white and terrified.

We turned back.

But coming away, I saw a band of men and women marching woodenly along toward the wall. They were old, most of them, and diseased. Some had been hurt—you could see the wounds.

They were heading straight for the lip. Silent, inexorable.

Ralph and I followed them for a while. As they approached, they started walking up off the sand—right into the air.

And over the tubes.

Just flying.

We decided to head south. Maybe the lip is different there. Ralph says the plan he'd heard, after the generals had studied the fast survey mission results, was to try to open the shield at the ground, where the Nile spills over. Then they'd get people out by boating them along the river.

Could they be doing that, now? We hear roaring sounds in the sky sometimes. Explosions. Ralph is ironic about it all, says he wonders when the Quarthex will get tired of intruders and go back to the source—*all* the way back.

I don't know. I'm tired and worn down.

Could there be a way out? Sounds impossible, but it's all we've got.

Head south, to the Nile's edge.

We're hiding in a cave tonight. It's bitterly cold out here in the desert, and a sunburn is no help.

I'm hungry as hell. Some Christmas.

We were supposed to be back in Laguna Beach by now.

God knows where Joanna is.

Dec. 26

I got away. Barely.

The Quarthex work in teams now. They've gridded off the desert and work across it systematically in those floating platforms. There are big tubes like cannons mounted on each end and a Quarthex scans it over the sands.

Ralph and I crept up to the mouth of the cave we were in and watched them comb the area. They worked out from the Nile. When a muzzle turned toward us I felt an impact like a warm, moist wave smacking into my face, for all the world like being in the ocean. It drove me to my knees. I reeled away. Threw myself further back into the cramped cave.

It all dropped away then, as if the wave had pinned me to the ocean floor and filled my lungs with a sluggish liquid.

And in an instant was gone. I rolled over, gasping, and saw Ralph staggering into the sunlight, heading for the Quarthex platform. The projector was leveled at him so that it no longer struck the cave mouth. So I'd been released from its grip.

I watched them lower a rope ladder. Ralph dutifully climbed up. I wanted to shout to him, try to break the hold that thing had over him, but once again the better part of valor and all that—I just watched. They carried him away.

I waited until twilight to move. Not having anybody to talk to makes it harder to control my fear.

God, I'm hungry. Couldn't find a scrap to eat.

When I took out this diary I looked at the leather case and remembered stories of people getting so starved they'd eat their shoes. Suitably boiled and salted, of course, with a tangy sauce.

I've got to keep moving.

Dec. 27

Hard to write.

They got me this morning.

It grabs your mind. Like before. Squeezing in your head.

But after a while it is better. Feels good. But a buzzing all the time, you can't think.

Picked me up while I was crossing an arroyo. Didn't have any idea they were around. A platform.

Took me to some others. All Egyptians. Been caught like me.

Marched us to the Nile.

Plenty to eat.

Rested at noon.

Brought Joanna to me. She is all right. Lovely in the long draping dress the Quarthex gave her.

All around are the bird-headed ones. Ibis, I remember, the bird of the Nile. And dog-headed ones. Lion-headed ones.

Gods of the old times. The Quarthex are the gods of the old time. Of the great empire.

We are the people.

Sometimes I can think, like now. They sent me away from the work gang on an errand. I am old, not strong. They are kind—give me easy jobs.

So I came to here. Where I hid this diary. Before they took my old uncomfortable clothes I put this little book into a crevice in the rock. Pen too.

Now writing helps. Mind clears some.

I saw Ralph, then lost track of him. I worked hard after the noontime. Sun felt good. I lifted pots, carried them where the foreman said.

The Quarthex-god with ibis head is building a fresh temple. Made from the stones of Aswan. It will be cool and deep, many pillars.

They took my dirty clothes. Gave me fresh loincloth, headband, sandals. Good ones. Better than my old clothes.

It is hard to remember how things were before I came

here. Before I knew the river. Its flow. How it divides the world.

I will rest before I try to read what I have written in here before. The words are hard.

days later

I come back but can read only a little.

Joanna says You should not. The ibis will not like if I do.

I remember I liked these words on paper, in my days before. I earned my food with them. Now they are empty. Must not have been true.

I do not need them any more.

Ralph and his science. It was all words too.

later

Days since I find this again. I do the good work, I eat, Joanna is there in the night. Many things. I do not want to do this reading.

But today another thing howled overhead. It passed over the desert like a screaming black bird, the falcon, and then fell, flames, big roar.

I remembered Ralph.

This book I remembered, came for it.

The ibis-god speaks to us each sunset. Of how the glory of our lives is here again. We are one people once more again yes after a long time of being lost.

What the red sunset means. The place where the dead are buried in the western desert. To be taken in death close to the edge, so the dead will walk their last steps in this world, to the lip and over, to the nether-world.

There the lion-god will preserve them. Make them live again.

The Quarthex-gods have discovered how to revive the dead of any beings. They spread this among the stars.

But only to those who understand. Who deserve. Who bow to the great symmetry of life.

One face light, one face dark.

The sun lights the netherworld when for us it is night. There the dead feast and mate and laugh and live forever.

Ralph saw that. The happy land below. It shares the sun.

I saw Ralph today. He came to the river to see the falcon thing cry from the clouds. We all did.

It fell into the river and was swallowed and will be taken to the netherworld where it flows over the edge of the world.

Ralph was sorry when the falcon fell. He said it was a mistake to send it to bother us. That someone from the old dead time had sent it.

Ralph works in the quarry. Carving the limestone. He looks good, the sun has lain on him and made him strong and brown.

I started to talk of the time we met but he frowned.

That was before we understood, he says. Shook his head. So I should not speak of it I know.

The gods know of time and the river. They know.

I tire now.

again

Joanna sick. I try help but no way to stop the bleeding from her.

In old time I would try to stop the stuff of life from leaving her. I would feel sorrow.

I do not now. I am calm.

Ibis-god prepares her. Works hard and good over her.

She will journey tonight. Walk the last trek. Over the edge of the sky and to the netherland.

It is what the temple carving says. She will live again forever.

Forever waits.

I come here to find this book to enter this. I remember sometimes how it was.

I did not know joy then. Joanna did not.

We lived but to no point. Just come-go-come-again.

Now I know what comes. The western death. The rising life.

The Quarthex-gods are right. I should forget that life. To hold on is to die. To flow forward is to life.

Today I saw the pharaoh. He came in radiant chariot, black horses before, bronze sword in hand. The sun was high above him. No shadow he cast.

Big and with red skin the pharaoh rode down the avenue of the kings. We the one people cheered.

His great head was mighty in the sun and his many arms waved in salute to his one people. He is so great the horses groan and sweat to pull him. His hard gleaming body is all armor for he will always be on guard against our enemies.

Like those who fall from the sky. Every day now more come down, dying fireballs to smash in the desert. All fools. Black rotting bodies. None will rise to walk west. They are only burned prey of the pharaoh.

The pharaoh rode three times on the avenue. We threw ourselves down to attract a glance. His huge glaring eyes regarded us and we cried out, our faces wet with joy.

He will speak for us in the netherworld. Sing to the undergods.

Make our westward walking path smooth.

I fall before him.

I bury this now. No more write in it.

This kind of writing is not for the world now. It comes from the old dead time when I knew nothing and thought everything.

I go to my eternity on the river.

STILL LIFE WITH SCORPION
by Scott Baker

Scott Baker is another writer who has made a large impact with a relatively small amount of published work. Primarily known for his short fiction, his stories have appeared in Omni, The Magazine of Fantasy and Science Fiction, Isaac Asimov's Science Fiction Magazine, Ripper!, Blood is Not Enough, Alien Sex, The Architecture of Fear, *and elsewhere. One of his* Omni *stories, "The Lurking Duck," has become something of an underground cult classic, and was published in French translation as a book. The story that follows, "Still Life With Scorpion," from* Isaac Asimov's Science Fiction Magazine *won the World Fantasy Award as Best Short Story of 1985; he also won the French Prix Apollo, in 1982, for his novel* Symbiote's Crown. *His novels include* Nightchild, Firedance, Dhampire, Symbiote's Crown, *and* Drink the Fire from the Flames. *His most recent book is a new novel,* Webs. *He lives with his wife, Suzi, in Paris, France.*

Here he sweeps us along with a party of unhappy and squabbling tourists on safari in Africa, and not caring much for it, for a chilling demonstration of that old saying, what goes around, comes around. . . .

The dust in the back of the open truck was as bad as ever, but the desert was getting a little greener-looking, with squat gray-green bushes scattered here and there among the twisted, bare-branched, black thorntrees. The truck lurched violently as they hit a hole, and the scarf Randy had tied inexpertly over his nose and mouth came loose just as he inhaled. He coughed, nose and throat coated with the thick hot red dust, and decided it was time to drink a little more water. He found his plastic canteen, took a cautious sip, swallowed and took another.

Looking up, he caught Cora watching him—the seats faced inward so she more or less *had* to look at him if she didn't want to strain her neck looking back over her shoulder all the time—and he held the canteen out to her. She shook her head and turned away, still not speaking to him.

On impulse he offered the canteen to the wizened little old man sitting next to him with his thick plastic raincoat buttoned to the neck.

"No, thank you." A thin, querulous voice, the kind of old man who enjoyed disciplining his grandchildren with a cane. "I spent twenty years in Africa—Egypt, not here—and you won't see me drinking that sort of water. I have three cups of tea with my breakfast, then nothing more until lunch, when I . . ."

Randy tuned him out and put the canteen back behind his seat. They were jolting across a dry gravel riverbed; about a hundred yards off to the right he could see a group of Samburu warriors in orange-red, toga-like robes watching their scrawny humpbacked cattle. Cora and half the other passengers waved happily at them. With the camera he wore slung openly on its shoulder strap, Randy got a good picture of them making condescending fools of themselves.

The truck labored up out of the riverbed and rounded a hill. Just ahead, the other truck was stopped by the side of the road with one of its middle wheels off. The Kikuyu driver was removing the brake drum while one of his passengers—the short man with the Jungle Jim safari outfit and the garage in Brighton—was giving him advice that he didn't need and wasn't listening to. The White Man's Burden.

One of the cooks had already set up the picnic table with its meat loaf and mango chutney sandwiches while the other two were dragging out the water cans and bottles of orange crush syrup. Nearby, a bare-breasted Samburu girl of fifteen or sixteen, with her neck and shoulders heaped with bright, beaded necklaces and collars, stood surrounded by her goats, watching the tourists as she chewed on a twig of the wood they used instead of toothbrushes.

Randy's truck stopped alongside the other as William, the engineer from Mombassa who looked like a bearded British Mephistopheles, started bargaining with the girl for a picture. She wanted fifty shillings; he was offering ten. Randy stood up and with a casual, practiced motion got a picture of the two of them with the camera concealed in the inconspicuous leather case he wore on his belt, where none of the Africans he'd photographed had yet noticed it.

"That's not fair," the nurse sitting by Cora said.

"Why not? As long as they don't know, what difference does it make? I'm not hurting them or anything."

"Some of them—I can't remember which ones, maybe it was the Masai—anyway, they think if you take somebody's picture you're stealing his soul. This is their country; you should respect their beliefs."

Cora was looking away, pretending to watch the Englishman bargaining with the girl, but Randy knew she was listening: She'd uncovered her face and he could tell from the tight, disapproving line of her lips.

"But the Masai let you take their picture anyway," Randy said, forcing himself to answer patiently. Cora had said almost exactly the same thing; if he could convince the nurse, it might help convince her. "As long as you're willing to pay them enough for it. So their souls can't really be worth all that much to them—and anyway, after the first picture somebody takes, they don't have any souls left to steal, right? So from then on they're cheating you."

"But they're so poor here. That's all they have to sell."

Randy shrugged. "They can still sell it to someone

else after I'm done. Or at the same time, even. They're not losing anything.''

"Maybe, but—''

One of the middle-aged women from the other truck shrieked and the nurse broke off in mid-sentence. The stocky German in the torn T-shirt was down on his hands and knees chasing a three-inch scorpion, one of the lethal black and yellow kind, under the picnic table and back out through the rapidly scattering group of women. Randy got two pictures of the confusion with the shoulder-strap camera, then ran out of film. He jumped down from the truck and managed to get a picture with his belt camera just as the German clapped his killing jar over the scorpion.

The scorpion writhed and snapped inside, arching its back to strike the jar repeatedly with its barbed tail and leaving a few drops of yellowish fluid on the glass each time, before the acetone fumes overcame it and it died.

By now everybody else was a good ways away from the picnic table. The German dumped the dead scorpion out onto the table, beside the heaped sandwiches, admired it an instant longer, then nonchalantly picked it up and injected it with glycerine from a hypodermic he carried in what looked like a doctor's little black bag.

Randy used his belt camera to get another two pictures of the German with his prize and a few of the crowd clustered around looking on—the Samburu girl as fascinated as the rest—before Joseph, Randy's driver, came around the truck and saw what was happening. He started yelling at the German, who didn't understand English, at least not Joseph's Kenyan English. The German nodded politely a few times, finally scooped up his scorpion and put it in another bottle.

Joseph wiped off the picnic table with a rag to reassure his charges. Most of the passengers from Randy's truck rather reluctantly drifted over and began taking sandwiches.

Randy looked around for Cora but couldn't find her. He considered getting her a sandwich as a sort of goodwill gesture, saw that her nurse friend was already head-ing around to the other side of the truck with a sandwich in each hand, and gave up for the moment.

William was still negotiating with the Samburu girl, who'd been joined by two other girls of about the same age. Curious men and women were drifting in from every direction. The desert landscape looked totally devoid of life, but Randy had learned by now that whenever the truck stopped for more than a few minutes it would draw a crowd, seemingly from nowhere.

"Wasn't it someplace around here that they speared the tourists in that lorry last month?" one of the British ladies was asking another. Joseph overheard her and said, no, that had been a few hundred kilometers away, near one of the areas where they were going to be camping on their way back from Lake Turkana.

Randy got a full roll of film of the three Samburu girls without any of them suspecting he was photographing them. Most of the pictures were sure to have something wrong with them, of course—for all his practice he still couldn't get the same kind of results with his belt camera that he could normally—but a few at least were sure to work out.

He half-turned so nobody outside the truck would be able to see what he was doing, opened the belt case and took out the camera, slipped the bright yellow roll of film out and put another in, then closed the case again. You had to look very closely to see that the case actually contained a functioning camera; most people who no-ticed it, even other photographers, thought it was just a spare lens case or something of the sort.

Randy's Uncle Phillip was vice-president of a tour company which was in the process of making the change-over from a small-time travel agency to something Uncle Phillip often said he was confident would be giving American Express stiff competition by the end of the de-cade. He'd seen three of Randy's photos in a group show in San Francisco—probably strong-armed into going by Randy's mother—and he'd told Randy he needed some photos for a new series of brochures his company was working up on Kenya, so would Randy like to do them?

Randy had said, of course, he would.

That had been three o'clock on a Friday afternoon. At six-thirty Cora had come storming back from the department store she was working in to tell Randy that she'd been sleeping with someone from work for six months and it wasn't any good but it was still better than sleeping with him, that she was sick of selling handbags to support him and his photography when she could be finishing up her M.B.A. and getting started on a real career, in short, that she was quitting her job and getting a divorce.

So he'd come up with the idea for the trip—a month together, just the two of them, in Romantic Africa, everybody's dream vacation. They could try to settle their differences and find renewed joy in each other's company away from their day-to-day problems and pressures; at the very least it would ensure that their last few weeks together would be something they could remember without bitterness, maybe even with pleasure.

Give me one last chance, he'd begged Cora, telling her he'd found a job that would provide the money for the trip—and, not for the first time, Cora had given him one last chance.

Only he'd somehow never managed to get around to telling her just what the job in question had consisted of, and when, the first day of the Turkana Bus Tour (See Vanishing Africa!), Cora'd seen him sneaking pictures with the belt camera and found out that their dream vacation was limited to the group tours his uncle's company was interested in and included none of the luxury lodges he'd told her about when he'd sold her the idea of the trip, she'd moved out of his tent and in with the nurse.

The whole problem with their marriage, she'd told him, was that he never faced facts or really tried to change; he always just came up with half-assed gimmicks and schemes when their problems together required real commitment, hard work, genuine solutions . . . and this trip, with his ridiculous hidden camera so he could rip off the starving natives to give her a cut-rate imitation second honeymoon, was the perfect example of what was wrong with him and with their marriage, and why there was no way she'd ever get back together with him again.

The el-Molo, when he saw them two days later, weren't worth photographing. A few huts of woven palm fronds patched with random trash, some women, children, and old men, all with rotten teeth, squatting in the shade among the fish bones and empty ten-gallon U.S. government surplus food oil cans. The men were supposedly great hunters, but as befitted great hunters, they were out hunting crocodiles and hippos, and so nowhere to be seen. Joseph claimed the el-Molo were the only totally nonviolent people in this part of Kenya, but whatever that might say for their inherent morality, it did little to make them photogenic.

Randy paid his twenty shillings to the village headman—making sure Cora saw him doing so—then wandered around with his visible camera, hoping for a half-skinned crocodile or something equally picturesque, even some bare hippo bones, but couldn't come up with anything. Cora was still doing her best to pretend he didn't exist. A wasted morning.

On the way back to the campground, two khaki-clad soldiers carrying antique-looking rifles probably left over from World War I, stopped the truck. They had a rapid conversation with Joseph in Swahili, then joined him up front in the cab. Randy could hear them laughing loudly together as the truck swung away from the lakeshore out onto the dead, barren wastes of jagged volcanic rocks with only the rutted track and the occasional cairns of smoother, light-colored stones to indicate that anything living had ever been there before.

Half an hour later they joined the other truck beside two small, water-filled holes in the rock. Between a pair of low, heaped black gravel dunes Randy could glimpse Lake Turkana's potash-encrusted shore a few hundred yards away, the lake's bitter, alkaline waters glittering in the noon sun.

Joseph was explaining that the two water holes were actually medicinal springs. The first one caused diarrhea and enabled you to clean out your digestive tract; the second counteracted the effects of the first. The ground around the springs was thick with dried excrement, some of it bovine, the rest presumably human.

Romantic Africa.

Cora was standing with the nurse, laughing at something William was telling them. Probably parodying the lecture and making Joseph look like a fool—the engineer had that kind of wit.

Randy left half-way through the talk—he'd had a few problems with dysentery already and the last thing he needed was water guaranteed to cause it—and made his way down to the lakeshore, hoping for some crocodiles to photograph. The Samburu and el-Molo had scared them all away from the bay near the campground.

Something bright flapping on the other side of a fold in the terrain caught his attention. He climbed onto some rocks for a better look, found himself looking down at a skeletally-thin but powerfully-muscled African wearing bright yellow robes with some sort of black design batiked onto them.

The man was crouched over a hole he'd dug in the potash with his spear, working something free with his hands. For some reason Randy thought of the Leakeys hunting for fossils on the lake's far shore. Seven swollen-looking calabash bottles were resting on the white crust beside the man, and as Randy watched he worked the body of a huge black beetle free of the potash and put it in one of them, then went back to chipping away at the white crust with his spear-point again.

Randy realized belatedly that the medicine man or whatever he was was impossibly photogenic, and Randy hadn't been taking any pictures. He twisted his hip into position so he could use his belt camera, snapped his first picture—

The African jerked, spasmed, started to fall forward, then caught himself with his spear. He levered himself laboriously back to his feet and glared up at Randy, his lips drawn back from blunt yellow teeth in a terrifying snarl. He was older than he'd first seemed, his wrinkled face disfigured with ceremonial scars and tattoos . . . and his eyes had no white in them at all, the dilated black pupils were set in eyeballs the color of tomato juice.

Randy's fingers were still resting on the belt camera. Reflex made him snap another picture—and once again the medicine man jerked as though Randy had hit him with an electric cattle prod. He fell to his knees, tried to stand again, still clenching his spear and glaring at Randy with terrifying, inhuman malice, mouth open in a soundless scream of rage or hate.

Staring at the *camera,* as though that were what was sending him into convulsions. But it was impossible, nothing like this could really be happening, Randy had to be undergoing some sort of bizarre delusion.

Randy kept on snapping pictures with his belt camera as the man jerked and spasmed on the snowy crust. The pictures would show what was really happening, that it wasn't his fault, that whatever it was, he hadn't done it, no matter how the man was looking at him. . . .

The African was bleeding from mouth and nose now. The black design on his yellow robes was a huge batiked scorpion. As he spasmed the black scorpion jerked and twisted like the scorpion in the German's killing bottle as it lashed out again and again in the glass.

He was having an epileptic seizure. Convulsions. He needed somebody to stick a spoon between his teeth, do something to keep him from hurting himself. Randy stared frozen at him an instant longer, unable to overcome his terror and go to the man's aid, then wrenched his hand away from the camera and yelled for Joseph.

Only then did he see Cora standing on the hill behind him. She had to have followed him away from the others, had to have been standing watching him as he took picture after picture of the man's seizure without even trying to do anything to help him.

Randy turned away from her, unable to meet the accusation in her eyes. The man was still now, sprawled face-down on the gleaming white, the scorpion on his flapping robes jerking and snapping with the wind.

The older-looking soldier turned the body over with his foot, knelt beside it and checked for a pulse. He said something in Swahili.

"This man is dead," Joseph translated. "What happened?"

The dead man's features were calm, peaceful, even handsome despite his scars, with none of that terrifying malevolence Randy had seen before. He felt ashamed of himself, of the way he'd hung back when he might have been able to do something to help.

Randy told Joseph about having seen the man digging things out of the crust with his spear and hands, about how all of a sudden he'd gone into convulsions as though he'd been having an epileptic fit. He didn't mention anything about the pictures he'd taken, the way the man had stared at him as though recognizing him, blaming him for what was happening, hating him for it. None of that was real. The pictures would prove it wasn't real when he developed them, the way that picture he'd once taken of what he'd been sure had been a flying saucer had proven it to be just a hot-air balloon and made him look like a fool to everybody else at the small-town California newspaper where he'd been working that summer.

Joseph translated. The soldier peered into one of the gourds, sniffed it, dumped a number of black beetles still encrusted with potash out of it, then gave the younger soldier an order. The second soldier slung the body casually over his shoulder and started back to the trucks with it. Most of the tourists seemed in a state of shock, but neither Joseph nor the soldiers seemed particularly upset.

"But . . . who was he?" Cora asked Joseph. "What was he doing, digging there?"

Joseph shrugged. The man wasn't anyone worth worrying about. He wasn't from around there, probably not even Kenyan. Another refugee from Uganda, probably, though he wasn't a Shifta or part of any tribe Joseph was familiar with. As for what he was doing there, a lot of the local tribes used the minerals and other things they found in the Lake Turkana potash deposits in their medicines; he must've been doing something similar.

The soldier dumped the body on the floor of Randy's truck, then went back up front. Joseph and the other soldiers joined him in the cab and in a moment all three were laughing and exchanging stories again as though nothing had happened. For them, nothing had.

Randy climbed into the truck, sat down by the body, stared at it without really seeing it. The other passengers milled around outside a moment, nervous, twittering and self-conscious, then most of them crowded together into the back of the second truck. Cora and the nurse were among the half-dozen or so others who finally ended up staying on Randy's truck.

The nurse, practical for once, found a blanket and covered the body, breaking Randy's trance. He looked up. Cora was watching him again.

"Cora, it just happened, I—" But it was no use, he hadn't done anything, he didn't have anything he could apologize for, there was nothing he could do to stop the way Cora was looking at him, what she was thinking about him.

Joseph started the truck. Randy turned away from Cora, stared back over his shoulder. Everything was dead and desolate, utterly hostile.

Back at the campground he checked the belt camera: He'd taken eleven pictures of the African on a fresh roll of film; he still had twenty-five left to go.

After lunch Joseph took them down to go swimming in the bay where the Samburu launched their fishing boats. Everyone seemed determined to stay together as a group, forget that anything out of the ordinary had happened. Randy went along but decided to stay dressed and on shore, both because he needed more pictures Uncle Phillip could use and because he didn't want to risk having his camera ripped off.

There was some sort of ceremony going on, perhaps a kind of christening for the brightly-painted red and blue boat which a half-dozen young Samburu warriors were paddling frenziedly away from shore while an equal number of adolescent Samburu girls stood in a line on the shore singing and dancing. They looked for all the world like a group of Hawaiians doing a commercialized hula dance: almost the same gestures, somehow the same spirit, though as far as Randy could tell the whole thing wasn't being put on for the tourists, of whom there weren't more than twenty at the moment anyhow.

Randy found himself hesitating, told himself he was being ridiculous, and took a picture of the girls with his belt camera.

One girl stumbled and had to be grabbed by another before she fell, but that was just a coincidence, the other girls seemed to think it was funny and went right on singing and dancing, and a moment later the girl who'd faltered was back singing and dancing with them.

Randy took eight more pictures of them and some of the men when they came racing back to shore to jump fully clothed out of their boat and prance the last few yards back to dry land, all of them laughing, and nothing bad happened to any of them, so Randy knew that everything was really all right after all.

Cora and the others had stayed in and around the truck, watching, but as soon as the ceremony—if that's what it had been—was over they stripped to their swimming suits and went in. Cora had her red and black bikini on, the one she'd bought for the trip to Jamaica that hadn't worked out, and she looked as carefree and beautiful as she had when Randy'd first met her, five years ago. As though she'd forgotten all about him, didn't even care enough to be angry or unhappy around him anymore. As though he no longer existed for her.

The water was muddy, akaline, clogged with some sort of water-weed; anywhere but in a desert it would have seemed totally uninviting. Yet Randy couldn't keep himself from feeling envious of the others, as they played a sort of water-tag they'd invented, with the one who was *it* sneaking up on the others with handfuls of mud and waterweed which he or she tried to slap onto his victims' heads. The whole thing soon degenerated into a free-for-all mud fight. Randy got a picture of Cora slapping a double handful of mud triumphantly down on William's thinning hair as William, unsuspecting, surfaced too close to her, another of William catching her in the back with a huge gob of mud as she tried to wade in to shore, forcing her to swim back out and submerge herself again to get it off, before Randy realized that pictures of mud-fights were going to do him no good whatsoever with Uncle Phillip's company. Uncle Phillip wanted pictures of glamorous, romantic Africa, not mud or poverty or men dying of epilepsy.

But even so Randy used his visible camera to take pictures of the naked children as they accosted the tourists to tell them in their surprisingly precise, mission-school English that they all wanted to be doctors, if only they could raise enough money to continue their educations, though that meant Randy ended up paying some of the children a couple of shillings apiece.

"The Samburu are all rich," the old man in the raincoat had informed Randy yesterday, as they'd driven through the hovels near the campground. "Like the Masai, only the Masai are a lot richer, of course. It's just that they put their wealth in cows and *like* living in filth."

One of the children had approached the old man in the raincoat and was trying to strike up a conversation with him . . . and the old man was gesticulating furiously, almost screaming as he drove the child off. He'd said something the day before yesterday about how all Africans were incapable of dealing with machinery, how the trucks wouldn't keep on breaking down if they could just get proper British drivers. . . .

Randy got in four pictures of the old man quickly with his belt camera, half-hoping taking his pictures would have some effect on him, though of course it didn't. With a little luck he'd get a whole photographic essay, maybe even a book, out of the old geezer and his tantrums. "Colonial Britain Face to Face with the New Africa" or something like that. . . . Even if he did get it published nobody'd ever see it except other photographers; he wouldn't have to worry about his subject seeing a copy and trying to sue him.

While he'd been concentrating on the old man Cora had intercepted the child the old man had driven off and was writing something down for him on a piece of paper. Her address, probably. At her parents' house in San Jose, not the apartment she'd shared with Randy.

Randy took a perfect picture of her talking to the child with the shoulder-strap camera, the brightly-painted Samburu boat in the background. Just the kind of picture Uncle Phillip wanted.

Randy awakened from a nightmare that night to the sound of a faint, dry scrabbling somewhere near his pack, and remembered the scorpion the German had unearthed. He grabbed his flashlight, used it to check out his shoes, backpack, the sleeping bag he'd been lying on top of, the rest of the tent. Nothing. Probably the wind rustling through the palm fronds overhead.

His watch said four-ten: He'd have to get up in another twenty minutes anyway. Resigned, he groped for his towel and toothbrush and headed for the shower.

The old man was already up, meticulously disassembling his tent. He nodded a curt hello as Randy passed him.

Noon found them in the midst of the Kaisut desert, eating meat loaf sandwiches again and drinking sickeningly sweet pineapple juice while Cora and William bar-

gained with a young Ariaal Rendille girl whose hair, an
elaborate cockscomb plastered with dried red mud, pro-
claimed her a mother. They finally persuaded her to accept fifteen shillings for all the photos of her with her
camel that the group could take.

Just after the tourists, with the old man in the raincoat
in the first rank, began snapping their pictures Randy
heard the sound of a car approaching, the first vehicle
they'd encountered since leaving Lake Turkana at five-
thirty that morning.

A candy-apple red Range Rover came into view,
stopped by their trucks in a cloud of dust while the driver
asked Joseph something. There was a blonde girl sunbathing topless on the Range Rover's roof, her skin glowing red with what was soon going to be a fierce sunburn.

The tourists who'd been crowded around the Ariaal
Rendille girl and her camel turned away to photograph
the blonde girl, who seemed delighted with the attention
and preened herself on the roof. The Brighton garage
owner yelled out ''Ten shillings!'' to her.

Furious at having had her audience stolen from her,
the Ariaal Rendille girl stalked over to the Range Rover
and began yelling at the blonde girl, while the overjoyed
tourists snapped pictures of their confrontation.

Randy got a picture of the old man's face as he took
picture after picture of the two bare-breasted girls with
the camera which Randy had noticed he only took out of
its plastic sack when there were African girls to photograph, then circled around behind him and managed to
get the two girls, the Range Rover, and the old man with
his camera in a single shot using the belt camera.

Cora and William were soothing the Ariaal Rendille
girl as best they could. It was another perfect picture for
Uncle Phillip—handsome, fun-looking young couple
talking with picturesque native girl—and Randy forced
himself to photograph the two of them laughing together,
just as he'd forced himself to photograph the two of them
laughing together as they'd disassembled the tent they'd
shared the night before.

If Cora was going to humiliate him in public like that, she might as well help him pay for the trip. Especially since the pictures he was getting of her with William would be more than sufficient to prove to his family—and to an eventual divorce court—that Randy, not Cora, had been the one wronged, and that Cora deserved neither sympathy nor alimony.

That evening, after fourteen hours of uninterrupted dust and desert heat, during which they'd passed nomads on camels and piles of bleached bones and been attacked by clouds of flies the size of clothes moths, they reached a mud puddle with a broken-handled pump at its edge: their camp site.

The old man in the raincoat had been unable to take the heat, and half-way through the afternoon had finally accepted a drink from one of the water tanks. Now he was sick and furious, yelling at Joseph that he'd been promised they were all going to get luxury showers that night, that there were animal tracks and dung all around the puddle from which he'd seen the cooks drawing the water for his tea, that there'd been gasoline—he said petrol—in the can they'd all drunk from earlier . . . that things had never been like this when he'd been in Egypt and that if they'd had the sense to put a white man in charge of the safari this kind of thing would never have been allowed to happen, as he intended to make perfectly clear to the management as soon as they got back to Nairobi. . . .

Joseph listened patiently as the old man went on and on, getting redder and shriller all the time, almost jumping up and down in his rage, like a withered infant having a tantrum. He was yelling, "I'm sick, damn you, and it's all your fault!" when the heat, exertion, and emotion proved too much for him and he collapsed.

Randy had run out of film for the belt camera a few moments before and had just enough film left in his shoulder-strap camera to get a picture of the nurse trying to give the old man artificial respiration.

He ducked back into his tent, broke two yellow rolls of film out of their boxes, changed the film in the larger camera, then hesitated.

No, he wanted to be able to take more pictures of the old man unobserved as soon as he recovered. Randy was willing to bet he'd try to blame Joseph for his fainting spell. Which wouldn't work; there was no way he could blame Joseph and get away with it, but it would make for an interesting confrontation, show the old man up for what he really was one final time. Just as the picture he'd taken through the tent flap that Cora and William had been too absorbed in their lovemaking to close would show Cora up for what *she* really was.

He fumbled the belt case open, took the camera out, cracked it open with one hand while he reached for the replacement roll of film.

And froze as the yellow and black scorpion that had been curled in the compartment where the roll of film should have been emerged in one rapid, dry scuttling motion. He dropped the camera but the thing clung to his forearm with its dry, clawed legs, staring at him from tiny globular eyes the color of tomato juice.

It was almost five inches long.

Randy tried to hold himself perfectly still; any movement might be enough to make the scorpion strike. He was sweating, his arm was shaking uncontrollably; he could feel the scorpion's tiny claws digging into his flesh, its dry, almost weightless body pressed against his skin.

Outside one of the women shrieked, then began weeping while someone else tried to calm her and the others began talking to one another in loud, hysterical voices which nonetheless contained a certain amount of thinly veiled relief.

Randy had just enough time to realize how much the scorpion on his arm resembled not only the African he'd killed with his camera but also the old man who'd just now died, just enough time to think, with a last desperate grasping at rationality, how impossible it was for a five-inch arachnid to resemble a human being at all, much less two specific persons at the same time, before the long jointed tail with the sting on the end came whipping up over the scorpion's back with a crabbed movement like the old man thrashing a child with a cane and buried itself in the soft flesh of his forearm, just below the elbow, where the school nurse had always given him his tetanus shots as a child.

His arm was burning, but he clenched his jaw shut, he kept himself from making any noise whatsoever as he jerked the scorpion from his arm and crushed it with his flashlight. He didn't want Cora to know, he wanted her with William when someone else found his body.

That was all he had left: the moment when all the old men and women would be staring at her, their unspoken accusations when they realized she'd spent the night in another man's tent while her husband was dying alone and in agony.

He lay down on his sleeping bag, legs together, arms at his side, and closed his eyes, keeping the image of Cora's coming humiliation, her slumped shoulders and frustrated anger, perhaps even her too-long delayed pity, between himself and the pain as the burning spread through his arm and body, as his vision blurred and the cramps began.

THE QUIET
by George Guthridge

George Guthridge lives in Dillingham, a small fishing town in Alaska, and is a professor with the University of Alaska Fairbanks, Bristol Bay. He has thrice been nationally honored for excellence in teaching, for his work with Alaskan Eskimo high school and junior high students during the 1980s. As a writer, he has sold over fifty short stories, most of them to The Magazine of Science Fiction, Isaac Asimov's Science Fiction Magazine, Analog, *and* Galileo, *among other markets, and is co author, along with Janet Gluckman, of the novel* Child of the Light. *Several more novels are in the works, including* Child of the Dark, *with Janet Gluckman, and* Black Mandragora, *with Janet Gluckman and George Harper.*

In the hard-hitting story that follows, "The Quiet," a Nebula Award finalist in 1981, Guthridge reminds us that good intentions are never enough. *Remember what they say about them and the Road to Hell, after all—although in this case, the Road to Hell leads* up, *to the cold and isolate Moon. . . .*

Kuara, my son, the whites have stolen the moon.

Outside the window the sky is black. A blue-white disc hangs among the stars. It is Earth, says Doctor Stefanko. I wail and beat my fists. Straps bind me to a bed. Doctor Stefanko forces my shoulders down, swabs my arm. "Since you can't keep still, I'm going to have to put you under again," she says, smiling. I lie quietly.

It is not Earth. Earth is brown. Earth is Kalahari.

"You are on the moon," Doctor Stefanko says. It is the second or third time she has told me; I have awakened and slept, awakened and slept until I am not sure what voices are dream and what are real, if any. Something pricks my skin. "Rest now. You have had a long sleep."

I remember awakening the first time. The white room, white cloth covering me. Outside, blackness and the blue-white disc.

"On the moon," I say. My limbs feel heavy. My head spins. Sleep drags at my flesh. "The moon."

"Isn't it wonderful?"

"And you say my husband, Tuka—dead."

Her lips tighten. She looks at me solemnly. "He did not survive the sleep."

"The moon is hollow," I tell her. "Everyone knows that. The dead sleep there." I stare at the ceiling. "I am alive and on the moon. Tuka is dead but is not here." The words seem to float from my mouth. There are little dots on the ceiling.

"Sleep now. That's a girl. We'll talk more later."

"And Kuara. My son. Alive." The dots are spinning. I close my eyes. The dots keep spinning.

"Yes, but. . . ."

"About a hundred years ago a law was formulated to protect endangered species—animals which, unless humankind was careful, might become extinct," Doctor Stefanko says. Her face is no longer blurry. She has gray hair, drawn cheeks. I have seen her somewhere—long before I was brought to this place. I cannot remember where. The memory slips away.

Gai, wearing a breechclout, stands grinning near the window. The disc Doctor Stefanko calls Earth haloes his head. His huge, pitted tongue sticks out where his front teeth are missing. His shoulders slope like those of a hartebeest. His chest, leathery and wrinkled, is tufted with hair beginning to gray. I am not surprised to see him, after his treachery. He makes num pulse in the pit of my belly. I look away.

"Then the law was broadened to include endangered peoples. Peoples like the Gwi." Doctor Stefanko smiles maternally and presses her index finger against my nose. I toss my head. She frowns. "Obviously, it would be impossible to save entire tribes. So the founders of the law did what they thought best. They saved certain representatives. You. Your family. A few others, such as Gai. These representatives were frozen."

"Frozen?"

"Made cold."

"As during gum, when ice forms inside the ostrich-egg containers?"

"Much colder."

It was not dream, then. I remember staring through a blue, crinkled sheen. Like light seen through a snake-skin. I could not move, though my insides never stopped shivering. *So this is death,* I kept thinking.

"In the interim you were brought here to the moon. To Carnival. It is a fine place. A truly international facility; built as a testament to the harmony of nations. Here we have tried to recreate the best of what used to be." She pauses, and her eyes grow keen. "This will be your home now, U," she says.

"And Kuara?"

"He will live here with you, in time." Something in her voice makes fear touch me. Then she says, "Would you like to see him?" Some of the fear slides away.

"Is it wise, Doctor?" Gai asks. "She has a temper, this one." His eyes grin down at me. He stares at my pelvis.

"Oh, we'll manage. You'll be a good girl, won't you, U?"

My head nods. My heart does not say yes or no.

The straps leap away with a loud click. Doctor Stefanko and Gai help me to my feet. The world wobbles. The Earth-disc tilts and swings. The floor slants one way, another way. Needles tingle in my feet and hands. I am helped into a chair. More clicking. The door hisses open and the chair floats out, Doctor Stefanko leading, Gai lumbering behind. We move down one corridor after another. This is a place of angles. No curves, except the smiles of Whites as we pass. And they curve too much.

Another door hisses. We enter a room full of chill. Blue glass, the inside laced with frost, stretches from floor to ceiling along each wall. Frozen figures stand behind the glass. I remember this place. I remember how sluggish was the hate in my heart.

"Kuara is on the end," Doctor Stefanko says, her breath white.

The chair floats closer. My legs bump the glass; cold shocks my knees. The chair draws back. I lean forward. Through the glass I can see the closed eyes of my son. Ice furs his lashes and brows. His head is tilted to one side. His little arms dangle. I touch the glass in spite of the cold. I hear Gai's sharp intake of breath and he draws back my shoulders, but Doctor Stefanko puts a hand on Gai's wrist and I am released. There is give to the glass. Not like that on the trucks in the tsama patch. My num rises. My heart beats faster. Num enters my arms, floods my fingers. "Kuara," I whisper. Warmth spreads upon the glass. It makes a small, ragged circle.

"He'll be taken from here as soon as you've settled into your new home," Doctor Stefanko says.

Kuara. If only I could dance. Num would boil within me. I could kia. I would shoo away the ghosts of the cold. Awakening, you would step through the glass and into my arms.

Though we often lacked water we were not unhappy. The tsama melons supported us. It was a large patch, and by conserving we could last long periods without journeying to the waterholes. Whites and tame Bushmen had taken over the Gam and Gautscha Pans, and the people there, the Kung, either had run away or had stayed for the water and now worked the Whites' farms and ate mealie meal.

There were eleven of us, though sometimes one or two more. Gai, unmated, was one of those who came and went. Tuka would say, "You can always count us on three hands, but never on two or four hands." He would laugh, then. He was always laughing. I think he laughed because there was so little game near the Akam Pan, our home. The few duiker and steenbok that had once roamed our plain had smelled the coming of the Whites and the fleeing Kung, and had run away. Tuka laughed to fill up the empty spaces.

Sometimes, when he wasn't trapping springhare and porcupine, he helped me gather wood and tubers. We dug xwa roots and koa, the water root buried deep in the earth, until our arms ached. Sometimes we hit the na trees with sticks, making the sweet berries fall, and Tuka would chase me round and round, laughing and yelling like a madman. It was times like those when I wondered why I had once hated him so much.

I wondered much about that during kuma, a hot season when starvation stalked us. During the day I would take off my kaross, dig a shallow pit within what little shade an orogu bush offered, then urinate in the sand, cover myself with more sand and place a leaf over my head. The three of us—Tuka, Kuara, and I—lay side by side like dead people. "My heart is sad from hunger," I sang to myself all day. "Like an old man, sick and slow." I thought of the bad things, then. My parents marrying me to Tuka before I was ready because, paying bride service, he brought my mother a new kaross. Tuka doing the marrying thing to me before I was ready. Everything before I was ready! Sometimes I prayed into the leaf that a paouw would fly down and think his penis a fat caterpillar.

Then one night Tuka snared a honey badger. A badger, during kuma! Everyone was excited. Tuka said, "Yesterday, when we slept, I told the land that my U was hungry, and I must have meat for her and Kuara." The badger was very tender. Gai ate his share and went begging, though he had never brought meat to the camp. When the meat was gone we roasted ga roots and sang and danced while Tuka played the gwashi. I danced proudly. Not for Tuka but for myself. Num uncurled from the pit of my belly and came boiling up my spine. I was afraid, because when num reaches my skull I kia. Then I see ghosts killing people, and I smell the rotting smell of death, like decaying carcasses.

Tuka took my head in his hands. "You must not kia," he said. "Not now. Your body will suffer too much for the visions." For other people, kia brings healing—of self, of others; for me it only brings pain.

Tuka held me beside the fire and stroked me, and num subsided. "When I lie in the sand during the day, I dream I have climbed the footpegs in a great baobab tree," he said. "I look out from the treetop, and the land is agraze with animals. Giraffe and wildebeest and kudu. 'You must kill these beasts and bring them to U and Kuara before the Whites kill them,' my dream says."

Then he asked, "What do you think of when you lie there, U?"

I did not answer. I was afraid to tell him; I did not want him to feel angry or sad after his joy from catching the honey badger. He smiled. His eyes, moist, shone with firelight. Perhaps he thought num had stopped my tongue.

The next day the quiet came. Lying beneath the sand, I felt num pulse in my belly. I fought the fear it always brought. I did not cry out to Tuka. The pulsing increased. I began to tremble. Sweat ran down my face. Num boiled within me. It entered my spine and pushed toward my throat. My eyes were wide and I kept staring at the veins of the leaf but seeing dread. I felt myself going rigid and shivering at the same time. My head throbbed; it was as large as a ga root. I could hear my mouth make sputtery noises, like Kuara used to at my breast. The pressure inside me kept building, building.

And suddenly was gone. It burrowed into the earth, taking my daydreams with it. I went down and down into the sand. I passed ubbee roots and animals long dead, their bones bleached and forgotten. I came to a waterhole far beneath the ground. Tuka was in the water. Kuara was too. He looked younger, barely old enough to toddle. Tuka, smiling, looked handsome. *He is not a bad person,* I told myself; *he just wants his way too much. But he has brought meat to our people, I cannot forget that. And some day perhaps he will bring me a new kaross. Perhaps he will bring many things. Important things.*

I took off my kaross, and the three of us held hands and danced, naked, splashing. There was no num to seize me. No marrying-thing urge to seize Tuka. Only quiet, and laughter.

"This will be your new home, U," Doctor Stefanko says as she opens a door. She has given me a new kaross; of *genuine* gemsbok, she tells me, though I am uncertain why she speaks of it that way. When she puts her hand on my back and pushes me forward, the kaross feels soft and smooth against my skin. "We think you'll like it, and if there's anything you need. . . ."

I grab the sides of the door and turn my face away. I will not live in nor even look at the place. But her push becomes firmer, and I stumble inside. I cover my face with my hands.

"There, now," Doctor Stefanko says. I spy through my fingers.

We are in Kalahari.

I turn slowly, for suddenly my heart is shining and singing. No door. No walls. No angles. The sandveld spreads out beneath a cloudless sky. Endless pale-gold grass surrounds scattered white-thorn and tsi; in the distance lift several flat-topped acacias and even a mongongo tree. A dassie darts in and out of a rocky kranze.

"Here might be a good place for your tshushi—your shelter," Doctor Stefanko says, pulling me forward. She enters the tall grass, bends, comes up smiling; holding branches in one hand, gui fibers in the other. "You see? We've even cut some of the materials you'll need."

"But how—"

"The moon isn't such a horrible place, now is it."

She strides back through the grass. "And we here at Carnival are dedicated to making your stay as pleasant as possible. Just look here." She moves a rock. A row of buttons gleams. "Turn this knob, and you can control your weather; no more suffering through those terrible hot and cold seasons. Unless you want to, of course," she adds quickly. "And from time to time some nice people will be looking down . . . in on you. From up there, within the sky." She makes a sweep of her arm. "They want to watch how you live; you—and others like you—are quite a sensation, you know." I stare at her without understanding. "Anyway, if you want to see them, just turn this knob. And if you want to hear what the monitor's saying about you, turn this one." She looks up, sees my confusion. "Oh, don't worry; the monitor translates everything. It's a wonderful device."

Standing, she takes hold of my arms. Her eyes almost seem warm. "You see, U, there is no more Kalahari on Earth—not as you knew it anyhow—so we created another. In some ways it won't be as good as what you were used to, in a lot of ways it'll be better." Her smile comes back. "We think you'll like it."

"And Kuara?"

"He's waking now. He'll join you soon." She takes hold of my hands. "Soon." Then she walks back in the direction we came, quickly fading in the distance. Suddenly she is gone. A veil of heat shimmers above the grass where the door seemed to have been. For a moment I think of following. Finally I shrug. I work at building my tshushi. I work slowly, methodically, my head full of thoughts. I think of Kuara, and something gnaws at me. I drop the fiber I am holding and begin walking toward the opposite horizon, where a giraffe is eating from the mongongo tree.

Grasshoppers, kxon ants, dung beetles hop and crawl among the grasses. Leguaan scuttle. A mole snake slithers for a hole beneath a uri bush. I walk quickly, the sand warm but not hot beneath my feet. The plain is sundrenched, the few small omirimbi water courses parched and cracked, yet I feel little thirst. A steenbok leaps for cover behind a white-thorn. This is a good place, part of me decides. Here will Kuara become the hunter Tuka could not be. Kuara will never laugh to shut out sadness.

The horizon draws no closer.

I measure the giraffe with my thumb, walk a thousand paces, remeasure, walk another thousand paces, remeasure.

The giraffe does not change size.

I will walk another thousand. Then I will turn back and finish the tshushi.

A hundred paces further I bump something hard.

A wall.

Beyond, the giraffe continues feeding.

The Whites with the Land Rovers came during ga, the hottest season. The trucks bucked and roared across the sand. Tuka took Kuara and hurried to meet them. I went too, though I walked behind with the other women. There were several white men and some Bantu. Gai was standing in the lead truck, waving and grinning.

A white, blond-haired woman climbed out. She was wearing white shorts and a light brown shirt with rolled up sleeves. I recognized her immediately. Doctor Morse, come to study us again. Tuka had said the Whites did not wonder about their own culture, so they liked to study ours.

She talked to us women a long time, asking about our families and how we felt about SWAPO, the People's Army. Everyone spoke at once. She kept waving her hands for quiet. "What do you think, U?" she would ask. "What's your opinion?" I said she should ask Tuka; he was a man and understood such things. Doctor frowned, so I said SWAPO should not kill people. SWAPO should leave people alone. Doctor Morse wrote in her notebook as I talked. I was pleased. The other women were very jealous.

Doctor Morse told us the war in South Africa was going badly; soon it would sweep this way. When Tuka finished looked at the engines I asked him what Doctor Morse meant by "badly." Badly for Blacks, or Whites. Badly for those in the south, or those of us in the Kalahari. He did not know. None of us asked Doctor Morse.

Then she said, "We have brought water. Lots of water. We've heard you've been without." Her hair caught the sunlight. She was very beautiful for a white woman.

We smiled but refused her offer. She frowned but did not seem angry. Maybe she thought it was because she was white. If so, she was wrong; accept gifts, and we might forget the ones Kalahari gives us. "Well, at least go for a ride in the trucks." she said, beaming. Tuka laughed and, taking Kuara by the hand, scrambled for the two Land Rovers. I shook my head. "You really should go," Doctor Morse said. "It'll be good for you."

"That is something for men to do," I told her. "Women do not understand those things."

"All they're going to do is ride in the back!"

"Trucks. Hunting. Fire. Those are men's things," I said.

Only one of the trucks came back. Everyone but Tuka, Kuara, and some of the Bantu returned. "The truck's stuck in the sand; the Whites decided to wait until dawn to pull it out," Gai said. "Tuka said he'd sleep beside it. You know how he is about trucks!" Everyone laughed. Except me. An empty space throbbed in my heart; that I wanted him home angered me.

Then rain came. It was ga go—male rain. It poured down strong and sudden, not even and gentle, the female rain that fills the land with water. Rain, during ga! Everyone shouted and danced for joy. Even the Whites danced. A miracle! people said. I thought about the honey badger caught during kuma, and was afraid. I felt alone. In spite of my fear, perhaps because of it, I did a foolish thing. I slept away from the others.

In the night the quiet again touched me. Num uncurled in my belly. I did not beckon it forth. I swear I didn't. I wasn't even thinking about it. As I slept I felt my body

clench tight. In my dreams I could hear my breathing—
shallow and rapid. Fear seized me and shook me like the
twig of a ni ni bush. I sank into the earth. Tuka and
Kuara were standing slump-shouldered in steaming,
ankle-deep water at the waterhole where we had danced.
Kuara was wearing the head of a wildebeest; the eyes
had been carved out and replaced with smoldering coals.
"Run away, mother," he kept saying.

I awoke to shadows. A fleeting darkness came upon
me before I could move. I glimpsed Gai grinning beneath
the moon. Then a hand was clapped over my mouth.

Doctor Stefanko returns after I've finished the hut. She
and Gai bring warthog and kudi hides, porcupine quills,
tortoise shells, ostrich eggs, a sharpening stone, an awl,
two assagai blades, pots of Bantu clay. Many things. Gai
grins as he sets them down. Doctor Stefanko watches
him. "Back on Earth, he might not have remained a
bachelor if your people hadn't kept thinking of him as
one," she tells me as he walks away. Then she also
leaves.

Later, she brings Kuara.

He comes sprinting, gangly, the grass nearly to his
chin. "Mama," he shouts, "mama, mama," and I take
him in my arms, whirling and laughing. I put my hands
upon his cheeks; his arms are around my waist. Real.
Oh, yes. So very real, my Kuara! Tears roll down my
face. He looks hollow-eyed, and his hair has been shaved.
But I do not let concern stop my heart. I weep from joy,
not pain.

Doctor Stefanko leaves, and Kuara and I talk. He bab-
bles about a strange sleep, and Doctor Stefanko, and Gai,
as I show him the camp. We play with the knobs Doctor
Stefanko showed me; one of them makes a line of small
windows blink on in the slight angle between wall-sky
and ceiling-sky. The windows look like square beads.
There, faces pause and peer. Children. Old men. Women
with smiles like springhares. People of many races. I tell
him not to smile or acknowledge their presence. Not even

that of the children. Especially not the children. The faces
are surely ghosts, I warn. Ghosts dreaming of becoming
Gwi.

We listen to the voice Doctor Stefanko calls the monitor. It is singsong, lulling. A woman's voice, I think.
"U and Kuara, the latest additions to Carnival, members
of the last Gwi tribal group, will soon become accustomed to our excellent accommodations," the voice says.
The voice floats with us as we go to gather roots and
wood.

A leguaan pokes its head from the rocky kranze, listening. Silently I put down my wood. Then my hand
moves slowly. So slowly it is almost not movement. I
grab. Caught! Kuara shrieks and claps his hands. "Notice the scarification across the cheeks and upper legs,"
the voice is saying. "The same is true of the buttocks,
though like any self-respecting Gwi, U will not remove
her kaross in the presence of others except during the
Eland Dance." I carry the leguaan wiggling to the hut.
"Were she to disrobe, you would notice tremendous fatty
deposits in the buttocks, a phenomenon known as steat-
opygia. Unique to Bushmen (or 'Bushwomen,' we should
say), this anatomical feature aids in food storage. It was
once believed that. . . ."

After breaking the leguaan's neck, I take off the kaross
of genuine gemsbok and, using gui fiber, tie it in front
of my hut. It makes a wonderful door. I have never had
a door. Tuka and I slept outside, using the tshushi for
storage. Kuara will have a door. A door between him
and the watchers.

He will have fire. Fire for warmth and food and U to
sing beside. I gather kane and ore sticks and carve male
and female, then use galli grass for tinder. Like Tuka
did. "The Gwi are marked by a low, flattened skull, tiny
mastoid processes, a bulging or vertical forehead, pep-
percorn hair, a nonpragnathous face. . . . " I twirl the
sticks between my palms. It seems to take forever. My
arms grow sore. I am ready to give up when smoke suddenly curls. Gibbering, Kuara leaps about the camp. I

gaze at the fire and grin with delight. But it is frightened delight. I will make warmth fires and food fires, I decide as I blow the smoke into flame. Not ritual fires. Not without Tuka.

I roast the leguaan with eru berries and the tsha-cucumber, which seems plentiful. But I am not Tuka, quick with fire and laughter; the fire-making has taken too long. Halfway through the cooking, Kuara seizes the lizard and, bouncing it in his hands as though it were hot dough, tears it apart. "Kuara!" I blurt out in pretended anger. He giggles as, the intestines dangling, he holds up the lizard to eat. I smile sadly. Kuara's laughing eyes and ostrich legs . . . so much like Tuka!

"The Gwi sing no praises of battles or warriors," the voice sing-says. I help Kuara finish the leguaan. "They have no history of warfare; ironically, it was last century's South African War, in which the Gwi did not take part, that assured their extinction. Petty arguments are common (even a nonviolent society cannot keep husbands and wives from scrapping), but fighting is considered dishonorable. To fight is to have failed to. . . ." When I gaze up there are no faces in the windows.

At last, dusk dapples the grass. Kuara finds a guinea-fowl feather and a reed; leaning against my legs, he busies himself making a zani. The temperature begins to drop. I decide the door would fit better around our shoulders than across the tshushi.

A figure strides out of the setting sun. I shield my eyes with my arm. Doctor Stefanko. She smiles and nods at Kuara, now tying a nut onto his toy for a weight, and sits on a log. Her smile remains, though it is drained of joy. She looks at me seriously.

"I do hope Kuara's presence will dissuade you from any more *displays* such as you exhibited this afternoon," she tells me. "Surely you must realize that he is here with you on a . . . a trial basis, shall we say. If you create problems, we'll have to take the boy back to the prep rooms until . . . until you become more accustomed to your surroundings." She taps her forefinger against her palm. "This impetuousness of yours has got to cease." Another tap. "And cease now."

Head cocked, I gaze at her, not understanding.

"Taking off your kaross simply because the monitor said you do not." She nods knowingly. "Oh, yes, we're aware when you're listening. And that frightful display with the lizard!" She makes a face and appears to shudder. "Then there's the matter of the fire." She points toward the embers. "You're supposed to be living here like you did back on Earth. At least during the day. Men *always* started the fires."

"Men were always present." I shrug.

"Yes. Well, arrangements are being made. For the time being stick to foods you don't need to cook. And use the heating system." She goes to the rock and, on hands and knees, turns one of the knobs. A humming sounds. Smiling and rubbing her hands over the fire, she reseats herself on the log, pulls a photograph from her hip pocket and hands it to me. I turn the picture right-side-up. Doctor Morse is standing with her arm across Gai's shoulders. His left arm is around her waist. The Land Rovers are in the background.

"Impetuous," Doctor Stefanko says, leaning over and clicking her fingernail against the photograph. "That's exactly what Doctor Morse wrote about you in her notebooks. *She* considered it a virtue." Again the eyebrow lifts. "We do not." Then she adds proudly, "She was my grandmother, you know. As you can imagine, I have more than simply a professional interest in our Southwest African section here at Carnival."

I start to hand back the photograph. She raises her hand, halting me. "Keep it," she says. "Think of it as a wedding present. The first of many."

That night, wrapped in the kaross, Kuara and I sleep in one another's arms, in the tshushi. He is still clutching the zani, though he has not thrown it once into the air to watch it spin down. Perhaps he will tomorrow. Tomorrow. An ugly word. I lie staring at the dark ground, sand clenched in my fists. I wonder if, somehow using devices to see in the dark, the ghosts in the sky-windows are watching me sleep. I wonder if they will watch the night Gai climbs upon my back and grunts throughout the marrying-thing.

Sleep comes. A tortured sleep. I can feel myself hugging Kuara. He squirms against the embrace but does not awaken. In my dreams I slide out of myself and, stirring up the fire, dance the Eland Dance. My body is slick with eland fat. My eyes stare rigidly into the darkness and my head is held high and stiff. Chanting, I lift and put down my feet, moving around and around the fire. Other women clap and sing the kia-healing songs. Men play the gwashi and musical bows. The music lifts and lilts and throbs. Rhythm thrums within me. Each muscle knows the song. Tears squeeze from my eyes. Pain leadens my legs. And still I dance.

Then, at last, num rises. It uncurls in my belly and breaths fire-breath up my spine. I fight the fear. I dance against the dread. I tremble with fire. My eyes slit with agony. I do not watch the women clapping and singing. My breaths come in shallow, heated gasps. My breasts bounce. I dance. Num continues to rise. It tingles against the base of my brain. It fills my head. My entire body is alive, burning. Thorns are sticking everywhere in my flesh. My breasts are fiery coals. I can feel ghosts, hot ghosts, ghosts of the past, crowding into my skull. I stagger for the hut; Kuara and U, my old self, await me. I slide into her flesh like someone slipping beneath the cool, mud-slicked waters of a year-round pan. I slide in among her fear and sorrow and the anguished joy of Kuara beside her.

She stirs. A movement of a sleeping head. A small groan; denial. I slide in further. I become her once again. My head is aflame with num and ghosts. "U," I whisper, "I bring the ghosts of all your former selves, and of your people." Again she groans, though weaker; the pleasure-groan of a woman making love. Her body stretches, stiffens. Her nails rake Kuara's back. She accepts me, then; accepts her self. I fill her flesh.

And bring the quiet, for the third time in her life. Down and down into the sand she seeps, leaving nothing of her self behind, her hands around Kuara's wrists as she pulls him after her, the zani's guinea-fowl feather whipping behind him as if in a wind. She passes through sand, Carnival's concrete base, moonrock, moving ever downward, badger-burrowing. She breaks through into a darkness streaked with silver light; into the core of the moon, where live the ancestral dead, the ghosts of kia. She tumbles downward, crying her dismay and joy, her kaross fluttering. In the center of the hollow, where water shines like cold silver, awaits, Tuka, arms outstretched. He is laughing—a shrill, forced cackle. Such is the only laughter a ghost can know whose sleep has been disturbed. They will dance this night, the three of them: U, Tuka, Kuara.

Then he will teach her the secret of oa, the poison squeezed from the female larvae of the dung beetle. Poison for arrows he will teach her to make. Poison for which Bushmen know no antidote.

She will hunt when she returns to Gai and to Doctor Stefanko.

She will not hunt animals.

DINNER IN AUDOGHAST
by Bruce Sterling

One of the most powerful and innovative new talents to enter SF in recent years, Bruce Sterling sold his first story in 1976, and has since sold stories to Omni, Isaac Asimov's Science Fiction Magazine, The Magazine of Fantasy and Science Fiction, Interzone, Universe, New Dimensions, *and elsewhere. His books include the novels* The Artificial Kid, Involution Ocean, Schismatrix *(a novel which, along with William Gibson's* Neuromancer, *can be regarded as one of the foremost achievements in the Cyberpunk cannon), the critically acclaimed novel* Islands in the Net, *and, as editor,* Mirrorshades: the Cyberpunk Anthology. *He has recently become one of the regular science columnists for* The Magazine of Fantasy and Science Fiction, *and is at work on a nonfiction book about the underground world of outlaw computer hackers. His most recent books are the landmark collection* Crystal Express, *and a new novel,* The Difference Engine, *in collaboration with William Gibson. He lives with his family in Austin, Texas.*

Sterling's work is always vivid and imaginatively supple, often told from unexpected perspectives, and often capable of throwing new light even on subjects and situations we thought *we knew well. This time, he takes us to Africa's remote and ancient past, at a time when the seeds of future Africas yet to come were being planted, and, in a cautionary tale with some disquieting implications for our* own *times, reminds us that while prophets may indeed be without honor in their own countries, they remain, after all,* prophets. . . .

Then one arrives at Audoghast, a large and very populous city built in a sandy plain. . . . The inhabitants live in ease and possess great riches. The market is always crowded; the mob is so huge and the chattering so loud that you can scarcely hear your own words. . . . The city contains beautiful buildings and very elegant homes.
—DESCRIPTION OF NORTHERN AFRICA,
ABU UBAYD AL-BAKRI (A.D. 1040–94)

Delightful Audoghast! Renowned through the civilized world, from Cordova to Baghdad, the city spread in splendor beneath a twilit Saharan sky. The setting sun threw pink and amber across adobe domes, masonry mansions, tall, mud-brick mosques, and open plazas thick with bristling date-palms. The melodious calls of market vendors mixed with the remote and amiable chuckling of Saharan hyenas.

Four gentlemen sat on carpets in a tiled and white-washed portico, sipping coffee in the evening breeze. The host was the genial and accomplished slave-dealer, Manimenesh. His three guests were Ibn Watunan, the caravan-master; Khayali, the poet and musician; and Bagayoko, a physician and court assassin.

The home of Manimenesh stood upon the hillside in the aristocratic quarter, where it gazed down on an open marketplace and the mud-brick homes of the lowly. The prevailing breeze swept away the city reek, and brought from within the mansion the palate-sharpening aromas of lamb in tarragon and roast partridge in lemons and egg-plant. The four men lounged comfortably around a low inlaid table, sipping spiced coffee from Chinese cups and watching the ebb and flow of market life.

The scene below them encouraged a lofty philosophical detachment. Manimenesh, who owned no less than fifteen books, was a well-known patron of learning. Jewels gleamed on his dark, plump hands, which lay cozily folded over his paunch. He wore a long tunic of crushed red velvet, and a gold-threaded skullcap.

Khayali, the young poet, had studied architecture and

verse in the schools of Timbuktu. He lived in the household of Manimenesh as his poet and praisemaker, and his sonnets, ghazals, and odes were recited throughout the city. He propped one elbow against the full belly of his two-string *guimbri* guitar, of inlaid ebony, strung with leopard gut.

Ibn Watunan had an eagle's hooded gaze and hands callused by camel-reins. He wore an indigo turban and a long striped djellaba. In thirty years as a sailor and caravaneer, he had bought and sold Zanzibar ivory, Sumatran pepper, Ferghana silk, and Cordovan leather. Now a taste for refined gold had brought him to Audoghast, for Audoghast's African bullion was known throughout Islam as the standard of quality.

Doctor Bagayoko's ebony skin was ridged with an initiate's scars, and his long clay-smeared hair was festooned with knobs of chiseled bone. He wore a tunic of white Egyptian cotton, hung with gris-gris necklaces, and his baggy sleeves bulged with herbs and charms. He was a native Audoghastian of the animist persuasion, the personal physician of the city's Prince.

Bagayoko's skill with powders, potions, and unguents made him an intimate of Death. He often undertook diplomatic missions to the neighboring Empire of Ghana. During his last visit there, the anti-Audoghast faction had mysteriously suffered a lethal outbreak of pox.

Between the four men was the air of camaraderie common to gentlemen and scholars.

They finished the coffee, and a slave took the empty pot away. A second slave, a girl from the kitchen staff, arrived with a wicker tray loaded with olives, goat-cheese, and hard-boiled eggs sprinkled with vermilion. At that moment, a muezzin yodeled the evening call to prayer.

"Ah," said Ibn Watunan, hesitating. "Just as we were getting started."

"Never mind," said Manimenesh, helping himself to a handful of olives. "We'll pray twice next time."

"Why was there no noon prayer today?" said Watunan.

"Our muezzin forgot," the poet said.

Watunan lifted his shaggy brows. "That seems rather lax."

Doctor Bagayoko said, "This is a new muezzin. The last was more punctual, but, well, he fell ill." Bagayoko smiled urbanely and nibbled his cheese.

"We Audoghastians like our new muezzin better," said the poet, Khayali. "He's one of our own, not like that other fellow, who was from Fez. *Our* muezzin is sleeping with a Christian's wife. It's very entertaining."

"You have Christians here?" Watunan said.

"A clan of Ethiopian Copts," said Manimenesh. "And a couple of Nestorians."

"Oh," said Watunan, relaxing. "For a moment I thought you meant real *feringhee* Christians, from Europe."

"From where?" Manimenesh was puzzled.

"Very far away," said Ibn Watunan, smiling. "Ugly little countries, with no profit."

"There were empires in Europe once," said Khayali knowledgeably. "The Empire of Rome was almost as big as the modern civilized world."

Watunan nodded. "I have seen the New Rome, called Byzantium. They have armored horsemen, like your neighbors in Ghana. Savage fighters."

Bagayoko nodded, salting an egg. "Christians eat children."

Watunan smiled. "I can assure you that the Byzantines do no such thing."

"Really?" said Bagayoko. "Well, our Christians do."

"That's just the doctor's little joke," said Manimenesh. "Sometimes strange rumors spread about us, because we raid our slaves from the Nyam-Nyam cannibal tribes on the coast. But we watch their diet closely, I assure you."

Watunan smiled uncomfortably. "There is always

something new out of Africa. One hears the oddest stories. Hairy men, for instance.''

''Ah,'' said Manimenesh. ''You mean gorillas, from the jungles to the south. I'm sorry to spoil the story for you, but they are nothing better than beasts.''

''I see,'' said Watunan. ''That's a pity.''

''My grandfather owned a gorilla once,'' Manimenesh said. ''Even after ten years, it could barely speak Arabic.''

They finished the appetizers. Slaves cleared the table and brought in a platter of fattened partridges, stuffed with lemons and eggplants, on a bed of mint and lettuce. The four diners leaned in closer and dexterously ripped off legs and wings.

Watunan sucked meat from a drumstick and belched politely. ''Audoghast is famous for its cooks,'' he said. ''I'm pleased to see that this legend, at least, is confirmed.''

''We Audoghastians pride ourselves on the pleasures of table and bed,'' said Manimenesh, pleased. ''I have asked Elfelilet, one of our premiere courtesans, to honor us with a visit tonight. She will bring her troupe of dancers.''

Watunan smiled. ''That would be splendid. One tires of boys on the trail. Your women are remarkable. I've noticed that they go without the veil.''

Khayali lifted his voice in song. ''When a woman of Audoghast appears / The girls of Fez bite their lips, / The dames of Tripoli hide in closets, / And Ghana's women hang themselves.''

''We take pride in the exalted status of our women,'' said Manimenesh. ''It's not for nothing that they command a premium market price!''

In the marketplace, downhill, vendors lit tiny oil lamps, which cast a flickering glow across the walls of tents and the watering troughs. A troop of the Prince's men, with iron spears, shields, and chain mail, marched across the plaza to take the night watch at the Eastern

Gate. Slaves with heavy water-jars gossiped beside the well.

"There's quite a crowd around one of the stalls," said Bagayoko.

"So I see," said Watunan. "What is it? Some news that might affect the market?"

Bagayoko sopped up gravy with a wad of mint and lettuce. "Rumor says there's a new fortune-teller in town. New prophets always go through a vogue."

"Ah yes," said Khayali, sitting up. "They call him 'the Sufferer.' He is said to tell the most outlandish and entertaining fortunes."

"I wouldn't trust any fortune-teller's market tips," said Manimenesh. "If you want to know the market, you have to know the hearts of the people, and for that you need a good poet."

Khayali bowed his head. "Sir," he said, "live forever."

It was growing dark. Household slaves arrived with pottery lamps of sesame oil, which they hung from the rafters of the portico. Others took the bones of the partridges and brought in a haunch and head of lamb with a side dish of cinnamon tripes.

As a gesture of esteem, the host offered Watunan the eyeballs, and after three ritual refusals the caravan-master dug in with relish. "I put great stock in fortune-tellers, myself," he said, munching. "They are often privy to strange secrets. Not the occult kind, but the blabbing of the superstitious. Slave girls anxious about some household scandal, or minor officials worried over promotions—inside news from those who consult them. It can be useful."

"If that's the case," said Manimenesh, "perhaps we should call him up here."

"They say he is grotesquely ugly," said Khayali. "He is called 'the Sufferer' because he is outlandishly afflicted by the disease."

Bagayoko wiped his chin elegantly on his sleeve. "Now you begin to interest me!"

"It's settled, then." Manimenesh clapped his hands. "Bring young Sidi, my errand-runner!"

Sidi arrived at once, dusting flour from his hands. He was the cook's teenage son, a tall young black in a dyed woolen djellaba. His cheeks were stylishly scarred, and he had bits of brass wire interwoven with his dense black locks. Manimenesh gave him his orders; Sidi leapt from the portico, ran downhill through the garden, and vanished through the gates.

The slave-dealer sighed. "This is one of the problems of my business. When I bought my cook she was a slim and lithesome wench, and I enjoyed her freely. Now years of dedication to her craft have increased her market value by twenty times, and also made her as fat as a hippopotamus, though that is beside the point. She has always claimed that Sidi is my child, and since I don't wish to sell her, I must make allowance. I have made him a freeman; I have spoiled him, I'm afraid. On my death, my legitimate sons will deal with him cruelly."

The caravan-master, having caught the implications of this speech, smiled politely. "Can he ride? Can he bargain? Can he do sums?"

"Oh," said Manimenesh with false nonchalance, "he can manage that newfangled stuff with the zeroes well enough."

"You know I am bound for China," said Watunan. "It is a hard road that brings either riches or death."

"He runs the risk in any case," the slave-dealer said philosophically. "The riches are Allah's decision."

"This is truth," said the caravan-master. He made a secret gesture, beneath the table, where the others could not see. His host returned it, and Sidi was proposed, and accepted, for the Brotherhood.

With the night's business over, Manimenesh relaxed, and broke open the lamb's steamed skull with a silver mallet. They spooned out the brains, then attacked the tripes, which were stuffed with onion, cabbage, cinnamon, roe, coriander, cloves, ginger, pepper, and lightly dusted with ambergris. They ran out of mustard dip and

called for more, eating a bit more slowly now, for they
were approaching the limit of human capacity.

They then sat back, pushing away platters of congeal-
ing grease, and enjoying a profound satisfaction with the
state of the world. Down in the marketplace, bats from
an abandoned mosque chased moths around the vendors'
lanterns.

The poet belched suavely and picked up his two-
stringed guitar. "Dear God," he said, "this is a splendid
place. See, caravan-master, how the stars smile down on
our beloved Southwest." He drew a singing note from
the leopard-gut strings. "I feel at one with Eternity."

Watunan smiled. "When I find a man like that, I have
to bury him."

"There speaks the man of business," the doctor said.
He unobtrusively dusted a tiny pinch of venom on the
last chunk of tripe, and ate it. He accustomed himself to
poison. It was a professional precaution.

From the street beyond the wall, they heard the approaching jingle of brass rings. The guard at the gate
called out. "The Lady Elfelilet and her escorts, lord!"

"Make them welcome," said Manimenesh. Slaves
took the platters away, and brought a velvet couch onto
the spacious portico. The diners extended their hands;
slaves scrubbed and toweled them clean.

Elfelilet's party came forward through the fig-clustered
garden: two escorts with gold-topped staffs heavy with
jingling brass rings; three dancing-girls, apprentice courtesans in blue woolen cloaks over gauzy cotton trousers
and embroidered blouses; and four palanquin bearers,
beefy male slaves with oiled torsos and callused shoulders. The bearers set the palanquin down with stifled
grunts of relief and opened the cloth-of-gold hangings.

Elfelilet emerged, a tawny-skinned woman, her eyes
dusted in kohl and collyrium, her hennaed hair threaded
with gold wire. Her palms and nails were stained pink;
she wore an embroidered blue cloak over an intricate
sleeveless vest and ankle-tied silk trousers starched and
polished with myrobalan lacquer. A light freckling of

smallpox scars along one cheek delightfully accented her broad, moonlike face.

"Elfelilet, my dear," said Manimenesh, "you are just in time for dessert."

Elfelilet stepped gracefully across the tiled floor and reclined face-first along the velvet couch, where the well-known loveliness of her posterior could be displayed to its best advantage. "I thank my friend and patron, the noble Manimenesh. Live forever! Learned Doctor Bagayoko, I am your servant. Hello, poet."

"Hello, darling," said Khayali, smiling with the natural camaraderie of poets and courtesans. "You are the moon, and your troupe of lovelies are comets across our vision."

The host said, "This is our esteemed guest, the caravan-master, Abu Bekr Ahmed Ibn Watunan."

Watunan, who had been gaping in enraptured amazement, came to himself with a start. "I am a simple desert man," he said. "I haven't a poet's gift of words. But I am your ladyship's servant."

Elfelilet smiled and tossed her head; her distended earlobes clattered with heavy chunks of gold filigree. "Welcome to Audoghast."

Dessert arrived. "Well," said Manimenesh. "Our earlier dishes were rough and simple fare, but this is where we shine. Let me tempt you with these *djouzinkat* nutcakes. And do sample our honey macaroons—I believe there's enough for everyone."

Everyone, except of course for the slaves, enjoyed the light and flaky *cataif* macaroons, liberally dusted with Kairwan sugar. The nutcakes were simply beyond compare; painstakingly milled from hand-watered wheat, lovingly buttered and sugared, and artistically studded with raisins, dates, and almonds.

"We eat *djouzinkat* nutcakes during droughts," the poet said, "because the angels weep with envy when we taste them."

Manimenesh belched heroically and readjusted his skullcap. "Now," he said, "we will enjoy a little bit of

grape wine. Just a small tot, mind you, so that the sin of
drinking is a minor one, and we can do penance with the
minimum of alms. After that, our friend the poet will
recite an ode he has composed for the occasion."

Khayali began to tune his two-string guitar. "I will
also, on demand, extemporize twelve-line *ghazals* in the
lyric mode, upon suggested topics."

"And after our digestion has been soothed with epi-
grams," said their host, "we will enjoy the justly famed
dancing of her ladyship's troupe. After that we will retire
within the mansion and enjoy their other, equally lauded,
skills."

The gate-guard shouted, "Your errand-runner, Lord!
He awaits your pleasure, with the fortune-teller!"

"Ah," said Manimenesh. "I had forgotten."

"No matter, sir," said Watunan, whose imagination
had been fired by the night's agenda.

Bagayoko spoke up. "Let's have a look at him. His
ugliness, by contrast, will heighten the beauty of these
women."

"Which would otherwise be impossible," said the
poet.

"Very well," said Manimenesh. "Bring him forward."

Sidi, the errand boy, came through the garden, followed with ghastly slowness by the crutch-wielding
fortune-teller.

The man inched into the lamplight like a crippled in-
sect. His voluminous dust-gray cloak was stained with
sweat, and nameless exudations. He was an albino. His
pink eyes were shrouded with cataracts, and he had lost
a foot, and several fingers, to leprosy. One shoulder was
much lower than the other, suggesting a hunchback, and
the stub of his shin was scarred by the gnawing of canal-
worms.

"Prophet's beard!" said the poet. "He is truly of sur-
passing ghastliness."

Elfelilet wrinkled her nose. "He reeks of pestilence!"

Sidi spoke up. "We came as fast as we could, Lord!"

"Go inside, boy," said Manimenesh; "soak ten sticks of cinnamon in a bucket of water, then come back and throw it over him."

Sidi left at once.

Watunan stared at the hideous man, who stood, quivering on one leg, at the edge of the light. "How is it, man, that you still live?"

"I have turned my sight from this world," said the Sufferer. "I turned my sight to God, and He poured knowledge copiously upon me. I have inherited a knowledge which no mortal body can support."

"But God is merciful," said Watunan. "How can you claim this to be His doing?"

"If you do not fear God," said the fortune-teller, "fear Him after seeing me." The hideous albino lowered himself, with arthritic, aching slowness, to the dirt outside the portico. He spoke again. "You are right, caravan-master, to think that death would be a mercy to me. But death comes in its own time, as it will to all of you."

Manimenesh cleared his throat. "Can you see our destinies, then?"

"I see the world," said the Sufferer. "To see the fate of one man is to follow a single ant in a hill."

Sidi reemerged and poured the scented water over the cripple. The fortune-teller cupped his maimed hands and drank. "Thank you, boy," he said. He turned his clouded eyes on the youth. "Your children will be yellow."

Sidi laughed, startled. "Yellow? Why?"

"Your wives will be yellow."

The dancing-girls, who had moved to the far side of the table, giggled in unison. Bagayoko pulled a gold coin from within his sleeve. "I will give you this gold dirham if you will show me your body."

Elfelilet frowned prettily and blinked her kohl-smeared lashes. "Oh, learned Doctor, please spare us."

"You will see my body, sir, if you have patience," said the Sufferer. "As yet, the people of Audoghast laugh at my prophecies. I am doomed to tell the truth, which is harsh and cruel, and therefore absurd. As my fame grows, however, it will reach the ears of your Prince, who will then order you to remove me as a threat to public order. You will then sprinkle your favorite poison, powdered asp venom, into a bowl of chickpea soup I will receive from a customer. I bear you no grudge for this, as it will be your civic duty, and will relieve me of pain.''

"What an odd notion," said Bagayoko, frowning. "I see no need for the Prince to call on my services. One of his spearmen could puncture you like a waterskin."

"By then," the prophet said, "my occult powers will have roused so much uneasiness that it will seem best to take extreme measures."

"Well," said Bagayoko, "that's convenient, if exceedingly grotesque."

"Unlike other prophets," said the Sufferer, "I see the future not as one might wish it to be, but in all its cataclysmic and blind futility. That is why I have come here, to your delightful city. My numerous and totally accurate prophecies will vanish when this city does. This will spare the world any troublesome conflicts of predestination and free will."

"He is a theologian!" the poet said. "A leper theologian—it's a shame my professors in Timbuktu aren't here to debate him!"

"You prophesy doom for our city?" said Manimenesh.

"Yes. I will be specific. This is the year 406 of the Prophet's Hejira, and one thousand and fourteen years since the birth of Christ. In forty years, a puritan and fanatical cult of Moslems will arise, known as the Almoravids. At that time, Audoghast will be an ally of the Ghana Empire, who are idol-worshipers. Ibn Yasin, the warrior saint of the Almoravids, will condemn Audoghast as a nest of pagans. He will set his horde of desert marauders against the city; they will be enflamed by righteousness and greed. They will slaughter the men, and rape and enslave the women. Audoghast will be sacked, the wells will be poisoned, and the cropland will wither and blow away. In a hundred years, sand dunes will bury the ruins. In five hundred years, Audoghast will survive only as a few dozen lines of narrative in the travel books of Arab scholars.''

Khayali shifted his guitar. ''But the libraries of Timbuktu are full of books on Audoghast, including, if I may say so, our immortal tradition of poetry.''

''I have not yet mentioned Timbuktu,'' said the prophet, ''which will be sacked by Moorish invaders led by a blond Spanish eunuch. They will feed the books to goats.''

The company burst into incredulous laughter. Unperturbed, the prophet said, ''The ruin will be so general, so thorough, and so all-encompassing, that in future centuries it will be stated, and believed, that West Africa was always a land of savages.''

''Who in the world could make such a slander?'' said the poet.

''They will be Europeans, who will emerge from their current squalid decline, and arm themselves with mighty sciences.''

''What happens then?'' said Bagayoko, smiling.

''I can look at those future ages,'' said the prophet, ''but I prefer not to do so, as it makes my head hurt.''

''You prophesy, then,'' said Manimenesh, ''that our far-famed metropolis, with its towering mosques and armed militia, will be reduced to utter desolation.''

''Such is the truth, regrettable as it may be. You, and all you love, will leave no trace in this world, except a few lines in the writing of strangers.''

''And our city will fall to savage tribesmen?''

The Sufferer said, ''No one here will witness the disaster to come. You will live out your lives, year after year, enjoying ease and luxury, not because you deserve it, but simply because of blind fate. In time you will forget this night; you will forget all I have said, just as the world will forget you and your city. When Audoghast falls, this boy Sidi, this son of a slave, will be the only survivor of this night's gathering. By then he too will have forgotten Audoghast, which he has no cause to love. He will be a rich old merchant in Ch'ang-an, which is a Chinese city of such fantastic wealth that it could buy ten Audoghasts, and which will not be sacked and annihilated until a considerably later date.''

"This is madness," said Watunan.

Bagayoko twirled a crusted lock of mud-smeared hair in his supple fingers. "Your gate-guard is a husky lad, friend Manimenesh. What say we have him bash this storm-crow's head in, and haul him out to be hyena food?''

"For that, Doctor," said the Sufferer, "I will tell you the manner of your death. You will be killed by the Ghanaian royal guard, while attempting to kill the crown prince by blowing a subtle poison into his anus with a hollow reed.''

Bagayoko started. "You idiot, there is no crown prince.''

"He was conceived yesterday.''

Bagayoko turned impatiently to the host. "Let us rid ourselves of this prodigy!''

Manimenesh nodded sternly. "Sufferer, you have insulted my guests and my city. You are lucky to leave my home alive.''

The Sufferer hauled himself with agonizing slowness to his single foot. "Your boy spoke to me of your generosity.''

"What! Not one copper for your driveling.''

"Give me one of the gold dirhams from your purse. Otherwise I shall be forced to continue prophesying, and in a more intimate vein.''

Manimenesh considered this. "Perhaps it's best." He threw Sidi a coin. "Give this to the madman and escort him back to his raving-booth.''

They waited in tormented patience as the fortune-teller creaked and crutched, with painful slowness, into the darkness.

Manimenesh, brusquely, threw out his red velvet

sleeves and clapped for wine. "Give us a song, Khay-ali."

The poet pulled the cowl of his cloak over his head. "My head rings with an awful silence," he said. "I see all waymarks effaced, the joyous pleasances converted into barren wilderness. Jackals resort here, ghosts frolic, and demons sport; the gracious halls, and rich boudoirs, that once shone like the sun, now, overwhelmed by desolation, seem like the gaping mouths of savage beasts!" He looked at the dancing-girls, his eyes brimming with tears. "I picture these maidens, lying beneath the dust, or dispersed to distant parts and far regions, scattered by the hand of exile, torn to pieces by the fingers of expatriation."

Manimenesh smiled on him kindly. "My boy," he said, "if others cannot hear your songs, or embrace these women, or drink this wine, the loss is not ours, but theirs. Let us, then, enjoy all three, and let those unborn do the regretting."

"Your patron is wise," said Ibn Watunan, patting the poet on the shoulder. "You see him here, favored by Allah with every luxury; and you saw that filthy madman, bedeviled by plague. That lunatic, who pretends to great wisdom, only croaks of ruin; while our industrious friend makes the world a better place, by fostering nobility and learning. Could God forsake a city like this, with all its charms, to bring about that fool's disgusting prophesies?" He lifted his cup to Elfelilet, and drank deeply.

"But delightful Audoghast," said the poet, weeping. "All our loveliness, lost to the sands."

"The world is wide," said Bagayoko, "and the years are long. It is not for us to claim immortality, not even if we are poets. But take comfort, my friend. Even if these walls and buildings crumble, there will always be a place like Audoghast, as long as men love profit! The mines are inexhaustible, and elephants are thick as fleas. Mother Africa will always give us gold and ivory."

"Always?" said the poet hopefully, dabbing at his eyes.

"Well, surely there are always slaves," said Mani-menesh, and smiled, and winked. The others laughed with him, and there was joy again.

A PASSIVE VICTIM OF A RANDOM GENETIC ACCIDENT

by Janet Gluckman

Born in South Africa, Janet Gluckman worked as a journalist there until she got into trouble with the government for her anti-apartheid views, at which point she escaped probable imprisonment by "immigrating" illegally to the United States—coming to the U.S. as a tourist, "and hiding, eating ketchup soup, moving around." She became an American citizen in 1966. Later, the publication of her first novel, Rite of the Dragon, *got her banned from returning to South Africa. She now works as a columnist and reviewer, lecturer, and editor, as well as a freelance writer. Her other books include the novel* Child of the Light, *coauthored with George Guthridge. Upcoming are several more novels coauthored with George Guthridge, including* Child of the Dark *and* Daughter of Madagascar, *a novel coauthored with George Guthridge and George Harper,* Black Mandragora, *a collection of her short fiction from Pulphouse called* Tigers Making Love, *and several solo novels. She lives in Richmond, California.*

South African Medical Journal, 1981:

"In the current survey of Huntington's Chorea in South Africa, there have been repeated instances of anti-social behaviour (by these) passive victims of a totally random genetic accident."

* * *

"Jakobus! Jakobus Van Schalkwyck!"

Jakobus crouched behind his rock and watched the *likkewaan*. The lizard wriggled slightly at the unaccustomed sound of a human voice. Then it lay still again in the sun which had only just broken through the fog that shrouded Dassen Island each winter morning. As usual, the Southeaster had gusted across from Yzerfontein Point, pushing the fog toward the horizon where it would lie in waiting until sunset called it back to the island.

"Jakobus, come out."

The woman's voice was thin against the shrill wind. Thin and urgent, like an island mosquito insisting it be heard over the susurrus of the ocean—and equally irritating.

Jakobus listened to the pattern of the waves on the beach and wondered if he could have imagined last night's storm. Perhaps it was spring after all, else why would the woman have come now. Dassen Island was separated from the Mainland by more than thirty miles of Atlantic Ocean. Only a fool would make the crossing alone in the winter, and she always came alone, bringing the spring. It was something he counted on, in the sameness of his days.

"Oh for God's sake, man," the physician yelled. "There are things I have to talk to you about."

Jakobus' anger rose. He felt the quivering begin in his right cheek, and with it the twisting that inevitably followed. The skin around his right eye and nose moved involuntarily and he covered it with his hand, pushing down on it as if the pressure could force it to lie still. When the convulsions ceased, he edged his way around the rock and peered at his visitor. The woman had aged; her skin had been sallow to begin with but smooth, like an olive. It was craggy now, the way he imagined his own to be after twenty years of exposure to the elements. He had not seen a mirror since they had brought him here, so it was hard to tell. Twenty years, Jakobus thought, looking at the woman. That meant she had to be in her mid-forties, too. He wondered how much longer she would be able to make the journey across to see him, and why she did it in the first place.

As if to remind him of why he was here, the twitching began again, in his right leg this time. As always, it left him unsteady. Still, Jakobus managed to straighten up to his full six feet. He would talk to the woman this time, he thought. Twenty years of silence was enough, unless communing with seals and penguins counted. And, of course, the sharks who shared his Atlantic bathtub. Or was it he who shared theirs?

"Will you come to my lighthouse, Dr. Lerner?" he said. "Or are you afraid of what I might do to you?"

Not that there was anything he could do to Anne Lerner in the lighthouse that he couldn't do out here, with only the lizards as witness, Jakobus thought.

"I could use a cup of tea," the woman said, apparently forgetting where she was.

"I can offer you goat's milk," Jakobus said.

Seeing the look of distaste on his visitor's face, Jakobus laughed. It was something he had not done in a long time, and the sound startled him; it was not unlike the bark of the hyenas he'd killed on border patrol in Swaziland in 1981, just before the hearing.

"I think I'll pass, thank you," the woman said. "You must have water. That'll do fine."

Yes, he had water, Jakobus thought. Plenty of it. And goat's milk, and penguin eggs, and fish. He even had meat, if he felt inclined to hunt it down. He had plenty of fresh fruit, too. Gooseberries, wild strawberries, even a delicious mutant grape it had taken him several years to find the courage to try. Food-gathering was one of his major occupations, that and carving with the tools the doctor had left for him on one of her first visits. The only thing he did not have was people. How he had longed for them at first, in the early years of his isolation. Now. . . .

Involuntarily, Jakobus' hand strayed to his face.

"How are you feeling, Jakobus?" the woman asked.

The man pressed down on his cheek in answer. Muscle and tissue moved under his fingers. "Scraped myself on a bramble," he said. Then, knowing he was not fooling her, he let go and allowed the tremors to run their course.

When he once again had control over his body, Jakobus clambered down from his rock. Without saying anything more, he led the way to the lighthouse. It pleased him to choose the long way around the island so that the city woman would have to struggle longer to move across the damp sand. His hardened soles slid easily over the surface, automatically avoiding the poisonous residue of jellyfish and the entanglement of seaweed and dead fish that had been washed up by last night's storm.

Once the lighthouse was in sight, Jakobus slowed down and turned around to watch his visitor. She had taken off her shoes and was walking gingerly—the way he had tiptoed across Shelly Beach his first time in the Transkei. He had been used to Capetown's beaches, the sand soft and dandelion silky.

"What do you want of me?" Jakobus asked, when the woman was at his side. He bent to retrieve two penguin eggs he had missed in his early morning gathering. "As you can see," he said, holding up the eggs, "I'm doing fine."

"Right now I'm too busy to see anything." The physician removed a baby crab that clung tenaciously to the sand-filled tip of her stockings. "I'm beginning to remember why I always loathed going to the beach."

"Maybe if you dressed appropriately," Jakobus said. "This isn't the operating room."

"Why don't these things stay in the water where they belong?" The woman flung the sand-crab into the closest rockpool.

Jakobus opened the lighthouse door and walked inside. It was warm and musty, and smelled of seaweed and salt.

"Why do you keep coming back year after year?" Jakobus motioned the doctor inside. "You can't still be studying Huntington's Chorea. Since I'm the last of the breed that would be pointless."

There was no need for the woman to say anything, Jakobus thought. He had not lost the art of reading eyes, and the answer was written there clearly, for anyone who cared to look: guilt; shame; anger at having been a part of the tribunal that had condemned him to this.

He walked over to the lighthouse window. It faced southeast. Somewhere out there lay Robben Island, and a little more than thirty miles away, Capetown. He tried to remember what Table Mountain looked like, imagining the layer of white cloud that draped it like a starched linen tablecloth. Closing his eyes, he groped for a vision of the slopes of Lion's Head, with its decoration of proteas and wild mountain daisies. He could see nothing except deserted lighthouses and the vague shadow of the occasional population of scientists who stopped in for guano samples, and left as hastily as possible. Straining, he listened for the sound of streets filled with cars and people and noise. All he could hear was the waves and the nameless birds that relieved the interminable silence of Dassen Island. The memories were just out of reach. When the scentless wild roses on the other side of the island had taunted him with the elusive memory of his mother's rose garden, he had uprooted them. This was not as simple. He could hardly dispose of all of the rocks on Dassen because he couldn't recall the triumph of climbing a real mountain, or kill every rabbit whose paws, rustling the grasses, did not approximate the whirr of tires on Adderley Street.

Angrily, Jakobus brushed at his cheek. The skin was stretching. Contorting. He watched the look of pity growing in the physician's eyes.

"When did it start?" the woman asked.

Jakobus jumped. He had forgotten she was there. "Three months ago," he said. "Four maybe."

"You know what that means, don't you?"

The physician's voice was calm, matter of fact, but the lines between her brows deepened. Jakobus stared in wonder that the years of dealing with death had not diminished the pain of this kind of exercise.

"It means I have at most fifteen years," Jakobus said, forcing himself to emulate her tone. If that were all, he thought, he could live with it. Even here. But it wasn't all, not according to the eminent panel of physicians and government officials who had passed judgment on him.

"You were a part of that panel," he said, facing the woman. "Was it really a unanimous verdict?"

The woman hesitated, tensing slightly as if a fine elastic band had pulled her shoulder blades together.

"Most people with Huntington's become violent, self-destructive if not destructive to others," she said at last. "At the very least you were 'at risk'. They . . . we . . . had no way to predict whether or not you would actually contract the disease."

"A potential criminal . . . wasn't that what they called me?"

Jakobus kept the anger out of his voice, but it showed itself in the tremors that shook his body. He could forget the scent of roses, or the exhilaration of climbing to the summit of a mountain, but there was nothing about that day he could forget, not if he lived forever. The contours of every face, the movements of their bodies, the nuances that drowned his hopes and dreams as the verdict was pronounced: banishment. The rest of his life to be spent on this barren island where he could neither pass on the disease nor pose a threat to their Afrikaner order.

He faced the woman. She'd been one of them, one of that tribunal who had declared him a "potential criminal."

"Tell me something, doctor," Jakobus said. He raised his shaking right hand. "You said most people. Most. If there was some margin of doubt, why did you give in to them?"

"There's always a margin of doubt," she said.

"Still you voted with them. They said the verdict was unanimous."

"It was. Eventually."

"How did they coerce you into agreeing with the them?"

"I couldn't afford not to," Dr. Lerner said simply.

"Why?"

She paused, as if she were listening to some internal debate. "I'll make this as brief as possible," she said finally. "It doesn't excuse me but. . . . Have you ever heard the name Linchwe?"

"I don't think so," Jakobus said, leaning against the wall.

"He was an African chief," the woman said. "He was sentenced to serve on a labor gang on Robben Island. He escaped. They found his body on the beach at Blaauwberg Strand. Drowned, or so they said."

"So?"

"Our family dropped the name a long time ago," Dr. Lerner said quietly.

"But you look. . . ."

". . . White? Yes. But it's in my blood. That's why I've never married. My children might come out Black . . . Coloured. If I ever give them cause to investigate me. . . ."

Suddenly Jakobus understood. They were kin, he and this woman, both of them haunted by a past that was none of their doing.

"It must make you happy that the committee was partially right," Jakobus said, holding out his shaking hand.

The woman turned away, but not before Jakobus saw the anguish on her face.

"Perhaps I should kill you and prove them right all the way. The trouble is, they'll never know, will they? Not unless they know about your housecalls and come searching for you."

The woman's shoulders shook almost imperceptibly, as if she were trying to dislodge tears too long buried.

"I'm sorry, Anne," Jakobus said, unaware that he was using her first name. "That was needlessly cruel."

She did not turn around.

"Why didn't you wait until the spring to come?" Jakobus asked.

The woman's next words were so soft that he had to strain to hear them.

"I came to tell you that they're coming for you," she said.

Jakobus felt his stomach lurch. He touched his cheek; it lay smooth and still. Suddenly, miraculously, all trace of the tremors had stopped. Home? Could he really be going home, away from this two hundred square mile prison?

"When?"

"I'm not sure. Nine months. A year at the outside."

Still the woman did not face him. Something was wrong, Jakobus thought. Very wrong.

"Why are they letting me go?" he asked.

She turned around. "They're not letting you go," she said slowly, the tears flowing freely now.

Jakobus sat down abruptly on one of the rude oak benches he had built during his first year on the island. His entire right side shook uncontrollably. He felt battered, a reed in the grip of a winter storm. "What are they going to do with me, Dr. Lerner?" he asked, when the tremors calmed down enough to allow his lips to form intelligible sounds. "Feed me to the lions as a tourist attraction?"

To his astonishment, the physician nodded. "In a manner of speaking," she said, avoiding his eyes. "They're building an arena inside Capetown Castle."

"What does that have to do with me?"

"The arena is to be used for the public disposal of . . . undesirables."

"You can't possibly be serious," Jakobus said, searching the physician's face for a sign of amusement. There was none.

"Oh, I'm serious all right," she said.

But Jakobus could not believe her. If this was her idea of a joke, he thought, her sense of humor left a great deal to be desired. Unless. . . . And then it came to him. There could only be one reason for this kind of cruelty. She was conducting an experiment. Testing him. Trying to provoke him into losing his temper to see for herself how far the disease had progressed.

"I have an idea," Jakobus said, pleased with himself for having caught onto her game so quickly. "Why don't you suggest that they use Robben Island? It's close enough to be cozy; big enough to build a high class resort. That way I can be the opening attraction. I mean, it's been a penal colony more than once. A leper colony . . ."

"It's being used as a military base. Besides, it's easier to bring in cameras and a crew on the Mainland," the woman said.

She was playing the game well, Jakobus thought. "All right, Doctor," he said. "Tell them I'm ready." He held his arms above his head. "Take me. I'm all yours."

The woman did not laugh. "Stop it, Jakobus," she shouted. "This isn't a game."

"Isn't it?" Jakobus said flippantly. "What is it then?"

"I told you. It's the government's way of disposing of the . . . undesirables," she said. "They're not just out to get you. The Blacks and Coloureds have all been sent to homelands; that was the plan, if you remember, even twenty years ago when you were around. Now they're starting to get rid of the criminals . . . the cripples. . . . They're calling it a process of purification."

If this was her idea of sport, Jakobus thought, she could go on playing alone. He was no longer amused. Still he decided to play one more round.

"What category do I belong in?" he asked. "Criminal or cripple?"

Anne Lerner looked directly at him. "They're calling you a . . . passive victim of a random genetic accident," she said.

Jakobus took a deep breath and steadied himself against the damp wall of his lighthouse. He was hallucinating. None of this was really happening, not here on Dassen where the springbok roamed free and the only order was what nature commanded.

The woman stepped closer and took his arm. Gently.

In the manner of a parent protecting a child who only thought he was all grown up. "Listen to me," she said. "It's all true. Every word of what I've told you."

"Suppose for a moment that it is," Jakobus said. "Why are you here? Have you come to protect me, is that it? First you condemn me and then you want to buy your way into heaven by saving my life . . . such as it is."

Shaking off the physician's hand, Jakobus began to pace. He had to drag his foot slightly.

Damn Willem Schalk Van Der Merwe, he thought. Damn him for coming to South Africa with Van Riebeek in 1652. Damn the doctors for isolating the disease he'd brought with him. Jakobus' right cheek twisted involuntarily and he grimaced.

Dr. Lerner looked the other way. "I could try to get you out of the country . . ."

". . . No!"

Jakobus did not pause to examine his instinctive response. He would do that later, out on the dunes where he could think most clearly. "There is something you can do for me," he went on, less emphatically. "You can tell me why it matters to you whether or not they use me . . ."

". . . As a human sacrifice? Of course it matters."

Slowly, Jakobus limped over to the window and looked down. For a moment, he imagined himself lying crushed between two rocks, decomposing along with the mussels and abalone. He shaded his eyes against the midday sun as it climbed toward its zenith but he did not move. This was his world now, the seals and the *likkewane* and the sharks that circled the island day and night. He looked at the physician's boat, moored at the lighthouse jetty and bobbing around like papier-mâché. If she left now, he thought, he could resume his life—what was left of it.

Scanning the ocean's rough surface, Jakobus made out one shark's fin and then another and another. He smiled. Maybe today he would hurl his gathering of rock calendars into the sea, making a gift of them to the sharks and the ocean bed. If he no longer marked the passage of time, perhaps it would cease to exist for him and he could escape the ones who were coming for him. The same calendars that had kept him in touch with their reality would protect him from them. He would live outside their time frame, safe from their distorted sense of right and wrong. Or there was always the possibility that if he discarded time, he could convince himself that the fifteen years left to him were over. . . .

"I thought you would refuse to come with me," Anne Lerner said. There was a new quality to her voice, a strength that spoke of words carefully rehearsed.

Jakobus waited for her to continue.

"You have no weapons with which to fight—not unless you can train an army of sharks."

"They won't take me alive," Jakobus said. "That will have to be victory enough for me."

"For you, perhaps, but not for me," the woman said.

"You sound as if you have a plan," Jakobus said. "Did you bring me a machine gun to aim at their helicopters? Remember, if I use violence I prove the committee right."

Anne Lerner shook her head. The sun, shining through the window, caught one of the strands of silver that hid in her dark hair. Jakobus, seeing it, wondered how he could not have noticed before how attractive she was. He moved closer, wondering if he dared ask her to stay until they came for him.

"I had a different kind of battle in mind," the woman said, "with a different weapon. If you destroy one helicopter they will only send another."

She angled herself at the stairs and moved toward them.

"Don't leave until you tell me your battle plan." Jakobus spoke quickly, his voice filled with fear that the spasms would take hold before he could stop her leaving. "You promised me a weapon."

"I'm not going, Jakobus," the woman said. "Not yet."

With that she began climbing the stairs.

Jakobus did not understand. ''There is nothing up there except my cot,'' he said.

''While you have been gathering food, I have been gathering an army,'' Anne Lerner said, turning around. ''Only, my soldiers are in training to give birth instead of death. That is our defense against their purification.''

''Your army? Are they . . . ?''

''One way or another, they are all passive victims of random genetics,'' she said, unbuttoning her shirt.

Jakobus threw back his head and laughed. This time the sound rang of triumph. By autumn, he thought, following his fellow victim of random genetics up the stairs, the sand would again be cool beneath his feet. Mornings would speak of the winter to come, and the occasional fog would descend on Dassen Island, waiting for the Southeaster to blow it away.

At first the wind would not come often, but the fog was patient. It would settle down and wait, content in the knowledge that, ultimately, the cycle would start anew.

And he, Jakobus, would also wait before he joined the horizon. Not for the Southeaster but for the noise of helicopters, and for one last look at the ignorance of men who believed that they had won.

THE PALE THIN GOD
by Mike Resnick

Here's another compelling African story by Mike Resnick, this one giving us a perhaps unwelcome—and definitely scary—look at some of the Powers that actually rule the world. . . .

He stood quietly before us, the pale thin god who had invaded our land, and waited to hear the charges.

The first of us to speak was Mulungu, the god of the Yao people.

"There was a time, many eons ago, when I lived happily upon the earth with my animals. But then men appeared. They made fire and set the land ablaze. They found my animals and began killing them. They devised weapons and went to war with each other. I could not tolerate such behavior, so I had a spider spin a thread up to heaven, and I ascended it, never to return. And yet *you* have sacrificed yourself for these very same creatures."

Mulungu pointed a long forefinger at the pale thin god. "I accuse you of the crime of Love."

He sat down, and immediately Nyambe, the god of the Koko people, arose.

"I once lived among men," he said, "and there was no such thing as death in the world, because I had given them a magic tree. When men grew old and wrinkled, they went and lived under the tree for nine days, and it made them young again. But as the years went by men began taking me for granted, and stopped worshiping me and making sacrifices to me, so I uprooted my tree and carried it up to heaven with me, and without its magic, men finally began to die.''

He stared balefully at the pale thin god. "And now you have taught men that they may triumph over death. I charge you with the crime of Life."

Next Ogun, the god of the Yoruba people, stepped forward.

"When the gods lived on Earth, they found their way barred by impenetrable thorn bushes. I created a *panga* and cleared the way for them, and this *panga* I turned over to men, who use it not only for breaking trails but for the glory of war. And yet you, who claim to be a god, tell your worshipers to disdain weapons and never to raise a hand in anger. I accuse you of the crime of Peace."

As Ogun sat down, Muluku, god of the Zambesi, rose to his feet.

"I made the earth," he said. "I dug two holes, and from one came a man, and from the other a woman. I gave them land and tools and seeds and clay pots, and told them to plant the seeds, to build a house, and to cook their food in the pots. But the man and the woman ate the raw seeds, broke the pots, and left the tools by the side of a trail. Therefore, I summoned two monkeys, and made the same gifts to them. The two monkeys dug the earth, built a house, harvested their grain, and cooked it in their pots." He paused. "So I cut off the monkeys' tails and stuck them on the two men, decreeing that from that day forth they would be monkeys and the monkeys would be men."

He pointed at the pale thin god. "And yet, far from punishing men, you forgive them their mistakes. I charge you with the crime of Compassion."

En-kai, the god of the Maasai, spoke next.

"I created the first warrior, Le-eyo, and gave him a magic chant to recite over dead children that would bring them back to life and make them immortal. But Le-eyo did not utter the chant until his own son had died. I told him that it was too late, that the chant would no longer work, and that because of his selfishness, Death will always have power over men. He begged me to relent, but because I am a god and a god cannot be wrong, I did not do so.''

He paused for a moment, then stared coldly at the pale thin god. ''You would allow men to live again, even if only in heaven. I accuse you of the crime of Mercy.''

Finally Huveane, god of the Basuto people, arose.

''I, too, lived among men in eons past. But their pettiness offended me, and so I hammered some pegs into the sky and climbed up to heaven, where men would never see me again.'' He faced the pale thin god. ''And now, belatedly, you have come to our land, and you teach that men may ascend to heaven, that they may even sit at your right hand. I charge you with the crime of Hope.''

The six fearsome gods turned to me.

''We have spoken,'' they said. ''It is your turn now, Anubis. Of what crime do you charge him?''

''I do not make accusations, only judgments,'' I replied.

''And how do you judge him?'' they demanded.

''I will hear him speak, and then I will tell you,'' I said. I turned to the pale thin god. ''You have been accused of the crimes of Peace, Life, Mercy, Compassion, Love, and Hope. What have you to say in your defense?''

The pale thin god looked at us, his accusers.

''I have been accused of Peace,'' he said, never raising his voice, ''and yet more Holy Wars have been fought in my name than in the names of all other gods combined. The earth has turned red with the blood of those who died for my Peace.

''I have been accused of Life,'' he continued, ''yet in my name, the Spaniards have baptized Aztec infants and dashed out their brains against rocks so they might ascend to heaven without living to become warriors.

''I have been accused of Mercy, but the Inquisition was held in my name, and the number of men who were tortured to death is beyond calculation.

''I have been accused of Compassion, yet not a single

man who worships me has ever lived a life without pain, without fear, and without misery.

"I have been accused of Love, yet I have not ended suffering, or disease, or death, and he who leads the most blameless and saintly life will be visited by all of my grim horsemen just as surely as he who rejects me.

"Finally, I have been accused of Hope," he said, and now the stigmata on his hands and feet began to glow a brilliant red, "and yet since I have come to your land, I have brought famine to the north, genocide to the west, drought to the south, and disease to the east. And everywhere, where there was Hope, there is only poverty and ignorance and war and death.

"So it has been wherever I have gone, so shall it always be.

"Thus do I answer your charges."

They turned to me, the six great and terrible deities, to ask for my judgment. But I had already dropped to my knees before the greatest god of us all.

TOWARD KILIMANJARO
by Ian McDonald

*British author Ian McDonald is an ambitious and daring
writer with a wide range and an impressive amount of
talent. His first story was published in 1982, and since
then he has appeared with some frequency in* Interzone,
Isaac Asimov's Science Fiction Magazine, Zenith, Other
Edens, Amazing, *and elsewhere. He was nominated for
the John W. Campbell Award in 1985, and in 1989 he
won the* Locus *"Best First Novel" Award for his novel*
Desolation Road. *He won the Philip K. Dick Award in
1992 for his novel* King of Morning, Queen of Day. *His
other books include the novel* Out On Blue Six *and a
collection of his short fiction,* Empire Dreams. *Coming
up is a new novel,* Hearts, Hands and Voices, *and a new
collection,* Speaking In Tongues, *as well as several
graphic novels, and he is at work on another new novel,
tentatively entitled* Necroville. *Born in Manchester, England, in 1960, McDonald has spent most of his life in
Northern Ireland, and now lives and works in Belfast.*

*In the vivid and eloquent story that follows, McDonald
takes us to a future Africa that is being threatened by an
ever-encroaching, unstoppably growing alien forest,
seeded from the stars, that is sweeping toward Nairobi at
a rate of one hundred meters per day . . . and takes us
along on a strange pilgrimage into the heart of the alien
jungle, to Kilimanjaro itself, to see if the seeds of love
can survive the heat of transformation.*

To every book its inscription. I have written my name
in black ink inside the cloth cover, but the syllables are

harsh and clashing in this land of whispered sibilants and strong consonants. How much better the name Langrishe gave me: *Moon*, generous, looping consonants, vowels like two eyes, two souls looking out of the page. One half of T.P.'s final gift to me, this journal, clothbound and intimate in Liberty print; I treasure it, hug it to me, companion and confessor. T.P.'s other gift I treated less kindly: black dragonfly wings shredded by the impact, struts snapped like the bones of birds. Already the forest is at work on it, converting the organic plastics into dripping stalactites of black slime.

It is over an hour since I lost the beat of the helicopters in the undersong of the Chaga; my crash-landing must have looked sufficiently convincing for them to abandon the hunt. Forgive me, T.P., but you would understand: skimming across the tree-tops toward the looming edge of Chaga with two Kenyan Army/Air Force Nighthawks behind me, expecting at any second to be smashed into nothingness by a thermal imaging StarStreak missile, one's options are somewhat limited. Sorry about the microlyte, T.P. But I will be good to the diary, I promise.

I look again at those four letters: Moon. How much of life is a search for our true names; the jumble of ideograms that spells us as we truly are? Some, like T.P. Costello, attain true personhood in being reduced to their initials. Some intimate, cozy souls never become more than their Christian names; to others, that name is a useless appendix, their true identity lies in their surnames, like you, Langrishe. And some only find personhood in the names they attract to themselves. *Moon*. They cannot see themselves; it takes another to tell them what they are. Moon. Langrishe, T.P. Our players. No, I have omitted one vital addition to the Dramatis Personae: the mountain.

"Wide as all the world; great, high, and unbelievably white in the sun," as Hemingway described it. To the Maasai, it is *Ngajé Ngai*, the House of God; but most simple and striking is its Swahili name: *Kilima Njaro*, the White Mountain.

You never forget your first view of the mountain, as you never forget your first, nervous, thrilling view of a lover's body. When I flew in to the Ol Tukai that first time, the clouds were hanging low across the mountain, but still its presence could be sensed, like God at Sinai. Interviewing Langrishe in his office, he noticed my attention being increasingly distracted as beyond the window the final rags of cloud dissolved and dispersed and that astonishing white tableland caught and kindled in the African twilight. Spellbound, I watched the shadows move up across the uncanny geometries of the alien forest until the final red glow was extinguished from the snows. You never forget; like that first, electrifying exploration of love, you keep it secret and warm in your heart.

And now, White Mountain, I make my exploration of you. Langrishe theorized (but then his theories were cheap and plentiful as flies on a beggar) that the symbiotic systems of the forest interlink so completely that the whole forty kilometer wide ring of life forms one great synaptic system: does the touch of my hand to a loop of tubing pulsing with warm oil signal a spark of recognition? Can you feel my approach through the groves of slowly turning windmill trees and the swaying fingers of pseudo-coral? Do you sense me as I spiral up through your northern foothills, do you know me?

Again, my name, inscribed in black ink inside the front cover of the cloth-bound journal. I have given much thought to what kind of journal I should keep. A neo-Victorian almanac of wonders and horrors, each neat copper-plate entry headed, Day the -th, Year of Grace 199-? Tempting. But my choice of traveling companions dictates otherwise. T.S. Eliot. Joseph Conrad. Thomas Merton. Not so much an expedition to the interior as a pilgrimage through the darklands of the soul. Langrishe as holy Grail? The comparison would please him, the arrogant bastard.

Early in the afternoon I came upon the remains of the old Ol Tukai Research Facility. Subtle transubstantiation:

I had been picking a path between the vegetation-shrouded bones for some minutes before the nagging tingle of familiarity became recognition. The voracious forest life had long since converted the organic materials to its own matrix of tubes and fans and flows of blue lichen. All changed, changed utterly. It is less than a year since the line of advance engulfed the center; now only the concrete-and-steel skeleton enforces some form of human geometrical discipline to the biological anarchy. I paused a while in the memory of Langrishe's office. Kilimanjaro was lost behind wave upon wave of forest, the mood strange, and I uncertain of my own feelings. From out of the wilderness came a twittering, chiming music, like a child's experiments with a synthesizer, un-canny and alien. I never saw what it was that sang that song.

I will not spend the night here. Memories too big.

Wide-eyed and clueless in the pick-up bay at Nairobi airport: I'd been in Kenya a whole half-hour and was still reeling from the *Africanness* of it all. Stepping off the plane into the sour grey pre-dawn drizzle, I'd almost kissed the tarmac; it was surely destined for canoniza-tion, the place where the astonishingly talented girl writer from Dublin town who was going to write *the* book on *the* phenomenon of *the* century first intersected with the surface of Africa. Now, two bags on the concrete, wait-ing and waiting while all around me taxis hire-cars lim-ousines shuttle buses were speeding my fellow passengers off to Sheratons Hiltons Intercontinentals Ramadas PanAfrics, the *Africanness* of it all was beginning to pall a little. Another flight came in, another disgorgement of travelers into the hinterland. I watched my own flight take off, onward bound, into a huge sunrise. The sun was well up and about its business when a dirty white Peugeot pick-up with what looked like a small greenhouse bolted to the back swung into the parking bay. The window rolled down, a face like an angst-ridden owl looked me up and down from behind immense spectacles and finally bellowed in dearest dirtiest Dublin:

"Bags in the back. You in the front, I'll get a ticket if I hang around here much longer; what'll I get?"

"A ticket?"

"That's correct."

T.P. Costello: East African correspondent of the *Irish Tunes;* liaison, contact, mentor, and, in the end, best friend; the only man in Kenya who was fool enough (or impecunious enough) to be prepared to share an office with me. And the worst driver I have ever known. Some people are born to bad driving. He aspired to it; to him it was a major social accomplishment. As we took a traffic circle at a speed that left rubber on the blacktop, he asked me, "What kind of underwear have you got on?"

Wondering just what kind of a pervert I had saddled myself with, I told him.

"Throw them out," he said. "Nothing but cotton. Nylon traps moisture. You can get fungus. What can you get?"

"Fungus?"

"That's correct."

Howling down the wide boulevards of downtown Nairobi, I noticed we were passing by shining skyscrapers with names like Sheraton Hilton Intercontinental Ramada PanAfric.

"Just where are we going?" (An explosion of hooting as the Peugeot pickup pulled out to overtake a lumbering green-and-yellow municipal bus straight into the path of an oncoming Nissan van: I'd never actually seen an expression quite like the driver's before.)

"The African Inland Church Guesthouse. It's comfortable, it's clean, it's central without you getting a noseful of diesel fumes every time you open your window, it's quiet—most of the guests are missionaries on R 'n' R—Mrs. Kivebulaya, the proprietrix, thinks Irish girls are polite, quiet, charming, and well-behaved—please don't disillusion her—and, above all, it's cheap. Given, the meat can be a bit chewy, but you can afford it."

We swung up a steeply curving drive and lurched to a halt in front of a relaxed red-tiled building, a genial mongrel of colonial and clinker-block ethnic. T.P. Costello busied himself in the back of the Peugeot and appeared with my cases and three chickens strung together at the feet swinging from one hand.

"My compliments to Mrs. Kivebulaya," he said handing cases and chickens to a geriatric porter dressed in a jacket of almost inspirational vileness. T.P. screamed the engine, preparing for another ballistic leap into the traffic. "224b, Tom M'boya Street," he shouted, and hurled himself into the streets.

I had never eaten chicken gizzard before. I enjoyed it much more than I should have.

Impressions from my notebooks: pen-sketches in that early light when we see clearest.

Woodsmoke, shit, and diesel. Street perfume; sweated from the red earth like a pheromone.

Wonderful incongruity: Colonel Sanders' patrician features intimidating the intersection of University Way and Koinange Street. Do all the black faces make him feel back on the ol' plantation again? Must order chicken gizzard with fries and buttermilk roll.

A man dressed Arab-style pushing what seems to be a small dog kennel on wheels along Kenyatta Avenue. The creeping horror when I glimpsed inside, the glitter of human eyes: a woman, wrapped in Muslim black, save for her hands; and eyes. . . .

The Hilton is extravagantly proud of its English fish and chips served in a copy of the London *Times*. T.P. tells me of a certain journalist who goes there every day to order the delicacy, throw away the fish and chips and read the newspaper.

The loping city: the people move like liquid in the streets, as if to the mental beat of drums and wires.

The casual bribery of the police: T.P.'s KitKat tin in the glove compartment of the Peugeot where he keeps the bribes for motoring offenses. The next best thing to a to-

tally honest police force is a totally corrupt one. Dame
Market Forces. . . .

For a city under siege, Nairobi is remarkably cavalier
about the fact. Since the package came down in the
Nyandarua National Park last year, opening a second
front, I reckon Nairobi has about a thousand days left
before the advancing walls of vegetation close. But life
goes on with a blythe disinterestedness that amazes this
European girl, who would be running round like Chicken
Little announcing the imminent fall of the sky. Disinter-
est, or African fatalism? Too much like a metaphor of
death for this white girl, this *m'zungu*.

To every city its municipal obsessions: Dublin's is
finding somewhere to park the car, Nairobi's is coin-in-
the-slot photo booths.

T.P.'s office was three rooms above the Rift Valley
Peugeot Service Depot on Tom M'boya Street where he
was apparently offering asylum to an entire family of
Asian refugees: mother on the telephone, daughter one
on the typewriter, daughter two in reception, father
bookkeeper, number one son fileclerk, number two son
runner, honored grandmother *chai*-maker. What amazed
me was that they were so infernally busy all the time. I
suspect that they were terrified of T.P. turning the lot of
them out onto Tom M'boya Street; certainly he ran his
office with the self-assured smugness of a minor, benev-
olent dictator.

For my thousand shillings per month I had use of what
T.P. called a "Captain Kirk Chair," a desk, a telephone,
a photocopier, a time-share of an asthmatic word processor, the occasional privileged glimpse into the specially
darkened room where the fax machine sat like a presid-
ing deity, unlimited *chai* and biscuits and the pleasure of
T.P. Costello's wit, wisdom, and virtually continuous
bitching about his immediate superior, one so-called Jacobellini.

And while I sat drinking *chai*, engaging in dubious
battle with the word processor and spending entire afternoons waiting for the operator to connect me with some

minor cog in the great wheel of scientists and researchers, humanity's first encounter with an alien life form was advancing toward me one hundred steady meters per day.

Sometimes I felt it would be easiest just to sit and wait for it to come creeping along Tom M'boya Street, up the stairs and into the office.

Even the professional imagination falters before the face of the Chaga. Description fails, only analogy can convey some impression of this landscape through which I am traveling. The experience that comes closest is the time with Langrishe on the coast, when I was working on the book; our explorations of the reef in snorkel, mask and flippers. Crucified on the surface tension, peering down like vacationing Olympians into the underworld. God, how I burned! That night in the banda; the wind in the palms and the rattle of the thatch; Langrishe's hands slicing lemons, rubbing the juice into my skin. . . . The gentle, painful, almost hallucinatory love-making, me riding him—was that the boom and crash of the surf on the reef, or the roar of my own blood and bone, or the song of Langrishe, inside me?

Shape yourself into some long-legged chitinous arthropod picking across a coral reef and you will have the feel of it. There is a submarine quality to the light that reaches you through the canopy of balloons, bladders, fans, umbrellas; submarine, and ecclesiastical, a cyclorama of colors like the light in a drowned cathedral. Analogy again.

I am beginning to wonder if my supplies will be sufficient. I had provisioned for twenty days; it may take that long just to reach the lower slopes of the mountain. The riotous Chaga-life confounds my sense of time and distance; I cannot judge how far, how fast I have come. I was so certain, then; now my stupidity at thinking that I can find one man in five thousand square kilometers of, literally, another world, astounds me. The sense of isolation is colossal.

Thank God for faithful fellow travelers! Conrad; brother explorer into the heart of darkness; Eliot, cartographer of the desert in the heart of man; Merton, pilgrim into the cloud of unknowing on the dawnward edge of faith. They know what it is to venture into an unknown region, into the utter subjective darkness of the interior wilderness.

Some spore is attacking my copy of *Seeds of Contemplation*, the vinyl cover is breaking out in tiny red warts. Amazing, the tenacity of these almost invisible flecks of life; despite my rigorous efforts to rid myself of all plastic and petro-chemical based materials, they still managed to bring the little acrylic aglets at the end of my spare pair of laces out in sulphur yellow blossoms. Ironic that after three years of the most intense scientific scrutiny anywhere on the planet, all the researchers can conclude is that the pseudo-vegetation (their word, not mine, please) of the Chaga is a carbon based form of life grouped around long chains of what seem to be polymers as opposed to the amino-acid/protein axis of terrestrial life. The phrase "Plastic Forest" entered the world vocabulary despite the protests of the researchers that really it wasn't plastic at all, rather a kind of long-chain self-replicating carbohydrate pseudo-polymer. Doesn't have quite the same ring, though.

Popular imagination perfumes the place like a decommissioned oil refinery. The reality is quite different; essential oils and musks, spices and incenses that seem maddeningly familiar though the memory can never quite place them exactly. . . . Sex. The Chaga smells like sex.

The industrial/chemical analogy may be very near the truth. The Chaga is only partly photosynthetic (and that part which is seems to operate by a system quite different from, and more efficient than, the green green grass of home); some exploit temperature differentials, others make use of catalytic chemical reactions, some employ wind power, others remarkably efficient heat pumps, others still generate electricity directly from what can only be described as solar panels. Some, like the corals they closely resemble, feed off aerial bacteria, some literally eat rock. All are linked together in vastly complex hierarchies of symbiosis. Benumbed biologists I interviewed for the book maintained that it might take decades to unravel just one symbiotic system. The most recent theories, which will form an appendix to the finished book, extend the factory analogy to the microscopic; at the cellular level, the organisms resemble machines more than biological entities.

If T.P.'s sources are anything to go by (and have they ever been anything other than reliable?) the executive singles of the Hiltons Sheratons Intercontinentals Ramadas and PanAfrics are hot-bunking Silicon Valley cyberneticists, brisk Teutonic micro-engineers, tofu-and-bran custom logic designers, and giggling Sony-Nihon chip customizers; all engaged in internecine warfare to be the first to bring home the flitch to their particular genus of *Homo Polycorporatus*. Sorry boys, but the Good News from the Chaga is that co-operation beats competition hands down, and is advancing toward your expense-account suites at one hundred meters per day.

I saw a vervet monkey today; nervous eyes in the shimmering canopy. A webbed sail of ribs, like some remnant of the time of the dinosaurs, grew from its back. I did not take it for a good omen.

I shall spend the night in the ruins of an old game lodge I came across unexpectedly; a memory of the days of zebra-striped Volkswagen minibuses bristling broadsides of Nikons. One thing the Chaga has done is restore peace and dignity to the land. These foothills of Kilimanjaro feel old in a way the land in Europe never can; it deserves the respect due age. I slung up my hammock on the verandah of an old game lodge. I had meant to write, cook, wash, do something; but a melancholy lassitude came over me. A calling of spirit to spirit, almost, as I lost myself in the shafts of green light. The fragile moment of self-unknowing when the consciousness is totally subsumed into the other, when the slightest tremor of self-awareness taps the still waters and the reflection

shivers into ripples. Time out of mind. I heard him. I
heard him, his voice, out there, a voice in solo flight
above the chords of the forest song. I hear you, Langrishe. I am coming.

Toward nightfall the small glade in which the abandoned lodge stood came alive and ringing with songs.
Twittering, rippling, passing into and out of phase with
each other. As the first of them came out of the gathering
dark, I rose to my feet; just the few at first, then the main
body, a procession of creatures like faintly luminous jellyfish rolling and undulating through the air. They separated around the lodge like a river around a rock; they
were still coming to break around me as I retired to my
hammock, out of darkness, onward into the darkness
again.

I could tell you the exact place and time I fell in love
with Peter Langrishe: March 17, 10:20 P.M., beside the
drinks trolley in the garden of the Irish Ambassador's
Residence. I could even tell you what we were drinking:
me: John Jameson's, neat, just a clink of ice; he: a Glen-
livet that had somehow found a niche on His Excellency's
strictly patriotic booze wagon.

The annual Ambassadorial St. Patrick's Day party is
the highlight of the expatriate community year. South-
erner or Northerner (everyone is an Irishman on St. Patrick's Night) voluntary workers, development engineers,
teaching sisters, rural midwives, Bible translators will
move heaven and earth to be there for His Excellency's
bash. Head of any queue was always T.P. Costello: it
was widely known and never officially denied that if His
Excellency really wanted to know what was happening
in the greater world he would do much better visiting
224b Tom M'boya Street than grinding himself exceed-
ing fine in the tedious mills of diplomatic intelligence.

An expatriate and colleague of T.P., my gilt-edged
invitation was assured; knowing my tendency to drink
myself horizontal—something I did not much want to do
in the presence of teaching sisters, rural midwives, Bible

Translators, Ambassadors, etc.—I had thought of declining until T.P. whispered that it might well be in my best professional interests to attend. I bought a dress for the occasion, the best my means and Nairobi's supply could achieve.

Two weeks of daily exposure to T.P.'s driving still hadn't immunized me to taking traffic circles at forty. Dodging red Kenatco taxis, he explained to me that he had come into certain information to the effect that certain highly placed individuals connected with a certain international research community could be in attendance at a certain Ambassadorial bash *ce soir*.

"I didn't know there were any Irish on the project."

"Oh, there aren't," said T.P., terrorizing a flock of pedestrians with his horn. "But it's good social and better political grace to be seen to be hospitable to the scientific community. Honorary Irishmen for one night."

Ghosts and illuminations: the assemblage of rented tuxes and almost-posh frocks was lit by outdoor candles on poles and lubricated by the ever-solicitous presence of the servants, all white smiles and freshly ironed cuffs. From the cover of a glass of J.J., T.P. steered me through the clashing rocks to the more noteworthy landmarks. An ectomorphic Norman Bates in animated conversation with a nun. "Nikolas Van Rensberg, Project Supervisor of the Ol Tukai Facility: Grand Poo-bah; between thee and me, he's a bit of a wanker." Laurel and Hardy arguing by candlelight, a raven-haired woman, in a dress that earned her my undying enmity, trying, and failing, to keep the peace. "Conrad Laurens from Ol Tukai, the Bouncing Belgian, and Hakko Lemmenjavi, the Frigging Finn, from Nyandarua. Lord High Executioner and Lord High Everything Else. No love lost between the two facilities. The fine, and exceedingly foolish, young creature between them is Annabelle Pasquali, Senior Botanical Supervisor from Ol Tukai. I once had a short, sweet, and altogether wonderful affair with her."

I wanted to know more about the short, sweet, and altogether wonderful affair, but T.P. had moved on to a small and typically astringent American woman in Nina Ricci frock and red Reebocks ("Honestly, these Colonials; bad taste is a national virtue,") holding court with a diplomatically bored Ambassador who was surreptitiously searching his pockets for cigarettes. "Dorothy Bazyn. Project Security. The military exclusion zones around the Chagas were her idea. I once tried, God knows why, to chat her up at a cocktail party in the Hilton and she asked me if I'd like a cocktail stick rammed up my dick." A solitary man by the drinks trolley with a pigtail and eyes like a Yeats poem. "Ah. Now. This one might be worth your while. In fact, of all the luminaries here foregathered, I would definitely say he would pay the best dividend. Peter Langrishe, Head of Xenobiotics, whatever that is; and a fellow Celt, though of the genus *Pictii* rather than the genus *Hibernii*. If you want a dash of vindaloo in your book, he's the boy to talk to. More wild and woolly theories about the Chaga than you can shake a stick at. Aliens are his pet obsession."

"Introduce me this instant, Costello."

T.P.'s smile froze on his face.

"Oh shit. Jacobellini has just waltzed in with two lumps of silicon implant on either arm. I thought he was well out of it down in Dar. Any excuse for a piss-up. I suppose I'd better go and pay me *devoirs*. Behave yourself. What'll you do?"

"Behave myself."

"That's correct."

Disgusting how like South Pacific it was, some enchanted evening, you may see a stranger, all that . . . just at that moment our eyes did meet, and hold. I attempted to match my orbit with his, weaving and apologizing through the teaching sisters rural midwives Bible translators.

Overheards: "I tried to get him to talk about the blood, but he wouldn't!" (Then, more vehemently,) "He wouldn't!"

"Are you sure you remembered the chain saw?"

"I mean, can you imagine, going out with the same girl for *ten days*?"

"And then he told me about the psychopath. . . ."

"Yes, but exactly *what* kind of a prick *was* Proust?"

"You know, some mornings I get up and I just feel so . . . Antipodean, you know?"

We arrived in each other's gravitational field. We circled, wrestlers trying to get a verbal grip on each other.

"Nice dress."

I wriggled, consciously counting every centimeter of bare flesh.

"Nice . . . ah, pigtail."

He told me his name, I told him mine; little hostages, exchanged.

"It isn't you at all," he said.

"What, my name? An unfortunate inevitability of being born in a Catholic country."

"No, you deserve better. You should be something more . . . elemental. A come-by-night. A *Moon*."

Sometimes you can *feel* your pupils dilate. Sometimes you possess the awareness of the exact state of every muscle in your body. Sometimes the fingers of unseen ghosts caress your spine.

"Moon. I like it. Moon I shall be, for the evening at least. And do you have an elemental name for yourself?"

"Just Langrishe."

St. Patrick's Day, 10:20, beside the drinks trolley on the lawn of the Ambassador's residence; where and when it began. Same place, two minutes later, where it almost ended; a gasp and a sigh from the gathered celebrants as a long slow streak of violet light drew a strict terminator across the sky above Nairobi. Twenty-five personal pagers exploded in frenzied beeping; needlessly, as the representatives of the Facility were already stampeding the cloakroom and calling taxis on their cellphones to take them to Wilson airfield.

Not even an apology.

I had to drive T.P. home. He interrupted a major monologue about the angers of dehydration and the virtues of ascorbic acid in ameliorating the effects of extreme inebriation only to throw up his entire night's consumption of John Jameson down the front of my party dress.

His arrival in the office on Tom M'boya Street at twenty to one was extremely wary. It took the offer of a late Indian lunch at the Norfolk Hotel to placate me. Over rogan josh, he told me that the satellite tracking station at Longonot had picked up the biological package coming in from orbit over the Solomon Islands. It had impacted somewhere in West Cameroun, and was currently under investigation by an advance team of international researchers.

He tried to make me pay half the bill.

The primal heart of the New Africa is shaped like a twin-deck CD twenty-watt-per-channel boom box. It beats in 4/4 time from Sony woofers and JVC bass drivers to the pulse of hy-lyfe guitars pickin' three-chord tricks. I have seen Rendille herdsmen, perched in the one-legged attitude of Biblical repose, wearing Walkman headphones; I have seen Nandi Hills coffee-growers in the fields with ghetto-blasters strapped across their backs. The first thing you hear when you arrive in Kenya is the Immigration Officer's radio; from that moment on, the general dance never ceases. The gaudy, hazy chaos of the country bus station. The voices and colors and perfume of the fruit market. The Asian store where seriously fat women fuss over *kangas*. Sam's Super Shine Stall on Kenyatta Avenue. Along Koinange Street, from every street vendor selling maize and kebabs grilled over Volkswagen hubcaps full of charcoal.

So familiar that I almost didn't realize the utter incongruity of what I was hearing. Sunny-Adé and his African Beats; thirty kilometers into the Chaga, on the lower slopes of Kilimanjaro.

The WaChagga may be the last proud people in the New Africa. The invasion of alien flora and fauna had dispossessed them of their ancestral lands on the slopes

of the mountain, it had even taken their name; all it had
left them was their stubbornness. Not the most obviously
useful asset against the advancing wave of life, but where
fire, chainsaw, Agent Orange, Agent Green, and finally
recombinant DNA had failed to stem the green tide, sheer
stubbornness, and infinite adaptability, had won a small
but not insignificant victory. In the general panic to evac-
uate when it became obvious that Moshi, Himo, and a
clutter of smaller settlements along the Tanzanian side of
the mountain were going to be engulfed, a few recalci-
trant WaChagga had slipped under the wire around the
resettlement camps and vanished from the twentieth century.

I know how Dr. Livingstone must have felt. . . .

The men of the settlement turned out to meet me, from
honored grandfathers to a five-year-old swinging the
boombox I had heard over the general voices of the forest.

(They insisted I call it that: the forest. *They* were the
Chagga, and they resented the forest having buccaneered
their name.)

Not so much Dr. Livingstone, I presume, as Dorothy
in Munchkinland. There was even a Yellow Brick Road
to follow, hexagonal tiles of hard yellow plastic that con-
cluded in a comically accurate spiral at the center of the
village.

We call tree-dwellers arboreals, but what do we call
flower-dwellers? *Floreals?* Sounds too much like a dead
bullfighter, but the word fits; the WaChagga lived, literally, in flowers. An impeccably mannered young gradu-
ate from the University of Dar es Salaam was assigned
as my guide to the wonders of the community his people
had created in the forest. Seen by daylight, the flower-
houses were wide parasols of zip-locked iridescent petals
atop a central trunk. In their shade, naked children scam-
pered and monolithic women sat, moving only their eyes
to look at the *m'zungu* woman. Passing the flowers again
by twilight, I saw the petals folding down into night-
proof bubbles of light and warmth. I was taken to join a

circle of women who were sitting and weaving what
looked like nylon thread on belt looms while watching a
ten-year-old American super-soap (courtesy Voice of
Kenya Broadcasting) on a portable Sony color set (somewhat scabbed and ulcerous, but nonetheless functional)
that was plugged into the trunk of the tree.

"The petals generate electricity from sunlight," explained my guide. Freshly graduated and already disil-
lusioned with the academic life, he had brought himself
and his European Studies degree home to the shadow of
the White Mountain—and then the biological package
came down. "The trunk stores power during the day for
us at night." Balloon-sized globes clustered near the top
of the trunk were bioluminiscent. "They somehow know
to come on when it gets dark. Look!" He turned a spigot-
like extrusion from the trunk; water splashed. "We have
hot as well; solar heating. Come!" The friendly impe-
riousness of the Africans. He guided me around the municipal plumbing system: the huge transparent gourds that
were the main cisterns, the obscenely peristaltic organic
pumps that maintained pressure, the stacked fans of solar
absorbers that heated the water, the distribution system
of plastic tubes and pipes to every house. The tour de-
toured via the municipal biogas plant to conclude in the
orchards that had sprung up around the settlement and
which now provided their entire diet.

I was the only woman guest at the dinner in my honor
that night; seated around the central spiral with the men
folk, while the women served up the fruits of the Chaga.
As an honorary man, I had debated whether I should
follow local fashion and undress for dinner. Casting
modesty to the devil, I turned up in old cycling shorts
and silver.

As we ate, Chief Webuye spoke to me through his interpreter. "We did not come to it. It came to us. It was
not easy in those early days; before the orchards grew,
we could not eat the food, many of us grew sick and
died, but the land was ours and the land still knew us,
and came to our need. From the bodies of the dead grew

the trees that keep us, from their water came our water, from their bones came our bread, from their skins the houses that shelter us. The forest, having taken from us, is bound to give back the homes it took.''

Traveler's wisdom from Chief Webuye: Where you see the color orange, you will always find water. Anything red will always be edible. Always shit before you sleep, and bury it, you will have food in the morning. A drop of blood on the ground and you will have fruit.

Behind me, the jack o'lantern glow of flower-houses closed up for the night, and the comforting jangle of guitars. Africans will always have their music. Not for the WaChagga the adolescent obsession with identity that mars modern African thought; they had found their identity in the very heart of the alienness. Eating with them, communing with them, I felt I was no longer a stranger in the forest.

Asleep that night in a pile of spun floss, I thought I heard my name called, very softly, very gently . . . *Moon*. . . . One, two, three times.

"Langrishe?" I unzipped the folded solar petals. My astral namesake was high and full and casting a silver unreality over the sleeping village. "Langrishe. . . ."

—*Moon*—

The Chaga was impenetrable as death. Haunted, frustrated, I retired to the house. My sleep ridden by incubus dreams. When next I woke, it was to the house petals unfurling to the sun.

Even before I heard the keening, wailing song of the women, I could feel the air stiff with fear and secrecy. They had gathered in a petal-house across the spiral, the women, slumped like black lava, rocking and nodding and moaning their song. One at a time they would rise and go forward to comfort the desolate young woman at the center of the ring. Totally absorbed with their mourning, they were oblivious to my approach; it was Tibuweye, the guide, who stopped me.

"Please. It is not for you. Constance, the young

woman, she gave birth last night, but the child was still-born. Please understand.''

''I understand. I am sorry. Please tell her that I am sorry.''

I glanced at the circle of women, at the mother wracked with the silent tears of complete grief, and, as the women swayed and rocked in their keening, at the baby at her feet.

The baby. . . .

One of the women saw my staring and whipped a sheet over the body.

The child had no arms, no legs; in their place, coiling green tendrils sprouted.

Before I left, they gave me two gifts. I am not certain which I treasure the more, the little glass jars that light up when I shake them, or the path that follows the path of the white man, the mad *m'zungu*, upward. All this morning I have climbed through the gardens of the WaChagga, the slopes ringing with the proud, animal cries of the men harvesting. I pause to eat some fruit from a tree; red fruit, it tastes of musk and sex, it tastes of the Chaga.

Did the apple in Eden feel *responsible*?

It must be one of those laws of universal perversity, the kind of thing you see in stick form in the rear windows of Fords, that when the thing you want most in the world happens, you don't believe it. When the phone rang and there among the hissing and scratching was Dr. Peter Langrishe of the Ol Tukai Xenobiotics Department extending a personal invitation to me to fly down to Amboseli and spend a week at the center, all I was capable of were a few mumbled acquiescences and a numb replacing of the receiver. T.P. said I looked like a victim of a good mugging. Four hours later, I was standing on the apron at Wilson airfield, bags packed (''nothing plastic, my dear, and that includes Walkman, film, and toothbrush,'') and fighting to maintain connection with my hat in the propwash from the Ol Tukai Twin Otter.

My first sight of the Chaga: glimpsed out of the cabin window as the aircraft banked into its final approach to the Amboseli airstrip. Half-hallucinatory, half-revelatory; a disc of rainbow-colored light which broke apart into flows and eddies, a pointillist sea of color, like a test for some new color-blindness. Then the plane banked again and we were down, scoring an arrow of dust across the dry lake bed.

He was waiting for me. God, but he looked good. I scarcely noticed the Kenyan soldiers treble-checking my security clearance on their portable datalink. Ol Tukai was ten miles away on dirt roads the texture of corrugated iron. Ten miles was the closest safe distance aircraft could come to the perimeter of the Chaga; early overflights with camera-loaded tourists had come to grief when the pilots found the fuel in the tanks turning to sludge and every scrap of plastic bursting into bloom. Langrishe fed me such little scraps of data and I sat grinning like a teenager, hanging on for grim death as the Daihatsu 4 × 4 took the ruts. Ol Tukai seemed to be in the process of dismantling itself into tea-chests and packing crates; both civilians and military were all check-lists and baling wire.

"Getting ready for the move." Langrishe nodded beyond the buildings. "Three kilometers is close enough."

My first four hours in Ol Tukai I had my security clearance checked eight times. "They're ashamed of it," Langrishe said. "Same goes for the Tanzanians. A kind of national disgrace. Right in the middle of their great and glorious task of nation-building, *this* happens, like a cancer in the body politic they'd rather the rest of the international community didn't know about. Want to come for a look at it before dinner? After you've finished interviewing, or whatever it is you do." Note for the book: no one in Ol Tukai ever called the Chaga by name, what was out there was a lurking, polymorphous "it."

I had not thought that it was possible to see the Chaga advance. One hundred meters per day, just over four meters per hour, sixty-six centimeters per minute. One and two-thirds centimeters per second. On the botanical scale, that's virtually relativistic. The line of advance was more subtle than I had envisaged, not so much a line of demarcation as an ever advancing graduation, from thorn scrub and grasses through increasing echelons of polygonal fungus and pseudo-lichen to low bladder plants and gourd-like growth, to tube bushes and small windmill trees and plants that sprayed water and lashed whip-like flails and spewed clouds of floating bubbles, to the towering columns and fans and webs of the false-corals and sponges, at which point the indigenous was totally absorbed into the full-climax Chaga. From his backpack, Langrishe took a squeaky plastic elephant.

"Carla Bly's kid's," he explained. "I did ask first." He placed the toy in the path of the advance. Following his example, I hunkered on my heels to watch. The smiling green elephant broke out in a psoriasis of yellow spots which multiplied with appalling speed to cover the entire surface. Within fifteen seconds the toy was a mass of sea-anenome-like extrusions. I watched the green elephant collapse and dissolve into a pool of oily sludge which, even as it seeped into the ground, was generating furiously reproducing clusters of sulphur yellow crystals.

"We assume they're alien biological packages because, given a plethora of impossible hypotheses, that seems the least improbable: that the earth is on the receiving end of an alien colonization program. Truth is, we have no evidence that this theory is any more credible than the more incredible ones. The packages appear out of nowhere on the deep-space trackers, make a couple of fast orbits, and then execute an aero-braked descent. We've been scanning the sun's Local Group of stars with our deep-space tracking facilities for the past five years without the slightest hint as to their point of origin. But they still keep coming: that one last month in Cameroun; the one six months back that splashed down in mid-Atlantic—submarine surveys say something's happening along the mid-Atlantic ridge, but they don't know exactly what. *Thus* was the first, that we know of; the second one came down in the Bismarck Archipelago, the third hit in the old Aberdare National Park up to the north, another took out a dam in the Amazon basin, another came down in the Ecuadoran Andes, three others in mid-ocean; but they all came down within three hundred kilometers of the Equator. Fancy a walk?''

He indicated the advancing Chaga. I shuddered. Where the green elephant had sat smiling, a bubble of ochre polymer was expanding.

"Dinner, then."

Dinner was a table out under the enormous African night; moon, wine, candles; picking at our food and feeding each other choice morsels of biography for dessert, the wheres, whens, whos of our lives. I loved every minute of it. I've never said a harder goodnight in my life.

And with the morning, we flew.

At the sight of the flimsy film wings, the eminently snappable struts and one's utter exposure to sky and gravity, this Moon very nearly chickened. Langrishe reassured me that they were equipped with smart systems that made it almost impossible to crash or stall them, they virtually flew themselves, and if I *really* wanted to experience the Chaga this was the only way I could get close, and because this Moon was going to impress or die that morning, I said, what the hell, yes, why not. While he was filing a flight plan with security, I put on my helmet and waggled my feet in the steering stirrups, and the solar wing fed power to the engine, and the next thing I knew we had shaken ourselves free from the wrinkled skin of Africa. Airborne, *flying*, at once terrifying and liberating. I wanted to laugh and scream as we banked (flash of iridescence as our wings caught the sun) and wheeled. Before us; the White Mountain, casting off its concealment of cloud, the eternal snows high and pure and holy; below us: birds and things that were not quite birds fled from the shadow our wings cast over the jumbled canopy of the Chaga. Langrishe waved, pointed: a flotilla of silver balloons bowled through the air just above the treetops. At his signal, we banked our drag-onfly craft to pursue—each blimp carried a passenger like a large silver octopus—banked again. Chaga, sky, Kili-manjaro, all whirled into crazy juxtaposition, and I was lost. Transported. I do not know how long I flew, where I flew, how I flew; I seemed at times a fusion of woman and wing, Icarus ascending on beautiful, foolish arms; the forest, the mountain, the high, white tableland dif-fracting refracting dazzling hypnotizing under the sun. . . . Mystical? Transcendent? I cannot say what I experienced, except to echo Thomas Merton's descrip-tion of God as the pure emptiness of light where the self dissolves into the cloud of unknowing, of which one can-not, of necessity, speak.

On our return to earth, we did not speak, we could not speak; the sexual, spiritual tension between us was too strong for words. In his office, we tore like vultures at each other, stripped each other, ecstatically, soul-naked for the long, deep, plunge into each other; kisses des-perate and naïve as ancient clay cuneiforms. Under the shadow of the White Mountain, desperate, desperate love. . . . God, Langrishe, I want you!

It has been several hours since the last skeleton of a baby. Like the others, it was wedged in a cleft of a fan-coral; like the others, it was terribly deformed. The pain was so old and eroded that I could pick through the bones with the same detachment that I would examine a dead bird. The tiny, eyeless skull, distended into a sweeping crest of bone; the jaws fused shut in one seamless ridge of enamel; the fingers long and delicate as those of a bat—the slightest touch snapped them—terminated in rounded open sockets. Like the others I had encountered on the WaChagga pathways, it had been deliberately abandoned. Ritual infanticide. Paradise exposed; the price of compromise of Chagga with Chaga?

Cooler now, higher. I have had to supplement my eth-nic fashions with my dearly loved leather jacket. I must look like a fetish-figure from a sword'n'sorcery fantasy.

The unremitting claustrophobia of the forest robs me of a sense of location: I find myself searching for some breach in the walls so that I can re-establish my relationship with the surface of Africa. Certainly I must be close to the heartlands; the density and diversity of the ecosystem is staggering. Writing this, I am overshadowed by stands of what I can only describe as giant toadstools crossed with oil refineries: caps and tubes; elsewhere on today's climb, I have encountered groves of coiled cornucopias, vagina-mouths wide enough to swallow me whole; miniature mountain ranges of what look like bright orange worm-casts, three times my height and waving feathery extrusions. Small estates of squat cylindrical pillars, an abandoned abode, seeping a semen-like froth from their open tops. Organisms as transparent and fantastic as marine radiolarin, magnified a thousand times. . . . What would the Ol Tukai researchers give just for me to have brought a camcorder with me!

Corresponding with the accelerating diversity of the flora, I am encountering new and quite alien forms of fauna. Creatures like aerial manta rays cluster around a tangle of vivid lilac intestines: the first sight of them winging through the forest toward me sent me diving to cover, two million years of instinct, but as they passed over, I saw they had no mouths. How do they feed? Too many mysteries, I haven't the time; as I have said, this is not an expedition, this is a pilgrimage. Heart of Darkness, eh, Conrad? You don't know the half of it. Mistah Kurtz, he dead.

You damn well better *not* be, Langrishe. You hear me?

There are others in this new land; like the WaChagga, they have *adapted*. As I progress toward the cloud layer, their presence becomes more and more evident: rafts of birds struggling to take wing, weighed down by sponge-like encrustations on their heads and legs, others ridden piggyback by objects like diseased organs. The vervet monkey I saw, with the parasitic dorsal ridge, is no freak here. Some monkeys possess octopus tentacles in addition to their own arms and legs, some sport antlers of green coral studded with hundreds of tiny blue abalone eyes. Some are carpeted in a green mold that I assume must enable them to photosynthesize like plants, for their mouths have fused shut under whorls and ridges of raw bone. Some of the young I have seen clinging to their mothers' backs bear the same deformities I saw in the abandoned children of the WaChagga. Yet none seem in distress from their mutilations, and all are obviously thriving. Is this their absorption into the symbiotic life of the Chaga? Is the law of the jungle being re-written?

More than monkeys and birds have come to terms with the aliens. A sudden crashing approaching through the understory, a stand of tall, brittle umbrella trees trampled down, and an elephant entered the clearing. It raised its trunk to test taste touch the air; around its neck was a red, veiny mass of flesh reaching down along the tusks to elongate into two prehensile tentacles, each terminating in something shockingly like a human hand. I remained hidden in the cover of a grove of translucent cistern-plants. Scenting the presence of its ancestral enemy, the elephant turned and withdrew into the bush. Another pact with the Chaga.

When I heard the movement in the hooting, trilling dark that night, I feared it was another visit of the long-legged tripod creature that had reconnoitered my camp two nights before, stroking my few intimate possessions with long feathery cilia. I have a deep and entirely proper dread of all things clicking and chitinous. I held my breath.

"Greetings to you in the name of the Lord Jesus. . . ." I almost screamed. "Peace, sister, I am only a humble servant of my Lord. Pastor Hezekiah, minister to the lost and light to the found. Tell me, sister, do you love the Lord?"

He moved into the range of my biolights.

Hezekiah: bifurcated man—your right side is flesh and blood, your left a garden of tiny white flowers, trumpet-mouths opening and closing flicking forked tongues to taste the air; your left eye observes the world from a half-

dome of blossoms and roots; your left arm is a swollen
club of green flesh fused shut upon a decomposing black
Bible. Too strange to terrify me, Hezekiah. To me you
were almost . . . beautiful.

He was dressed in a memory of old Anglican vest-
ments. His speech was deeply beautiful, enriched by decades of exposure to the towering cadences of the
Authorized Version. I did not feel any threat or darkness
about him, rather, a sad holiness that made me move my
little jars of biolight into a circle as an invitation to enter.

He had evolved a complex and curiously satisfying theology around the Chaga, in which God had cast him in
the role of a latter-day John the Baptist: the voice crying
in the wilderness, prepare ye the Way of the Lord! With
reverential fervor, he expounded his credo that, in the
shape of the Chaga, the millennium was at hand, the
Kingdom of Heaven come down to Earth: "Is it not written sister, that a star shall fall from heaven, and its name
shall be Wormwood, and that one third of all the growing
things and creeping things upon the earth shall be destroyed? Does it not say that the New Jerusalem itself
shall come down out of the heavens?" His brother
preachers had been blinded to this truth by Satan and had
denounced it as ungodly; to him alone had been granted
the vision, and in obedience he had come out from the
midst of the scoffers and unbelievers, left his small parish
near Kapsabet, and walked the five hundred kilometers
to the mountain of God. In the towns he passed through,
he would preach his new revelation and call the orphans
of Babylon to the slopes of Mount Zion and the advent
of the Second Adam and Eve. "Eden!" he declared, including the singing forest with a wave of his Bible-hand.
"The new Eden! The Earth redeemed and cast in the
perfect image of God. What we had seen previously as
in a glass darkly, we shall now see clearly and without
distortion." His pilgrimage followed a divinely-ordered
spiral around the mountain, each level corresponding to
a new degree of spiritual grace and enlightenment: as he
reached the summit and the pinnacle of transfiguration,

his own personal transfiguration would be completed, changed from glory into glory, into the likeness of Christ his master. It was a mark of God's grace that he was half-transfigured already. He touched his mantle of flowers, eyes shining with ecstasy.

I envied him his fine madness. I asked him were the WaChagga disciples of his. "Degenerates," he denounced them. "They would not receive the Lord, so I have shaken their dust off my feet. God has spit them out of His mouth, they shall not see the glory." I asked him had he seen a white man, a *m'zungu,* in the forest. "Yes, many months ago, a *M'zungu,* from the Research Facility." When I asked where the *m'zungu* had been headed, he pointed up into the mists. He prayed a blessing over our sleep and in the morning he was gone, moving from glory to glory. But I could not rid myself of the sensation that he shadowed all that day's march: a half-glimpsed suggestion of a figure that could as easily have been a delusion of the prismatic perspectives of the forest. I stopped, called his name, waited for him, several times during today's climb, but the Chaga kept silence.

T.P. knew it. Mrs. Kivebulaya knew it. Phylis at the Irish Embassy, who let me have her day-old copies of the Cork *Examiner,* knew it. The entire office, from venerable tea-lady to junior runner, knew it.

Moon was in love.

The Celts invented the concept of romantic love.

He actually left messages for me pinned to the Thorn Tree in the cafe of the New Stanley Hotel, a thing no one has in any seriousness done since the shadow of Hemingway stalked the bars and country clubs; dates and arrangements for champagne breakfasts overlooking the Rift Valley, night trains to Lake Victoria (a teak and brass time machine focused fifty years in the past), hiking expeditions in the N'gong Hills, camera safaris to Lake Turkana, microlyting over the Maasai Mara. Impossibly romantic. Horrendously expensive. Moon loved every second of it. T.P. found it simultaneously hilarious and pitiable.

Suddenly the five hundred pages of notes, the hundred and twenty two hours of taped interviews, the twelve box files full of associated documents that I had been avoiding like a persistent creditor, seemed to spontaneously combust under my fingers. T.P. watched in dumb amazement from his Captain Kirk chair as the spirit of the Chaga reached out and possessed me. Finally, to save me from myself, and save his afternoons of contemplative crossword-solving and street-watching, he ordered me out of his office and sent me to pursue my demonic muse in the sultry climate of the coast. He obtained an indefinite lease on a beach-edge *banda* half an hour's drive north from Mombasa and sent me off on the overnight train with a ream of A4 and a Remington portable that barely qualified for the description.

Silence and solitude unbroken. I drove that Remington portable into the ground; well after dark, homeward-wending shell-sellers were surprised to see me working chthonically on the verandah by the light of oil lamps. At two o'clock, I would tumble through the mosquito nets into bed and sleep until dawn, when I would rise and run, or swim, before breakfast in the hotel up the beach. Then I would plunge into the book and not surface until dinner time. By Friday, I would be exhausted but glowing and waiting eagerly for the headlights of the Ol Tukai 4 × 4 to come weaving through the palm trees, the herald of two days of swimming, sunbathing, sleeping with Langrishe.

We all carry around a box of snapshots of our loves. Riffle, shuffle, deal them again.

Two figures running down the surf-line, running for the joy of using their bodies to push at the limits of their selves; the dawn coming up behind black thunderheads out of India and the world waiting, crouching in the indigo, waiting to be reborn. They make love in the shower, licking the salt sweat from each other's skin.

An ebony bed, brought down by dhow from Moga-

dishu for the Sultan of Mombasa's pleasure. After centuries, the wood had not lost its perfume.

Sudden, savage rain, beating on the palm thatch.

The moon, huge on the seaward edge of the world.
The call of the moonpath: to the sea! to the sea! The man
and the woman burst from the water like creatures newly
created, like drops of fire from the fingers of God, before
they sink again into the amniotic embrace and each other.

Still life: she, absorbed in her book with the moths
butting softly against the globe of the oil lamp; he, in his
wicker chair, watching. Just watching.

All things were a prelude to sex. Respighi's symphonic
poems amongst the trees at the batflight. Wading thigh-
deep through the blood warm ocean. Hands lovingly oil-
ing me against the sun. . . .

After, in that black Arab bed, he would explore that
land of heart's desire, the high, white tableland beyond
the clouds.

"Who are they? A day doesn't dawn that I don't ask
myself that question a dozen times: who *are* they? The
satellite cameras have looked through the clouds to show
us the things that are up there—amazing things, forms
and systems more complex than any we've yet discovered—entire tracts of forest that seem like animate cities.
Why? For whom? When? Are *they* already abroad in their
living cities, have we seen them and not recognized them?
Have we indeed seen the faces of the masters of the
Chaga, in those satellite photographs, and not recognized them?

"Or then again, it may be that the time is not yet right
for them: all is prepared, the stage set, but the principal
performers have yet to make their entrances. How could
they have put an entire world into something not much
larger than this room? Will they make themselves known
to us? One day, will our survey expeditions go to the
edge of the Chaga and find *them* waiting? Will they come
soon, will they wait until their grip on our world is more
secure? Are they delaying so that they may deal with us
as equals, or is that moment centuries distant, when the

whole earth is changed into their likeness? Who are they?
Most of all, *that* question; every day, every minute, that
question casts its shadow over everything else: *who are
they?* Moon . . . Moon?''

He would never notice that I had turned away from
him, staring at the tracks the beetles left on the wall.

With the morning, he would be gone. I was not woman
enough to hold him—the mountain had a more primal
claim on him. I knew he would leave me, at the last, for
that other love. I almost told him to go, rather than bear
the pain of having him leave me. To love someone so
much you will give him away rather than lose him, does
this make sense? Yet every time that 4 × 4 came swinging through the palms, I would throw myself on him and
drag him down, into that Arab bed.

I could smell it in the wind, the day the houseboy from
the tourist hotel half a mile up the beach came panting
to my verandah to tell me there was a telephone call for
me, most urgent. I followed in a daze of numb serenity.
When Dorothy Bazyn regretted to inform me that Peter
Langrishe had failed to return to the Oloitiptip Research
Facility after a microlyte survey of the northwestern sec-
tor of the Chaga, I experienced a colossal sense of guilty
relief, of a kind I have not felt since my mother finally
surrendered to the cancer that had taken six years to kill
her. I almost laughed, but a preventing hand around my
heart restrained me, like a mailed glove. That same
glazed calm accompanied me home on the train, until I
saw T.P. waiting for me amid the porters and taxi drivers
at Nairobi Station and all restraint fled. I was shattered
like a soapstone pot; the interior emptiness it had shaped
was lost in the greater emptiness without. I cried for an
hour all over his pure silk suit.

I sank into a deep, dark depression. Weeks, months,
disappeared behind me. The book sat three-quarters
complete on my desk at 224b Tom M'boya Street. T.P.
was always there, to listen when I wanted to talk, to
merely *be* when I could not talk. He preserved me from
some of the more disgusting excesses of self-pity: stop-

ping me drinking myself stupid, flushing the cocaine I had bought from an American consular official down the *choo*. I think he would have slept with me if that would have helped the healing. Over tea at a questionable Chinese restaurant tucked behind the Kenyatta Conference Center, I asked him why it hurt so much, still. He said it was because I was in love with Langrishe, still. We toyed with the mottoes from our fortune cookies, pretending all sorts of things.

"T.P."

He lit one end of his motto in the candle flame.

"You're right. I still love the bastard, so bad I know I will never, never be free of him. God, I love him. I am going mad without him. What's the line from that old song?"

"I can't live, with or without you."

"T.P., will you help me find him?"

I think that was the only time I ever succeeded in surprising him.

The very next day: "I have a little something for you. Out back, if you would care to take a look?"

I don't know how he had managed to put the thing up in the postage-stamp backyard; certainly his office staff looked very pleased with themselves. The microlyte was black and green, like a proud and beautiful dragonfly. I could not speak, merely run my hands over the wings, the struts, the power unit; appreciating it by touch.

"T.P., it must have cost a fortune."

"It did. Presuming that, as a typical romantic, you haven't the least idea about how to bring your plan to fruition. I took the liberty of engaging in a little logistical thought: great amusement, by the by. You can dismiss immediately any thought you might have entertained of obtaining a security clearance from Oloitiptip. Dorothy Bazyn does not want a second Missing in Action on her quarterly report, and I presume you have enough wit not to even *think* of trying to make it past the perimeter patrols on foot; the odds of you ending up in a bodybag, that is, after the soldiers gang-rape you, is in the region

of 98 percent. However, if you were to find a secluded
spot, say, fifty kilometers from Kilimanjaro, and fly in
just above ground level underneath the radar net, the odds
are a little more favorable. At least, if they open up with
twenty-millimeter cannon, you won't feel anything. So,
I made a few, ah, purchases?'' I almost kissed him.

We worked fast, furious, we did not stop to consider
what we were doing; the face of our madness might have
turned us to stone. Deep dark truth in the mirror. *The
Last Safari*, T.P. christened it, but I told him that had
been a film with Stewart Granger. ''That was *King Solomon's Mines*,'' he said. ''With Deborah Kerr.''

We drove down to a place on the road south, just outside of Ilbisil township; a bend, a baobab, and a lot of
sky. T.P. unpacked the microlyte—he had borrowed the
Irish Ambassador's Range Rover for the occasion (''He
owes me, the Garibaldi affair,'')—and assembled the aircraft under the watchful gaze of a dirty, gawky Maasai
kid, materialized out of five hundred square kilometers
of nowhere, as they tend to. All three of us were most
impressed when the propeller actually turned.

''Well, aren't you going to give Deborah Kerr a kiss
for luck?''

Hands in pockets, T.P. contemplated the landscape.
''Among the Dinka tribesmen of Sudan,'' he said, ''the
baobab is known as the Tree Where Man Was Born. In
Kenya, there is a common belief that the baobab disobeyed God by growing where *it* wanted to, in punishment for which, God uprooted it, turned it upside down,
and thrust it back into the earth again. I think there may
be a moral in that somewhere, Moon. What is there?''

''A moral, T.P.''

''That's correct.''

I kissed him anyway.

Five minutes later, I was airborne.

In the cloud forest, we face the final confrontation, the
ultimate consummation. An appropriate enough stage for
it, this high shoulderland of Kilimanjaro. In this season,

the clouds hang unbroken for weeks on end. A landscape of moral ambiguity, all shades of gray . . . is this the Cloud of Unknowing? The Daliesque geometries of the Chaga, the ripples and veils of fog—suitably Macbethian for a Scot like Langrishe.

I came upon the clearing at the end of a heavy day's climb. The air was thin, every footstep was a shard of migraine exploding through my brain. When I found myself on the edge of the small, rocky defile that cut a jagged gash through the ubiquitous Chaga, I knew instinctively that this was to be the place. As I made camp, the fog capriciously swirled and dissolved; I found myself looking through a tree-lined window over the cloud-speckled plain of Amboseli. To be able to *see*! The many-colored land swept away beneath me to merge almost imperceptibly with the tawny earth-shades of Kenya. Those winks of light, that scattering of antiseptic white like spilled salt; the new facility at Oloitiptip; those plumes of dust: vehicles, perhaps aircraft taking off from the dry lake bed; those specks of black moving through the middle air: Army helicopters.

It is not good for the soul to look down from the mountain too long: I lingered until nightfall, and the more I looked, the more I felt myself despising the monotonous, starved landscape beyond the mountain, the more I rejoiced in the color and diversity of the Chaga. I did belong here.

He came that night. I was expecting him.

"Moon."

No doubt, no uncertainty this time. I was already reaching to shake my biolights into luminescence.

"No. No light."

"Why?"

"No light. Or I'll go. . . ."

"No! Don't go. Langrishe, where are you? Don't hide from me. . . ."

"Moon . . . oh Moon. Don't make this difficult for me. I want to come to you; more than anything, Moon.

Just to see you, here . . . why did you have to come, why
could we not have left it where it lay and let wither?"

"Langrishe, I couldn't leave you. I couldn't let it
wither and die; it isn't like that, you know. It won't die,
it can't die. Langrishe, listen to me. . . ."

A silence. Alone, in the dark, with the whole forest
listening, I sat and hugged my knees to my chest. After
a time, he spoke again.

"Those living cities along the snowline that we have
seen in the satellite photographs . . . I've been there, up
in the snows, Moon, I've explored those cities. The word
'city' barely describes what is up there; I've seen things
that beggar the human imagination, things far beyond my
comprehension; but *one* thing I understand—there is no
race of aliens waiting buried in the soil to step forth and
inhabit them. In a sense, we were right when we hypoth-
esized that we might not be able to recognize the aliens;
we do not recognize them because, Moon, we *are* the
aliens. . . ."

I waited the rest of the night for him to return, shaking, and shaken, in my protective circle of biolights. The
clouds were low and cold and drizzling the next day.
Miserable hours; wrapped up in my sleeping bag in my
hammock, I picked and pecked at Thomas Merton, but
my mind was too full of birds and doubts to mirror the
Benedictine's tranquility of solitude. Too long since I last
read him; the vinyl cover of the book was a nauseating
mash of pulpy crystals and froth. I ripped it off, threw it
away, read the master in the nakedness of his own pages.

He came at nightfall, in the dripping, freezing twilight.

"*Evolution,* Moon, catastrophic shifts to new levels of
complexity. Do you understand? You must understand,
it's vitally important that you understand. Evolution does
not plod through history one steady gene at a time—
Evolution dances, evolution leaps, from level to level; on
the biological clock, the second hand does not move
continuously—it clicks from one minute to the next.
Changes occur simultaneously throughout an entire pop-

ulation; within one generation, a population may shift to a higher level. Do you understand? Moon, you *must* understand!''

''Langrishe!'' Empty, dripping darkness. I dreamed about his eyes all that night, terrible, terrible eyes, without a face.

Washing in the lukewarm waters of a cistern next morning, I heard my name in the mists.

''Go away, Moon. Before you came, there were never any choices to make, never another consideration; and when I left to come here, it was that way again. I knew what I wanted, what I was searching for, and now you have turned everything inside out again. I want to be with you, I want to run away from you, I love you, I am terrified of you.''

I turned around slowly, scanning the gray silhouettes of undergrowth.

''Langrishe . . . where are you?''

''Here, Moon.'' Shadow among the shadows, a man-shaped patch of mist. ''No. No nearer. Please. Listen. I can't stay long. This is important. Fire will not burn it, poisons will not kill it, it thrives on our wastes and pollutions and can provide technological man with his every need: is the Chaga the next evolutionary step forward? Technological man fouls his nest with glee; will the nest reject him, or will the nest *adapt* itself so that he can live there without destroying it and himself?

''The protein life has had its day; now the new life has come and is sweeping it away. The change, Moon, the change.''

As he spoke, I had closed the distance between us, one cat-cautious step at a time. I was within a handful of meters of him when he awoke from his self-absorption and noticed my proximity. He gave a cry as we saw each other, face to face. Then, in a flicker of movement, he was gone.

My heart pounded. Black phosphenes exploded noiselessly in my retinas, my blood roared. Those fears and dreads that had stalked my dreams. . . . Langrishe was still human.

That night, in my hammock, a touch on my cheek, a kiss. Mumbling like a great contented cat, I turned over and looked into his face and the soft sensual mass of his body pressed on mine. Mouths parted, lips met; I unzipped the sleeping bag to welcome him within, lifted my hands to touch him. "No," he said. "Please. Don't touch me. Promise me that, Moon."

"But why?"

"Because of you. Because I don't understand what it is about you that drives me mad. I'm mad to even *think* of doing this. Mad. Mad! What is it about you, woman?" I laid a finger to his lips; one second later our mouths met, and before I was even aware he had slipped inside me. I gasped in surprise, his tongue was at my nipples, his breath hot on my skin. He smelled of Chaga, musks, essential oils, the intimate perfumes of the orifices. His hands held mine above my head, sexual surrender as we plunged and pulsed in the absolute darkness of the senses. As his thrusts grew more frantic, his pace more urgent, his fingers released mine and my hands automatically fell to stroking his body, over the thighs, nails lightly raking the buttocks, tracing little spider-feet along the flanks, onto the gentle syncline of his back.

At my scream, the song of the Chaga fell silent for a minute.

My fingers were entwined in a holdfast of veins and tubes rooted in the base of his spine; a throbbing umbilical that bound him to God knows what out there in the darkness. He leapt away from me, naked, shivering, dripping; I vomited endlessly, emptily.

"Oh God oh God oh God oh God. . . ."

"I told you I told you, I *told* you not to touch. . . ."

"You bastard, you bastard, what have you done, oh my God. . . ."

"*Why* did you have to come here, why did you not go when I *asked* you, *why* did you have to reawaken all the things I had forgotten, why did you have to make me *human* again?''

"Human?" I screamed. "Human? My God, Langrishe, *what are you?*"

"You want to see?" he screamed back. "You want to know? Look! Look well!" He pointed a quivering finger at me. A ponderous crashing from the night-forest, something huge, that knows it can take forever to get where it wants. "Look!" screamed Langrishe again, and suddenly the ravine was bright with biolights. "I can do anything with it I like. Who do you think fed you, watered you, watched you, guided you?" Into the amphitheater of light came a great mound of flesh, taller than a man, wider; ribbed with veins and arteries and patches of scabrous yellow mold. Clusters of organs swayed as it advanced on two massively-muscled legs. Lacy antennae feathered from barnacle-like warts along its back; it turned toward me, raised itself up on its clawed feet, and extended an array of mandibles and claspers. Its belly was an open vagina, connected to Langrishe by the umbilical cord.

I felt I was going mad.

The umbilical retracted, drawing Langrishe into the raw red maw. It closed around him, advanced another step on me. Langrishe's face regarded me from a cowl of red flesh.

"I tried to tell you Moon, but you refused to understand. Evolution. The future, Moon. The *future* man. *Homo Symbioticus*. The orthobody. A completely self-contained environmental unit. Imagine an end to sickness and disease, bodies that will heal our every illness, that will repair and regenerate our bodies; why, I am effectively immortal! Imagine no pain, no war, imagine the very *ability* of one human to cause another human pain abolished; we can have that, the orthobodies have a system of neurological checks that make it impossible to translate a violent thought into violent action. Imagine— no more want, no more hunger, for the orthobody lives on sunlight, air and water like the plants, and every man

will be able to draw what he needs from the endless re-
sources of the forest. Imagine—a world without ignorance; my brain is linked with the orthobody's brain,
which can process information with the speed of a computer; what is more, it can link into another orthobrain,
so that the total of all human knowledge is accessible by
every man, woman, and child; knowledge is no more the
privilege of an educated class, the heritage of humanity
is the *right* of all humanity. Imagine—the richness of experience and emotion of a Shakespeare or a Michaelan-
gelo the birthright of *everyone*; imagine eyes that can see
into the infra-red and the ultraviolet, new spectrums of
hearing, the ability to taste, smell, touch things you never
conceived of before; in addition to new senses, new
awarenesses that I cannot even begin to describe to you,
Moon!''

"Horrible!" I cried. "Horrible!"

"No, *glorious*! The next evolutionary leap! If man
cannot live harmoniously with his planet, his planet must
adapt to live harmoniously with man. Moon, I understand your fear; it looks dreadful, it seems monstrous;
believe me, it is more wonderful than you can ever imagine. I feel like . . . a god, Moon. A god!''

Eyes I dare not meet in dreams.

"God, Langrishe. . . .''

"So, what will Moon do, then? Will she go back? Will
she come down from the mountaintop; to *that*? Can you
go back, after what you've seen, after the wonder and
glory you've touched here? Or will she stay, with me?
You loved me enough to come here to find me; do you
love me enough to *stay*? Am I any more monstrous than
I would be if I lay paralyzed in an iron lung? If I had
leprosy? You would love me *then*—can't you love me
now?''

No, not a god, Langrishe, a devil, and a subtle one at
that, a driver of devil's bargains. My mind was a fire-
storm of doubts and confusions; through the conflagra-
tion, the numb roaring, I reached out to touch him, lay

a hand on the red ridged flesh beside his face. "Oh, Langrishe. . . ."

"You said we were one. You said we were inadequate parts of a unity, each incomplete without the other. I'm not saying that you have to become like me; you don't have to pass into an orthobody, you can just stay with me, as you are, and we can know each other as we did, before. . . ."

"Langrishe. . . .

"Moon, I love you."

But I had already fled into the night.

The sifting of the ashes: all the emotional underpinnings upon which the life of Moon had been built have collapsed into embers. If only he had not said that. If only he had not said that he loved me, it might have been bearable then. Why did you always have to make *me* the guilty one? Was it *always* like this, was our love mere explorations of new ways of causing pain to each other? Was all we needed from each other a mirror in which to examine ourselves?

He will come again for me, soon, come calling, through the mist and the forest that lies across the shoulders of Kilimanjaro. And I do not know what I will do then. That is why I am completing this journal: the fury of the condemned man's diary. The longest journey is the journey inwards; it is also the journey from which return is least possible. Of all travelers, it is most true for the pilgrim that you can't go home again.

The pilgrim that comes down from the mountain will not be Moon: Moon died, up there under the breath of the snows: what returns to earth will be as changed within as Langrishe is without. And if I stay . . . I cannot become like that. I cannot accept that this is the future for humanity—an eternity of graceless hedonism, browsing in the great world-forest, each man an island entirely sufficient unto himself? No, I reject it. Do you hear me, Langrishe, I reject it!

I must finish now. I can hear him calling, he is coming

for me. I have not much time to complete this record, and still I am undecided. Maybe this will not be my last entry after all. T.P., if this journal should ever find its way back to you, by my hand, by the hand of another, even if you may not understand it yourself, try to make the world understand. It is possible to love the heart of darkness even while being repelled by it.

He is here now, I must put down my pen for today. Tomorrow? Tomorrow. . . .

FURTHER READING
ABOUT AFRICA

Peter H. Beard, THE END OF THE GAME, Chronicle, 1988.

David Ewing Duncan, FROM CAPE TO CAIRO, Weidenfeld & Nicholson, 1989.

John Heminway, THE IMMINENT RAINS, Little, Brown, 1968.

John Heminway, NO MAN'S LAND, E. P. Dutton, 1983.

Mark Hudson, OUR GRANDMOTHERS' DRUMS, Minnerva, 1989.

Elspeth Huxley (editor), NELLIE: LETTERS FROM AFRICA, Wiedenfeld & Nicholson, 1973.

Elspeth Huxley, WHITE MAN'S COUNTRY (2 volumes), Chatto & Windus, 1935.

Marion Kaplan, FOCUS AFRICA, Doubleday, 1982.

David Lamb, THE AFRICANS, Vintage, 1983.

Charles R Larson (editor), AFRICAN SHORT STORIES.

Patrick Marnham, FANTASTIC INVASION, Penguin, 1987.

Thomas Pakenham, THE SCRAMBLE FOR AFRICA, Random House, 1991.

Mort Rosenblum and Doug Williamson, SQUANDERING EDEN, Harcourt Brace Jovanovich, 1987.

SCIENCE FICTION STORIES
WITH AFRICAN THEMES

Jim Aiken, "My Life in the Jungle," *F&SF*, Feb. 1985.

Brian W. Aldiss, "North of the Abyss," *F&SF*, Oct. 1989.

Mary C. Aldridge, "The Andinkra Cloth," *Marion Zimmer Bradley's Fantasy Magazine*, Winter 1989.

Poul Anderson, "Ivory, and Apes, and Peacocks," *Time Patrolmen*.

Clive Baker, "How Spoiler's Bleed," F&SF, Oct. 1988.

Michael Bishop, "Apartheid, Superstrings, and Mordecai Thubana," *Full Spectrum 3*.

John Crowley, "Great Work of Time," *Novelty*.

Thomas M. Disch, "Casablanca," *Alpha Four*.

David Drake, "Out of Africa," *From the Heart of Darkness*.

George Alec Effinger, "Marid Changes His Mind," *IA Science Fiction Magazine*, May 1989.

Joe Haldeman, "Lindsay and the Red City Blues," *Dark Forces*.

Sterling E. Lanier, "His Only Safari," *F&SF*, February 1970.

Judith Moffett, "Surviving," F&SF, June 1986.

Michael Moorcock, "The Cairine Purse," *Zenith 2*.

Chad Oliver, "Far From This Earth," *The Year 2000*.

Frederick, Pohl, "Waiting for the Olympians," *IA Science Fiction Magazine*, Aug. 1988.

Mike Resnick, "Bully!" *IA Science Fiction Magazine*. April 1991.

Mike Resnick, "Bwana," *IA Science Fiction Magazine*. Jan. 1990.

Mike Resnick, "Kirinyaga," *F&SF*, Nov. 1988.

Mike Resnick, "The Manamouki," *IA Science Fiction Magazine*, July 1990.

Mike Resnick, "One Perfect Morning, With Jackals," *IA Science Fiction Magazine*, March 1991.

Mike Resnick, "Song of a Dry River," *IA Science Fiction Magazine*, March 1992.

Charles Sheffield, "The Serpent of Old Nile," *IA Science Fiction Magazine*, May 1989.

Charles Sheffield, "Tunicate, Tunicate, Wilt Thou Be Mine?" *IA Science Fiction Magazine*, June 1985.

Robert Silverberg, "Born with the Dead," *Born With the Dead*.

Robert Silverberg, "Lion Time in Timbuctoo," *IA Science Fiction Magazine*, October 1990.

Robert Silverberg, "To the Promised Land," *Omni*, May 1989.

Norman Spinrad, "Lost Continents," *The Star-Spangled Future*.

Michael Swanwick, "The Feast of Saint Janis," *New Dimensions 11*.

Howard Waldrop, "He-We-Await," *All About Strange Monsters of the Recent Past*.

DAW

Science Fiction Anthologies

☐ **FUTURE EARTHS: UNDER AFRICAN SKIES**

UE2544—$4.99

Mike Resnick & Gardner Dozois, editors

From a utopian space colony modeled on the society of ancient Kenya, to a shocking future discovery of a "long-lost" civilization, to an ingenious cure for one of humankind's oldest woes—a cure that might cost too much—here are 15 provocative tales about Africa in the future and African culture transplanted to different worlds.

☐ **MICROCOSMIC TALES**

UE2532—$4.99

Isaac Asimov, Martin H. Greenberg, & Joseph D. Olander, eds.

Here are 100 wondrous science fiction short-short stories, including contributions by such acclaimed writers as Arthur C. Clarke, Robert Silverberg, Isaac Asimov, and Larry niven. Discover a superman who lives in a *real* world of nuclear threat . . . an android who dreams of electric love . . . and a host of other tales that will take you instantly out of this world.

☐ **WHATDUNITS**

UE2533—$4.99

Mike Resnick, editor

In this unique volume of all-original stories, Mike Resnick has created a series of science fiction mystery scenarios and set such inventive sleuths as Pat Cadigan, Judith Tarr, Katharine Kerr, Jack Haldeman, and Esther Friesner to solving them. Can you match wits with the masters to make the perpetrators fit the crimes?

ISAAC asimov PRESENTS THE GREAT SF STORIES

Isaac Asimov & Martin H. Greenberg, editors

☐ **Series 24 (1962)**   UE2495—$5.50
☐ **Series 25 (1963)**   UE2518—$5.50

Buy them at your local bookstore or use this convenient coupon for ordering.

PENGUIN USA P.O. Box 999, Dept. #17109, Bergenfield, New Jersey 07621

Please send me the DAW BOOKS I have checked above, for which I am enclosing $_____ (please add $2.00 per order to cover postage and handling. Send check or money order (no cash or C.O.D.'s) or charge by Mastercard or Visa (with a $15.00 minimum.) Prices and numbers are subject to change without notice.

Card #_____ Exp. Date _____
Signature_____
Name_____
Address_____
City _____ State _____ Zip _____

For faster service when ordering by credit card call **1-800-253-6476**

Please allow a minimum of 4 to 6 weeks for delivery.

DAW
FANTASY ANTHOLOGIES

☐ **ALADDIN: MASTER OF THE LAMP**　　UE2545—$4.99
　　edited by Mike Resnick & Martin H. Greenberg

All original tales of Aladdin and his lamp—and the promise and perils the lamp's wishes can bring.

☐ **CATFANTASTIC**　　UE2355—$3.95
☐ **CATFANTASTIC II**　　UE2461—$4.50
　　edited by Andre Norton & Martin H. Greenberg

Unique collections of fantastical cat tales—original fantasies of cats in the future, the past, the present, and other dimensions.

☐ **CHRISTMAS BESTIARY**　　UE2528—$4.99
　　edited by Rosalind M. Greenberg & Martin H. Greenberg

A rollicking new collection of all-original holiday tales about mermaids, selkies, golems, sea serpents, pixies and other creatures of enchantment.

☐ **DRAGON FANTASTIC**　　UE2511—$4.50
　　edited by Rosalind M. Greenberg & Martin H. Greenberg

All-original tales of the magical beasts which once ruled the skies, keepers of universes beyond human ken.

☐ **HORSE FANTASTIC**　　UE2504—$4.50
　　edited by Martin H. Greenberg & Rosalind M. Greenberg

Let these steeds carry you off to adventure and enchantment as they race, swift as the wind, to the magic lands. . . .

Buy them at your local bookstore or use this convenient coupon for ordering.

PENGUIN USA　P.O. Box 999, Dept. #17109, Bergenfield, New Jersey 07621

Please send me the DAW BOOKS I have checked above, for which I am enclosing $_____ (please add $2.00 per order to cover postage and handling. Send check or money order (no cash or C.O.D.'s) or charge by Mastercard or Visa (with a $15.00 minimum.) Prices and numbers are subject to change without notice.

Card #_____ Exp. Date _____
Signature_____
Name_____
Address_____
City _____ State _____ Zip _____

For faster service when ordering by credit card call **1-800-253-6476**
Please allow a minimum of 4 to 6 weeks for delivery.

DAW

Eluki bes Shahar

THE HELLFLOWER SERIES

☐ **HELLFLOWER (Book 1)**　　　　　UE2475—$3.99

Butterfly St. Cyr had a well-deserved reputation as an honest and dependable smuggler. But when she and her partner, a highly illegal artificial intelligence, rescued Tiggy, the son and heir to one of the most powerful of the hellflower mercenary leaders, it looked like they'd finally taken on more than they could handle. For his father's enemies had sworn to see that Tiggy and Butterfly never reached his home planet alive. . . .

☐ **DARKTRADERS (Book 2)**　　　　　UE2507—$4.50

With her former partner Paladin—the death-to-possess Old Federation artificial intelligence—gone off on a private mission, Butterfly didn't have anybody to back her up when Tiggy's enemies decided to give the word "ambush" a whole new and all-too-final meaning.

☐ **ARCHANGEL BLUES (Book 3)**　　　　UE2543—$4.50

Darktrader Butterfly St. Cyr and her partner Tiggy seek to complete the mission they started in DARKTRADERS, to find and destroy the real Archangel, Governor-General of the Empire, the being who is determined to wield A.I. powers to become the master of the entire universe.

Buy them at your local bookstore or use this convenient coupon for ordering.

PENGUIN USA　P.O. Box 999, Dept. #17109, Bergenfield, New Jersey 07621

Please send me the DAW BOOKS I have checked above, for which I am enclosing $_____ (please add $2.00 per order to cover postage and handling. Send check or money order (no cash or C.O.D.'s) or charge by Mastercard or Visa (with a $15.00 minimum.) Prices and numbers are subject to change without notice.

Card #_____ Exp. Date _____
Signature_____
Name_____
Address_____
City _____ State _____ Zip _____

For faster service when ordering by credit card call **1-800-253-6476**

Please allow a minimum of 4 to 6 weeks for delivery.